THE LONG VIEW

Elizabeth Jane Howard was the author of fifteen highly acclaimed novels. The Cazalet Chronicles – *The Light Years*, *Marking Time*, *Confusion* and *Casting Off* – have become established as modern classics and have been adapted for a major BBC television series and most recently for BBC Radio 4. In 2002 Macmillan published Elizabeth Jane Howard's autobiography, *Slipstream*. In that same year she was awarded a CBE in the Queen's Birthday Honours List. She died in January 2014, following the publication of the fifth Cazalet novel, *All Change*.

ALSO BY ELIZABETH JANE HOWARD

Love All
The Beautiful Visit
The Sea Change
After Julius
Odd Girl Out
Something in Disguise
Getting It Right
Mr Wrong
Falling

The Cazalet Chronicles

The Light Years
Marking Time
Confusion
Casting Off
All Change

Non-Fiction

The Lover's Companion
Green Shades
Slipstream

THE
LONG VIEW

ELIZABETH
JANE HOWARD

With an introduction by
John Bayley

PICADOR

First published 1956 by Jonathan Cape Ltd

This paperback edition published 2015 by Picador
an imprint of Pan Macmillan
20 New Wharf Road, London N1 9RR
Associated companies throughout the world
www.panmacmillan.com

ISBN 978-1-5098-0424-5

1 3 5 7 9 8 6 4 2

A CIP catalogue record for this book is available from the British Library.

Typeset by Palimpsest Book Production Ltd, Falkirk, Stirlingshire
Printed and bound by CPI Group (UK) Ltd, Croydon, CR0 4YY

Visit **www.picador.com** to read more about all our books
and to buy them. You will also find features, author interviews and
news of any author events, and you can sign up for e-newsletters
so that you're always first to hear about our new releases.

For E.M.

INTRODUCTION

In an essay of the early thirties a witty and benevolent critic, Desmond MacCarthy, observed that all women's fiction began with the same sentence: 'Robina was glad she had lighted a fire.' He was being deliberately unfair of course. It was the period of *The Waves* and *Mrs Dalloway*, of *Lolly Willowes*, *A View from the Harbour*, *The Weather in the Streets*, *The Death of the Heart* – to name but a few; and Desmond MacCarthy was himself the friend and warm admirer of the talented novelists who had produced these masterpieces. But he had a point. Less talented writers were inclined to be indulgent with themselves, to feel that feminine consciousness, like a new green growth, had only to be seen uncoiling and expanding to give the reader a new sort of aesthetic satisfaction, and one far removed from the mechanical plots and ideological contrivances of men.

There is an important distinction looming in the background here, one which attends all novel writing at all times and is not confined to any difference between the masculine and the feminine. Some novelists – Graham Greene for example – are natural manipulators, whose characters are stereotyped to behave in particular ways in exciting or unusual situations. Some novelists appear to let their characters develop naturally, so that they surprise the reader, or even cease to interest him, because their individuality is not established for a particular purpose but seems to come and go, opaque at some moments and clear at others. When managed in a masterly fashion, as it is in *The Long View*, this creative process can be very rewarding indeed.

It is also very difficult to do, and to control. Control in the kind of novel Desmond MacCarthy was thinking of tends to be exercised all too simply, by the perpetual presence of the writer as heroine as consciousness. Robina was glad she had lighted a fire, and then she was distracted about this, and delighted about that, and wondering if she was really in love with Charles, and so forth. A modern Robina is found in the novels of a writer like Margaret Drabble, and her consciousness is carefully assessed in relation to the outlook and feelings of a changing society. Nowadays she is sensitive and caring, and the reader is invited to care for and with her; but while this can easily be done, and a large measure of interest taken, there lurks somewhere in the presiding consciousness an equally large measure of complacency, a lack of sharpness and detachment. Indeed the reader is invited to find such an absence of sharpness admirable in itself, a sign that being warm and caring are virtues in our society, which the novel's consciousness must imitate and embody.

That may be all very well, but an alternative strategy is to cast a cold eye, or seem to do so. Elizabeth Jane Howard does not require us to sympathise in a facile way with her Antonia, or to become instantly intimate with her. The art of the novel does indeed lie in making us take the long view. We come gradually to know, to like, to respect the heroine, and our sense of her varies in the reversed perspective so that at times she seems a stranger and at times familiar, sometimes vulnerable and touching, sometimes distant and difficult to understand. It is as if Anna Karenina were to be revealed gradually from the moment of her death back into her girlhood, so that we begin to understand (in a way that Tolstoy of course never tells us, leaving us instead to make our own inferences) now a certain kind of personality comes into existence. Antonia is not a 'portrait'; she is not on display like Dorothea Brooke in George Eliot's *Middlemarch*, or Henry James's Isobel Archer in *The Portrait of a Lady*. The indirection with which the reader is made increasingly aware of her is a technical triumph, and one of a very unusual sort, depending neither on the calm relationship in which the author demonstrates her heroine to the reader, nor the intimate one in which the reader is invited to enter the heroine's stream of consciousness.

The triumph is created by means as subtle as they are unobtrusive. We first know the heroine as Mrs Fleming, and we do not even know she is the heroine; she seems a capable and helpful person arranging a dinner party and coping as best she can with a house and husband and grown-up children. Gradually she becomes a pronoun – she – but without losing that indeterminate mildness ('Mrs Fleming said mildly . . .') which seems inappropriate to the persona of a heroine. Gradually, as she is younger and more unformed, and as time is carrying us steadily backwards, she becomes Antonia, the young girl of the novel's final section. But she could never be like Desmond MacCarthy's Robina, thrust upon us by the author, a girl in the company of whose consciousness we have to remain as if we had been brought together by a too-officious hostess.

Antonia is not mysterious: she is more interesting than that. Her passivity and her helpfulness have been exploited by life, by the conditions and expectations such a girl grows up with. But here again Elizabeth Jane Howard quietly confounds the reader's own expectations of how he or she is required to react, for this is neither a case of *pitié pour les femmes* nor of the hard but rewarding growth of experience, the *ingénue* learning with pleasures and pains about the world of men and marriage. Rather it illustrates, and in a complex and scrupulous way, how instinctive is the process by which we co-operate with destiny, finding 'what something hidden from us chose' and making a life of it without too much surprise or reflection. Antonia's marriage is beautifully suggested in its desolation and its humdrum intimacy. Her husband Conrad becomes a part of her without ever letting her become a part of him. With most marriages in novels there is a blur left, as it were, in the area of the two partners' closeness. The novelist finds himself having to concentrate upon one individuality or the other. The achievement of *The Long View* is to dissolve the heroine in the necessities and acceptances of marriage, and yet retain her, by means of the backward look, as a personality on her own.

Conrad himself has much to do with this. A remarkable and wholly convincing projection in himself, he is also a symbolic figure of man in marriage, accepted as such by his wife, who, we infer, comes to depend on and to need just that side of him which is ill-suited to the domestic relation. The woman accepts, the man chooses: but her acceptance is not necessarily of what he chooses, which is why they have two children he never wanted. There is a great deal of buried humour in this situation, which the narrative insists on no more than it does on the symbolic role of wife and husband – she prepared to accept what happens, he determined to create everything for himself in his own life, his wife included. He takes a mistress on the same terms, and we see the process undergoing there its own variations. Equably, without bitterness or insistence, the novel shows how many women find it hard to resist a man like Conrad, just because he is so capable of loving them 'for themselves', that is, of creating a self for them which they can welcome and inhabit with love. Young Imogen, the mistress, is pleased to destroy her drawings, because Conrad had given her an image of herself which no longer requires them. 'Sweet to myself that am so sweet to you' as the Victorian poet Coventry Patmore put it with his usual rather embarrassing insight. Yet there is something touching in the process, and the novel admirably reveals how it is a potential for growth and joy, as well as for sterility and imprisonment. This novel is also far too realistic to tread mechanically in any of the now well-worn paths of 'women's lib'.

It is a sad novel, but with a sadness well earned and never exploited. Humour and fun are never far away, and even when, quite early on, Antonia finds herself sitting at her solitary dinner-table with her married life over, she is not a pitiable figure but a strong resigned mild one, who will do her best to help her children survive the usual ghastly mistakes in love and marriage, or their modern equivalents; and who will go on being as cheerful as she can. None the less, the cocktail party she goes to before that solitary dinner has tragic overtones and moving effects of a very original kind. She has met there someone who seemed as unhappy as herself, who seemed to intuit for that reason what her unhappiness was. She was frightened by the way in which he had recognised what was wrong with her, and as she sits down to her supper she is overwhelmed with a sense of the 'passionate gravity' of the present.

> If she had known, then, how to find the man
> who had so frightened her at Leila's party,
> she would have gone to him. But she did not
> know.

The past stretches behind into the rest of the book, the future is unknown. But its promise still exists, for anyone who is prepared to take the long view.

John Bayley, 1986

PART ONE
1950

ONE

This, then, was the situation. Eight people were to dine that evening in the house at Campden Hill Square. Mrs Fleming had arranged the party (it was the kind of unoriginal thought expected of her, and she sank obediently to the occasion) to celebrate her son's engagement to June Stoker. The guests were asked at a quarter to eight for eight. On arrival the men would be politely wrenched from their overcoats, their hats, umbrellas, evening papers, and any other more personal outdoor effects by the invaluable Dorothy, until, reduced to the uniformity of their dinner jackets, they would be encouraged to ascend the steep curving staircase to the drawing-room. The women must climb to Mrs Fleming's bedroom on the second floor, where she would afterwards find strange powder spilled on her dressing-table, mysterious hairs of no colour she associated with the heads of her guests caught in her ivory comb, and a composite smell of unremarkable scents. When the women had confirmed before Mrs Fleming's mirror whatever they had thought a little while earlier of themselves before their own; when one of them, perhaps, had made public some small disparaging discovery about her appearance, and heard it indifferently denied, they would troop cautiously down the stairs (it was easy to tread on one another's skirts round the sharp vertiginous corners) to the drawing-room, where they would find the men drinking, and eating glazed dazed little pieces of food. June Stoker would be introduced to a company which had otherwise long ceased to discover anything about themselves likely to increase either their animation or their intimacy, and her immediate future with Julian Fleming (a honeymoon in Paris and a flat in St John's Wood) outlined.

In due course they would descend to the dining-room and eat oysters and grouse and cold orange soufflé, and drink (in deference to June Stoker) champagne. The conversation would consist of an innocuous blend of the world situation, and the St John's Wood situation of June Stoker and Julian Fleming. In neither case would enough curiosity or information be supplied to provoke real interest. After the soufflé the women would retire to the drawing-room (or Mrs Fleming's bedroom) to match up June's potential experience with their own: and the men would continue over brandy (or port if Mr Fleming turned up at his own house in time to decant it) to turn the Korean situation to economic, not to say financial, account. The party would merge again in the drawing-room, until, at eleven, the prospect of another day exactly like the one just spent, would transport them in their mind's eye to the last-minute hitches of the evening – their garage doors sticking; urgent incomprehensible telephone messages left by their foreign servants; their reading-lamps fused – perhaps even the necessity of discussing with one familiar person the threadbare subject of something done mutually and without pleasure. Then they would leave the delightful party: Julian would see June home; and Mrs Fleming would be left in the drawing-room scattered with ashtrays, brandy glasses, exhausted cushions, and, possibly – Mr Fleming.

That, reflected Mrs Fleming, was the only factor of the evening in the least uncertain; and even then there was merely the alternative. Either he would stay, or he would go. How the alternative reduces one's prospect and petrifies the imagination in a way that the possibility can never do. Possibilities, innumerable and tightly packed, could shower forth like mushroom spore between such alternatives as being here, or there; alive, or dead; and old, or young.

Mrs Fleming shut the book she had not been reading, uncoiled herself from the sofa, and went upstairs to dress for dinner.

The view, even from the second floor of the house, was beautiful and disturbing. From the front windows the steeply declining square crammed with lawn and bushes, and the massive trees, which were fading and yellowing in the chill silent sunlight, filled the eye, so that the houses straight across the square were scarcely visible, and a little to the right down the hill were quite out of sight. At the bottom were no houses: the square opened straight on to the main road, like the 'fourth wall' of a theatre, or the 'Terrible Zone'. The effect from Mrs Fleming's bedroom was mysterious and satisfying: the great metropolis knowing its place, and rumbling distantly back and forth.

From the back windows the view was almost a miniature of the front: but instead of the square, narrow strips of back gardens dropped away until only the black tops of their walls could be seen. Beyond the gardens was a sloping row of mews cottages, all a little different from each other, and beyond them lay London, under a sky left hyacinth by the vanishing sun. She glanced down at the mews attached to her garden and observed that her daughter had returned from work. A man's hand, at least not Deirdre's (her daughter did not like women), twitched the scarlet curtains together. Mrs Fleming was genuinely without curiosity, salacious or moral, about her daughter's private life, knowing only that it was conducted with a dramatic symmetry of conflict. There were always two men involved – one dull, devoted creature whose only distinction was his determination to marry her, in the face of a savage series of odds (the other, more attractive, but even more unsatisfactory young man). She suspected that Deirdre was not happy, but the suspicion was an easy one; and since Deirdre herself was clearly convinced that a mutual ignorance was all that held them tolerably apart, Mrs Fleming never attempted to force her daughter's lack of confidence. She supposed that whoever had twitched the curtains was probably coming to dinner, but she could not remember his name . . .

∞   ∞   ∞

Louis Vale let himself into his ground-floor flat in Curzon Street, slammed the metallic door, threw his briefcase on to the bed or divan (he preferred to call it a bed), and turned on his bath. His room, one of an enormous block, resembled the cell of some privileged prisoner. Bare but very expensive essentials were symmetrically arranged in a room so small and so dark that colour, untidiness, or time-wasting trivia of any kind would have been lost or unusable in it. Everything possible was flush with the walls. The cupboard for his clothes, the shelf for his alcohol, the wireless: even the lights clung like white bulbous leeches to the grey paint. There was a cringing armchair and a small double-tier table on which lay an ashtray, a telephone, and the current copy of *The Architec-*

tural Review. The curtains were grey: he never drew them. His bathroom, equipped like a small operating theatre for the business of bathing and shaving, and now slowly suffusing with steam, was a bright uncompromising white. He emptied his pockets, flung off his clothes, and bathed. Ten minutes later he was in his dinner jacket swallowing whisky and water. There was a single drawer set into the wall above the head of his bed. It had no handle and opened with a minute key. Inside the drawer were three unsealed white envelopes. He selected one, shook out of it a latch-key, and locked the drawer.

He parked his car outside the mews in Hillsleigh Road, and let himself into Deirdre Fleming's flat. It was very small, and, he observed with distaste, in a transitional, very feminine state of untidiness. A pile of clothes lay in one corner of the room awaiting the laundry or cleaners. Plates and glasses (the ones they had used two nights ago) were stacked on the draining board by the sink. The bed, or divan (Deirdre preferred to call it a divan), had been stripped of sheets and was now loosely covered by its loose cover. Two half-written letters lay on the table with an unaddressed brown paper parcel. The waste paper basket was full. The only chair was hung with stockings, almost dry, laid on dirty tea-cloths. In a large saucepan he discovered the wreck of an old chicken soaking in water. He read the letters. One was to her father, thanking him for the cheque he had given her on her birthday – and the other, he found with quickening interest, was to him. She felt she must write to him, he read, since he would never allow her to talk. She knew that she irritated him, but he made her so unhappy that she could not remain silent. She knew that he did not really love her, as, if he did, surely he would understand her better. If he really knew the effect that he had upon her when he failed to ring up or to stick to any arrangement, and thought her simply absurd, would he please tell her; but she could not really believe that he knew. He could not possibly want to make anyone so unhappy: she knew what he was really like underneath – an entirely different person to the one he made himself out to be. She knew that his work meant more . . .

Here she had stopped. Here we go again, he thought wearily, and put the letter back on the table, with a sudden vision of Deirdre naked, trying not to cry, and waiting to be loved. She has to be stripped of her self-respect in order to dress me in it. By the time she has grown out of being a romantic, I shan't want her. I am a stinking cad to go on living on her emotional capital. Perhaps, he concluded without much conviction, I thought that she would infuse me with her belief. If she had succeeded, I should have made it worth her while – but she will not succeed. She hasn't got what it takes, and I haven't got what it makes.

Suddenly, old and sad about her, he drew the curtains, so that she should think he had been in the dark, and had not noticed her letter. Then he lay down on the uncomfortable bed, and slept.

He heard her cautiously intruding upon his sleep: opening the door carelessly, shutting it with elaborate calm; trying the ceiling light – on, and off – and then lighting the standard lamp. He felt her motionless in the middle of the room, watching him, and nearly opened his eyes, to interrupt her private heart about him – then remembered the letter, and remained still. He heard her move towards him and halt – heard her fingers on the paper; her sudden little breath which had always charmed him, and the indeterminate noises of concealment. Then, because he did not want to be woken up by her, he opened his eyes . . .

∞ ∞ ∞

June Stoker emerged from the Plaza Cinema in a dim tear-soaked daze, stopped a taxi and asked it to go to Gloucester Place as quickly as possible. She felt in a confused way that she was late: not for anything in particular – her dinner was not until a quarter to eight, and she intended skipping the Thomases' drinks party – but simply late: what in fact she always felt when she had been doing something secretly of which she was rather ashamed. For she would *die* sooner than tell her mother how she had spent the afternoon; alone in a cinema watching a film which in any company at all she would have condemned as sob stuff. To her it seemed frightfully, frightfully sad, and possibly even quite true, if one was that sort of girl. To June the essence of romance suggested the right man in the wrong circumstances – but somehow she could not imagine Julian in those circumstances, in spite of his father, whose behaviour really did seem to be rather odd. She was rather afraid of meeting him: even Julian, who was so calm about everything, seemed a little uncertain about the prospect. His mother had been easy, although June supposed you couldn't really tell in one meeting. Mothers-in-law were supposed to be awful, but one need not see them much. She opened her compact, and powdered her nose. Anyone observant could tell that she had been crying. She looked exactly as though the tears had sprung from all over her face, and not simply from her eyes. She would slip into her room and say that she had a headache. She had a sort of headache now she came to think of it. Home. But it won't *be* my home much longer, she realized: I shall have a different name, and a different house, and all my clothes will be new (well, nearly all), and Mummy won't possibly be able to ask me where I am going all the time; but I *do hope* Julian will ask me when he comes back from the office: and we shall have our friends to dinner – I'll be a marvellous cook, he'll keep finding unsuspected qualities in me . . . I wonder what it will be like spending a whole fortnight alone with Julian . . .

She had paid the taxi and shut herself into the lift. She would have to ring Julian to tell him to pick her up at home, instead of at the Thomases'. She wondered what the dinner party with his parents would be like. Full of awfully clever and interesting people to whom she would not be able to think of anything to say. She sighed, and felt for her latch-key.

Angus, her Aberdeen, yapped mechanically round her feet, and of course her mother called her into the drawing-room. She was having tea with her old school friend, Jocelyn Spellforth-Jones. June first submitted to being told by her mother that she was late, that she looked hot, and that she never shut doors behind her, and then to a general and very unappetizing invitation from Jocelyn Spellforth-Jones to 'tell her all about it'. Nobody but Mummy would think of telling Jocelyn anything: perhaps that is why she always wants to know so badly, thought June, the inevitable blush searing her face and neck, as she protested weakly that there was nothing much to tell, really. Mrs Stoker looked with mock despair at her best friend. Jocelyn returned the look, and invited Angus to search her. He was a sensible little dog and declined. Jocelyn then reminded Mrs Stoker of how absurd they had been when they were June's age, and told a really revolting story about a set of blue china bunnies which she had insisted when she married on transporting from her bedroom mantelpiece in her old home, to a shelf built especially for the purpose by her new bed. Mrs Stoker remembered the bunnies perfectly, and June felt she might reasonably escape. Murmuring something about a headache, she rose to her feet. Immediately, her mother began bombarding her with questions. Had she found a pair of shoes? Did she remember the Thomases? What had Marshall's said about her nighties? Well, what *had* she been doing all afternoon, and why did she suddenly have a headache? June blushed and lied and eventually fled to her bedroom feeling cross and tired.

Everything in her bedroom was pale peach coloured. She liked this; but when she had suggested repeating the colour in their flat, Julian had said that cream was more suitable. It was more neutral, he had said, and she expected that he was right. She slipped out of her pink woollen dress, kicked off her shoes, and emptied her bag on to the end of her bed. Angus (he was getting much too fat) waddled aimlessly round her shoes and then jumped on to his chair which was covered with a greasy car rug of the Hunting Stewart tartan.

If she had not spent most of the afternoon in tears, June would certainly have cried now. Just when everything ought to be marvellous, it somehow actually wasn't. Of course it was largely that awful woman sitting there with Mummy and talking about her marriage with a deathly mixture of silliness and nastiness – and Mummy (although of course she wasn't really like that) at least putting up with it – not noticing it. What was there to *say* about Julian anyway? He worked in an office, advertising things; she didn't know much about it, and honestly it didn't sound awfully interesting, and 'they' said that in view of his uncle, and his general ability for the position, he was certain to be a director before he was thirty. Which, 'they' said, was very good indeed. Julian would not have been able to marry so young without such a prospect, and to start with they would certainly have to be careful. She tried hard to imagine what being careful meant, but she could only think of cottage pies, and not going to the Berkeley. Julian was determined to keep his car, and she simply could not set her own hair. It was dark brown, thick, and rather wiry – frightful hair – although her friends said how lucky she was to have a natural wave. But Julian . . . Well, he was rather good looking, and they thought the same about things, like not believing much in God, and thinking circuses were rather cruel, and not bringing up children in a new-fangled way – and – all that kind of thing. Masses of things really. They had met at a dance and got engaged in Julian's car by the Serpentine. That evening was only a month ago; it had been simply wonderful, and she had thought about it so much since then, that now she could not remember it properly – which was a bore. One ought to remember the night of one's engagement. Julian had seemed a little nervous – she had liked that – and he had talked very fast about them, except when he had touched her, and then he had not talked at all. She could still remember his fingers on the back of her neck just before he kissed her. He had never held her head again in the same way, and she had not dared ask him in case, when he did, it would be different. She lived nostalgically on that little shiver, and the hope that it would return and envelop her when circumstances permitted.

Well, in a week she would be married, and everyone, except that foul Jocelyn (and she didn't matter), was being very nice about it. After all she was an only child: Mummy, for all her frenzied co-operation, would probably be a bit lonely when it was all over, and Julian was the only son. Rather rotten for parents worrying away for years and then getting left. She wondered whether Mrs Fleming minded. Julian did not seem to be especially what her mother described as 'close' to his mother. Perhaps Mrs Fleming preferred Julian's sister. Or perhaps she concentrated on her extraordinary (probably glamorous) husband. One heard all kinds of things about him. He did not seem to lead much of a family life, which had made Mummy like Mrs Fleming much more than she would otherwise have done. June knew that her mother distrusted women of her own age who did not look it; but Mr Fleming's frequent absences from both of his houses made Mummy sorry for Mrs Fleming.

She had been sitting in front of her pink dressing-table removing her make-up; her clear red lipstick, and the film of pink powder which bloomed unbecomingly on her flushed face. She wore no rouge – if one blushed much it was fatal – and her eyelashes were dark and thick like a child's. She scraped her hair back from her wide, shallow forehead, and fastened it with a piece of old pink chiffon. She looked attractive because she was so young, and because she was so young, she felt, like this, very un-attractive. How should she employ these rites with a husband always about? What would he think when he first saw her like this? Impossible to pin up her hair and put cream on her face at night: but how could one expect to remain attractive if one never did these things? She would ask Pamela, who had been married for nearly a year: but Pamela looked ravishing, different, of course, but still ravishing without any make-up at all, while she simply looked like a schoolgirl who was not allowed to know better. And then, as if to convince herself that she no longer was a schoolgirl, she ran to her door and shot its bolt, peeled off her remaining clothes, and lit a cigarette. Now, she thought, she resembled some awful French picture. She certainly did not look like a schoolgirl. Now she would ring up Julian.

Only when she reached the telephone did she realize with a shock which filled her brown eyes with sudden tears of discretion, that she would not, even if he asked her, tell Julian that she had spent the afternoon alone in a cinema.

She pulled the counterpane round her shoulders, and lifted the receiver.

∞   ∞   ∞

Mr Fleming replaced the telephone on its shelf, and sank back into his bath. He had had an exceedingly tiring afternoon, and he felt much the better for it. He regarded his wife's dinner for their son calmly, and decided that he would arrive late. One of his secret pleasures was the loading of social dice against himself. He did not seem for one moment to consider the efforts made by kind or sensitive people to even things up: or if such notions ever occurred to him, he would have observed them with detached amusement, and reloaded more dice.

An unorthodox master at his public school had once written neatly across the corner of his report: 'Brilliant, but bloody minded.' This had delighted Mr Fleming at the time, and he had stuck to the formula ever since. It had really got him a very long way. Throughout his several astonishingly successful careers (he had roared through the examinations for chartered accountancy, fought a courageous war in the service of the Navy – ending up in the trade, gambled his prize money on the Stock Exchange with spectacular luck or ingenuity, and almost as casually begun his term as law student) he had concentrated on himself with a kind of objective ferocity; until now, at an age which merely added to his fascination, he had constructed a personality as elaborate, mysterious, and irrelevant, as a nineteenth-century folly. In turn, he had cultivated information, power, money, and his senses, without ever allowing one of them to influence him exclusively. His incessant curiosity enabled him to amass a quantity of knowledge which his ingenuity and judgement combined to disseminate, or withhold, to the end of power over ideas and people. He made money out of both without people clearly recognizing it, since they were usually so dazzled by his attention that their own ends were blinded. He had a heart when he cared to use it. But on the whole, he did not care in the least about other people, and neither expected nor desired them to care about him. He cared simply and overwhelmingly for himself: and he felt now that he was at last a man after his own heart. The only creature in the world who caused him a moment's disquiet was his wife, and this, he thought, was only because he had at one period in their lives allowed her to see too much of him. This indirectly had resulted in their children: who, though clearly a case for Shaw's theory of eugenics, were, in his opinion, otherwise the consequence of mistaken social exuberance. The boy bored him. He had no doubt that Julian was marrying an exceptionally, even a pathetically, dull young woman; and the only mitigating feature of the affair, Julian's extreme youth, was not likely, in view of his work and disposition, to count for very much. He would probably attempt to extricate himself at thirty, or thereabouts, by which time he would have two or three brats, and a wife, who, drained of what slender resources had first captivated him, would at the same time be possessed of a destructive knowledge of his behaviour. This would inevitably lead to his leaving her (if indeed he were to achieve it) for entirely the wrong reasons.

He considered his daughter to be a more subtle disaster. She was undoubtedly attractive, but although not a fool, she was not equipped with enough intellectual ballast for her charms. Hers was an impulsive intelligence, and she had not the reason either to sustain or to reject her impulses. She would confuse her life with men who exploited her, and work that did not; until, her attractions waning, and her judgement impelled by fear, she would marry. This last, short of a miracle. Mr Fleming believed only in miracles wrought by himself: 'by hand' he would explain with an ingenuous expression, that appeared on his face quite devilish. All this was the result of his wife trying to be a good mother; and he, he was perfectly sanguine about it, trying not to be a father of any kind.

Innumerable women had enquired why he had married his wife; and it had fascinated him to hear the varying degrees of curiosity, solicitude, and spite with which they contrived to put the damaging little question. It had fascinated him no less to reply (throwing contemptuously aside such reportorial excuses as youth or inexperience) with fantastic, and apparently circumstantial detail; in such a way as to defer their hopes, excite their interest, or disprove their theories: discovering, each time (and he never told the same story twice), that there was no limit or horizon to the human capacity of belief. He did it, he considered, in the best possible taste. He never deprecated his wife, even by implication. He simply added, as it were, another storey to the structure of his personality, and invited the lady in question to put herself temporarily in possession: there she might perch precariously, in what she could be easily persuaded was an isolated castle in a rich and strange air.

He was bathed; he was dressed.

In the bedroom he regarded a tangle of sheets, damp silky hair, and bare sulking arms, with faint, with very faint, interest. When he had said hours ago that he would not be dining with her, she had started to make emotional capital out of it. His remark that to her monotony was the spice of life had reduced her to an injured dramatic silence which he knew very well she expected him to break. Instead he put two five-pound notes and some small change on the dressing-table, secured them by her bottle of Caron, and left. It amused him to see how women reacted to this: he always maintained that the theatrical insult of pennies thrown upon the stage related strictly to the value of the coins. Sovereigns would produce a different result. The sentimental women (they were legion) returned the notes and kept the change. The professional kept the lot and never alluded to it. The romantic and inexperienced returned the lot and discussed it for weeks with varying degrees of tortuous indignation (he had learned to avoid them). One woman had left it lying on an hotel dressing-table for days, and then, when they had left the hotel, announced that it was a tip for the chambermaid; and one had kept the notes and sent the change back to him as a donation to the cause of his sensibility.

He collected a taxi and drove to his club for a drink and a little telephoning. The time had come, he felt, to make several, drastic changes . . .

∞　∞　∞

Leila Talbot telephoned her house to tell her maid to tell her nanny that the children were not to wait up for her as she would be late at the hairdresser, to ring up the Thomases to say that she would be late for her drink (oh dear, and they had asked her to be early), and to ring up the Flemings to say that she would be late for dinner as she would be late at the Thomases'. Then, with a little groan of pride at her administrative ability, she cautiously encased herself in the electric hair-drying machine. Most people were late without warning people; they had no manners nowadays . . .

∞　∞　∞

I should like to be really rude to him. Really outrageous, Joseph Fleming thought, his gouty fingers struggling with his black tie. He had disliked his elder brother so intensely for so many years that even at the prospect of seeing him he indulged in a preliminary orgy of hate. His mind ebbed and flowed and broke again over the rock of his brother's insolence, his success with other men, with any woman, with money (his profession seemed exasperatingly to combine streams of women and the acquisition of money), and finally with that collective mystery, the world. He

18

did not like Mrs Fleming either; but then, he did not like women, he disliked other men liking them, and he loathed anyone who had ever liked his brother.

It was characteristic of Joseph that he suffered badly from gout, particularly in his hands, without drinking red wine. He knew that the angry variations upon which he was now engaged would make him very hungry; that he would eat too much too fast at dinner, and that he would spend a night sleepless with indigestion. It was also characteristic of him that however little he thought he wanted to go to dinner at Campden Hill Square to meet some hard-boiled chit that damned young puppy his nephew was to marry (and probably a small crowd of dreary people he had so frequently met there before), nothing would have induced him to miss it. As it was, he believed he had one of his gargantuan colds coming . . . but still, he would go, although how anybody could expect the evening to be enjoyable was utterly beyond him.

TWO

They all sat round the table eating oysters. June said she adored them. Leila Talbot said how exciting it was to eat them for the first time every September. Joseph said that he had met somebody at his club who had lived in New Zealand where all one had to do was to put one's hand into a pool and pull them out. Mr Fleming had remarked that if they were quite so easily come by, he did not think that he would want them. Deirdre said anyway there ought to be *some* compensation for living in New Zealand. Louis, who had been very silent, said that he had been born there, and that, with Deirdre subsiding into an agony of sensibility, was that.

Mrs Fleming, as a result of formal interest, learned that Louis Vale was an architect, a member of the Georgian Group, and a contributor to several sympathetic journals on such subjects as the ground plans of great houses long since demolished. The conversation flowered, as monologues of intelligent young men on the subject of their careers to an intelligent and sympathetic woman will do; until, at the point when Deirdre was softening under the influence of her lover acquitting himself so well (she had not listened to what Louis had been saying, but only to the effect of what he had said), and Joseph, unable to command Leila Talbot's attention against such competition, was rumbling and snarling inside like a volcano, Mr

Fleming leaned forward and, with deceptive delicacy, asked Louis what he was designing, or doing.

Louis, pulled up – floundered – said that he taught second-year students, and that (he spoke very fast) he was designing prefabricated public conveniences . . . to be used, of course, all over the country.

During the moments that followed, Georgian, or what they conceived to be Georgian, images fell to ruins in the pit of a silence so small but so deep, that at the end of it all of them were made violently aware of one another, as people who have survived an earthquake. Joseph thought: Stevenson could have written him: only Stevenson. He's a villain – an intellectual villain.

Deirdre, subject to a battery of emotion – hatred of her father, and resentment of her mother – suddenly saw Louis separate from herself; as he must have been before she knew him – as he was now, without her; the part of him that was recoiling from her father might envelop him to the exclusion of herself. A waste of emotional despair overcame her; so that for a moment she was positively, destructively, beautiful – her eyelids weighted to Botticellian proportions – her baroque mouth simplified by her unhappiness. Instinctively, she glanced at her mother; but every thread of her face was controlled. *Her* thoughts, *her* feelings were so much her own business, that she had no time for those belonging to anyone else. But miraculously, she had. She leaned forward, and with perfect conventional manipulation, she restored Louis's faith in himself. Architecture was again safe: Joseph was again possessed of Leila Talbot; and Mr Fleming, unmoved, proceeded to dissect June, who, almost everyone knew, including Mr Fleming, was hardly fair prey . . . it was indeed a minute admission on his part. June was quickly reduced to the public uttermost depths of an unformed mind. Dark green and bright red reminded her of holly, which reminded her of Christmas, which reminded her of her childhood. Had she been less simple, she would have realized that these reactions were uniform. If she had been more adept she would have prevented these discoveries relating to herself. As she was (and Mr Fleming intended she should be), she blushed amid high school clichés and indestructible platitudes which she had read and spoken since she had been taught to read and speak: but her limitations and her embarrassment were so routine that they afforded Mr Fleming little pleasure. She was a nice, ignorant, repressed, anxious, unimaginative girl, designed perfectly to reproduce herself; and regarding her, Mr Fleming found it difficult to believe in *The Origin of Species*.

Julian enjoyed his grouse, and wondered what the hell he was going to *do* with June in Paris. After all, there were limits, pretty stringent ones, if she'd never been to bed with anyone before. He approved of that, but it made the prospect of a honeymoon with her something of an ordeal. He reviewed his own experience rather defiantly to reassure himself: the local intellectual tart at Oxford; that extraordinary woman he had met at a shoot in Norfolk; and Mrs Travers, who had been at least forty, and infinitely stimulating. It was odd that although he had been to bed with her four times, he still thought of her as Mrs Travers. Sometimes he tried saying 'Isobel' carelessly to himself, but he never felt happy about it. Mrs Travers had had a husband, a lover who lived in her house, and a stream of young men. She was very good tempered, and told them all extremely careless lies; but as long as they pretended to believe her, she was very kind to them. From her he had learned that everything took twice as long as he had thought necessary; but except for her irritating habit (when she was otherwise carried away) of calling him Desmond, the incident had proved as enjoyable as it had been educative.

Fortified by these fleeting exaggerated recollections, he considered grandly whether he had better not sack Harrison. Harrison was their office manager, and had been for nearly twenty years. Julian was not really in a position to sack him, but anyone with any imagination could see that Harrison's methods were hopelessly antiquated, and that his sole concern (that of keeping down overheads) was beginning seriously to cramp developments, and even giving the firm a bad name. Harrison owed his position to a crablike ingenuity with Uncle Joseph, consisting chiefly in a nauseating Dickensian act of worthless feudal memories, which Julian's uncle, who could never remember anything, greatly enjoyed. Well, in Paris he could think about sacking Harrison. He half wished that Paris was over; June said that she did not really speak French, and neither of them knew anyone there at all well – still they would have the car, and they could go to films. June said that French films were much better than English or American ones – she was saying it now to his father; and he, damn him, was asking her why she thought so. Poor darling, she was blushing, and of course she didn't know why. Suddenly protective about her, he felt for her hand which was nervously twisting her napkin under the table. When he touched her, she turned to him with such a radiance of gratitude that for a moment he knew that he loved her.

Mrs Fleming, while she listened to Deirdre's difficult, attractive young man, examined her husband's face, which was now blatantly, almost insultingly, expressionless, as he enquired into June's prejudices and predilections. It was a lack of expression so complete, that although she had observed it many hundred times, she was never able to believe it; and she searched now a little more urgently than usual (perhaps because she wanted to protect June?) for some trace of his mind on his face. But his large pale forehead was smooth; his pale blue, nearly round eyes had not even the familiar intense quality of glass eyes; and his lips – so unlike one another, so little a pair that it was impossible to think of them as a mouth – touched one another and parted for food and speech as though they had no interest in either. She believed that at such moments his mind was working furiously; but the insulation was so practised and complete that she was never certain. He was probably bored. After their first three years she had spent the remaining twenty fighting the battle of his boredom, and, she realized suddenly now, never with any hope of success; since from the first he had been freakishly and inexorably ranged against her. It had been he who had suggested this dinner party; he had resisted her slightest attempt to enliven it with less accountable guests; and she, in the solitary and dangerous position of knowing half his mind, had not persevered.

Now, suddenly finished with June, he was leaning towards Deirdre and saying in his soft pedantic voice: 'But you, my dear Deirdre, never answer letters until your recipient's anticipation has been blunted by despair. You will never make a Clarissa. You will lose your voice on the telephone, and your virtue, unable to prevaricate by any civilized means, will turn uneasily in its double grave.'

And Deirdre, who knew her father well enough not then to thank him for his birthday present, replied: 'My dear Papa, of what possible interest can my voice or my virtue be to you?'

To which, with the faintest gleam of malicious acknowledgement, he said: 'None, excepting that I am a student of strife,' and stared gently at his orange soufflé.

Mrs Fleming hastily relinquished Louis Vale for Deirdre's reinstatement. How many times had she sat at this table blocking her husband's sorties – a little too soon, and he was resentful; a little too late, and the guests were damaged; perhaps, worst of all, at exactly the right moment, when he felt challenged to more murderous and ingenious attacks: always upon people without the wit or assurance to respond (as he might have liked) against him. She had threatened once to throw him out of countenance, but ignoring the impossibility of such a proposition, he had silenced her by saying simply that the situation between two people married was so painfully familiar to them, that the need for it to be an enigma to everyone else was surely obvious. She was not exactly afraid of him, but in twenty-three years he had literally exhausted her, and she had therefore never attempted publicly to confound him. He must, she supposed, have had a trying afternoon. She turned now to Joseph, who, she knew, disliked her in a simple uncompromising manner that she found pathetic and sometimes even endearing.

Louis, aware that he had been thrown into the breach, gathered together the warp and woof of his aggression and his self-control; sized up Mr Fleming (and got him wrong) – and was immediately outfaced by Mr Fleming selecting the works of Bellamy, to which he brought the full weight and variety of his mind. Soon they were lost in the heights of Tiahuanaco. Deirdre unwisely attempted to introduce the Pyramids, but Mr Fleming waved them gently aside as so many castle puddings, and continued to expound and elaborate Bellamy's theories with an amiable brilliance of which, earlier, Louis would not have thought him capable.

Leila Talbot was a woman who talked to men about themselves and to women about other people. When she was doing neither, she applied stern concentration to her own appearance, or a more frivolous appraisement to the appearance of any other woman present (she was seldom alone). She had accounted for June – she had observed that June was inexperienced or conscientious or rich enough to wear her best stockings with a long dress; that she veered unhappily and unsuccessfully between Victorian and Edwardian family heir-looms and 'costume jewellery'; that she clearly experienced trouble with her hair; and that she had lost weight since she had bought the buff-coloured jersey silk she was wearing. Now, Leila, as she ate her soufflé, turned, as on these occasions she always did, to her hostess. She had known Mrs Fleming for a very long time and their friendship, never intimate, uncharged by either competition or sympathy of interest, afforded them none the less a certain pleasure as women who have known each other for anything more than twenty years, without either side divulging any of the ephemeral misleading details of their private lives. Even when Mrs Talbot's husband was killed in an air crash, she had not confided to Mrs Fleming how little she had cared, and how guilty she had felt for not caring; but Mrs Fleming had been quietly imaginatively kind to her at the time, she remembered. Leila kept any speculations about Mrs Fleming's life with her husband to herself, which was more than she did for anyone else. Mrs Fleming, she felt, stimulated the best in her, and though this meant that she did not want to see too much of Mrs Fleming, she enjoyed being accepted as reserved, disinterested in personal affairs, reliable, and more intelligent than she was.

At the moment, however, she was characteristically concerned with her friend's appearance: with her hair, which though still dark and thick, was laced with single pure white hairs apparent now even in the candelight – showing more, Leila thought, because she wore it gathered neatly to the back of her head without a parting; with her skin, which was smooth, and of an even parched colour; with her eyes, which looked as though they had once been a brilliant temporary blue, and had bleached to the texture of water by some violent light. Except for her eyes, none of her features was remarkable – but the absolute regularity of their disposition gave her a kind of distinction, a pleasing and rare elegance, perhaps more prevalent, at any rate more consciously aimed at, in the time of Jane Austen, than now. That was the answer, Leila concluded, to her mysteriously ageless quality; she was quite simply out of another age . . . and now she was fast on the way to becoming a grandmother. Leila considered her own three children, all identically unattractive, sized ten, twelve, and fourteen, like horrible mass-produced clothes, and thanked God that at least they were far from an age when they would be likely to bombard her with grandchildren.

Her speculations were finally brought to an end by her hostess's eye. The four women went upstairs, and having seen them on the way to her bedroom, Mrs

Fleming retired alone to the drawing-room to make the coffee.

There were four cups on the tray by the fire, which meant that Mr Fleming was performing the same operation on the floor below. Mrs Fleming made excellent coffee, but never to her husband's liking. When he made it, it became mysteriously a foreign drink, tasting of its colour, and unbelievably hot, so that one half-expected the brittle cups to explode. She made her coffee, and thought she thought of nothing at all: but when June entered the room, and, on her invitation, advanced rather timidly to share the long stool, she realized that her husband, and Julian, and Deirdre, had been running through her head like some endless unsatisfactory fugue, which would not, could not, stop, unless it was resolved or interrupted.

June seemed nervously to expect this tête-à-tête to become a cross-examination of her ability to look after Julian. In vain did Mrs Fleming discourse with mild kindness of Paris and the new flat; June closed each attempt with defensive assertions about her domestic, and even maternal, talents. When she asked whether she might be taught to make coffee like Mrs Fleming, to whom the gaucherie of such ingratiation was both alarming and disagreeable, Deirdre joined them, remarking that Leila was telephoning the Thomases', where she thought she might have left her cigarette case. She then asked affectionately for some of her mother's perfectly filthy coffee. 'You make it like some health-giving tea, and Papa makes it like a drug: same coffee, same apparatus. I don't know how you do it.'

Mrs Fleming said: 'I expect people's natures obtrude upon their coffee,' and smiled at June, who looked as

28

though Deirdre had dropped a brick on her. 'The cigarettes,' she said severely to her daughter, 'are on the mantelpiece.'

Deirdre reached for the box, handed it to June, and lit their cigarettes.

'Are dozens of horrible presents still rolling in?' she asked, with a kind of commiseration that was none the less aggressive.

'Quite a lot.' June smiled unhappily. She was terrified of Deirdre, and did not like her.

'I haven't given you anything yet. What would you like?'

Stretched on the rack of this heartless generosity, June was reduced to saying that Deirdre had better ask Julian.

'Oh, *Julian*. He never really *wants* anything.' She rose suddenly, and threw her barely smoked cigarette into the fire. 'Mamma, may I have some brandy?'

'They can't find it, but they are looking. If they fail, I shall work steadily backwards over yesterday!' Leila left the door ajar, and sank into a chair.

Mrs Fleming murmured: 'It sounds like a play by Mr Priestley,' and handed her coffee.

'Thank you. Yes, I should love some. But really, it is too depressing. This is the case that I only found last week, after losing it for all that time before.'

June thought that obviously Leila's mother had never told her that she always left doors open. She shivered, and Mrs Fleming, who had been warming glasses, gave her some brandy.

Deirdre continued mercilessly: 'We were trying to decide what I should give June for a wedding present.'

'Oh my dear, it's a dreadful problem. But, I warn you, what you get in the way of revolting objects and fulsome congratulation when you are married is nothing to what you get when you have a baby. Could I have a cigarette?'

Deirdre supplied her, lit another herself, looked at it, and laid it on an ashtray.

'Dreadful books about its age and weight at every conceivable moment, and ghastly yellow knitted matinee coats (why *are* they so often yellow?) and letters from hospitals, and photographs of other people's babies so that you can see exactly how awful it's going to look when it's larger, and little brushes and combs and things covered with pixies; a sort of undercurrent of Margaret Tarrant and Walt Disney, glazed with God. Oh! I shall send you two dozen Harrington Squares.'

Mrs Fleming was amused; and June, though faintly shocked, was laughing, when Deirdre, with a sudden clumsy movement, knocked her brandy glass over on to the hearth, where it smashed to the stem. Ignoring it, she walked to the door. 'The most appalling draught,' she said, and returned to the broken glass.

Mrs Fleming was about to speak; looked at her daughter's stormy face, and was silent. Something is very wrong: but I shall never know what it is until it doesn't matter whether I know or not; which is probably quite right. I only think I can save her some needless extravagance of the heart; or perhaps I only think I ought to save her. Oh dear, oh dear, what a mistake it is to listen to one's thoughts. But it is a mistake of such infinite variety that making it constitutes a chief pleasure in life. Aloud, she said: 'Clear away the bits, darling. You know what your father feels about anything broken.'

'I don't believe he feels about anything until it *is* broken.'

But she picked up every single fragment that she could see, and wrapped them in the evening paper.

Leila and June were happily engaged upon the absorbing and uncontroversial subject of how much too expensive everything was. Deirdre's mouth curled, and she looked desperately round the room. She has his capacity for boredom, thought Mrs Fleming anxiously, I wonder whether she has . . .

But at that moment the men entered the room: returned from the mysterious technical conversations about money, about sex, about the murderous propensities of the North Korean – having discussed the fundamentals as superficially as the women in the drawing-room discussed the superficialities fundamentally. After half an hour's uneasy amalgamation, the party broke up.

Mr Fleming showed no signs of breaking with them, but accompanied them to the door in an obtrusively hostly manner; leaving Mrs Fleming in the drawing-room. He was sure she was tired, he said . . .

∞ ∞ ∞

Julian shut June into the car and walked round to his door saying something that she could not hear. As soon as he had switched on the ignition she asked him what he had said. (This was a ritual they were to repeat until the tedium of it provoked them to conduct all their quarrels in cars.) Now, however, he thought it rather sweet of her to care what he had said.

'I said it's a good thing we have this hill to start on, because she hasn't been charging properly for weeks.'

He released the brake and they slid down the hill, jolting a little as the motor started.

'What about Paris?' June asked.

'What about it?'

'Not being able to start.'

'Oh *that*. She's going on charge tomorrow morning.'

There was a pause, and then June said carefully: 'I like your mother. But all your family are a bit frightening.'

'Oh well, the only course open to in-laws is to be frightening or dull. It's better if they start frightening, I should think.'

'But your mother *is* nice,' persisted June, wanting to know how nice Julian thought his mother.

However, he answered indifferently: 'She's all right. A perfectly blameless creature. My father is no joke though.'

'Everybody is to *him*.'

'You know, I believe that's true. That's *clever* of you!'

He said it with such surprise that she might have laughed, but she was so young, and knew so little about people, that she was hurt, and said: 'I do know about people. People are my thing.'

'Oh darling! People are your thing!'

The chain of lights down Bayswater Road were strung before them like Douglas's bad sonnet on London.

'Aren't they pretty?'

'What?'

'The lights all down the centre of the road.'

'Awfully pretty. No policemen about, are there?' He began to drive fast.

A minute later, June asked: 'Did you have a tiring day?'

'Not specially. Tiresome. Clearing things up.'

She waited for him to ask her what sort of day she had had, so that she could tell him quickly about the cinema; but he did not ask her. They were at Marble Arch, and he said: 'Damn. I should have turned left.'

Outside her house, he switched off the engine and took off his hat. She had planned at Marble Arch to tell him at this moment – quickly – just before he kissed her, because his wanting to kiss her would make it all seem less shameful or less absurd: but his deliberation, which seemed to her both practised and heartless, frightened her again. She did not know that he was deliberate simply because he was nervous.

So she did not tell him.

∞   ∞   ∞

Deirdre and Louis left hurriedly together. They left Leila and Joseph waiting for the taxi for which Julian had telephoned. Louis left with regret, and Deirdre with relief exacerbated by Louis's obvious reluctance to finish the evening. She knew that he had been impressed by both of her parents; but while this was something that part of her passionately required, she as passionately wanted to be regarded by Louis 'for herself' as women say, which means for some elusive attraction which they do not feel they possess.

They walked in silence the few yards up the hill and round the corner to the Hillsleigh Road mews outside which stood Louis's car. The sight of it threw Deirdre into a state of defiance which was very like panic. She determined to say nothing aloud; but her secret self gabbled and implored, alternately abject and bitter: her immense distrust of everyone which began with herself completed its circle, until, by the time they were arrived outside her door and Louis's car, nothing she said would have had any meaning, and she might have said anything, if Louis had not forestalled her.

'I'll see you safely inside, and then, I *think*, home to my own bed. Darling,' he added. He had been praying (in more measured terms) that Deirdre would also be tired – be calm, but tired. Now, however, she swung round on him, her hand on the uncomfortably high door-knob, her eyes dilated, blazing with entreaty. He moved nearer to her, ready to want her, but she flung out the fingers of her left hand in a minutely passionate denial (she had hands like her mother's – elegant, eloquent hands); her eyebrows rose and settled in quivering drifts of humiliation, and she turned away from him to the door.

For a moment he was really afraid of her . . . of her perilous depths of emotion, which seemed to sweep her desolate of pride, and to strand them both in a desert of anxious silence and nervous hands: then he remembered the letter, and thought angrily that her sense of drama made her ridiculous, and life with her intolerable – why even her despair was in some sort erotic, so what could she *expect* him to feel?

Trying to eliminate the exasperation from his voice, he said: 'But I shall see you tomorrow evening,' and then, when she did not reply: 'Deirdre, what is it?' (That surely gives her an opening.)

Without looking at him, she said: 'It is having to *ask* you to stay. I find that unbearable. Being forced to ask you. Then it simply makes you think that . . .'

She had spoken very slowly, as though her words were difficult to choose, and when they became easy, she stopped, obviously afraid of where they might lead her.

Louis thought: Women are sensitive to temperature in exact proportion to the amount they are bored. He was extremely cold himself. Aloud, he said: 'Well darling Deirdre, quite often, I am glad to say, you *do* want to go to bed with me. And, quite as often, you think you don't, and find you do. If you just want to talk to me, couldn't it wait until tomorrow? I do promise you, I shall listen far better . . .'

'But I have something to tell you!' she cried, as though this cleared and precipitated the whole situation.

Christ, that damned letter, he thought: remembered how young she was, how little versed in the subtle laws of emotional demand and supply, and resolved to be gentle with her, but to go through with it in such a way that she would never abandon them again to further situations of the kind.

'Right, well if only you'll open the door, I will walk up into your parlour.'

She opened the door, started up the steep rickety stairs, and then, before she reached the top, she turned round to him, and said with an effort of lightness: 'My dear Louis, I do assure you that in this particular instance, *I* am the fly.'

He noticed then that she was shaking from head to foot, and with a kind of unwilling fear, for the first time he took her seriously. The letter, he remembered, had not been finished . . .

∞ ∞ ∞

'Since she *knows* that I live in Chiltern Court, and she in Pelham Crescent, why does she expect me to share a cab with her? In order to have someone to chatter at, and pay the fare for her, damn her.' Joseph eyed Leila Talbot morosely as they waited for the cab; and managed during those interminable minutes, to pin this feminine contrivance on his brother. He particularly disliked Mrs Talbot because she was not only a woman, but a widow, and he regarded all widows with egocentric suspicion: irrespective of their age, they were predatory and *passé* like man-eating tigresses. The fact that Mrs Talbot throughout the evening had divided her attentions among her fellow diners with indifferent partiality only made him angrier, and he rationalized her behaviour venomously as yet another instance of her cunning.

Their drive in the taxi was therefore not enjoyable. Leila was both nervous and bored. She attempted three or four topics sufficiently uninteresting to merit some sort of reply, but he grunted her out of countenance. She knew he was passionately interested in something . . . (was it coins or caves?) but serious conversation in a taxi cab was to her an anachronism.

At Pelham Crescent she thanked him, made some move to pay her share of the fare, and then without in the least meaning it, said as she climbed out: 'I know there was something frightfully important that I wanted to tell you, but I simply can't remember what it is.' There was a pause, and then she said, 'I shall have to ring you up.'

She immediately forgot this, but Joseph pondered it with exhaustive distrust all the way to Chiltern Court and throughout his ensuing indigestible night.

∞ ∞ ∞

Mr Fleming bolted the door on the last of his guests, and walked thoughtfully to the ebony table where he had earlier observed a pile of envelopes addressed to him. He put them in his pocket, returned to the door, unbolted it, and climbed the stairs to the drawing-room.

She looked up from her book – he suspected that she had not been reading it – and he shut the door gently behind him . . .

THREE

Mrs Fleming sat perfectly still where Mr Fleming had left her. Her mind remained as motionless as her body: poised for some movement which she felt must be collected and designed if she were not to perish. All the words and thoughts and shivering sensation attributed to a shock of this kind poured through her, rejected by the age of her reason as inadequate. The fear of doing, or saying, or being something annihilating to the pride which she had guarded for so long, through the agonizing sequence of smash and grab and compromise against which she had been ranged, was paralysing in its strength. It was not a simple question of tears, or vituperation, of the beautifully easy blame which children and political agitators release in their predicaments: she had no violent facile conviction to support her; no private place where she could vanish from self-consciousness: no godlike creature brimming with objective love and wisdom to whom she could turn . . . simply the skeleton of perhaps twenty-five years ahead of her on to which she must graft some fabric of her life.

So she sat, perfectly still amid the coffee cups and brandy glasses, until, long after the fire had died, and a fine even chill had settled imperceptibly on the room like ashes, she became aware that she was very, very cold; and that he had been gone nearly three hours.

∞ ∞ ∞

Waking was like being born: 'We are worthless to one another,' he was saying – but not once – again and again, and tears were streaming down her face.

She considered leaving Julian to breakfast downstairs alone, and then as sleep and the damning reiteration receded, realized the folly of such an indulgence. She had woken at her usual hour, and as she proceeded with the routine of beginning the day, she reflected how inexorably people as they grew older become set in the mechanics of their lives. When Dorothy arrived with tea and lemon juice, she was already in a very hot bath.

In her bath she discovered two things: that her mind, usually able to play freely on her favourite theme of relating ideas she had read to things she had seen, or people she had encountered (often resolving in some grandiloquent notion – frivolous, but pleasant exercise to one who enjoyed the morning), was now leashed in an immediate introspective manner to herself. It crowded in a frenzy of ghoulish anticipation, round the naked reclining body of Mrs Fleming; as though she had suffered some accident, and it was awaiting unhelpfully further developments; her removal from the scene – her actual death.

The other discovery was her age. One applied age to other people, generally and precisely: they were older than they looked; they were only twenty-two; they were remarkable for forty-three: but the growing up with oneself – the stiffening of the body and the loosening of the mind; the selection and rejection of what could or could not be done, or said, or thought; the accretion of experience and habit was so gradual: there was such a quantity of these moving pictures, that one did not seem (and was not) very different from another, until something happened which forced the whole private collection upon their owner; discrepancies of behaviour and appearance shouted down the years which make age, echoing in vault after vault of memory that they had changed – that they were new – that they were old. That she was forty-three.

She brushed and combed and dressed her hair, wondering at what age people were most vulnerable: when they were very young, with a daring beautiful resilience, in love with themselves and anyone who loved them; or later, when experience could be compared, and future opportunity was diminished; or later still, in the middle of the wood, where the trees ahead so horribly resembled the trees behind, and the undergrowth of their past caught and clung and tore at them as they moved on. Perhaps they were most vulnerable of all very late, when the end at least, even for the short-sighted, was inexorably in sight – the small clearing in which to lie down and be still and sleep like the dead.

She put on enough make-up to render her face familiar to those who did not really know it, and went down to breakfast with her son.

Julian, balked of his *Times* by the number of congratulatory letters his engagement still provoked, was in his usual early morning temper. When Mrs Fleming arrived he was annihilating toast, and ripping envelopes which he cast from him unread in silent resentment. He hated writing letters, and, being a consistent young man, he hated getting them.

'I say, Mamma, were you afflicted like this when you married?'

Mrs Fleming finished pouring her coffee before she replied: 'I expect it was worse, because people had more leisure; but mercifully I cannot remember it at all.'

There was a short silence, during which Mrs Fleming thought how old Julian must think her not to remember the letters she had got when she was married. Then, he said:

'I really think June might cope with them. She hasn't got to work all day.'

'She has all her own letters, and her clothes, not to mention the new flat. Anyway, can you imagine how outraged some of your friends would be if they were answered by her. Really, Julian, your sense of indecorum is . . .'

'Remarkably developed: you might be a bloody Bohemian,' he finished. It was the remark of one of his great-uncles thus frivolously handed down. It did not make either of them laugh; it was a kind of ritualistic trap into which from time to time they and Deirdre fell.

'Oh well, Porky can answer then.' He began sweeping them into jagged heaps.

Mrs Fleming said: 'I sometimes wonder whether even she likes being called that.'

'Porky? Well she's been called it for twenty-two years; she must be used to it. She's the only secretary in the office with a nickname. I expect you'd find she's proud of it.' He got up from the table in a cloud of envelopes. 'Women like Porky, Mamma, get used to *anything*. They have to. I'll be out to dinner,' and he went.

No, she wouldn't, she couldn't tell Julian.

She went upstairs to write to her husband that Julian need not be worried by their private affairs until after he was married and back from Paris. 'Of course, he need never be *worried* . . .' she wrote: 'but he need not even be told. I imagine that you will attend his wedding.' This last was, in their currency, a desperate plea that he should attend: so complex, dull, and indirect had become thoughts and desires between them.

The familiar uncertainty which these uncharacteristic demands always induced stopped her now for consideration, and her consideration was interrupted by the telephone. Her heart made a violent unpleasurable leap, and she picked up the receiver.

But it was Louis Vale.

He sounded very much older than he was, older, and more responsible. He wondered whether he might see her. Well, yes, it was rather. He knew that it sounded extremely odd, but could she possibly lunch with him? He meant odd because it was such short notice and she hardly knew him, he added. He spoke with the kind of calmness which suggested long-term agitation. Mrs Fleming proposed that he lunch at Campden Hill Square. He accepted with a gratitude which, she detected, at the back of his manners, was desperate. He thanked her thoroughly, but noncommittally, for her dinner the night before, and rang off.

'I believe if I had not asked him here, he had keyed himself up to propose it.' Then suddenly she thought of Deirdre, and in unthinking panic dialled the number of the place where she worked. It was engaged, and while she waited for the line, Louis telephoned again. This time he sounded really embarrassed. He knew that it was a preposterous thing to ask, but would she very much mind not telling anyone that he was coming to lunch? *Anyone*? Of course, he didn't expect her deliberately to rush about telling people, but he hadn't made it at all clear that he wanted to see her privately . . . by the way, he was not inconveniencing her, was he: she would be alone? She reassured him, and then asked if he knew whether Deirdre was at work? No, it wasn't one of her office days, he replied, and then said: 'As a matter of fact she's out for the day. She'll be back in the evening, I think.' Mrs Fleming, relieved, said that she would expect him at twelve thirty. 'You are exceedingly kind. Exceedingly kind,' he repeated, and rang off.

'I suppose he wants to discuss Deirdre. But really, what a fuss.' She felt the slight irritation which so often succeeds unwarranted panic; signed the letter to her husband, addressed it to his club, and went downstairs to arrange about luncheon.

Louis arrived at twelve twenty-five.

The first thing they each privately observed of the other was that he and she looked as though they had not slept. He put this down to her age, and she to his youth and obviously nervous disposition. They drank sherry and tried to make allowances for one another (she had looked such a very attractive woman the night before: now she seemed parched – drained of her particular degree of attractiveness – daylight, and unromantic clothes?): and she tried to walk them through the conversational prelude to whatever it was he had really come to talk about (he looked positively haggard; as though he had been humiliatingly drunk, or killed somebody by accident, or been told that he was to die six months hence), until finally she found that they were both looking desperately at the clock, in an effort to calculate and arrange the time. She realized then that he wanted to begin, but was afraid, and that he was considering their removal to the dining-room in a few minutes.

'Would you rather wait until we go downstairs before telling me whatever it is you want to tell me, or would you rather start now? We are lunching at one.'

He looked at the clock again, and back at her. She had a way of looking at him at the end of her sentence – an absolutely direct unimpassioned gaze, which lent a kind of dignity and significance to her most commonplace remarks, and which seemed to him then the most intricate blend of charm and good manners. If he had not been so desperately nervous and generally sick at the prospect before him, he might have enjoyed lunching with her. As it was . . .

'The difficulties are,' he said, 'that if I don't begin very soon, I shall not have the courage to begin at all; but if I start, and we are interrupted, I shall find it . . . the whole thing will become . . .' He flicked the ash off his cigarette on to the carpet, and pounced on it with his foot. 'Oh, damn, what an awful thing to do . . .' He was too much distressed to say anything more, and the general situation began to rock and tremble and lose its balance.

Mrs Fleming said: 'If you will carry it, I think we had better move our lunch up here where it is much warmer, and we shall not be disturbed by Dorothy.'

He stumbled gratefully to his feet, and carefully carried two vast trays round the narrow corners on the stairs, while Mrs Fleming established their privacy with Dorothy. Eventually, they were seated on either side of the fire with food on their plates and whisky in Louis's glass. Mrs Fleming began calmly eating her lunch which she did not in the least want. The moment had suddenly arrived.

'If you accept the fact that at least I think I am right to tell you all this, perhaps you will forgive the way I tell it. You see, I've thought and thought and rehearsed in my mind how to begin, and it all seems hopeless now. I think, in spite of the shock, I'd better try to be simple and brief.'

'I must, of course, reserve my judgement of whether you are right to tell me at all.'

'You must, of course, do that.' He drank some of his whisky, and stared at his untouched food.

'Deirdre has started a child. The child is undoubtedly mine. Apparently she has known about it for some time, but she only told me last night. She has not said so, but I know that she wants me to marry her. She didn't tell me about the child sooner, and she hasn't said that she wants to marry me, because she knows that I do not want to marry her.'

There was a little silence: he cleared his throat and looked at her. She was not looking at him, and there was no expression on her face. Oh God, I could not have put it worse, he thought. Where has she gone from here? He raced along all the possible avenues of her mind in vain pursuit. He found nothing; he could feel nothing.

'Of course, there are one or two ways out of this situation,' he said, 'but they are not so simple as one might think. Possibly they seem more complicated to me than they would to you.'

Mrs Fleming drank a little water.

'Listen,' he said; her silence was stripping his mind to a point where he felt she ought not to remain alone in the room with it. 'I haven't come here to justify my behaviour or elude my responsibilities. But there is no point in my telling you this unless I tell *all* of it, and you believe me.'

'Why *are* you telling me?'

'Because I honestly don't know what to do,' he said.

45

'I've got to do something, and you seemed to me . . . last night, that is . . . someone who would know what to do. In any crisis. Last night. Do you despise me very much for that?'

She felt him almost unconsciously trying to lighten the atmosphere, which, in the circumstances, was hardly his prerogative, and said: 'Do you know why it is so easy to make decisions for other people? It is not simply because one is objective. It is because if I make a decision for you, I shall not have to carry it out. If I make a wrong decision, the responsibility will still be yours.'

'Yes?'

'Perhaps you had better describe your behaviour and responsibilities. I am not very clear about how you regard either.'

He thought this was sarcasm, and looked at her expecting to see it dirtying her face; but it was not; and he thought again – She is simply exact in her language, and I hope to God I shall be honest and accurate to her. Aloud, he said:

'The obvious solution in a sense would be for me to marry her. The trouble about that is that I don't love her, and I should make her very unhappy. I don't want to marry anyone at the moment, and I am not faithful to Deirdre even now. But I don't think it would be dishonest to say that she doesn't love me. She has made something of me in her mind, which I do not in the least resemble, and she suffers frequently from my failure to be what she wants to think I am. All things being equal, she would eventually have despaired of me, and created the same image of another man.' He paused, and tried in the silence to gauge her interest and disapproval; but again, he could not. He could only feel that she was very intent.

'Another solution would be for her not to have the child. I'm afraid last night that I began by assuming that she would not want to have it, and, of course, I offered to arrange all that for her. But I found her absolutely determined to go on with it. Before I say anything more outrageous, I do want to tell you that although I do not love Deirdre, I care very much about her; I do feel responsible for her, and am prepared, if that seems the best thing for her, to marry her. I am also, of course – I know I said this before – prepared to see to – to look after . . .'

'It is not, in fact, a question of love or money,' Mrs Fleming said calmly.

He looked up sharply from his cigarette-case (he had not attempted to eat), his rather dully tragic features enlivened by dismay. Whatever she offered – comfort, resentment, advice, assistance – might well be beyond his intellectual powers to grasp. Louis had always applied the best of his mind, his intelligence, perseverance, and intuition to his career, confining his private relations (and this was easy) largely to women whose emotions and senses dominated their lives. He was, in fact, at twenty-seven, in a fair way to becoming a success; in the case of this particular piece of human mass production 'untouched by human heart'. Faced with a predicament, however, he was sincerely concerned to employ principles, which, although he did not thoroughly understand them, were not, he knew, necessarily conducive to his advancement. He was only twenty-seven.

Something of this penetrated Mrs Fleming's mind as she sat making coffee and trying to understand him. She had suggested coffee in lieu of the food that neither of them seemed to want, in a manner which allowed them to be silent while she made it.

Taken separately, people were not difficult, if one took the trouble to take them separately. It was people in relation to one another that baffled her. What had brought her daughter to her knees before this young man? She tried to consider this; but the jokes about village girls and bad limericks about abortionists . . . *mariages de convenance* . . . the very short-term bliss of ignorance, and fragments of the conversation she had had so late in the night with her husband, dispersed untidily . . . nothing, she felt, is so unhelpful as experience when it seems irrelevant . . . and she needed to be single-minded with a fixed point of view – like Pinero or Elgar.

With some curiosity, she asked: 'What do you expect me to say to you?'

'If I knew that, I should not be waiting here, because the whole thing would not seem so immensely difficult. I thought you would probably want to ask me more about it. You might just want to tell me how badly I have behaved towards your daughter.'

'Your assumption that Deirdre does not love you seems to me rather unfair.'

'Perhaps it is. Perhaps she does love me.'

His willingness to agree shifted a little more moral ground under Mrs Fleming's feet. Morality, she felt, was like sand. She said:

'It seems to me something you should know. Presumably this child was an accident.'

He put his coffee cup carefully back in its saucer before replying, and, in the instant of his doing it, Mrs Fleming's heart sank.

'I'm sure that it was,' he said.

For the first time she really liked him.

'I think perhaps that I had better talk to Deirdre.'

'Oh.' She could not tell whether he was more apprehensive or relieved. 'Of course, she doesn't know that I have talked to you.'

'I suppose she would mind that very much,' said Mrs Fleming.

'I'm afraid so. Would it be at all possible for you to discover what is happening . . . I don't really know whether she talks to you I'm afraid . . .' he was tentative, apologetic.

'No, she does not talk to me at all, and that would be very difficult. I'll try, but something must be done about this you know. I cannot leave it because you are afraid that she will be angry with you. Deirdre is only nineteen.'

'I only meant that if I am to marry her, it would be better not to start with her feeling . . .'

'But you *have* talked to me behind her back. Much better tell her that yourself. I shall do everything I can to persuade her *not* to marry you.'

He looked astounded.

'My dear Mr Vale,' Mrs Fleming said gently, 'it is not possible to teach children not to make the classical mistakes. But children should not be brought into the world at all for reasons of social blackmail or moral compensation: only if they are wanted by the people who beget them. I do know this. Neither the children nor the parents ever recover from the guilt of compulsion. You do not want to marry Deirdre, and you are therefore very unlikely to make her happy. You most certainly do not want this child. I shall try to make both these things very plain to her.'

There was a short silence, and then he stubbed out his cigarette and said: 'Yours is not a usual point of view. You seem, forgive me saying so, extremely certain.'

She answered: 'I have two very good reasons.' And for the first time he observed that she did not look at him.

They parted with mutual respect and relief; with Mrs Fleming promising to telephone Louis when she had seen Deirdre. ('The aspirin of social intercourse', somebody had once described the telephone to her.)

Now, she stood alone in the narrow hall. The little new air that the opening and shutting of the front door had introduced hurried round her, and then settled, with the faint tinkling of the small chandelier, to the weight and texture of the house: becoming not quite transparent, and not absolutely cold: an atmosphere with a suggestion of consommé, set in the familiar silence of a London house on a foggy afternoon.

In the basement, Dorothy, having dismissed the morning daily, would be sitting in an ancient basket chair seemingly made of brambles, as whenever she sat in it, it snarled her stockings and cardigans. She nevertheless refused to exchange it for anything more comfortable; and padded it from time to time with cushions filled with dust or oozing an occasional improbably exotic feather. In this chair she sat every afternoon of the week (except when she went to Brixton to see a sister suffering from mistaken, but absolutely intractable illusions of grandeur). She sat chain-smoking Goldflakes, with the wireless belching incessant quantities of entertainment and information: knitting some huge pale pink or lemon coloured garment which mysteriously disappeared on completion to be replaced by another (she was never seen wearing one). On a chair opposite her sat a colossal common cat. Both of them endured the wireless with impartial indifference – hoots of canned laughter – dreadful news – unintelligible plays – sentimental songs – jokes – orchestrated signature tunes – the vicarious excitement of football and racing commentaries – comforting heart-to-heart talks on silage, national health, or chicken incubators . . . not a muscle of their faces moved; no shred of the information they must both have absorbed ever escaped either of them, or appeared to influence their lives in any way.

At four o'clock, the wireless would be turned off, Dorothy would make tea, and the cat would leap lightly through a small and widely barred window.

Above the basement, however, the house was thickly quiet, patient and desolate. Mrs Fleming returned quickly to the drawing-room. The letter that she had written to her husband lay on her desk beside her diary. The diary reminded her that she was to have tea (that horrible unnecessary meal designed to make unsatisfied women still more unsatisfactory) with Mrs Stoker at Gloucester Place. The wedding was, after all, only a week off, and there was much to arrange. She had nearly two hours in which to start upon the immense and baffling task of clearing up.

As she climbed the further two flights to the top floor where Deirdre had slept until she had moved to the mews, and Julian had a room for six more nights, she reflected, a little wearily, that at least the house had always possessed far too many stairs . . .

FOUR

Ten hours later, Mrs Fleming sat in her bedroom watching her daughter's mews. She sat in the dark, except for a small electric fire which burned with a heartless local heat and neither warmed nor illumined her

It was long past midnight; she had left Deirdre nearly an hour ago, but the light in the mews still burned, and Mrs Fleming had reached a point of fatigue and anxiety when she felt constrained to watch a light which in reality could tell her nothing. If it was put out, or if it continued to burn, she would not really know whether Deirdre slept, or wept, or went out, or tried to do anything more desperate. The last, she told herself again, Deirdre would not do. Deirdre's unhappiness was an acutely vital business: she was half in love with it – she did not want it to end. She did not possess the matters of fact to render her hopeless. It was therefore futile to watch the light; but Mrs Fleming drew her coat round her shoulders and watched. It had been a frightful day. The panic and agony at the back of her mind had lain in wait for just such a moment as this – to catch her tired and alone, free of other people's superable problems. It had been a frightful day, she told herself soothingly, and this curiously comforted her.

She remembered that in her youth, she had been enjoined always to think of others less fortunate than herself; relativity in any misfortune had been employed as a successful counterirritant by her family. She had always resisted the sadistic complacency of such a creed, but now, although she did not approach the dangers inherent in comparison, she was none the less thankful that there were people who patently needed thinking about.

After such a day, she could ruminate on the general predicament of mothers and daughters: June and her mother, and she with Deirdre. The ghastly sterility behind the scene she had witnessed between Mrs Stoker and June at tea had struck her with terrifying force. They had seemed two women bound together, having in common nothing in particular, and everything in general; who, were they not related, would not willingly have spent five minutes in each other's company; but who, because of their relationship, had spent nineteen years, irritating, modifying, interfering with, decrying and depending upon each other. The scene had begun by Mrs Stoker announcing with a kind of angry roguishness that she knew how June had spent the previous afternoon; and had ended, interminable minutes later, with June scarlet and near to tears, crying why shouldn't she go to a cinema if she wanted to, she had her own life to lead – and leaving the room. As she had returned soothing noises to Mrs Stoker's circle of apologies, excuses, and aggression, Mrs Fleming had tried to consider her relationship with Deirdre; but what she found she felt about her own daughter appeared so uncertain and intangible, that she had stopped in fright. She felt simply unhappy, embarrassed and inadequate; and very much afraid for Deirdre. (She also made a private resolution never again to have tea with Mrs Stoker in her beige and peach-pink flat.)

Now she had seen Deirdre – they had gone through the whole business – they had broken down fence after fence of suspicion and reserve, and found nothing but a waste of tears and shame. For Deirdre's utter inability to see the affair in relation to anyone but herself had filled Mrs Fleming with a kind of miserable shame which amounted almost to revulsion. She discovered that she was caring about her daughter with deliberation; finding reasons for her love, bolstering it with all the protective sense she possessed. This, she was well aware, was not what Deirdre wanted. Deirdre had seemed to expect a violent parental outcry, emotional, and totally uncomprehending, of what she evidently considered to be uniquely mitigating factors of her affair. 'You don't understand!' she had cried over and over again: long after, if she had thought about it, she must have seen that Mrs Fleming did.

Louis, whom Deirdre described as heartless (Mrs Fleming suspected that this was part of his attraction), had assessed both Deirdre's nature and the situation with surprising accuracy. It was impossible, Mrs Fleming thought wearily, not to blame herself for the whole affair. One wanted children; had them, and brought them up: and then, in spite of all the calculations of time and care, they defeated one by producing a result which seemed, to say the least, almost mathematically incorrect. It was Deirdre's attitude that demoralized her: this wilful manipulation of circumstances, followed by complete subjection to them. She had wanted to shake Deirdre – to utter some of the bracing platitudes with which her own youth had been so frequently braced. She remembered that at one point she had said things of the kind: had earnestly implored Deirdre to pull herself together, to think a little about Louis and the child; to remember that life seldom finished for anyone at nineteen – above all to control herself and *think*. Deirdre had stared at her with resentful streaming eyes, and then reiterated that if Louis was really determined not to marry her – if he couldn't see how desperately right that would be – she would still have the child, because she would never love anyone else, and at least then she would have the child: adding inconsequently that a lot of very nice people were illegitimate, so if Mummy fussed about that . . .

Apart from what either of them felt about illegitimacy, Mrs Fleming had interrupted, there was the question of supporting and educating the child: bastards, in her opinion, tended to be rather more expensive than the ordinary kind – if one was to protect them adequately from that section of society unable to distinguish between cause and effect. Deirdre had seemed thoroughly shocked.

'You are talking like Papa! *Have* you talked to him?'

'Of course not,' Mrs Fleming had replied; and caught herself wondering for how many years she would have said 'of course'. From that moment, however, things had seemed a little easier between them: until Mrs Fleming, after a general discourse on the folly of marrying without mutual enthusiasm, had made the mistake of mentioning that Louis was not absolutely unprepared to marry Deirdre, if Deirdre really saw no alternative. Then they were off again: 'Why not? Why *not*?' and more tears. But Mrs Fleming saw that Deirdre's ground had shifted, had dissolved a little; and began to see her reasonably, as very young, and pregnant, and pathetic.

After some comforting, however, Deirdre's pendulum had swung again: she blew her nose defiantly and said: 'Of course I could marry Miles,' and when her mother simply stared at her, trying to think who on earth Miles was – she said: '*You* know Miles. He's been around for ages wanting to marry me – *he* doesn't mind anything: he wouldn't even mind Louis's child.'

Mrs Fleming said sharply:

'Have you told him about it?'

'No: but of course I would if I married him. It would be all right I suppose as long as he didn't get *duller* married, but I've an awful feeling that he would and then I might literally *die* of boredom.'

This necessitated more desperate advice; giving it, she did not feel that it would be taken, but having given it she thought that perhaps her daughter had merely been determined to shock her at all costs.

It had all ended by Deirdre promising to consider carefully everything that her mother had said. Mrs Fleming had tried very hard to get her to sleep in the house that night, but had failed so immediately, that she thought it wiser not to persist. She had left Deirdre with two sleeping pills and a box of cigarettes.

Back in the house, she had attempted to telephone Louis, but had found him out.

No, certainly she could not tell Deirdre.

This meant another letter to her husband. The thought of writing again to him faintly nauseated her, recalling the Duchesse de Praslin; but at least, she reflected, *her* letters enjoyed the dignity of the post . . .

FIVE

The very early morning was the worst time: the frightful half-conscious moments when catching up with the present – becoming awake and aware – lacerated sleep; when half the mind craved oblivion and the delusions surrounding it, and the other half struggled and sought for complete consciousness, until the whole painful situation took possession of mind and body; the present day leapt suddenly into life, and as suddenly, sleep was gone. It was then that she would find herself in tears, which seemed terrible to her because she could not remember their beginning. Then, she found, she wept because she found herself weeping . . .

She lay, watching the ribs of shallow sunlight which fell listlessly on the carpet, trying to make them symmetrical, or to complete some pattern: encouraging her mind with all the minute detail of the room that she could see or hear without turning her head, as though she was ill or a prisoner. The Morris wallpaper of green leaves and clear red berries which she had chosen years ago in a determined effort to make this room, at least, uncompromisingly her own (William Morris, her husband had then said, made him howl with laughter), was remarkably satisfying. When she felt safer, and steadier, she could risk looking at her watch, or finding a handkerchief: it was odd how the smallest movement made too soon after tears provoked them again.

It was seven o'clock, and she found her handkerchief.

In the bath, she found herself, via random speculation on Deirdre and Julian, facing the next hurdle with which her particular brand of introspective honesty was bound to face her. She had wondered whether Deirdre and Julian would ever succeed, if they were to try, in communicating to each other their feelings about Louis and June: and had come to the conclusion that they would fail, or that they would not try, because their ideas and requirements concerning people were utterly dissimilar. Then, suddenly, as she was idly turning over the thought that the word 'love' had as many implications as the word 'light', her mind was blocked by the petrifying fear that the first word meant nothing to her – absolutely nothing. What, for instance, did she feel for her husband, about whom she was extremely unhappy? Did she love him? Or was she subject simply to fear and pride: of being left alone, and of other people seeing this happen to her? She had been taught, she realized, to regard life in four stages. One stored extreme youth, in order to expend it in the twenties; and one banked the middle part of one's life, in order that one might live on a minimum of the accrued interest in one's old age. One was, in fact, permitted a butterfly extravagance with youth or beauty or pleasure for a shorter time in relation to one's whole life than a butterfly in relation to its metamorphosis from an egg to a caterpillar to a chrysalis. There was something wrong somewhere. But then, she had never regarded marriage, or ideal marriage, or perhaps simply her own marriage, in the light of saving up, or banking.

While she dressed, she reflected that after twenty-three

years she could hardly expect her husband to desire her
– even were she as desirable as she knew she had been
twenty-three years ago: that it would be indeed remarkable if after twenty-three years there were segments of
her mind which he had not either thoroughly assimilated
or ignored because he disapproved of them; that her
accomplishments during that time had progressed by the
twilight of nature, and thus imperceptibly – there was no
sudden glare or sunlight of achievement upon her ability
now to run two houses and bring up two children, to
decorate herself, or anything surrounding her: that Mr
Carroll's penetrating remark about running very hard to
stay in the same place applied to marriage as to so much
else; but that the achievement of this naturally got one
nowhere; and that therefore there was no earthly reason
why she should expect the same man to continue spending
a day in her ageing and familiar company.

She breakfasted, and dispatched Julian. There was a
postcard from Leila Talbot which she said she had written
ages ago and forgotten to post asking her to a cocktail
party that evening. Mrs Fleming noticed that she was
asked by herself, and wondered how long this had been
so, or whether Leila knew that now this was the way she
should always be asked to parties. The curtains in Deirdre's flat were still drawn. Dorothy was in a bad temper
about the number of silver-fish that wriggled deathlessly
all over the basement. These curious creatures appeared
from nowhere at unspecified intervals, infuriating Dorothy,
and delighting her cat, who killed them by dozens with
a kind of oriental dispassionate intensity.

Mrs Fleming arranged for the death of the silver-fish,
and went to the very top of her house, to the floor where
Julian and Deirdre kept their possessions. For two hours

she struggled with the infantile, schoolgirl, and adolescent welter of her daughter's things. Objects such as a one-eyed rather nebulous animal called Strickland were revealed (she recalled how passionately Deirdre had wanted to be renamed Strickland); a scrap-book half-filled with pressed wild flowers, little jars filled with green dust (a relic of the days when Deirdre had feverishly made face-cream from white of egg, and sold it to unsuspecting and spotty school friends); a letter from a quite hideous little boy who had lived across the square, saying that he was collecting enough string to tie her to a tree in Kensington Gardens; a brush and comb bag embroidered with Mrs Fleming's initials, in red and green – unfinished – and stuck with a rusty needle; four mercifully unfinished diaries (she did not read more than the first sentence of each): 'Elizabeth Tomkinson will always be my greatest nearest friend.' 'I am afraid that I am more sensitive than anyone else I know,' and so on. Mrs Fleming threw them away. There were boxes and boxes of clothes, half-knitted jerseys, unstrung beads, lipstick cases, and theatre programmes. These, she felt, must be sorted by Deirdre herself. Almost everything was either half broken or half finished. When she had reached the gymkhana ballet era of Deirdre's life, Dorothy suddenly appeared with a cup of warm brown tea – a mark of forgiveness and solicitude which Mrs Fleming knew she must accept to the dregs. Dorothy felt that people *ought* to want tea: if they refused it, they did not know what was good for them; they were poorly, and needed more tea than ever. She stood over Mrs Fleming now, repeating everything she had said about the silver-fish; to show Mrs Fleming that she was no longer angry, but that the silver-fish had been important enough to warrant anger two hours ago. Dorothy's cat, who always accompanied her, ostensibly out of affection, but really, Mrs Fleming thought, with the subconscious desire to trip her up, had gone comfortably to sleep in a cardboard lid on John Gielgud and some metal hair curlers. 'I'll leave my boy with you,' Dorothy said, pretending that she had any control over him, and departed.

Mrs Fleming slowly drank the tea, and permitted the other side of her mind its elaborate (and, she secretly felt, more convincing) point of view. Why should anybody expect to collect one either in the prime of life, or, worse, before one had had time to reach a prime, cut a pattern for one, pin one down for years and years until one had entirely become a compromise of their original ideal, and their increasing indifference; if at the end, one found oneself the wrong creature in solitude? It was too late to mourn any private intentions she might once have had towards herself – she had been loved, and touched and fashioned; dominated, protected, and ignored, until even her enjoyment of the wallpaper that her husband despised was coloured by the fact that he despised it. Even the few occasions when she had thought that she had asserted herself were direct results of her association with him. The wear and pull and take of human relations suddenly appalled her: she did not feel able, at forty-three, to assume an equal share of responsibility about them. It is fatal, she thought, to grow up with anybody: one must remain young with them, or begin old. I was not grown up when I married – I was very little older than Deirdre – different, but very little older. I could manage the whole situation now, if only I could start at the beginning: what is difficult, is the end of a situation that I began so badly.

Dorothy called reproachfully that Miss June was on

the telephone. Mrs Fleming, who had heard it ring, apologized for not hearing, and went down to speak to her future daughter-in-law.

In spite of the fact that she spent a great deal of her life on the telephone, June used the instrument rather as a means to general than specific communication. This, for anyone who disliked telephones, was one of her most tiresome habits: Mrs Fleming, who had not previously encountered it, was now plunged into a stream of disjointed small talk; apologies for not having written about the dinner party, speculations about the forthcoming wedding, and even a short account of the canker in Angus's ears. Among all this, Mrs Fleming gathered that June had to go that afternoon to the new flat where various irrevocable decisions about its decoration must be made: that Julian was unable or unwilling to accompany her; that they did not agree about pink or cream distemper; and that in any case June felt unable alone to select either a pink or a cream. As she had not yet seen the flat, June thought that perhaps Mrs Fleming might be free that afternoon to look at it and advise her. It would be frightful if, by herself, she went and chose the wrong pink or cream. Mrs Fleming accepted this depressing aesthetic responsibility, wondering how many years ago she would passionately have persuaded June to use and enjoy colour.

During luncheon, a woman, nearly in tears, and with a Viennese accent, telephoned and asked for Mr Fleming. On hearing that he was away, she uttered some tragic exclamation in German, broke down altogether, and rang off.

Mrs Fleming arrived at the flat before June.

The third floor could be reached by a lift, which resembled a cavity in a tooth; exuding an air of breathless discomfort which, she felt, would ascend a pinnacle of agony if she touched it. She walked up, and, having rung the bell, stood in a draughty vomit-coloured gloom, mentally adding unpunctuality to her knowledge of June.

June arrived panting in a pink woollen dress and a beaver lamb coat that was a little too short for her. She groped about in her bag for the latch-key, explaining and apologizing; feverishly at a disadvantage. She had vaguely meant Mrs Fleming to be reassured and gratified by this plan of seeing the flat, and now it was all going wrong: she was not, as her mother would put it 'gaining Mrs Fleming's confidence', or approval, or anything of the kind. Her mother constantly said, 'Oh June, don't be so *silly*'; and now, when she least wanted to, here she was being very silly indeed – oh thank *goodness*, the key – but she was by then so nervous that she was unable to turn it in the lock.

Mrs Fleming, remembering the scene at tea with Mrs Stoker, and conscience-stricken at her conclusions before June's arrival, opened the door for her, and they entered the flat.

It was small; it was cheerless; it was unexpectedly dark. The three rooms were so designed that any piece of furniture of the slightest use must either crowd or ridicule their proportions. It would, Mrs Fleming thought, afford passable comfort for people about four feet high. She exhausted herself, however, by creating the flat's advantages to June, who, in turn, pointed out such disabilities as she could envisage: these were varied, and surprising, in that none of them had occurred to Mrs Fleming, and now stuck the needle of her taste into the groove of June's practical requirements. They both wanted so desperately to be kind.

When they had thoroughly surveyed the dirty almost empty rooms, they perched uncertainly upon a pair of trestles left by the decorators in the bedroom, and June produced shade cards of distemper and paint. The colours began with those suited to the strings of pastel wooden beads which confound so many small babies; proceeded to a selection of the heartless vivacity associated with tiny village sweets; and ended with the monumental drabness, the grandiose olive, mud, and damp chocolate, endured in so many institutions. There was, as June said, so very much to choose from – although one honestly wouldn't actually be able to *live* with very many of the shades. Mrs Fleming suggested mixing a colour and getting it matched, but June, clearly terrified at the idea, said that there was no time, as the painters had to start work the next morning if the decoration was to be finished by the time she and Julian returned from Paris.

A silence ensued, during which June fingered unpleasantly possible pinks, and Mrs Fleming noticed her pretty nails. Eventually, as it seemed that the silence was not to be broken by a choice being made, Mrs Fleming, after the impulse of finding them attractive had waned, remarked on the pretty nails.

June blushed deeply, and dropped the shade card on to the floor.

'Oh, honestly, they aren't really. I mean Julian hasn't noticed them.'

'I'm sure that he has.' Mrs Fleming detected that the nails might be symbolic, and that the fact that Julian had not observed their attraction had rushed suddenly into June's mind, tugging a stream of similar omissions in its wake. She intended reassurance, but she was immediately confounded.

June had descended from her trestle to pick up the card which had skidded out of reach across the dirty parquet floor. Now she seemed to crumple, she was actually on the floor, twisting the card in her hands, and looking away from Mrs Fleming.

'I do sometimes feel,' she said, attempting to weight her sudden panic with the appearance of habit, 'sometimes – not always, of course – that he ought to notice things like – well, anything that he finds . . .' the card fell on to her lap, 'I mean people *always* notice what is bad about one, don't they? Even if they don't *say* anything, they notice everything. And if, when people marry, they don't notice any of the good things – at the beginning, I mean – then they'll just get used to them, and only notice the bad things. It's something that has been worrying me for a long time,' she added hesitantly, having just discovered what had been worrying her.

Mrs Fleming, treading water very gently, said:

'People very seldom say all that they feel.'

'But how does one know that they feel anything?'

'Julian wants to marry you. You know that.'

'I don't believe he really does! I don't believe he really *wants me* at all! I might be anyone, and *he* might be anyone. It's – oh, awful!' Her eyes were so full of tears that it seemed impossible they should remain in her eyes.

Mrs Fleming, not daring to move, lest she unwittingly propel June still further out of her depths, sat silent.

'People don't – I thought that when two people were marrying each other they were frightfully happy. Like discovering something – oh, you know, marvellous, I thought that was the point of it: like the very end of books – not simply the next thing you do in your life – except with Julian I think it is.'

'You haven't begun your marriage yet: this is the worst part . . .'

But June turned suddenly to her like a creature whose instincts were at bay; a hunted exhausted expression which utterly subdued any such middle-aged claptrap, and shamed Mrs Fleming out of continuing it.

'I'm not at all clever or interesting. I'm not beautiful, or even especially pretty. I do see all that quite clearly. I can't really see why he should want to marry me.' She found it difficult to speak: her slow painful blush spreading, it seemed, all over her body, as she saw more and more of herself for the first time in her life. 'But if he *does* want to marry me, surely he ought to find at least one particular reason? If I don't seem special to him in any kind of way, I shall always be the same, shan't I? And nobody will find anything special about me because it won't be there. He – he doesn't seem to *expect* anything – and Mummy says I'm dull, so I'm afraid – I'm afraid,' she repeated, and a tear dropped on to the colour card of paints. She ignored her tears with unexpected arrogance.

Mrs Fleming, recognizing this piece of honesty, took refuge in curiosity.

'Do you tell Julian why you want to marry him?'

'I?' She seemed really startled. 'I – I thought that I could – oh, cook, and things like that. Look after him, you know. It isn't that part of it – the separate bits of our lives. It's – living together – not his work, or this flat, but our *lives*. I don't mean bed, of course,' she added rapidly, and Mrs Fleming saw that she did not: that that aspect seemed set by itself; so mysteriously remote, so utterly unpredictable, that to June it was meaningless.

What was there to say? That they were like two people on a desert island – aware that food was a necessity, and consequently prepared to eat berries which might equally sustain or poison them? But they were not on a desert island. June, Mrs Fleming thought, is perhaps a pathetic version of the princess who must sleep until anyone cared to discover her – and then kiss her awake. But the princess's pride had been protected by the magic forest of brambles, and June had no such protection: a foolish mother who had no thought for her but marriage, and who therefore set her, without purpose or interest, in an arid waste where anyone might approach her – where she was no attainment, because even the most indifferent could attain her. But is Julian so indifferent? Have I been so foolish a parent that any household seems preferable to mine? Julian, however, had been free to live where he chose, and he had apparently chosen June. This act of folly, for so it appeared to her now, did not seem to be graced by a spark of romantic selection, desire, or bravado – seemed nothing more, as June had said, than the next thing these two were to do in their lives. They seemed to have no reason behind them; no intentions before, but simply to have drifted in a vacuum of social intercourse as close to one another as the vacuum would allow, with the consequences that society presumably expected of them.

Looking at June (she was frowning in an effort to check her tears which seemed now to have become the very texture of her face), Mrs Fleming wondered what on earth was expected of either of them. The fundamental unnecessity of the situation perplexed her, but her proximity to Julian, and now to June, prevented her from objective criticism. 'What a piece of work is a man,' indeed – but one could not criticize any piece of work with which one was not in sympathy, and here all she could do was cry down their marriage, without, at least in June's case, presenting her with an alternative. However, there seemed nothing else to be done; and, very hesitantly, she suggested that, in view of June's uncertainty about Julian's feelings, and even, Mrs Fleming ventured, possibly June's feelings about the whole affair, it might perhaps be wise to postpone the marriage until . . . But here the appearance of June forestalled her. She looked as though someone was attempting to take a toy, of which she was very afraid, away from her.

'Oh no!' she cried; and, 'It's all *arranged*! I didn't mean . . .' She got up, and walked to the window.

'You must think me frightfully silly,' she said a moment later, and Mrs Fleming's heart sank.

'No, I did not think that, at all.'

'Saying all those awful things. After all, you are Julian's mother.' This, almost as though Mrs Fleming had been deliberately concealing the fact.

For a moment Mrs Fleming considered retorting that indeed she was, and for that reason was justifiably anxious; but she realized, before the sentence cleared her mind, the danger of saying anything of the kind. The marriage would go forward; and June would merely be convinced that her mother-in-law opposed it. She could perhaps talk to Julian – a prospect which filled her with weary alarm, as she had not attempted it since the night before he went to prep school – but here and now she must perforce revert to claptrap. She rose to her feet.

'Not at all,' she said. 'Everyone gets exhausted with being engaged. I remember feeling exactly the same.'

June glanced at her uncertainly, but Mrs Fleming's face preserved a good-natured blank which comfortably reduced June's earlier revelations to a small (but understandable) display of nerves.

It remained to choose the pink or cream. June, whose judgement was now apparently reinforced, selected the cream for the drawing-room and pink for the bedroom. 'It's a compromise!' she exclaimed to Mrs Fleming as though presenting her with an original triumphant achievement.

She really is awfully understanding for a mother-in-law, June thought, relaxing in her cab. She felt *much* better: oh, as though there had been a thunderstorm, or she'd passed an examination at school, or arranged some flowers and somebody had asked whether Mummy had done them (Mummy was absolutely *wonderful* with flowers).

Mrs Fleming, having successfully evaded sharing a taxi with June, drove back to Campden Hill Square, repeating again and again with a kind of horrified revulsion: 'I did *not* feel like that. I *never* felt like it. I did not: I did *not*.'

SIX

Leila Talbot gave cocktail parties distinguished, so far as Mrs Fleming was concerned, in one respect. With remarkably few exceptions, they were attended by a stream of people one had never met at her house before, and who, experience proved, one would never meet again. Mrs Fleming, having gone to parties at Pelham Crescent for nearly twenty years, had by now run her speculative gamut about them: she had assumed that Leila must give parties every night, and wondered how she contrived to have so many friends; she had once, before a bad attack of influenza, conceived the morbid notion that they were all really the same people whom she was unable to identify or remember; she had considered the statistics of cocktail party gate-crashing – but with all these reflections, and many too idle to record, she had never reached any satisfactory conclusion. What mystified her most was the way these ceaseless streams of guests seemed to know their hostess with exactly the same enigmatic degree of intimacy: it was impossible to tell whether they also had known her for twenty years, or whether they had merely met her the previous week. Sometimes, Mrs Fleming thought that they had perhaps known her very well twenty years *ago* – had perhaps played together as children – but then she reflected that even Leila could hardly have played with, and then reassembled, quite so many and such diverse people (apart from their hostess, they had little in common). It was possible, occasionally, to observe some specific professional or cultural undertow; such as doctors when Leila had been working as an almoner and playing a lot of golf – or architects when, after her husband's death, she had nearly built a house in the Isle of Wight (in order, Mr Fleming had remarked, that she might more decently conceal her lack of grief). There was usually one man, whose satisfied isolation from everybody else – whose apparent lack of personality coupled to his rather eager familiarity with the contents of the cocktail cabinet – proclaimed him to the interested and observant as Leila's current lover. Leila invariably called him 'darling', whoever he was, and never introduced him to anybody. He moved about the room in an anonymous haze – he always knew where everything was, from angostura to the lavatory – and, *he* was hardly ever the same man from party to party – which was confusing to the observant, although they might have comforted themselves with the oral reflection that Leila never called two people 'darling' at one party.

There were about a dozen people assembled when she arrived, only one of whom she knew, as having vaguely occupied the background of Leila's life; a bright thin stringy woman, parched with sunburn, looking now with her dry bleached hair like an old little girl of fourteen; although she had herself told Mrs Fleming that she had had two husbands and four children.

The professional undertow at this party seemed to be cultural administration of one kind or another: people were being introduced to each other either as Mr Gordion the painter, who was now engaged upon organizing the exhibition of British Sea Shells for the '51 Festival – or, alternatively, as Mr White, who, having run the house organs for the Ministries of Wealth and Welfare during the war, and been Secretary to the Association for the Prevention of Internal Anxiety after it, was now entrusted with the delicate task of designing a ton of plastic tropical fish, to be dropped from aeroplanes on to the artificial lakes in public parks at the opening of the Festival.

Mrs Fleming, having met four people engrossed in discussing these and similar activities, having refused three cigarettes and accepted a glass of Tio Pepe from a sallow little man whose anonymity was if anything enhanced by a soft ginger beard, found herself sitting in a large armchair, on one arm of which perched Leila's stringy friend.

'But it's ages since I *rode* a bicycle!' she was exclaiming, throwing one stringy little leg over the other, and staring brightly into the face of an enormous man in a bow tie and striped trousers, who laughed with a kind of baritone lechery and said, 'You should try, my dear Esmé, you should try.'

More people were arriving, and Leila forestalled the ginger beard's determination to offer Mrs Fleming her fourth cigarette. 'She doesn't smoke, darling. See if Nanny has managed to open the American nuts.'

Somebody standing alone by the fireplace threw a half-smoked cigarette sharply into the fire. The gesture caught Mrs Fleming's attention, reminding her suddenly of Deirdre after dinner two nights ago. It had been, she realized, the beginning of all the subsequent revelations: the first occasion of Deirdre's distress, which even then, had meant almost nothing. Now, a cigarette thrown away unfinished had for her a private significance, which means, she thought, that in a room containing approximately fifteen people, the private significances must occur in such quantity as to drive Providence mad . . .

Leila interrupted her with a young couple called Fenwick who had just arrived. 'They're house-hunting, and are mad about Campden Hill.'

Mrs Fleming found herself embarked upon a discussion of houses in that area. The Fenwicks were recently married, and frequently said so. It seemed the only fact of which they were sure, as the necessity they evidently felt for substituting 'we' for 'I', made both of them so tentative, hesitant, and self-conscious, that their plans and requirements were a perpetual compromise. Mrs Fleming politely battled with the pair of them, feeling that they would be much better alone together, or alone separately, until they had learned how to be together with other people; feeling also more and more like a social worker, until the arrival even of Leila's twelve-year-old daughter brought a merciful relief.

Mrs Fleming could never believe that Maureen was as unattractive as she looked: she looked like a small pig dressed by Daniel Neal; but her repertoire of unattractiveness was considerably more extensive than any pig's. She now stood bulging and hostile in front of Mrs Fleming.

'What foul earrings,' she remarked; 'just like bird's mess – give me some of that.'

Mrs Fleming favoured her with her famous glassy stare reserved for revolting children, and did not reply; but young Mr Fenwick smiled weakly and said: 'It's not good for little girls.'

'Go on, give me some. You'll be drunk if you drink all that. Give me the olive, then.'

Mr Fenwick gave her the olive. He wanted his wife to see how good he was with children. Maureen ate it, and spat the stone back into his glass. 'It looks like a piece of rat's mess in your glass. I say, have you noticed the piece of rat's mess in your glass?' Delighted with this, she proceeded round the room extracting other people's olives, and repeating her performance with them. The Fenwicks smiled guardedly at one another, and murmured something about a difficult age.

'Nonsense!' Mrs Fleming heard herself say – so clearly above the room's conversation – that in some confusion she turned away from the Fenwicks to meet the eye of someone standing across the room by the fireplace. He gazed at her for a moment with enquiring interest: she felt that he had heard her say 'Nonsense!' and that he faintly wanted to know what she found so positively nonsensical; then somebody moved and he was obscured from her.

The Fenwicks had retreated: culturally administrative talk hemmed her in, and she felt isolated in the midst of the noise.

'The beauty of the whole design is that it can be executed *entirely* in paper.'

There was an appreciative grunt.

'With a little plastic, of course.'

'Of course.'

'Of course, there was trouble with the insurance people, but I said to Braithwaite – you know Braithwaite?'

'We did all those posters on hygiene together.'

'Of *course* you did – Well I said to Braithwaite, "My dear chap, that's *your* department's job to departmentalize. Not mine." My department, I mean. I mean one cannot be eternally hamstrung on a point like selection of materials because another department can't delegate responsibility. What is Braithwaite *for*? I mean, we all know he's a good chap, keen and conscientious and all that, but he will *not* delegate. I don't know whether you found that with the hygiene job. He will try and do it all himself. Puts everyone's back up – after all, he's not *supposed* to *know* anything.'

'Good Lord, no!'

They both smiled indulgently, while the ginger beard filled up their glasses.

'But it's fascinating in the big cities. They walk up and down all night – literally all night, below one's windows, and one can't get a wink of sleep. They *never* go to bed.'

'My *dear* Esmé!'

She laughed brightly, and fitted a cigarette into her holder. 'I adored Spain. Every inch.'

Mrs Fleming accepted a second glass of sherry. She could see nobody to whom she wished to talk: indeed the room seemed fuller than usual of people she would prefer to leave unmet, but she felt she could hardly continue sitting in the most comfortable chair, drinking in a silence which in any case Leila would probably observe and inappropriately break. Perhaps she should go home and see Julian. She looked down at her sherry. At that moment, there was a loud thud, a sound of breaking glass, and a wail from Maureen. Everybody turned in the direction of the fireplace. Two people picked Maureen up, now howling and shouting, 'He tripped me up. You beast! You tripped me up!'

She was immediately removed bleeding at the nose by Leila. The room seemed clearer, and Mrs Fleming saw the man whose eye she had met, collecting pieces of glass off the carpet, and putting them into what looked like the *Radio Times*. It was only then that she identified him as the one who had thrown the cigarette into the fire. When he had finished, he ran his hand over the carpet, and rose slowly to his feet. He was tall, and immensely thin. Then he picked a cigarette-box off the mantelpiece and walked over to her.

'Do you smoke?'

'No, thank you.'

'Do you drink?'

'I don't smoke, because I do drink.' She indicated her glass.

'I must sit down.' He cast about him for an empty chair, which there was not. He picked a plate of nuts and a vase of flowers off a small table, gave the nuts to her, and put the flowers on the mantelpiece. When he returned, he had a glass in his hand.

'So do I. But I don't suppose you like nuts. Shall I put them on the floor?'

'Your talents in that direction are remarkably useful.'

He smiled then, rather tiredly, and said, 'Oh yes. I never spill things; I only trip them up, or dispose of them.'

There was an amiable silence between them. Then he said:

'I don't find alcohol very insulating.'

She noticed that he was drinking brandy. 'Do you want to be insulated?'

His hand, which had lain stretched out along the arm of her chair, closed up, and he said: 'Well, yes, at times. Everybody wants to be insulated at times.'

'From what?'

'Oh – from "the thousand natural shocks", I suppose.' He had retracted altogether; he had decided not to talk about that. He smiled.

His hands were very large, but unmuscular: with long

bony fingers; not a good or a bad shape, but noticeable, because they were unusually large, and in proportion.

Someone was extolling Ernest Hemingway's new book, and someone else was decrying it. They listened for a minute; then Mrs Fleming said: 'Somebody told me that he was writing another book, but that in the middle of it he was told that he had only a little while to live, so he abandoned the first work, and wrote a second: and now he has been told that he will not die.'

He looked up suddenly, and she saw that he was both astonished and angry. 'How do you know that?'

'I do not know. I cannot even remember who told me. I don't expect that it is true.'

'In any case, his state of mind – or body, can have nothing to do with the intrinsic merit of the work. Either it is a good book, or a bad one. Whether he was dying when he wrote it, or thought himself dying, can have nothing to do with the book afterwards.'

Mrs Fleming said mildly: 'If it was true, it must have had a good deal to do with the book while he was writing it.' She could not understand what she had said that had so disturbed him. 'Anyway, I have not read it. Do you write books?'

'No. I wrote one book a long time ago; a reference book, bristling with information that nobody wants, and so heavy that the average student would not have wanted to lug it home from the library. The kind of book one finds being auctioned by the yard at sales. It cost twenty-five shillings even then, and was fearfully dull. Before I wrote it, I used to wonder who wrote them.' He had a habit of smiling when he had finished speaking: the rather tired illumination of his features was his full stop.

'What was it about?'

He considered her gravely for a moment. 'No, if I tell you, it will spoil the story. You do not write books?' He was not really asking her; he was sure she did not.

'No. I don't do anything. My life is rather an indirect business.'

Again, she saw him regarding her with a shock of interest or enquiry (what was it – passionate curiosity, disapproval, agreement with what was surely this time a rather gauche remark?). At any rate she found these sudden halts, with the full weight of his mind upon her, a little unnerving, and, as she turned away from him silently, he spoke.

'It is clear to me that you do not like nuts.' He disposed of them. 'Would you prefer dinner?'

'Thank you, but I am already dining. Do you know the time?'

'I no longer wear a watch, but I'll find out.'

Before he had returned, Leila was upon her, saying:

'Lunch, we simply must have lunch; but I suppose it will have to be after the wedding. What a thoroughly nice girl – how *sensible* of Julian. You must be so relieved. Did you meet Erasmus White? I meant you to – over there, not listening to Percy. Twenty-five to eight, darling. I won't keep you – I *so* understand how you feel about punctuality.'

So when he returned, she knew the time.

She told him that she was going, and wished for a fleeting instant that she was not. They shook hands; and then he said with an impassivity that made the words more startling:

'Of course, no amount of alcohol would insulate either of us as we are at present.'

She stared at him, wanting to laugh at or dislike him,

but she could do neither; she was simply, horribly, afraid: she was so frozen with terror, that she could not withdraw her hand.

'So am I,' he said gently, 'but there is nothing whatever that we can do about it.'

∞ ∞ ∞

Even the ancient taxi she picked up at South Kensington failed to jolt her into any sense of reality. All the way to Campden Hill she sat with the immediate effect of his words continuing – not ending and beginning again in her mind, but continuing at the same pitch; without allowing her to draw the breath of memory, without her being aware even of time rushing past her, or streets accumulating behind her; making some distance between the moment when she had heard him speak, and now, when she remembered what he had said.

Her taxi drew up behind Julian's car: she paid her fare and let herself into the house. There was a letter from her husband on the ebony table. As she slit open the envelope, Julian and Dorothy appeared on the stairs above and below her. Julian said:

'Awfully sorry, Mamma, but something's cropped up. I've told Dorothy. I say, what's the matter? You look *awful*!' Then he saw Dorothy, and added: 'I shan't be late. See you later, perhaps,' and almost ran out of the house.

Dorothy, who was brandishing a blue envelope, said: 'Dinner is ready, but I'll give you a few minutes. Miss Deirdre came round and left this. She asked me to tell you that she's gone away to the country for a few days – to *think*, she said.' Dorothy frequently made it clear how much she disapproved of both practices, and now lingered, ready to discourse on her aversion from the country, and her contempt of thought – Deirdre's coupling of the two providing her with a unique opportunity, but Mrs Fleming simply plodded silently upstairs, a letter in each hand.

She read her husband's letter in her bedroom, sitting in front of her looking-glass. He said nothing of his intentions about Julian's wedding, but simply asked her to lunch with him at what she recognized to be his dreariest and least frequented club. She put the letter back in its envelope. 'You look *awful!*' Julian had said. She remembered, suddenly, Tolstoy's remark about Karenin being 'offensively, disgustingly' unhappy; smelling to heaven in his grief at Anna's departure. This must be true, and not simply of Karenin, or that man (even now she did not know his name) would not have said what he had said at the end of Leila's party. It must be true of her, for all her age, her experience, her life behind her. She was a positive freak of unhappiness – indecent, and absurd – she should not be seen: it forced people either to conceal their discomfort, or it exposed her to the humiliation of their pity which they must feel that she did not really deserve. Dependence is not pretty after twenty. Crustacean self-containment was the order of her years: a self-containment, progressing until the passing dignity of death had been accomplished. At over forty one was no longer lightly accorded excuses for grief, for illness, for any frightened demands one might attempt of other people. One was supposed to have found a place in the world, and if one had not, the world ignored one's failure, and put one into what it regarded as one's place. Even when she was being most hysterically unhappy, Deirdre contrived to appear attractive: her beauty mysteriously justifying the pity and protection she evoked. (Have I appeared as I did just now to Julian – *all day*?)

Her eyes strained at her eyes in the glass; in this light they seemed to have died, were almost without colour; and they had once looked the imperishable origin, the very height, the immortality, of blue. She had learned – years ago now – to continue looking at people after she had spoken to them; thus she had been able to say the simplest things and invest them with a beauty, significance, or a wit, which everyone had been eager to believe. She had been able, as the books say, 'to shun admiration', because she had been so sure of it that she was enabled to select. The intricate, the elaborate, homage given to a fascinating and intelligent woman had been hers; and she seemed now to herself never to have enjoyed it, to have been barely conscious of it.

And now, even such private ruminations were despicable; she found them not even pathetic; to have lived her life on the timbre of her voice or the colour of her eyes seemed commonplace extravagance, deserving nothing. Many people had to live without such ephemeral qualities. (But they were not the whole reason for my existence – at no time in my life were they that: they were simply – attributes – which I did not waste. *He* did not marry me for my eyes or my voice – although perhaps without their attractions he would not have observed me. I was provided with greater choice, and so there is now perhaps less excuse for my having chosen wrongly. Or more excuse?)

Dorothy was ringing the little clamorous handbell which Julian had brought her from Geneva. Mrs Fleming rose from her dressing-table, and the blue envelope fell to the floor.

Deirdre's writing sprawled reproachfully at her: wearily, she opened it.

Darling Mummy,

I am just off to the country. Miles is taking me to somewhere called Burford where we can stay for a bit and I can think things over. I've told him everything and he wants to marry me immediately – but of course I must think seriously before doing that – so we are going to stay away a week while I think. Miles is really frightfully kind which is much more important than a good many things, and he's terribly understanding about the whole thing. Of course it will mean starting one's life again – completely washing out everything that has ever happened to me, but I do feel safe with Miles and I shall have the baby. I'm sorry about missing Julian's wedding but June seems to me so enfantile that honestly I can't see why he's doing it and this does seem more important. I'll send him a telegram. She doesn't like me anyway and I'm sure Miles would loathe her – he likes people to be more interesting than him which is rather sweet of him. Miles said that he wants to meet you when we come back. Don't be put off if he doesn't say a word – he's frightfully shy about meeting people – it really is an ordeal for him and he loathes it. He never talks much anyway. Thank you a million times for trying to help.

> *Love,*
> *Deirdre*

Don't tell Papa, but his birthday cheque will be madly useful for shapeless garments for me! Now I must fly to start my new life.

The letter was dated '4 p.m.'. She put it back in its envelope. Nothing now was needed to endorse her sense of futility and failure. She knew dimly – dumbly – that she would try to prevent Deirdre leaping into this fresh classical disaster, and knew also that she would fail. The blackmail of the alternative was too strong – the lure of a 'new life' too potent.

The war-time, music hall, American phrase (she did not know its origin) 'Where do we go from here?' slipped neatly into her mind like a coin into a slot machine which was empty, for she had no answer. The desire to go backwards, to retire into her life she knew, was very strong. But she was living; and so unable to escape from the passionate gravity of the present, which physically, is always now.

So, she went downstairs to dine alone.

If she had known then, however, how to find the man who had so frightened her at Leila's party, she would then have gone to him. But she did not know.

Dorothy had cleared the second place from the table. *My* new life, she thought, and sat down to it.

PART TWO
1942

ONE

'The situation is perfectly simple. All you have to do is to meet me from the 7.38 at Euston.'

Thus Mr Fleming on a trunk call from the previous night from goodness knows where. Indeed, put like that, what could be simpler? With the world at war, meticulously grinding vast cities exceeding small; with such catastrophes as Singapore and Dunkirk behind one; with such feats of administration and of the spirit as the fifth column in France or the battle of the RAF over Britain; with the ubiquitous removal of men, women, and children into more or less danger as the immense situation demanded; with the value of lives rocketing up and down like shares on a crazy stock market – the mere meeting of a train seemed almost inanely simple. Mrs Fleming slung her gas-mask over her shoulder, delved in her bag for her torch, and went to meet the 7.38.

She picked up a taxi in Holland Park. Of course he had meant her to meet him in the car, but he did not realize that the petrol ration would not begin to last for the journey up from Kent and back. He would be annoyed about it, and he would be exasperated at the explanation. He would, she reflected, almost prefer the car to have blown up than to have run out of petrol. The worst of her (very representative) wartime existence was that it did not efficiently provide for even such a small emergency as a trunk call from her husband. Their house near Tenterden now contained Deirdre, and the little girl who was parked on them for the war; three convalescent naval officers, one badly shell-shocked; a bombed-out mother and her terrified and dirty family of three; and Dorothy, to whom even a succession of invalid young men did not compensate for the horror of living in the country. There was also a glamorous, sulky, and altogether improbable Land Girl. Each of these ill-assorted, more or less unhappy people constituted an emergency of one kind or another; and while it is generally agreed that a crisis often brings out the best in people, and in particular, the British Press constantly averred, of the British people, the crisis was usually assumed to be of a few hours', or perhaps days', duration. The duration of the war, however, already an immense quantity of time, yawned and stretched before Mrs Fleming now as drearily as old age and death; and everybody in her household (with the possible exception of the children) had long ceased to live up to their new-found national characteristic of being magnificent in a crisis.

Mrs Fawcett *might*, she supposed, have been magnificent the night her house was bombed; indeed, poor woman, she was reputed, though garrulous, to have behaved with a presence of mind, which had had, none the less, the elements of courage: but now, deprived of her home and neighbouring enemies, whose reputations she could only continue to impair in retrospect, and her husband, who for years had been the chief inspiration of her invective and contempt ('a few more like '*im* in the Army and we shan't win the war, they must be daft!'); all remnants of her glory had vanished – the village had run its gamut of admiration and envy at her bomb story, and she was reduced to falling (in every possible direction) upon her three unfortunate children, whose fear of their mother far exceeded any they had experienced in a blitz. She quarrelled with Dorothy and the Land Girl, and hit her children continuously with a kind of expert wildness, which, practised though they were, they hardly ever managed to evade. She refused to clean her part of the house, and swapped her children's rations for cigarettes. This was her third billet 'and here they tell me I've got to stay whatever it's like which won't be much as I can see', she had remarked on arrival.

Dorothy lived a life dominated by Hitler, and reinforced by the wireless. So far as she was concerned England had no government: everything was badly organized and therefore Hitler was personally responsible for it. The blackout, the rations, the shortage of soap, of petrol, of fuel for the boiler, of knitting wool – everything – was contrived with fiendish ingenuity by Hitler. She was convinced that nothing but the murder of him would end the war; and as she imagined him sleeping in bullet-proof pyjamas at least forty feet below ground, attended only by satellites who were drugged into agreeing with him, her ruminations about his possible death were consistently gloomy. Sometimes, Mrs Fleming thought, she was even beginning to doubt his mortality. She listened incessantly to the wireless, and proclaimed her utter incredulity of everything it told her. She worked from morning till night, and adored the naval officers and children between whom she made no distinctions at all. They were all untidy, all careless, and they all liked chocolate semolina, which she made them with persistent devotion.

Mrs Fleming regarded the Land Girl with urban apprehension, feeling that the girl's proximity to Nature could only result in natural but (for Mrs Fleming) embarrassing consequences. She exuded sex; spent all her spare time in the house on her appearance; and concentrated exclusively on men, with a single-minded candour that evoked terror in the debilitated convalescents. The only point on which both Dorothy and Mrs Fawcett were agreed was on disliking Thelma. In spite of the fact that Thelma had to get up at six in the morning in order to bicycle to her farm, she was frequently out all night. The other Land Girls did not like her. Mrs Fleming had great difficulty in liking anyone so unaccountable and unresponsive. She sighed. Leaving such a household, even for one night, filled her with experienced misgiving. Getting away was like beginning to thaw one's frost-bitten mind to the point where one began to perceive its degree of paralysis – and then returning to the frost.

Euston Station in the dark concentrated for its effect almost entirely upon smell: fish, smoke, lavatories, coal dust, sweat, oil, newsprint, cheap scent (carnation or violet), animals, disinfectant, and furniture polish. The immediate effect, as Mrs Fleming got out of the taxi, was so overpowering as to be almost tangible. Like a curtain of fog, she felt one could stretch out a hand to touch it, and if the sudden flash of a torch illuminated her hand, it would be mysteriously and deeply ingrained with soot.

The taxi refused to wait, and she went in search of her husband's train. Inside the station, she became aware of its noise: a vast conglomeration of harsh and dissonant sounds – an orchestration of finality, of departure (for at first she was unable to discover any indication of an arrival); doors slamming, whistles blowing, shouting, platform gates clanging, opening for a power-driven luggage truck, and clanging again – an endless train moving endlessly away out of the bleary undertow of light into the dark; leaving behind it a disembodied suburban voice intoning its destination through a faulty microphone.

She discovered the board indicating arrivals, and found that her husband's train was well outside London and already forty minutes late on schedule. The taxi would never have stood for that. She went in search of coffee.

The buffet was very full. She stood at the marble-topped counter which glistened with innumerable liquid or sticky circles where wet glasses had stood, waiting for the coffee which she knew would be undrinkable. Beside her was a silver three-tier food stand covered with a glass dome. She was asked whether she wanted anything to eat. Beetroot sandwiches, and structural pieces of pastry shaped like bombs (Cornish pasties), reposed on charming paper lace mats. The beetroot gleamed between thick bread with the dull resentment of alligators' eyes. She did not want anything to eat.

Anyway, she reflected, keeping the house in Kent had provided a reasonably safe home for Deirdre, and Julian in his holidays. Her husband had wanted to send them to America or Canada, had, indeed, made all the arrangements, and then faced her with them; and she, guilty in her need of her children's company, had nearly succumbed to this opportunity for them to be safe, properly fed, kindly cared for, and travelled. But she had chanced, the week before, to go with a friend who was seeing her children off to Canada, and the experience had been painfully unforgettable, fragments of it returning to her whenever she went to a railway station . . . Parents coaxing their children on to the train: one little boy had asked:

'Will it be a *long* time?'

'Oh, no, a *very* little while.'

'Until Christmas?'

'We'll see, but it won't be very long.'

'You'll love it anyway,' his father had said; and suddenly the child had known that they were lying, and that the time was utterly beyond all three of them: he had not cried, but had stared silently at them with a kind of helpless grief and resentment until the train had left.

One child had had to be torn from her mother by an escort, and carried into the corridor crying out the bitter discovery of her homesickness.

'She *said* she'd like it. She *said* she *wanted* to go,' her mother repeated over and over again. People kept telling her that the child would forget; would be all right even by the time they reached Liverpool – and meanwhile it screamed and screamed that it wanted to go home – it *didn't* want – it *didn't* want . . .

When the train had disappeared, its mother leaned over a luggage truck and was violently sick.

Then there were the ones who had been toughened – who had been told that they were not to be afraid of school, of the dark; that they must not cry. They said their farewells, and climbed into the train like disciplined little troops, feeling furtively for their handkerchiefs, or holding very tightly to their bears and dolls. And many of course found it gay and exciting. It was *their* parents who collapsed afterwards, or who walked away telling each other the same lies that other parents had told their children. It wouldn't be for long. It was much better really . . .

Anyway, she had Deirdre. Julian had had to continue at his prep school, which he finished at Christmas. She had him in the holidays. The framework provided by school terms and holidays was curiously comforting to her in her present life. It helped to justify the monotony of petty day-to-day anxieties (What on earth can we have for lunch? Why does the Petroleum Board never answer letters? etc.): it comforted her in the gradual loss of that other framework: the tenuous but uneasy relationship she had had in London with her husband, which now seemed perceptibly to be draining away. She saw less and less of him, and consequently he seemed at short irregular meetings such as the one she now awaited both strange and familiar in entirely the wrong proportions. He refused to talk about his work, which was clearly very exhausting and moved him constantly all over the country. She knew dimly that he did trips in bombers and a wide assortment of naval craft, but she did not know why, and he refused to tell her. Occasionally, he rang her up to tell her that he was back, or all right; which simply confirmed her fears without informing them. Whatever he did occupied his mind entirely, as on the rare occasions when he came down to Kent, he was either preoccupied or bored. But above all, the children, and particularly Deirdre, enabled her (sometimes, at least) to see her life as dull, but not meaningless: the selfish private panic that she sometimes felt about being nearly forty dissolved a little as she watched Deirdre growing up. After all, what was one supposed to be doing with one's life at thirty-five? Indeed, if it were not for the war, what *would* she be doing? This, in the middle of Euston Station surrounded by khaki, by uniform of every description, was beyond her imaginative powers: indeed, she found it as difficult even to remember what her own life had been like in 1939, as to strip all the people in the buffet of their war clothes and dress them for peace. That pre-war life, by the very phrase, now seemed a frivolous inconsequent dream, of which

93

leisure and pleasure had been natural phenomena. She stopped pretending that she was going to drink her coffee, and decided that if she could find somewhere to sit, she would abandon herself to nostalgia.

It was very cold outside the buffet, and suddenly she began to dread meeting her husband; the absence of a waiting taxi; their strained and inadequate conversation while they waited for one; and their return to the desolate half-shut house. Now, she almost wished that she had accepted Richard's offer to accompany her, although she had refused it for what still seemed excellent reasons. Her husband resented the convalescents *en bloc*, and ignored her argument that the alternative was more Mrs Fawcetts, as a piece of feminine unreason.

She went to look at the indicator board, from which, she discovered, her particular train seemed to have disappeared. An ancient dyspeptic-looking man whose job it was to alter the details on the board, met all her enquiries with a sardonic smile, which only enraged her because it was obvious that he could hear what she asked, and knew the answer. Eventually, an equally ancient fat porter took pity on her, and told her that the train had come in a few minutes ago. 'Platform 18, you ought to find it over there,' implying that she would be very lucky if she did. She ran for the train with the indicating ancient glaring malevolently after her.

He was at the barrier when she arrived. He had given up his ticket, and stood motionless in his black velvet-collared overcoat, which always looked too big for him, clutching what she knew would be an exceptionally heavy small suitcase. He did not seem to see her as she approached him, and when she called his name he shook himself and blinked.

'Ah,' he said.

She explained about the indicating board, and as she did so, she knew that the explanation was unnecessary, and sounded foolish and pointless. She interrupted herself by saying it didn't matter and realized that she would have to tell him that she had been unable to bring the car.

They were still standing where they had met, with the end of the crowd off his train filtering past the ticket barrier into the dark. She said:

'Sorry I couldn't bring the car. We'll have to try and get a taxi.'

'Not if we have to try very hard. I'll ring up for a car.'

She turned to him in surprise, but he was searching in his pockets for change. He pulled out a bundle of five-pound notes, and she knew that mysteriously, as usual, he would possess no other money.

'I've got it,' she said, praying that she had – that that much of their life would be smoothed for them by her possessing twopence.

He took her arm, and propelled her towards the call boxes.

She *had* twopence, and he went into a box with it, leaving his case with her.

'Ten minutes,' he said, when he joined her. 'What about food?'

'There is a meal at home.'

'Any meat?'

'Bacon. And eggs.'

'I need meat,' he observed. 'We'll pick some up on the way back.'

She followed him outside the station feeling unaccountably depressed. The feeling of dread at meeting him had not disappeared, had, on the contrary, increased. Three times already she had felt ineffective and improvident, and as though she was old enough to know better.

Eventually, a car appeared which he said would be theirs, and it was. He packed her in, and said something to the driver, who covered her knees with a rug which felt dirty even in the dark. They drove off.

'Where on earth are you going to get meat?' she asked, but he touched her sharply through the rug, and his reproachful pale blue eyes gleamed with mocking conspiracy.

'Tell me how it is with you,' he said a moment later.

'It is all exactly the same, which I suppose is a good thing. And you?'

'It is all exactly different.'

'Another job?'

'Possibly. It will not affect *your* life in any way,' he added. He did not in the least mean to console her, and a little angry, she retorted:

'But yours? It must affect *your* life.'

She felt him grin suddenly in the dark, and then stop grinning. Then he said: 'Oh yes, it might radically affect *my* life.'

She knew immediately that he was thinking about death, and the incompatibility of her present continuing existence, and his possibly mysterious death, jolted about her mind in passionate disagreement, preventing even such conversation from continuing. This vast graveyard of private relations she thought, and wished suddenly for the day to have ended – for sleep to conceal her solitude. She glanced at him. His head was sunk into the collar of his coat, and it was too dark to see his face.

She roused herself to continue being the right kind of wrong companion.

'Deirdre is still convinced that you are really a spy.'

He was silent.

'It is all the Buchan she has been reading.'

'I am glad that she can read,' he answered politely.

'Oh Conrad, don't be so ridiculous: of course she can read. She is ten.'

The car was stopping – she thought they were in Soho, but she was not sure. They were stopped, and she was sure it was not Soho. He got out of the car and knocked and rang at a narrow little door. After a long wait, he was admitted, and the door shut. She became ridiculously afraid that she would have to make conversation to the chauffeur of the car. But he sat, immobile and silent, and seemed to expect nothing. It was very cold. She realized that she had had nothing to eat since a sandwich at the National Gallery after a lunch-time concert with Richard. And when we get back, she thought, the kitchen will be freezing cold, and I shall be so hungry that I shall not even want meat – but surely he won't be able to get *meat*.

The narrow door opened; he appeared, and for a moment she saw silhouetted behind him the figure of a very pregnant woman in an overall, who was either laughing or coughing convulsively – she could not determine which: and then the door was shut, and he had returned to her.

'Now home,' he said: and put a parcel on the floor of the car.

'I do try to live up to my daughter's literature,' he added a moment later, and she knew that he was trying again. Then he touched her, and wrote something on the window with his little finger. The word was 'Stake'. They had always had a private convention of misspelling single simple words (she could not remember how it had started), but he had not employed it now for a very long time. She wrote: 'Good: I love Staik' (the word was always endowed with a capital letter). He watched her write, read it with intense gravity, and then wrote as quick as lightning: 'Steyk is good for you'. Then the windows were used up.

The silence back to Campden Hill thereafter was an easier one.

TWO

The kitchen was dankly cold. The fire had gone out. Most of the cupboards and shelves were bare of stores and utensils, making the low stone-floored room more largely unattractive. The wooden shutters over the windows did not seem to quench the raw draughts, and the harsh ceiling lights with white china shades did not cheer the room – seemed merely and heartlessly to show it up in all its uninhabited discomfort. A calendar for 1939 hung on the wall: the days had been torn off it until September – a piece of ostentatiously subtle detail which was like the cinema.

She began cooking their meal. She was neither an experienced nor a natural cook; her husband minded very much what he ate, and she was now extremely tired. She had brought vegetables from the country that morning, and had prepared them in the afternoon. She unwrapped the steak. It was a very large steak; she had no onions, and the lack of them seemed suddenly all-important. If she did not warn her husband that there were no onions, everything would be spoiled. She went to the foot of the basement stairs and listened for him. Whenever he returned to either of his homes, he immediately prowled, like an animal, all over them – he did not unpack his luggage, or go to his study, or read his letters, he simply occupied the entire house, and then took up his life in it exactly where he had left off. Oh dear, she had not told him about Richard coming up for the night. Richard was out, but his things must be somewhere; Conrad would come upon them, and then she would feel she ought to have told him first. Such was the state of her mind racing about in the bottom gear of anxiety, when her husband reappeared.

'Oh Conrad, there are no onions and the fire is out. I am sorry.'

He looked at her carefully.

'You are grossly overtired. Go and change.'

'I cannot change *and* cook dinner!'

'If you think you are presenting me with that alternative, I would infinitely prefer you to change. If you stand about you will feel much worse. Where is the food? Ah!' He seized a large knife. 'You are alone in a basement threatened by a comparative stranger with a murderous weapon. What choice have you?'

'None at all,' she answered gratefully and retired.

She heard him drop the knife as she climbed the stairs.

In her room she found her corduroy long coat for dining laid out on her bed, and the electric fire switched on. She knew then that although he had never done so before, he would cook the meal and relight the kitchen fire, and that she was not meant to feel merely ineffective and improvident. She changed with the utmost attention to detail (he always maintained that living consisted of no fundamentals, outlines, basic truths, or principles, even for one person, let alone society, but simply a vast quantity of detail, endlessly variable and utterly unrelated). His most satisfactory and astonishing aspect was his capacity to astonish her.

She discovered strands of his dry brown hair in her

comb – even his hair was unexpected. She wished suddenly that she could change her appearance – that she could join him unrecognizably different. But she did not possess that talent, as some women possessed it – the mysterious ability to recast the shape of their heads, or emphasize a new aspect of their faces – to seem what hitherto they had never seemed – her extreme simplicity of appearance permitted almost no variation that did not fall below her standard.

At the end of her changing, she stepped back from the long mirror to look at herself with the kind of professionally objective scrutiny that she had evolved from years of this ritual. The tall thin creature in peacock blue that the ribbed velvet rendered almost black, stared back at her with a solemn and minute curiosity; observed dark hair impeccably drawn away from the face; collected for a second the startling eyes; paused at the pale velvet shadows thrown on to the crest of the cheekbone; hesitated as the earrings of cut steel swayed faintly; considered seriously the redness of the mouth; then travelled swiftly down the long dark lines from which the narrow white nervous wrists shot out like pieces of separate life. She was ready.

She had recently read in a magazine an article called 'Be Forty and Enjoy It'. She had read it carefully, wondering why the fact of being forty constituted such a menace to enjoyment. The article evidently thought so; but all she could glean was that the unfortunate women of forty should try very hard to look thirty-five, and not think about it. She *was* thirty-five; if it had not been for Richard, she would not have thought about her age at all, and when she did, it seemed merely a statement of fact like the date, by itself, and meaningless by itself. She went downstairs to join her husband.

He had relighted the fire which now blazed, and he was seated in one of Dorothy's old basket chairs, with a glass on the table beside him. As she entered the room, she knew that he had been asleep, but he slept and woke with such lightning facility, that only she would have known it.

'Now,' he said, 'have a large glass of duty-free gin.'

His suitcase, she noticed, was on the kitchen dresser.

'What about our dinner?'

'You must first drink enough to stop worrying about things that don't matter. I have cooked us the most delicious meal.'

'You are a very gifted man,' she said, subsiding into the other basket chair with the glass he gave her.

'I have bushels of lights,' he replied. It was the kind of remark that really amused her, without making her laugh.

'I shall never do it again,' he added a moment later.

He had been watching her with a detached gravity which she knew was the token of his approval. And I must make no move, she thought, not thank him for choosing my clothes, or warming the room; I must remain apparently calm and indifferent to anything he does, and everything will be all right.

'I want to shop tomorrow morning. What would you like?'

'I should like some earrings,' she said at once. He liked her to have some requirement immediately available – he liked to gratify some wish of hers that had lain for a while on the surface of her mind – he did not like her to be detached from material longings – from a kind of childlike greedy acquisitiveness – although there were, of course, infinitely secret rules to this live-and-let-give aspect of them both. She must want something in which he was interested – and it must be something which he could possibly give her. She knew that the earrings would be beautiful, and would become her.

'And a penknife?' she asked. He loved penknives, and possessed an enormous collection that she was not allowed to touch.

'Why do you want a penknife?'

'It would be very useful,' she said with the weakness of truth, and knew that she had lost all chance of getting a penknife.

He snorted, and finished his gin. He had a theatrical snort.

'Does anything matter now?'

'Absolutely nothing. I have a lovely hot corkscrew going down my throat. I haven't had gin for weeks.'

He was getting dishes out of the oven.

'You have worked hard,' she said, watching him.

'I have,' he agreed. 'But then it is much more exhausting seducing somebody one has known for a long time.'

The corkscrew, burning, shot suddenly down to the end of her spine. She said: 'What made you think of wrapping the steak in paper?'

'Hot *buttered* paper. It would have dried up if I hadn't. That unpleasant little spilt-milk quality – common sense. Come and eat.' The remarkable meal was on their plates.

She asked what he had done with the potatoes – they were brilliant, and there was no milk.

'I can't remember. I expect I used alcohol of some kind. As I shall never mash potatoes again they had to be brilliant.'

'You are a valedictory cook.'

He laid down his knife and fork. 'But *think*,' he said, gazing at her with an earnestness in which she was not intended to believe. 'Understand how fortunate you are to be present on such occasions. Supposing I was a dogged, far less talented little man, trying something new, but determined to get the hang of it, think of the potato you would have to endure – and how little it would matter to you in the end that I had got the hang of it. One should do everything not wisely, but a little too well.'

'With such consequences?' She was half laughing, half perplexed.

'Of course. Then one need never do it again.'

'I entirely disagree with you, and I do not at all see how the world would go round.'

He stretched his hand palm upwards towards her across the table.

'My dear,' he said, 'the world will continue to rotate whatever you do. It has its own axis to grind. You and I have no hand in it at all.' His fingers curled into his palm and straightened again.

'Do not identify yourself with this business. You have nothing to do with it. It is not, even indirectly, your guilt. I will fight because I hate, and because I choose to fight, not because I feel that I could have prevented the war. I will buy you earrings, but not a knife.'

She gave him her hand. She felt then distinctly that she was a part of him, not, perhaps, the part she would have chosen, but then perhaps it was not a question of choice. The notion (it seemed extraordinary because it had never struck her before), that perhaps *he* could not really choose the part she played for him, occurred to balance their uneven intimacy.

'I shall buy myself a knife,' she said.

He smiled seraphically.

'You'll choose one which is perfectly useless.'

And as she was allowing him to get away with that, the front door slammed. Oh Lord, I never told him about Richard, she thought. Oh damn, why did I forget? Aloud, she said:

'It's Richard Corthine, he came up for the night. Sorry darling, I forgot to tell you.'

He withdrew his hand. The footsteps, heavily hesitant, sounded above them.

'He'll probably go straight to bed.'

The footsteps had reached the head of the basement stairs: she was wrong. She looked at him – his face was already devoid of any expression.

When Richard Corthine came into the kitchen they were looking at the food on their plates but not eating. He had intended simply to say good night, but the air of tension was so apparent to him, that he determined not to leave her alone in it.

'I just looked in to say good evening. Good evening, sir. I imagine your train must have been madly late.'

'Madly.' Mr Fleming's lips hardly moved.

'You are back very early, Richard. Have you dined?'

'Oh yes, thank you. The other chaps wanted to go to a cinema afterwards so I came home.'

'Do you dislike the cinema?' Mr Fleming enquired.

'No, I don't dislike it, but it's not much good to me at present I'm afraid.'

A shadow crossed his lean unshadowed face, and he moved with deliberate cheerfulness to the fire. 'You've no idea how cold it is out.'

'Richard came up for them to see how his eyes are getting on.'

'How *are* they getting on?'

There was a short silence and Mrs Fleming looked at Richard.

'Sorry, I thought you were asking your wife. Oh, they don't say anything, you know. They never really tell one anything. I tried to get a chap to gang up with me on the tests, but he wasn't in favour. They said if they (my eyes I mean),' he screwed them up apologetically, 'if my eyes improve over the next few months they might give me a shore job.' He cleared his throat. 'In fact they'll probably sling me out at the end of the war. It's their usual form.'

'And how is the rest of you?' It was impossible to ignore the malice so barely concealed in this question, but Richard had good manners which he used even when they were not required.

'It *was* only my eyes, sir. My eyes and these headaches,' he answered, with a steadiness which somehow increased the malice of the enquiry.

'Of course. It is sometimes a little difficult for me to keep track of my wife's invalids.' He was working his way through his steak and did not look at either of them.

Richard thought: God, she looks wonderful in that dress: bloody little man; if we have coffee I can stay awake until we're all so tired she won't have much of him to put up with.

Aloud, he said: 'Are you back for long, sir? Have they given you a proper leave?'

'My dear Corthine, I am not a Naval Officer – I don't get leave, definite or indefinite.'

Mrs Fleming said abruptly: 'What about some coffee? Shall I make it?'

'You have not finished your steak.'

'It was delicious, Conrad, but I can't eat any more.'

Richard said: 'One never wants food one has cooked oneself.'

'Ah, but she *didn't* cook it. *I* did. I hope you are confounded?'

Richard said that of course he was, and then Mr Fleming continued gently: 'You know, I don't believe I would have *trusted* her with a steak.'

'Well, whether you trust me or not, I am going to make coffee.'

'Have a bit of Icelandic cheese?' He seemed to produce it from nowhere. She shook her head, and went to light the gas under the kettle.

Richard thought: Good, she wants coffee too. I wish I'd never come downstairs – no, I don't, that's selfish – she ought to have let me come to the station with her – she was tired out before she went, and obviously dinner wasn't going with a swing. What shall I talk about? What's a nice uncontroversial subject, although *he'll* argue about anything if he's in the mood: better if he argues with me, then she can have her coffee in peace. Funny how living in a house with a woman gives one insight. A year ago I'd have had no *idea* what was going on. He said:

'Were you in Reykjavik, sir?'

But Fleming, at precisely the same moment suddenly shot at him: 'You must be extraordinarily tidy!'

'Oh?' Richard was immediately and unreasonably defensive. (What the hell is he after now?)

'I do not recall any trace of you about the house. Is that the result of Dartmouth? Has the habit been instilled in you since you were thirteen – everything shipshape and above or below board as the occasion demands?'

Mrs Fleming said: 'One doesn't necessarily have to go to Dartmouth to be tidy. You look tired, Richard. Do you want to wait for coffee, or would you rather go to bed?'

'I'd love some coffee.' Damn, now I can't even take my dope with it, although she always knows when the pain starts. He had a headache which reminded him always of making fishbones of a chestnut leaf: every time he moved, another strip of leaf was torn out from behind his ears up to the sides of his forehead. The uneven tearing pain was so sharp that if he was thinking at all, he always felt at those times that he was able to think with unusual clarity. But perhaps it is simply that *she* has taught me to be discerning. Whenever he had this kind of headache (there were two other kinds, one not so bad, and one infinitely worse), he imagined himself remaining in the Navy, rising to great heights solely on account of his integrity with people.

Mrs Fleming, with an attempt at lightness, said, 'Oh this watched pot business. It *won't* boil.'

Richard thought: Yes, he's watching me, but I won't boil either – that'll fox him. He made one more effort – this time selecting the degree of stability which an old destroyer mounted with a number of new guns might be expected to have in the North Atlantic – a subject about which he suspected that Fleming knew a good deal. He was eager, he was genuinely interested, he was even tolerably informed – when he had served in the particular class in question there had clearly not been enough armament – on the other hand he knew somebody who had recently been in an old ship when she had rolled ninety degrees with a heavy sea running – he had not heard the results of the subsequent enquiry into the efficacy of existing stability tests – perhaps Mr Fleming . . . ? But he got nowhere. Fleming remarked that one could not indefinitely continue putting new guns into old destroyers. Then they both realized that the coffee was made. A relief, thought Richard, and then felt that no, of course it wasn't a relief, because here they all were sitting round the table again.

She said: 'I wish we had some brandy.'

'Have we none?'

'We moved what there was to the country. You remember.'

'An extremely foolish move. What have you *done* to this coffee?'

She made a little gesture of weariness, but her hair was still perfectly neat. 'The usual things. Do you dislike it very much?'

He drained his cup. 'Very much. It was revolting.'

She tried hers. 'It is so hot that I cannot taste it.'

'Well, drink it quickly before you can.'

Richard drank some and scalded his tongue.

'It seems very good coffee to me,' he said.

The sharp smaller pain of the scald was a relief from the uneven strip tearing in his head. The evening is nearly over, he thought, and, in spite of trying, I don't seem to have done much good.

The evening was over. On the stairs, Fleming halted, looked down on the others and said: 'Does Richard know where he is sleeping?'

'Of course he knows.'

'I'm on the top floor.'

'Go right down if there is a raid.' When she said that, he knew that she knew about his headache, and a wave of the comfort and security which her knowledge and solicitude always engendered in him, stopped him, while the others had continued to climb.

They were waiting for him on the landing outside their bedroom.

He said good night, and climbed the last flight alone to the attic floor where the children had slept. There is nothing I would not do for her, he thought, wanting to do everything. He did not realize at all that he could do nothing.

THREE

Mrs Fleming sank on to the stool before her dressing-table. She was speechless with apprehension and fatigue. There was no point in being angry, either with Richard or with Conrad: each saw the other strictly in their own terms, in relation to themselves in relation to her. She had become used to beginning and ending her day alone, and the knowledge that she was now trapped with the remnants of the evening until sleep released one or both of them (and sleep, she well knew, was not easily achieved in such conditions), added to her nervous agitation. She resolved to work her way through it all with amiable bravado; she knew from long experience that it could not be ignored, and she did not choose to postpone it until they were embarked upon the eternity after the lights were out. But he forestalled her.

'How very much I dislike the young. Their complacent certainty that their infantile dependence will be met. Their utter lack of self-containment. Their determination to be compensated for the disastrous consequences of their casual curiosity. Their greed for indiscriminate approval – their lack of technique – their senseless demands – they will pick endless watches to pieces and expect others to mend or replace them – their inability to profit by the experience of others and their refusal to experience anything for themselves. Their contempt of reserve – their ceaseless searching for somebody before whom they can swagger and be saved – their brash resolve that each time they are burned is the first – their ridiculous belief that they are Adam – the first new specimen of their species, magnificently unique, when they are only one more pathetically identical detail turned off the bench. Their faith in their own indispensability – their tiny wisdom and their colossal impatience—' He had stopped.

'Yes?' she said. 'Go on.'

'There is no point: I have undressed. I do not like that young man.'

'And there is now no point in my saying that after all he is only young.'

'None whatever. There is no point in your saying anything. What, or should I say who, has possessed you to design anything so badly?'

She said: 'I did not design it.'

He seized his bottle of hair lotion and shook it furiously.

'I will not spend my evenings with you in an atmosphere of Freudian night nursery. I will not play down to that adolescent's Italian comic opera. Give me gout and a little more money, and a few more doors to the kitchen and we should have been complete.'

She had unpinned her hair, and now, laying her earrings in their niche of bruised velvet, considered the tiresome necessity of taking off her clothes. She hated undressing in these conditions; becoming, she felt, more and more vulnerable and literally thin-skinned, while he always managed to follow the most commonplace ritual – even absurd little things like rubbing lotion into his hair, without losing control of any situation he was making at the time.

'You should be more discriminating in the flattery you require. Or if that is beyond you, more selective as to time.'

She heard herself saying: 'I thought Richard had gone out for the evening. What *does* it matter anyway!'

'You spend ninety per cent of your time with children, invalids, fools, and animals. What a mind will yours become!'

'I thought that was the company approved for women by most men!'

'You are so intent on becoming most women that you forget who I am. If you had sent the children away as arranged you could now be living an intelligent life.'

'I thought you said that I must not identify myself with the war!' Almost afraid that she had scored, she swung round on her stool and said: 'Conrad: I am disliking this so much. It is not simply this evening that exasperates you – what is it?'

'These young men with their persistent nagging devotion, constantly presenting you to me in a light which I find unattractive. If they had reached an age where they were capable of discovering romantic inspiration in someone more than their mother or their nurse I should bear with them.'

'If they were encouraged to see me in any other light, the position in Kent would become impossible.'

'Exactly. That is what comes of burying yourself in Kent. You should travel for your affairs. Look at Marseille.'

'What about Marseille?'

She felt all the blood in her halt, and then jerk forward again to catch up: then she repeated: 'What about Marseille?'

He was brushing his hair now, but he stopped to say

pensively: 'Isn't it odd that while affairs are on, there is everything in the world to say about them, and one can't; and when they are off, it doesn't matter saying anything in the world, and one doesn't.'

Glad of this generalization she said: 'There is always poetry.'

'Poetry?'

'People write it when they are in love.'

'My dear, what *years* since you were in love. They use the telephone. Or does that young man write poetry to you?'

'He writes poetry. I've never seen it. No, I expect it's all about the sea.'

'I'm damn sure it isn't. Does he do *everything* badly?'

'You sneer so much, like someone perpetually exhaling. You never absorb a breath of anybody. It is so – so *dull* of you!'

She had managed to undress, and now she went into their bathroom and shut the door. He had the capacity to make her incurably angry, with herself and with him. Why had she told him that Richard wrote poetry? Why give him that handle? Poor Richard – whose life was the Navy, which was in all probability going to divest him of his life. She knew that Richard regarded his future with a kind of panic: he simply saw all his competence, his knowledge, and his status removed from him, and he could imagine nothing in their place. When she had once inveighed against a Service that could act so harshly, he had immediately contradicted her, unholding any decision they might see fit to make. 'You see,' he had said earnestly, 'that is their strength. Never to have men who are anything less than I was. That was what made one – oh, proud, you know.' He had frequent nightmares of

114

his trying unsuccessfully to sell vacuum cleaners or washing machines, and sometimes, he said, the object he was trying to sell got smaller and smaller each time that he failed, so that the failure was smaller too, but felt worse because it ought to be easier to sell something small. He had been told what to do all his life; the very channels for his initiative had been charted: he might perhaps have questioned decisions made for him to act upon, but he would follow them at all costs with an impersonal loyalty which required no recompense, not even any acknowledgement but permission to continue his service. She remembered one of his fellow officers who came to see him in Kent saying that when, after hours of searching, they had found Richard and dragged him out of the water, frozen and unable to see because at that point he was blind, they had asked him how he was and he had said, 'I'm in it up to the eyes,' and laughed. Everybody had laughed, and it wasn't until they handed him a flask of whisky that they realized he couldn't see it. Well, he could see again; and perhaps he wouldn't get chucked out. She made a little prayer to the Royal Navy to allow him to continue risking his life in their employ, and went back into the bedroom.

Her husband was in bed, reading Donne.

'You need more scent,' he observed.

She glanced at the bottle: it was half full.

'I mean, now.'

She sat obstinately on the bed, her dressing-gown round her shoulders. He threw his book aside, fetched the scent and stood over her.

'I am too tired to care.'

'I will care for you,' he said, immediately: 'lie down.' His hands were comforting in contrast to his eyes which were now fixed on her with soothing, faintly satirical, detachment.

'You are like a gardener spraying his favourite rose bush.'

'A good gardener sprays *all* his rose bushes,' he replied, and then added, 'few people can avoid a gallantry as I can. I am saving my breath to warm your ardour you see.'

'I see,' she said, but she did not feel anything.

He put a little scent on the corner of her pillow, and returned the bottle. 'There. I like you to enjoy the good things of your life. Now you will have some faint echo of your smell.'

'I suppose there are rows and rows of bushes,' she said drowsily. She did not very much care. He had an hypnotic effect upon her: when he intended her to feel soothed, almost immediately she was. 'Perhaps that is because you do it so seldom,' she said aloud, and realized that he would not know what she meant. 'The contrast,' she added as though that explained it. She heard him laugh a little as he turned off a light, and with a flicker of curiosity she asked him why he laughed.

'I was remembering you climbing into bed reeking sweetly of toothpaste. A long time ago.'

'Was that absurd?'

'It was simply charming. How little you knew! How little you cared! I don't know which charmed me most.'

He was lying beside her, and now he leaned over her, reaching for the other light. When he found the switch, he paused, looking down at her with a serious, almost fanatical, expression.

'I was extraordinarily in love with you – once.'

'A long time ago.'

She thought she was smiling, but she was not.

'I remember it more completely in the dark,' he said, and made the room dark.

He did not speak to her, which rendered their anonymity complete; except that she recognized his hands breaking down the familiar resistance of her mind, until the moment, when, without knowing it, without love or affection, she kissed him. The kiss was not returned – she would have cried out or died for it, but there was suddenly no time to lose or spend: her mouth was covered and she was not alone.

The tide, which for so many hours had been making, eddying, creeping up to its height – struggled with all its irresolute strength; and then violently turned – sweeping her out in hurrying darkness to the wide estuary where separate bodies lie in an accomplished silence.

Out of that silence she thought he said:

'I shall never do that again, either.'

But she had already drifted too far from him in sleep.

PART THREE
1937

ONE

The situation had been growing steadily worse for days. The facts that they had achieved the journey from England in a heat wave, with both children, their nurse, and a very great deal of luggage, to a villa which with the Talbots they had rented blind; that the villa had surprisingly displayed almost all the assets of beauty and comfort passionately listed in a series of letters which its agent had mistakenly written in English; that the children had suffered the minimum of sickness, heat spots, and diarrhoea, and their nurse had so far only managed to work in one of her customary bilious attacks; that they had not quarrelled with the Talbots, and that they were all agreed about the desirability of St Tropez, were beginning to count for nothing. Like the sun which shone with gentle tireless determination, drenching the sea with its brilliant glancing power: drying their hair, soaking into their bodies, glinting, gilding, bleaching, burning, permeating, strengthening the light and heating the atmosphere; dominating colour and smell and almost all sound but the cicadas, who seemed the very tick, the frantic mechanism of heat: like this sovereign element they had come so far to seek, Mr Fleming's boredom which they had come so far to avoid, pervaded the whole party, beginning to touch and to cling to everything they touched. They were not all aware of it, of course, but to Mrs Fleming it was so urgently alive, it was growing so fast that she felt it must destroy all of them in the end. There were another ten days of the holiday to run; fourteen of them had already been spent. Certain people literally spend holidays, she thought, and he is one.

At first it had not been so bad. He had been very tired when they arrived, and the combination of his fatigue and the change of environment had entirely occupied his mind with his body. But he had slept so furiously, had bathed and eaten and drunk with such scientific attention to his own rehabilitation, that now he was spoiling for some stimulating experience. He was bored by Leila's husband; Leila, who sometimes amused him, was pregnant; he was (naturally) bored by her, and the children had always bored him, he said, since nine months before they were born. He was now engaged upon becoming bored with St Tropez: using up the beaches, eating steadily through the repertoire of cooking, drinking so much of the delicious *vin du pays* that any moment he would, she knew, morosely take to boiled water; methodically exhausting every topic of conversation; declaring that it was unfair of green Penguins to be identical within as without; even quarrelling with the sun, which, he had begun to claim, oversimplified everything. He did not quarrel with her, or with any of them. He merely defied them to amuse him, at the same time making it clear that it was essential he be amused.

She supposed it was all her fault; by which she meant that she was responsible for their being in St Tropez with their children and the Talbots. The holiday had been planned months before: she had wanted to take the children abroad, the Talbots fell in gratefully with a plan which did not involve their being alone together, and at first she had not minded very much whether Conrad accompanied them.

But the last three months had been very difficult; and under the unexpected strain of violent and internally uncontrollable jealousy, she had succumbed to the pallid pleasure of dominating external events: she had got him to say that he would join them, and she had made it impossible for him honourably to evade his promise. She was consequently very unhappy; and the discovery that it had taken her thirty years thoroughly to understand that nothing is worth having if one schemes, if one dislocates the character one hair's breadth by imposition or manipulation, haunted her in this full sunlight as relentlessly as that other discovery had haunted her during the dusty summer evenings in London.

She had known, of course, that he was not faithful to her; but previously she had thought his attentions had been so casual and diffused that they had not seriously interrupted her life with him. Now, she was bitterly uncertain. She reflected that usually in the summer when she retired to Kent for the children's holidays, he appeared at odd intervals, and that her decision to remain in London this year while electric light was installed in the country house had irritated him profoundly. He had at once proceeded to be out or away: she knew that his work was exhausting him to a point where he always behaved badly, but almost immediately she behaved so badly herself that she could not forgive him for being responsible. She had taken to going alone to the opera, where, one evening, she had seen him in a box with a ravishing young woman. She had waited in her drawing-room for him until past two in the morning, and inspired him by her evening dress, her tears, and the hour to lose his temper with her.

He had begun calmly by saying that the whole scene was horribly dated, and that were she to attend the opera more often she would learn that such behaviour as hers invariably led to disastrous consequences; but when these remarks merely elicited from her a flood of ill-considered and conventional allegations he became dangerous: whole-heartedly agreed with her, ignored her tears, and left her on the discouraging note that there were only two kinds of people – those who live different lives with the same partners, and those who live the same life with different partners; a remark, he said, to which she could not possibly object, since she had so perfectly created the situation which provoked it.

She was left feeling that she had had just enough reason for behaving badly to make her having done so intolerable. During the ensuing week's silence she ceased going to the opera. When, after the week had elapsed, he returned to Campden Hill Square, she asked no questions and he told her no truths: they did not try to approach one another, and she worried frantically about whether, at thirty, she had ceased to be attractive. At a dinner given by the Talbots to discuss the holiday, she had contrived to make him tacitly agree to joining them, and now here they all were . . .

It was the middle of the afternoon, and she lay naked between sheets, awake, and very much alone. The shutters were closed and she lay in the dark. She disliked using a lamp, and when earlier, as she always did, she opened the shutters, the burning light almost struck her as it always seemed to do, and the room immediately became stifling.

They had bathed and sunbathed all the morning and now they were all supposed to sleep: 'To have a good old siesta', as Don Talbot said every day. He slept with the Continental *Daily Mail* over his face on the terrace, and Leila lay stupefied for hours in their bedroom. The children slept like exhausted puppies, while their nurse covered pages of violet-coloured paper with a post office pen (what did she find to say, Mrs Fleming wondered: her description of anything being usually confined to its being 'nice', or 'not nice', and to people 'kind', or 'unkind'?).

And he, what was he doing? Often he chose these burning hours to sunbathe alone in the garden or on the beach, returning at five for a shower: apparently refreshed, recharged by the sun and the silence. After the shower he would drink quantities of the local absinthe or pastis, stuff which in this native state was so potent that she dared not drink it at all; and as his eyes sharpened under its influence, he became incredibly amusing, in a manner so far over the Talbots' heads that she was constantly and helplessly divided between her amusement and their exclusion. All the time, of course, this intellectual clowning was a show: with the Talbots she was nearer to him – or at least as near as the front row of an appreciative audience; but when they were alone together, the show ceased, all the lights went out, and she did not know where she was. She tried to be calm and patient, but their leisure and the climate were not conducive to either intention. Tempers would rage here, she thought, turning to find a cool patch of sheet in her bed, as violent and meaningless as the local thunderstorms. Very often, at least twice a day, she resolved to talk to him, but she was so afraid that she would perpetrate any of her desperate folly in London that she dared not try. Each day, and particularly each afternoon, she thought that if he made love to her

they might be able to talk; but as each night and particularly each afternoon drifted by and he did not, she imagined herself resisting him more and more completely,
until to achieve her, he would have entirely to want her.
Thus the mirage of his desire for her shimmered in her
mind, vanishing each night with the sun, returning each
day in the desert of these long, solitary afternoons, when
her body lay stretched on her bed, and her mind was
stretched over those interminable sun-baked hours until
he came in for his shower. Then it was that she suffered
defeat; day after day as he entered the room she knew
that the situation was unchanged, and was therefore,
illogically, worse. Sometimes, she thought that she hated
him: sometimes, that she loved him so much that she
would wither and die from the private shock of his indifference. Always she clung to him and to herself; she was
unable to face the abstract of their emotions; of love,
desire, or indifference – they could not be translated into
any other terms – as though in banishing her jealous
imagery of the girl at the opera, she had banished the
whole world of possibilities, leaving them with nothing
but each other. She built this stockade against the attacks
of humiliation, and each day as she made the same
discovery afresh, the attacks and her defence developed
with a frightful equal efficiency, like weapons of war
designed to combat one another.

Each day, after the discovery, and while he had his
shower, she would get up and dress for the evening with
a passionate, an almost fanatical, care. She washed her
long thick hair free from salt every day; her skin was
becoming an even gold which darkened smoothly,
enabling her to wear paler and paler colours, until at any
moment now she would be able to reach the final contrast

of white. That was the kind of decorative timing which he had taught her – not to wear white until her skin was of a colour perfectly designed to carry it.

She looked at her watch, faintly luminous in the gloom. It was twenty minutes to five. She was listlessly considering the possibility of leaving her hot bed and having a shower, when she heard a door below shut with a distant decisive click. She leapt out of bed and opened one shutter. She did not want to feign sleep, but she could not bear the thought of his coming into the room and finding her awake in the dark.

When he entered the room she was brushing her hair, holding her head over the side of the bed in order to get a satisfactory sweep.

He watched her for a moment, and then said:

'The Egyptians polished theirs with silk.'

'They had Egyptians to polish it then,' she replied, continuing to brush. She waited for him to introduce some fantastic thesis on hair – he seemed in the mood for it, but now he proceeded to fill his fountain pen without saying anything. The strain of having minded being alone frayed and snapped gently in her – she felt wonderfully, suddenly peaceful watching his deliberate neatness with his pen. She put down the brush in order that she might touch her hair, so that if in a minute he touched it, she would know how it felt to his hand.

He said: 'Do you want a shower?'

'I might this evening. Eventually.' She stretched in the bed until the well-being reached down her body to her feet. 'You are taking a long time with your pen.' It was the nearest she ever got to inviting his attention.

'All three pens,' he said, 'and then I'll come and talk to you.'

She seized the hairbrush, and resumed her brushing. But he began to talk where he was.

'Either one marries a woman who gradually sharpens, intensifies, exaggerates herself, to the essence of her original appearance – or a woman brimful of a kind of beauty that runs over and dissipates – that blurs and diffuses until there is no constant picture of her at any one time, but simply a vast series of impressions – even asleep, she is not a picture of herself, but of someone who *was* like her, asleep. The first is intellectually aesthetically desirable: her men can watch her becoming more what at the beginning they hoped she would be; only that was at the beginning and in the end they no longer want it. The second is always elusive, always disappointing, fascinating because there is no contrast, maddening because nothing is ever attained. There is merely a choice between the woman with a bone structure, a core, an architectural personality that will wear; and a creature of light and colour and shadow who requires all the senses to enjoy her; whose character is so freckled with feminine possibility that it can never be defined; who will shame the intellect, and outface the desire for beauty – but who will always unconsciously accentuate the difference between the men she attracts and herself – a most comforting charm, since it provides a structure for social and erotic behaviour. One need never pretend to treat her as one would another man. She has nothing to preserve since she cannot preserve her youth; she can stand up to being courted and married and raped as she would never clearly envisage an alternative. She would not torture herself with the rigorous standards of intellectual romanticism – she would not relate any one thing to another except when she indulged in such orgies of inconsequence that it was amusing. On seeing her for the first time ten years after marriage people would ask why on earth did he marry her—'

'With the other kind of woman people say meaningly that they quite understand why he *married* her.'

He looked up. 'That is what they say.'

'But do you really think that there are only two kinds of women?'

'Only two kinds that I should marry. I always talk about myself. Other people's opinions are so dull that I am never sufficiently informed to discourse upon them.' He put his pens on the dressing-table. 'You see, you have not asked which kind of woman you are.'

'I have not asked because I know.'

'You have not asked because you want me to tell you. The second kind of woman would have asked because she thought I wanted to tell her.'

He leaned out of the window to fasten back the shutter which had been slowly closing, and said: 'I am going to Paris tomorrow. By air from Marseille.'

She checked the little cry of astonishment and despair. She picked up her comb and said: 'It was silly to fill all your pens. They will flood in the aeroplane.'

'I thought perhaps you might drive me there.'

She made a minute gesture of indifference and examined her comb.

'There is a plane leaving Marignane at about seven o'clock. You will have to stay the night in Marseille. Would you mind that? Because if you would, I'll drive myself, and send someone back with the car.'

His solicitude about her minding the drive hardened her artificial indifference. She said:

'Surely Nice is nearer? Why don't you go from there?'

'I prefer Marseille. I prefer the drive.'

'Are you coming back?'

'No.' He sat on the end of her bed. 'I didn't want to come here at all. You know that. The thought of even one more evening with the Talbots appals me. I am prepared to work in tedious conditions, but I will not attempt to play in them. You presumably like it, or you would not have elected to come here with them in the first place. I shall see you in London in – how long is it – ten days' time.'

'And supposing I said that I wanted to come with you!'

'It wouldn't be true.'

'How on earth do *you* know?'

'You have made it perfectly clear that you want me to stay here with you. I have now made it perfectly clear that I want to go to Paris. I have not invited you to come with me for two reasons. One, I want to be by myself, and two, you are responsible for the children who have still ten days of their holiday to go.'

She put down the comb and hid her shaking hands under the sheet.

'My dear, very often two people want two different things that cannot be reconciled. You must accept that, because I won't have a lot of sandy compromise thrown in my eyes. It doesn't suit either of us. Do you understand that?'

'It is all unanswerable.' Her mouth felt so dry and rigid that she could hardly speak. She wished desperately that he would go out of the room, but she felt with the insanity of pride that she would never ask him to do anything again – not even to go out of the room. If she said anything at all, some of the shocked, pent up, blistering, miserable emotions would spill out and flood them – he would suddenly see her as she really was, and she would be over this crumbling precipice.

He was looking away from her out of the window during this silence; now he got up from the bed.

'You make such intolerable alternatives for yourself. It would probably be better to cry.' And then he did leave her.

∞ ∞ ∞

On the terrace before dinner she said: 'Conrad has to leave us tomorrow: isn't it sickening?'

The Talbots agreed that it was absolutely *sickening*. They did not really feel it was.

After dinner when she said good night to the children, she told them that he was going, and they immediately asked whether she was going too. When she replied that she was not, Julian said: 'Well, that's all right then,' but Deirdre, balked of the drama of her mother suddenly leaving her, cried: 'But you said he would go dark black here, and now he won't have time!' and burst into tears. 'Don't be silly,' said her brother severely, 'he's going to Paris – well, that's French – he can get black there,' and Deirdre was instantly consoled.

Much later, when they were in their room again, she broke the exquisite pain of their silence by saying:

'I – will drive you to Marseille – if you like.'

It did not sound at all like a concession, but an appeal.

She was sitting on the edge of her bed, barefoot, twisting her hair out of the way for the night.

He picked one of her hands from her hair, and stared down at her. He looked suddenly, hopelessly, sad.

'Good,' he said, and put her hand back, on to her lap.

∞ ∞ ∞

131

The next morning she bathed before coffee. There was a little beach near the villa, and good for early swimming, although too small to be much use later in the day, when even half a dozen people made it seem crowded. This morning she shared it with a large black Labrador, an expert swimmer, and very friendly.

It was very early and beautiful. There was a self-assurance about this climate, she thought – it had none of the pale trembling transitory quality of an English summer morning – a beauty that would take the breath and vanish with the dew, would dissolve, as like as not, into any one of a variety of undistinguished days. Days here began like Juliet; with a bewitching blend of freshness and maturity. It was cool, but the faint throb of heat left from the evening before had not stopped: colours were throaty, full pitched, and perfectly balanced – they did not seem to experiment with one another – there was none of the secret glancing uncertainty of early morning light in England.

She swam in the small lagoon, and then lay on a flat rock over which the sea washed with irregular lazy after-thoughts.

She had not really accepted the fact that Conrad was going to Paris. Ever since he had told her, she had recoiled from the shock – since she had first checked her initial cry of despair – since after that she had not wept, or implored – she had strung herself along from one event to another – telling the Talbots – telling the children – the servants – and finally the offer to drive him to Marseille: this last because she knew that he loathed driving himself, and because it prolonged the time before he had really gone – and because she had wanted to break the intolerable silence and unbalance of feeling between them. (But he had come exactly half way towards her mind – which is never far enough – touched her hand and retreated again) – and now she was strung up for the drive, she was thinking in terms of Michelin, of petrol, and where they would stop for lunch. She carefully did not consider the long drive back alone, or her return in St Tropez for ten days without him. In the night, while she had not slept, while she had lain deliberately still because she had not wanted him to know that she was awake – she had struggled with what she recognized to be childish illusions about this holiday – she had tried not to separate it from the rest of her life but to see it in proportion – three weeks out of ten years with Conrad: out of – what was it – twenty years before him. Put like that – three weeks were nothing. It was foolish to indulge in elaborate preconceptions: anticipation was a featherweight, doomed to compete with the inevitable, convincing bulk of reality. The trouble was that one had to face reality without knowing beforehand precisely what it was to be. One had somehow to discover and tread the hard, between the sloughs of fearing the worst and hoping for the best. Anything more complex and one fell into the trap laid for imagination – anything simpler and one existed in a kind of vacuum of mediocrity, where one refused to play the game at all in case one lost . . .

When, at a quarter to eight, her husband joined her on the terrace for coffee, she had washed out her hair, and packed. She was wearing a white silk shirt that had belonged to him and a coarse black linen skirt. Her damp hair was tied to the back of her head with a scarlet sash. He remarked upon her simple magnificence, and she, drawing out the flat gold watch which she wore round her neck on an exquisite chain he had given her, replied evenly that he had better say goodbye to the children as they ought to leave in six minutes.

Five minutes later, as he handed her into the driving seat, he laughed, and said, 'Yes?'

'I was wondering whether a woman could *ever* continue to be mistress of herself, a man, *and* a situation.'

'Only, I think, when either the man or the situation are not worth having. Now N98 to Toulon. Then, I thought the coast, in case we want to bathe, and because of Cassis.'

'Let us do whatever you would most enjoy.'

This made them both actually laugh; it was his age-long preface to doing exactly what he would most enjoy.

TWO

They reached Marseille a little before five. Exactly twenty-four hours, she thought. They were driving down the wide dusty road edged with exhausted plane trees which, pollarded, and clipped into a jaunty shape, looked none the less dirty and fatigued – by the dust from bicycles, from the gigantic lorries, from the little rattling battering trams that journeyed ceaselessly out from Marseille to Mazargues, and back. The road, like all main roads into any big city, achieved a kind of vast squalid importance – everyone travelling upon it was either hurrying to get into the city or out – it was a life line with a low opinion of life. The petrol stations, the huge crude advertisements, the little cafés right on the road, the crowd of factory workers pouring out of irrelevantly elegant iron gates, the scattering of large French mongrels – everything seemed designed to be seen at the rate of forty-five kilometres an hour – it being a point of honour with all traffic to exceed the speed limit by a minimum of five kilometres.

They were approaching the square where the trams stopped.

'Air terminus?'

'We have an hour. Let us get you fixed up at an hotel,' he answered.

'I will do the fixing,' he added a moment later. 'Then we'll have a drink.'

It was very hot, and with the car stopped, almost intolerable. Their bathe in Cassis seemed fantastically long ago, and she began to regret her decision to stay even one night in Marseille. Well, in an hour he would be gone, and she could do anything she liked. And I shall do *anything* I like, she thought, without any clear idea of what she would like to do.

He emerged from the hotel looking so actively, so intensely, impassive, that she knew he had achieved something.

'They showed me a cupboard looking on to an open sewer which I have naturally refused. I have secured you instead an enormous double room looking on to the harbour – Come and see.'

'But I don't need a double room!' she said, as the small lift gave a deep gasping sigh and moved slowly upwards.

'What a ridiculous thing to say. If you lived your life on the principle of only having what you strictly needed, you wouldn't enjoy a moment of it. By eleven o'clock tonight you may be very glad that you have a room large enough' – he glanced at the lift boy whose face was ominously inexpressive – 'to watch a thunderstorm from with somebody to stop you being frightened.'

'One has to marry to ensure an irregular sex life,' he hissed in her ear, as they walked down a dark corridor behind the boy.

The room, which faced south-west, was, of course, dark. The boy turned a switch, and the room flickered with a tinselly Victorian light, which suited the heavy white bedspread and the damp smell of clean laundry.

'It is now the same price as the cupboard. I don't suppose the taps work. No. Cold from the hot, and nothing from the cold. Now. You wash, and then we can have a drink outside.'

He opened a shutter, and went out on to the blazing balcony.

Her mind had reached a state of immediacy when looking for her soap entirely occupied it. When she had washed, and done her hair, she turned this full shallow attention to the drink they were to have.

'Half an hour,' he said, as they settled themselves at a table below her room, and looking straight on to the harbour.

She looked at him vaguely.

'I shall have to go in half an hour.'

'Oh! Oh yes.'

'What will you drink?'

'A *fine*.' She looked as though she was watching the people who surged and lounged, and spat, and stared, and skulked on the road and the quay before them, but she did not see them. She was suddenly, and with bitter sharpness, remembering Paris with Conrad: she realized that he was leaving her, and going – to Paris of all places – and a wave of jealousy submerged her, so violent that she could neither see nor speak. Through the sick faint haze she heard him say, 'There's Thompson!' and by the time she had regained control of herself, another man was sitting at their table with them. She realized that she had been introduced to him, and smiled. Her brandy had arrived; she drank it and leaned weakly back in the cane chair.

'. . . only arrived this afternoon,' the man was saying.

'By air? And what will you drink?'

'What I should really like is a whisky and soda. And your lady would like some cognac or whatever it was.'

137

He extracted a battered packet of Gold Flake from the breast pocket of his shirt and handed it politely to her.

'Do you use these things?'

'No, thank you.' (Boring little man: where on earth did Conrad pick him up?)

While they waited for the drinks, he scratched the back of his neck and then wiped it carefully with a dirty silk handkerchief covered with anchors.

'I've been bringing a boat down for somebody,' he said, stuffing the handkerchief into a trouser pocket. 'Warm here, isn't it?' He selected a limp cigarette and looked enquiringly round. 'I wonder if I could trouble you for a light?'

'What sort of boat?' asked Fleming instantly: he seemed really interested, she noticed with resentment.

'Converted Brixham trawler – and how. Skinned her, they must have – teak throughout, fancy aluminium mainmast – two new suits of sails, a blooming great engine fitted this spring – a *bath* – about eleven burgees and a monkey. Took a year to refit her, and now her own builder wouldn't know her – she's such a fancy job. Businessmen playing sailors. He's only had one game, and then he got stuck on the Brambles. He'd have had the crew playing football round her if they could have got a side to play against.'

The cigarette, which had hung unlit from his mouth throughout this speech, now dropped limply on to the table. He picked it up, pulled out a few straggling wisps of tobacco and flattened the end with his thumb.

'Are you leaving her here?' Fleming asked.

'Nope. Cannes is my terminus. But I'm ahead of schedule. Thought I'd look round here for a couple of days. Buy some bananas for the monkey.' He looked over the back of his chair and said: 'Pouvez-vous m'obliger avec une lumière?' The Frenchman smiled with weary scorn, and gave him a box of matches. 'Merci beaucoup. Years since I've tried to speak this. But I can always get m'self around.' At last he lit the cigarette: it ceased to be the uniquely squalid object that had begun to obsess Mrs Fleming. He was rather like a monkey himself, she thought, an English monkey – if that was not too great a contradiction in terms. He had small unselfconscious animal movements; he concentrated extremely on the cigarette, and the box of matches, and wiping the sweat from the back of his neck with his handkerchief. He said what came into his head the moment it arrived, and when he had nothing to say, he watched them with a calmly childish curiosity which seemed entirely physical – 'What colours are you wearing? Are you as hot as I am?' – nothing more complicated than that. For the rest he was small and very brown and gave the impression of being furry.

He had thought of something else.

'Tell you what,' he said, 'why don't you come and see my boat?'

'Unfortunately I'm leaving almost at once.'

'He has an aeroplane to catch,' she said, trying to be nice about it. She had drunk her second *fine* and felt much better.

'What a shame!' He seemed really deflated. He finished his drink carefully and then turned to her: 'I suppose you wouldn't care to come and see her? She really is a lovely boat—' he added with a kind of eager friendliness – as though, if she had not been such a lovely boat, he would not have dreamed of asking her.

She looked up, hesitating – she did not at all want to

see the little man's boat – and caught her husband's eye snapping with satirical amusement – waiting to see how she would get out of that one – and determined not to help her. She pulled her watch out of her shirt and looked at it.

'First I must see that Conrad catches his plane.'

'My wife would have made an admirable secretary.' He hitched his chair nearer Thompson. 'Isn't it fascinating that all wives resent being told that, and all secretaries resent being told that they would have made admirable wives.'

'It's the past tense that does it,' said Thompson calmly. 'No woman would like being told what she was, or would have been. They like the future – the future and the present.' And he smiled suddenly at her showing most perfectly dazzling teeth.

'Whereas for a man, without a past you have no future at all.' Conrad seemed to have forgotten about his aeroplane – he did not seem surprised at Thompson's (to her) unexpectedly penetrating remark – and he was savouring what he had himself just said in the leisured considerate manner which, she knew, prefaced hours of conversation. For a minute she thought of letting him miss his plane: but then he will catch another later on, and by then I shall cease to feel strung up, and simply be muddy and bad-tempered about his going. She rose from the table.

'I am going to make sure they haven't taken your bags out of the car. Three minutes?' she said, and then to Thompson, 'Do keep him up to it, I've driven him miles to get him here in time.'

Oh dear, even that sounded faintly hysterical, she thought, walking through the hotel. She had begun to feel acutely self-conscious – as though she was too tall, and her arms hung in a curious manner, and her eyes could look at nothing easily: as though she was walking too loudly fast, hearing her footsteps pounding so hideously out of time with her heart. 'Too full of herself,' she remembered a nurse saying of her when she was a child, and she thought now, what an agonizing thing to be, and how she would give any of herself away, in order that there might not be so much – but nobody would take it – she finished, fumbling in her bag with cold clumsy fingers for the key of the car.

Her husband appeared, minutes later, and with Thompson. In spite of knowing that it was a good thing not to be alone with Conrad, she resented his bringing Thompson, as she would have resented any third person. The car had stood in the shade and she had become unreasonably cold sitting in it. Fleming hesitated outside, until Thompson said, 'No, you go in front': a harmless remark that she knew ought not to exasperate her.

'Make up your mind anyhow,' she said, 'or you'll miss the wretched bus.'

They got in.

They had missed the bus. They saw the end of it disappearing up the hill as they reached the terminus.

'Thompson will drive me,' said Fleming.

She ignored this, and proceeded to drive unnecessarily fast to Marignane.

Fleming talked to Thompson all the way: she noticed that he answered monosyllabically, and wondered what on earth he must think – but then there wasn't anything for him to think, and he didn't think anyway.

In spite of her driving, the bus beat them to it – largely because she was unable to pass its formidable lurching bulk – and they arrived almost together. They all got out, and Thompson brought the bags and put them on to a waiting truck. They were all standing outside the door through which the passengers from the bus were hurling themselves.

'Let them go,' said Thompson. 'They all travel like that.'

They waited until the (presumably weakest) last had sulkily jostled through, and the doorway was empty. An aeroplane was coming in to land. When it had roared over their heads, Fleming turned to Thompson and shook him warmly by the hand.

'I'm delighted to have met you again. Come and see us in London. My wife will tell you where. Look after her for me. I'm sure you could if you tried.'

And Thompson shook his hand and said: 'Have a good trip.' Fleming turned to her, and put his hand on her shoulder. She, stupidly thinking that he meant to kiss her, lifted her face. But he said simply: 'Enjoy yourself,' dropped his hand, and went through the door.

He had gone. Deeply mortified, she turned to Thompson: he was staring at the aeroplane which had just landed on the runway to their right. She knew he had seen her expect to be kissed, and scalding tears of humiliation burned her eyes.

It was too much to be left like that, and with this odd little man there to see. She pretended to watch the aeroplane – and heard him walking the little way back to the car – she could not really see the aeroplane – the worst of ridiculous or shameful behaviour was stopping it – the mere stopping accentuated it for anyone else to see – even that little Thompson man.

She walked slowly back to the car trying to adjust her mind.

He was leaning against the car grinding something

into the ground with his foot. He wore espadrilles that had faded from dark blue to streaky mauve.

'Want to move?'

'I don't think there is much point in staying here,' she replied, and heard her voice stiff with the effort not to tremble. (Damn; take another turn on the screw.)

'Do you want to drive or shall I?'

'I should think I'd better.'

He gave her a friendly, speculative look, and opened the door for her.

When they were both in the car, he said:

'Do you mind if I smoke?'

She shook her head.

He extracted the battered packet again.

'Is there a match in this motor?'

'Try the front pocket.'

He pulled the knob, and it fell off.

'Sorry about that. It *was* loose, you know.'

He picked it off the floor of the car and looked at it critically. 'A botched job. I could do it better myself.'

'You can still open the pocket with it if you're careful.'

'Yep: I know. But it beats me how they've the face to make anything so badly.'

'It doesn't matter,' she said. 'You light your cigarette. I'll have it mended some time.'

He looked at her hands lying slack on the wheel. She had not attempted to start the car.

'Shall we find somewhere and have a drink?'

One of her hands shot out suddenly for the knob which he was slowly sliding back into its socket. She pressed and turned, the pocket opened, and the knob fell out again.

'There,' she said. But there were no matches. The pocket was empty. After he had looked, he looked at her.

'You do feel awful, don't you?' he said.

She did not move or reply. He touched her arm and said:

'You let me drive. You've had enough of it.'

The moment that he touched her, tears streamed from her eyes – she resolved before him without a word.

She put back her head as though to stop the tears from running out of her eyes, and her hands suddenly tightened on the steering wheel with the same effort. He waited a moment; then carefully loosened her fingers and held them. He did not speak to her. He merely soothed her hands as though she was some nervous animal that had taken fright – he did not treat her as a complex sophisticated woman whom he did not know, and whose tears would be an impossible embarrassment – but simply as he would treat any distraught creature, with a natural, physical kindness which was instinct in him.

Gradually, as the first shock of tears ceased, and the remaining few slipped more slowly, still silently, away, she moved her head and shook it as though finally to release herself. He put her hands one upon the other, and that was, she found, a comforting thing.

'Sorry about that.'

'So am I.' And he got out of the car for her to move into his place. In the driving seat he leaned across her, picked up the knob from the floor, and stuffed it in his pocket.

'I'll mend that later on,' he said, and started the engine.

'Plugs need cleaning,' he said, later, 'another little job for me.'

'Do you *like* cleaning plugs and so on?' she asked.

'I like an engine to run sweet. She can't if she's not serviced. I like to do that myself, because then I know it's done right. Shall we find ourselves somewhere for a drink? Then you can have a bit of sleep.'

'How do you know I want to sleep?'

'Because if you have a drink and a little sleep you'll feel like a proper meal,' he replied seriously.

She nearly laughed.

'Would that be such a good thing?'

'Would what be such a good thing?'

'My drinking and sleeping in order that I should want to eat.'

'Of course it would. You must take my word for that. You see I'm not an intellectual type at all – not highly strung or what have you, so naturally I think about eating and drinking and sleeping a lot of the time.'

'You like people to run properly, like engines.'

'That's it.'

He drove the car well. Perhaps she ought to make some more conversation between them.

'Do you find it tiresome remembering to drive on the right?'

'Nope. Roads are easy. England and Scandinavia on the left – everywhere else on the right. Rivers are much worse – you get whopping big tankers bearing down on you for a joke if they think you don't know the passing rule – heading straight for you – then if you're in a small craft you get the wash.'

'Are boats your profession?'

'No. I haven't got one. I just do what comes to hand. We could drink here. Looks all right, don't you think?'

It was a small café with a *terrasse* covered with wide trellis and creeper.

They drank Cinzano and cognac. The tablecloths were grass-green check and on one table crouched a thin wild-looking cat. 'Il a peur – toujours peur,' said the girl who served them, when they remarked on its glaring abstract terror. 'C'est affreux,' she added indifferently as after she tried to touch it, it drew back almost snarling with frightened dislike.

Thompson snapped his fingers at it – casually once – but he had been watching it, and it turned to look at him. Now it leapt off its table, walked slowly to his feet, and looked carefully up at him with unblinking yellow-glass eyes. Then, neatly and perfectly, it jumped on to him, settled, and folded its paws with its head pressed against his shirt.

She watched his hand stroking its bony back, and the cat seemingly soothed and reassured, fluffed its meagre fur and tried to look luxuriant.

'Doesn't look as though it has much of a life, does it?' he said.

'Is it an intellectual cat?' she asked.

He looked uncomprehending. 'How do you mean?'

'I've never drunk brandy with Cinzano before.' She felt suddenly self-conscious and also relieved because she felt that with him there was no need to feel self-conscious.

'I think it's a good drink,' he said. 'Do you want another?'

'Yes please.'

While they were waiting for it, she made up her mouth, and he watched her with the same friendly interest and curiosity she had first observed in him. With most people she would not openly have painted her mouth; but he was different – so easy it didn't matter – he was not the kind of man to regard it either as an intimate gesture, or simply as bad taste. Nevertheless, when she had finished, she gave him a little worldly smile, admitting the necessity but faintly deprecating what she had done, and he smiled back.

'That's fine now,' he said.

'You'd better buy some matches,' she said a minute later, trying to identify herself with his requirements as she felt he had tried with hers.

He paid for the drinks and his matches in his atrocious French. He put the cat gently on to their table, and they returned to the car.

'What time is it?'

She looked, and told him.

'I must get back to my boat. 'I'll drop you first at the hotel for your sleep.'

'I thought I was supposed to inspect your boat.' She discovered suddenly that she did not want to be abandoned.

'You can see her tomorrow if you like. If I take you there tonight with no warning, the crew I've left on board will take all their clothes off, and I shan't be able to show you anything.'

'Why will they do that?'

'It's just one of the things they do if they are faced suddenly with a woman on board when they haven't had notice to clean up. I gave half of them shore leave tonight – I've got to see they haven't all gone off – taken French leave I suppose one might call it.'

He laughed and she began to find his continuing practical enjoyment of everything he did restful and endearing. She did not want to dine alone.

'If I go to sleep now I shall never wake up for dinner.'

'No, you probably wouldn't, left to yourself. But I

thought I'd slip back to the boat, see to the crew, collect some tools for your repairs, and wake you when you've had an hour. Then we'll go and find some good sea food. Does that suit you?'

'Yes,' she said simply, because really it was exactly what she wanted. His face had screwed up more like a monkey than ever in the effort to make all those plans. When she agreed, he turned to her and smiled, his polite friendly smile – his eyes, she noticed, were like small warm brown chestnuts.

'Hooray,' he said, and it did not sound a silly thing for him to say.

THREE

Back in her large room, she had a shower, undressed her hair and opened the shutters. The sun had gone; the grey airy twilight slid into the room, and almost at once, began perceptibly to darken and retreat. She wrapped herself in the spare white peignoir and lay on the bed to sleep.

She woke very slowly – aware of the distant tinselly light by the basin – of the sharper sounds of night begun in Marseille coming up from the street – of the windows framing a soft dark sky, now hectic with lightning, silent, without thunder – and then of Thompson standing beside her bed.

'Don't hurry,' he was saying, 'it's awful waking up.'

But she stretched and enjoyed the return of her senses gradually until she was wholly awake.

'I've brought you something to drink.'

He had poured it out, whatever it was, and handed her a glass.

As she sat up, she saw dimly reflected in the mirror across the room and facing her bed, a figure, golden brown – almost naked except for the gleaming white wrap round one shoulder and dark hair streaming into shadow. Had it not been for the gold watch slung round her neck, and the arm stretched out for the glass, she would not immediately have recognized herself, so unexpected was the reflection, so marvellously unlike her idea of herself did she seem. The blacks and the brown and the richness of the white – even the attitude of this savage, beautiful reflection, filled her with a sudden ravishing conceit.

And there was Thompson, holding out the glass to her. She pulled the wrap round her and took the glass. He did not say anything, and as the blush which seemed to begin in her mind came out all over her skin, she thought thank goodness it was only he, and not anyone else. The thought, like the rest of her, was utterly confused.

They drank, and then, while she dressed, he sat on the balcony smoking, and telling her what he could see. 'A black man selling tortoises – he's got them all on top of one another in an orange box – poor devils.' And, 'Two children doing conjuring tricks – they aren't much good though.'

'Is it still warm?'

'Balmy. You won't be cold.'

Really, she might have known him for years. She took a great deal of trouble over her appearance – the vision in the looking-glass, which it seemed to her on closer examination she did not in the least resemble, prompted her, none the less, to compete in some measure with its exotic improbability.

He came in from the balcony just as she was screwing silver rings on to her ears.

'I've found out where to eat. Are your ears pierced?'

'No. Ought they to be?'

'*I* don't know. But I'll do them if you want them done.'

'Oh really, Thompson! Did you fetch tools for that from your boat?'

'I've done it before,' he said.

'Then you'd have to alter all my earrings. Twenty-four pairs.'

'I could only manage the ones without enamel. Enamel flies if you fire it,' he said. He was perfectly serious.

'I'll tell you if I ever change my mind.' She was not sure whether she had hurt his feelings.

'What a lot of things you can do,' she added, as they left the room.

'I have my uses, you know.' He had her white peignoir over his arm.

'Why?'

'That has its uses too.'

They ate: they talked. Their conversation was easy – almost desultory – the food was very good. They did not argue or discuss, or tell one another the story, or any story, of their lives. He was neither very amusing nor dull. He did not, she felt, expect, or even want to be amused. They concentrated on their dinner – not with the ferocious apathy of the French couples round them, but with the greedy enjoyment of people who do not customarily eat either so well or together.

They reached the end of their meal, and she said she wanted a very sticky liqueur, knowing that he would neither blench nor treat her as a tasteless cretin. They had two each, and then he bought a bottle of cognac.

'I would like a French cigarette,' she said suddenly.

When the girl brought some packets on a plate she picked out a blue one, and looked at him enquiringly.

'Very strong those,' he said, 'have the yellow. Unless you want them extra strong,' he added.

'I liked the colour of blue.' But she took a yellow packet. He lit her cigarette for her and watched her enjoy the beginning of it.

'You don't smoke much, do you?'

'I used to smoke far too much, so now I don't smoke at all.'

She smiled at him and thought: How odd, what ought to seem too intimate is easy between us; but that conventional disclosure seems very intimate. She had forgotten these minute inversions of feeling, that with certain kinds of experience shift all the contours of any settled view.

He asked for the bill, and she began to worry about the amount of money she was costing him, and, rather diffidently, she said so. But he pulled out his dirty battered note-case stuffed with dirty battered money, and said: 'Don't. I was paid an advance on this trip and this is how I like to spend it.'

'Yes, but you are spending it twice as fast.'

'Oh no, I don't think so,' he answered carelessly, and then added, 'I'd probably be drinking it if I was by myself.'

'But you wouldn't be,' she said, discovering this.

He smiled the same ingenuous amicable smile.

'Not if I could help it.'

Outside, in the air which was like warm velvet, they hesitated. The sky, now phrenetic with stars, was not entirely dark; the people in the street were substantial shadows – their talk, clear but unintelligible, the echo of daylight talk.

They were immediately absorbed into this atmosphere and appearance of blood heat, and got silently into the car.

'Would you like to drive out somewhere? I thought we might swim.'

She nodded, and then realized that he probably couldn't see her and said yes.

'Do you know where to drive?'

'I think so. I had a good look at a map while you were sleeping. Anyway I can usually feel my way about.'

'I'll get you back all right,' he said a minute later; 'I can always find my way back.'

'Like a cat, or a pigeon,' she murmured. 'I wasn't worrying about it.'

'I drove in on this road today,' she said some time afterwards. It was the only reference she had made to anything that had happened to her before she met him.

By the time he had found them a little bay, the moon, very late and lovely, had appeared. The rocks on either side of them curved sharply round, making a small lagoon, and the water ended in warm white sand.

'All right?'

'Incredible. Of course in a way one gets used to it.'

'To what?'

'Oh it being like – oh – *Coral Island* or *Adrift in the Pacific*.'

'Those are books, aren't they?'

'Children's books. But there isn't a grown-up equivalent for them except fragments like the beginning of *Erewhon*.'

'You like reading then,' he said. It was not the envious accusation of the illiterate – simply a statement.

'Yes. It creates new requirements: and sometimes the very good books fulfil them.'

They had been picking their way down the path from the road, and now their feet sank soundlessly into the sand. There were no other people in the bay.

'I was apprenticed to a firm of boiler-makers once,' he said. 'I had to read then. Awfully dull stuff with diagrams.'

'And before that?'

'We read a play at school. I can't remember much, except that it started with a shipwreck. Funny thing; trying to start a play like that, don't you think?'

'Very difficult.' Dear Thompson, she thought: he hasn't

got another name – dear Thompson. Now he was pleased because he had found a comfortable rock: he arranged her peignoir, his towel, and the brandy, and invited her to climb up to it.

'Might have been hewn out for me.'

'Are you going to smoke another of your cigarettes?' He felt in his pockets for her Gauloises, and the silk handkerchief covered with anchors appeared. She eyed it with affection.

'Thompson, it is a wonderful handkerchief. Where did you get it?'

He was still searching for her cigarettes. 'I put them in the pocket of the car, I'll get them.'

'I don't really want one at all.' She was watching the sea. She felt him preparing to disbelieve her and repeated: 'Really I don't want one.'

'I mended that knob,' he said. He had lit a Gold Flake.

The sea seemed varnished with silver oil which stretched thinly and broke to black water before and after each rhythmic, vastly gentle, undulation. Further out, these dark ribs narrowed and seemed less restless, until right out, up to the horizon, it was a sheet of stern un-moving silver.

'Good,' she said. She roused herself, and put her hands behind her head. 'I mean, thank you, of course.' She wanted suddenly to be out in the silver, beyond the rest-less ribs, right out to the streak below the sky. She rose to her feet.

'I want to bathe.' She jumped down the seaward side of their rock. The water was only a few yards away, but the sand was dry. Her desire to be in the sea was so urgent that she heard her shirt tear a little as she wrenched it over her head. When she was free of her few clothes, she remembered the watch round her neck, and with a little choking sigh of impatience she felt for the clasp on the chain. She put the watch in the pocket of her shirt, kicked off her shoes, and ran into the water. When it reached her knees she could not run – she took several long, dragging steps, and looked down at her body – it had gone white with the moon, and the water was half way up her thighs. The beads of splashed water stood silver on her skin. She looked once more at the beautiful distance, and flung herself towards it.

He joined her, very soon, or a long time after, and swam beside but not near her, but he left her the silence. Each time she looked ahead, the silver edge of the sea seemed as distinct, as remotely perfect as it had seemed from the shore. But later, when she looked again, the edge had narrowed, and then suddenly it was not there; the waters had darkened to an infinity of black, and there was no horizon. She cried out, and turned in the water – a soft black wave washed over her head; after the wave, she had no sense of direction or desire for it – she knew only that she must breathe air and that breathing involved continuous, difficult movement.

When he reached her, she was treading water, and the waves, broadside on, were slapping her hair down over her face. She felt his hands under the pit of her arms holding her up. 'The moon went out!' her voice was pierced with distress. 'It was all the same – all dark.'

'Not too dark,' he replied. He pushed her hair to the back of her neck and turned her round. 'Land,' he said: 'can you manage it, or shall I do it for you?'

She did not say anything, but obediently began swimming as he directed. The waves were running behind her now, washing through her with a kind of spectral ease, and then riding away into the dark; each wave losing identity just before it was replaced by the new, soft, hurrying bulk of another. He swam with her – holding back her streaming hair – she was moving slowly – very tired now, he thought.

After a while he said: 'Rest for a bit?'

'How far is it?'

'Not much further.' They had been a long way out, but surely it couldn't be much further.

She made some small, inarticulate sound, and continued. His arm ached with the effort of holding back her hair, and for a moment he wondered whether they were, in fact, making any headway, or whether they were being swept out or very much to one side by a current.

The shore happened suddenly – there seemed nothing but sea ahead – and then, suddenly – only a few yards away there was shore. They both saw it at the same moment – the uneven end of the sea and the stillness of the faintly white sand. He wanted to try the depth, but he felt her weakly increased effort and did not halt her. She swam into the shallows until her head and shoulders and her arms were out of the water. He got to his feet, and stretched out a hand to help her, but she lay still, almost on her face, with her arms thrown out on the sand above her head, and the sea swaying gently up and down over her back. He looked for their rocks: they were an indeterminate distance to the left. He bent over her; she was shuddering faintly; he thought that perhaps she was crying; but when he told her the rocks were near and tried to help her to her feet, she turned to him with the small supplicating smile of utter exhaustion.

As he carried her slowly across the bay, the moon began to reappear, and by the time he laid her down on their rock the sea was again like marcasite, and her body drenched in the cold light. He covered her with the peignoir and started looking for the brandy. He was beginning to feel very cold; he wrapped himself in his towel, found his knife, and got the cork out of the brandy bottle.

She lay propped against the rock, exactly as he had left her. Her eyes were closed. He put an arm round her and raised her head.

'Come on. Brandy.'

She opened her eyes, drank a little, and choked. He waited a moment, and then tried again, but she turned her head away.

'I knew I'd choke.'

'I'll clear the bottle a bit for you.' He drank, and felt the liquid searing down his throat, and some cold brandy dripping down his neck.

She had begun to shiver violently; her whole body shook, and her teeth chattered against the glass rim of the bottle – he poured a certain amount of brandy down her, spilling at least as much as she drank in his desperate attempt to stop the paroxysms. Her shivering frightened him as nothing else had done: he felt that she would shake to pieces. He put down the bottle, and began rubbing her furiously. After a moment she sat with her head resting on drawn-up knees, and he worked hardly, methodically, up her back, until he gradually felt the lassitude of their mutual returning warmth.

'Drink some more, and I'll get your clothes.'

When he came back to her she was leaning against the rock again, and immediately she offered him the brandy. He put the clothes beside her and took the bottle.

She said: 'Thank you for holding back my hair.' She spoke calmly, but her eyes were trembling with some

157

entreaty which, because he did not thoroughly under-stand it, he decided entirely to misunderstand.

'Have a Gold Flake?'

'You have one. I should think you need it.'

He smoked a cigarette and dressed. They each drank some more, and she tried to comb her hair.

'I should leave your hair for the moment.' He looked at her clothes and then enquiringly at her, and with an immediacy that he found deeply touching, she put down her comb, pulled her wrap from her shoulders, and began weakly searching among the small heap beside her. Her nakedness and her fatigue seemed to him almost unbear-able, and, without a word, he began carefully putting on her clothes.

When he had dressed her, he kissed her.

She drew a little away from him.

'I wasn't trying to – anything – when I went out into the sea—' Her eyes were filled with anxiety.

'I knew you weren't.'

'All the time?'

'People walk when they do that: they don't run.'

She gave a little sigh of recovery and acceptance.

'We live on this, don't we?' She indicated the bottle.

'It's all we've got. Are you hungry?' She doesn't want to talk about it, he thought, give her a free rein.

'No, I simply feel deliciously, noticeably warm. You treated me like a horse. Have you looked after horses too?' He's so simple – he's easy to deflect, she thought, he won't think of asking me about the sea now.

'I was brought up with them. I think I'll groom your hair next, or you won't go on feeling warm: it doesn't last, you know.'

'My mane.' She inclined her head.

'I'll rough dry it, and then we must go.'

'Must we?'

'I thought it would be more comfortable if we did,' he said simply.

She remembered that after the salt and brandy, he had tasted unexpectedly, wonderfully sweet – something between honey and nuts, and she shivered once.

'You'll lose your pretty watch,' he said. He felt in the pocket of her shirt for it, and fastened the chain round her neck. She looked down at his hands. Hands were never simply one thing – she discovered, looking at his – never simply practical, or sensitive, or sensual . . . He was tucking the watch into her shirt, and, involuntarily, she shivered again.

He got up and held out a hand to her.

'I'm not really cold,' she said as she stood up.

'You are not in the least *cold*,' he said, 'but if we don't go now, I shall kiss you till you won't be able to stand.'

She turned to him, and he was smiling the same polite friendly smile that was her first recollection of him. Heavens, she thought, I know nothing; nothing at all.

He collected their things, and they walked slowly back to the car.

He drove, and she slept. He drove fast because by then he wanted her very badly indeed.

∞　∞　∞

Back in the bedroom with the tinsel light, they surveyed one another. In their clothes they felt as many people do for the first time together without them – a self-conscious apprehension, a kind of mutually nervous appraisal, as each private anticipation meets with reality, recoiling or adapting, justifying or delighting.

'I think I shall wash the salt off me,' she said uncertainly. She wanted a separate reason for getting out of her clothes.

'No need,' he said. He said it carefully: he felt the situation getting out of hand.

She moved restlessly to the dressing-table and started brushing out her hair. She was beginning to feel unaccountably angry.

'Anyhow I must dry this out a bit.'

He did not answer, and, when she looked in the glass for him, she saw that he was methodically undressing, folding things and putting them on a chair in the corner of the room. Sure of himself, she thought – but then I want him to be that – but not so sure of me. Perhaps by now he can't separate us.

'I don't know your name,' she said coldly across the room.

'It's Thompson, t-h-o-m-p-s-o-n, and the sooner you get out of your clothes the better.'

There was silence after that; she was both angry and frightened at feeling so miserably self-conscious – of the distance between her and the bed – of his being now naked and she not – of her inability to associate him with the desire she had felt earlier – of exasperation with him for not bridging these distances, and anger that she should need him to do so – and finally fear that her desire had entirely escaped her and vanished. She heard him go to the bed.

'You get in,' she said, 'I'll join you.' (That is sufficiently, clearly, squalid: I don't care any more, so it's easy. You cannot lead a man to expect this of you and then fail him.)

She got up from the dressing-table and went quickly into the room or cupboard containing the shower.

When, washed of salt and wrapped in the second peignoir, she emerged, ready to be calm and deliberate, and, she told herself defiantly, experienced; she found him lying on his face on the bed: pretending to be asleep – trying to save her, she thought, more of this disgusting embarrassment. She walked over to the bed, but he seemed really asleep. He lay uncovered, with his head on one arm, and the other stretched out across the bed. He had a wiry elegant body – small and tough – the limbs well turned at wrist and knee and ankle. She stared down at him – her hostility and her defences evaporating – the sight of him gave her a feeling of peaceful affectionate pleasure. She slipped out of the peignoir and lifted his arm carefully so that she could lie down in the bed where it had lain. She hardly remembered pulling the sheet over them before she slept.

∞ ∞ ∞

He woke her very slowly in the night to make love to her. She discovered then the ecstasy which lies far beyond any false summit of delight: he guided her throughout the difficult ascent; waiting for her, honouring her with his absolute attention and care, until when the final moment came, his entire body had communicated itself to hers – the journey had ended, and they met perfectly as lovers.

FOUR

Like a dream the hours came and were there and went, totally disregarding the time they were supposed to represent. She discovered, much later (she discovered much else at the time), that any emotion, if it be sufficiently strong, is elusive, not accurately memorable – that only the small practical fringe – the attendant commonplaces remain vividly in the mind – and that the memory of them only serves to conceal the core or essence of violently felt experience.

So, for a short while she could remember lying as it were on the summit of their mountain; the mists lifted from a vast panorama below, which displayed itself to them as endless, as beautifully comprehensible – a magnificence which they alone were seeing together – and then, very soon, they were left remembering that they had seen it. For longer, she could clearly remember waking, in streaming sunlight, with such a sense of her own comfort and peace, such well-being and delight in herself, that the fleeting revelation of this being the first time she had ever woken thus was almost impersonal – seemed remote and insignificant; she did not stop to question it, although she remembered turning to him, finding him awake and saying: 'I feel like – exactly as though—' and his replying: 'I can see, but you feel much much better than that.'

She could always remember the point-to-point obstructions – telephoning Leila and saying that there was something wrong with the car and she would be stuck for another day or two – was that all right? Leila (she sounded more depressed than incredulous) saying but wasn't it ghastly in Marseille in the heat? No, no, she had found some people Conrad knew with a boat who were being very kind to her. Well, do come back soon: Don's awfully bored without you. – She asked about the children. – *What* about them? – Were they all right, was Nanny being good? – The children were divine: Leila simply never saw them, but oh, my dear, *pregnancy* – you simply feel as though you're never alone, not a minute to oneself, and it's no good my telling Don that he's getting just as fat but in different places – he comes out in a sort of prickly heat with rage – and I've lost my passport so I suppose I'll be stuck here till the baby's old enough to let me travel on *its* – no, darling, the children are at the beach or somewhere, but I'll tell Nanny about your wretched car. Don't worry about us, we're perfectly all *right*; weren't French telephones *awful*? Did Conrad catch his plane? she added, and do be careful of the *sailors* in the boat. Sailors were devastating, especially in foreign parts. Esmé, she knew who Leila meant, had had the most extraordinary time in Tenerife, *quite* extraordinary – if Esmé hadn't kept her head she would have lost everything else – not, darling, that Leila thought *you* need worry – you're far too sensible, but still, all alone – but, of course, you aren't alone, are you . . . ?

At this point, she had had enough, and stemming what was clearly the consequence of Leila being denied an English telephone for a fortnight, cut herself off.

After that the day was hers – or theirs.

'Do I look too sensible for sailors to devastate?' she asked Thompson much later.

'Do you what?'

'Look as though I wouldn't – you know perfectly well what I mean.'

'Nobody looks sensible all the time.'

She watched his face after he said that, and recollected the same expression, as when, with Conrad, he had made the remark about women liking the present and the future – after which he had smiled at her. He smiled now in exactly the same way, and she shivered. Instantly he was solicitous. He observed, and seemed fascinated by, her slightest physical reaction.

'Are you cold? Do you want my arms round you?'

She shook her head: 'A goose walked over our bed.'

He did not understand what she meant.

She never saw his boat. There was the afternoon: there was the night. She had never before felt so refreshed, and so exhausted.

The next day she said she must go. He asked her to stay, and she explained about the children.

'I'll drive back with you then,' he said.

'How will *you* get back?'

'I'll get back.'

They started from Marseille at about four in the afternoon. The gap in time between this drive and the drive with her husband seemed so enormous, that she was surprised she could remember the first drive at all.

When they were nearly arrived, he said:

'This hasn't been very long, has it?'

'Let's go up to Gassin.'

'Where's that?'

'It's a village on a hill. There's a road up to it somewhere along here on the right. We could drink up there.'

'That's what I like about this country,' he said, 'you can drink anywhere.'

This was the first time she remembered Leila's telephone conversation, and her remark about telephones, and *that* also seemed weeks away in time. Marseille had begun to slip into the past. The present trembled on the brink of unreality; and the future – she could not think beyond the week ahead at St Tropez – but she knew that she dreaded it.

They found the road, which climbed with a steepness only made possible by its tortuous method. The sun was subsiding into the wooded hill as they climbed; the atmosphere was neutral. The village, perched extremely on the summit, and held there by the confidence of time, and a small parapet, seemed at first to be very quiet, to be almost deserted. But when they had stopped the car, and started to walk up the narrow cobbled slopes through the little bunch of leaning yellow-grey houses, they became aware first of the animals, and afterwards of the people. Tortoiseshell and tabby cats regarded them with inscrutable indifference; a number of dogs all clearly related, but otherwise unlike any known breed of dog, followed them a few snuffling steps; there were chickens sententiously picking their way from grain to grain; goats were picketed outside open doorways, and there was a wild fox on a chain running up four steps and down three – up three steps and down four, with a kind of frenzied perpetual motion: it did not seem to look where it was going because it miserably knew – always it moved a little too far in each direction, so that the chain choked it back. 'I hate that,' Thompson remarked without heat, and they saw a very old woman with a face like a walnut watching them watch the fox. She nodded and called something unintelligible, but she had no teeth and her voice seemed to crack out of her face. When she saw that they did not understand her, she nodded again with courteous resignation, and pulling her black shawl round her shoulders, resumed her unimpassioned study of the fox.

On the south-east side of the village was a wide terrace, flanked by the parapet, below which the hill dropped sharply away. There was the smooth glinting gulf: across it, the lights in Ste Maxime flitted uncertainly, and below the terrace heavy woods bloomed with dusk. They sat on the parapet and drank a bottle of wine. It was then that they had their only conversation.

It began because she was so possessed with a panic of unreality, that she thought the sound of their voices would help. And so, without real curiosity, she said:

'You said you just do what comes to hand. Does that mean that you do *anything* – that you don't care what it is?'

'I choose, you know. I can choose because I don't mind doing nothing – unless I'm cleaned out for money.'

'Then you have to take any job?'

'Well, I can't afford to be so choosey then—'

'But what are you *really* interested in?' she persisted.

His face screwed up in the effort of consideration.

'My main interest. Oh, women. Women, every time.' He drained his glass and leaned towards her with the bottle. He was smiling – defensively – ('I wouldn't have told you that, but you asked for it').

'Crowds and crowds of different women?'

'I expect so. I don't think of them like that.'

'Simultaneously? Or consecutively?'

'What do you mean?'

'I mean, do you like several women at once, or one at a time?'

'Oh, I see. Oh, one at a time – of course.' He looked shocked. 'Have some more wine?'

'Please. And each woman imagines herself the glorious exception?'

He smiled again, unhappily: 'That's right. Of course, she is, in a way.'

'But not in the way she thinks.'

'I don't know what she thinks, you see,' he answered. He was now harassed into his original politeness.

Still cut off from being herself, she said:

'Is it vulgar of me to ask you all these things?' And he answered simply:

'I don't know the meaning of that word.'

She had never felt so vulgar in her life.

Later, he said: 'It doesn't make you happy, though, does it?'

'It doesn't make me anything.' Then she added with a rush: 'I'm sorry. I don't feel real. Everything seems a long way ahead or a long way behind, and I seem in the very middle of a vast vacuous interim. Do you understand that?'

He shook his head. 'Never mind. What do you do in London?'

'Why?'

'I just wondered what you did.'

She took a deep breath. 'I run one house in London and another in the country.'

'What country?'

'Kent.'

There was a pause while she waited for him to say

something about Kent; but he said nothing, and she continued faster and more defensively: 'I look after my children. Julian's at his prep school and Deirdre goes to a day school near London. I—'

'So they are away or out all day,' he interrupted.

'Yes. That's what all children do at that age. Many children,' she corrected herself – obviously he had not done it. 'Then we entertain a good deal. Conrad likes streams of people.'

'So you have a lot of cooking.'

'I don't do the *cooking*. I couldn't possibly cook well enough for Conrad. I do the arranging of it. There *is* a lot of arranging, you know. I read, and look at pictures, and garden, and listen to music – and Conrad minds awfully about clothes so I spend a certain amount of time on them—' She stopped: she knew dimly how it all sounded to him and she knew dimly what it was all like – equally and differently unsatisfactory and incomprehensible to them both, and her talking only made it more irreconcilable.

'I suppose I'm a sort of scene shifter for Conrad,' she finished. 'He likes an elaborate setting, and he likes it to vary. I try to do that for him.'

'I'm sure you're very good at whatever you try to do,' he said; and they surveyed one another worlds apart across the small table. Anyway, I can leave him, she thought; it will not be difficult at all, and years hence it will simply be a surprising and friendly thing to remember. We have nothing in common, she thought, and if we go on now, I shall be back before the children are asleep.

They had paid for the wine, it was drunk; and they got up to go.

'Let's go back that way,' he said.

At the end of the terrace they found a narrow archway
– a covered alley. It was very dark, and she slipped on
the uneven stone. He put out his hand, holding her elbow
to steady her: his hand felt like a distant memory, until
he said:

'Shall I see you in London then?'

The blazing present flashed upon her; she came back
to her senses, and in the illumination of being herself, she
saw him again quite clearly – him and herself and nothing
else at all.

She faced him without answering and kissed him with
all the violence of their lives suddenly returned to her.

'Still want to go back tonight?'

'I must go back.'

They walked in silence to the car.

They drove in silence almost to the villa. Then she said:

'Isn't this a foolish place to drop you? How will you
get back from here, it isn't a main road.'

'I shall have a meal somewhere, and look round. Get
a lorry tonight, or early in the morning.'

'But you'll have to get back to the crossroads for a
lorry.'

'Don't worry about me, I'm an old hand at this.'

She stopped the car.

'Shall you go tonight or tomorrow morning?'

'Depends: don't worry about me,' he repeated.

She wanted badly to know whether he would go from
St Tropez that night or in the morning, but knowing that
such a requirement would seem inexplicable to him, she
resigned herself to the extreme discomfort of uncertainty.

'I won't worry,' she said.

He got out of the car, and then, with a natural unconsidered grace, picked up first one of her hands and then

the other and kissed them. The gesture reminded her suddenly of a longshoreman on the Thames, who, standing in the stern of his craft, and propelling himself down the river with a single scull, had looked up at her just as he was about to shoot the bridge from which she watched him, and, with inimitable gallantry and timing, had taken off his large black hat, flourished it, and bowed.

Now – Thompson.

He said: 'Goodbye, and thank you.'

'Thank you,' she said, 'for having me.' And he answered with unexpected urbanity:

'A delight which I hope to repeat in London.' He gave one of her hands a little shake. 'Bless you,' he said: 'I'm gone.'

She did not watch him go. He had contrived his departure too well for anything but a disconsolate little drag of the heart back into neutral – a blank screen in the mind's eye, and an imperceptible evaporation of the spirit.

From a standing position the car did not pull well up the hill.

∞ ∞ ∞

Leila said she was looking quite marvellous. Don Talbot looked curiously at her and said nothing.

'Are you glad I'm back?' she asked her children – hearing herself courting their approbation, and Deirdre, flinging herself on to her mother, cried:

'Oh yes, I am! I *am*! I *am*! Darling darling Mummy – ages and ages – I *am*! I *am*!'

But Julian, hunting in his bed for a spare piece of Meccano, simply said: 'I knew you'd be back.'

FIVE

During the hectic uneasy week that he spent in Paris, Fleming had conscientiously tried to get rid of his desire for Imogen Stanford. He employed all the usual methods, but they proved unusually unsuccessful. He tried not to think about her, and found it as breathlessly difficult as the amateur's effort entirely to empty the mind. He embarked on a heavy programme of intellectual amusements, but whenever he thought that he had successfully distracted himself, some exasperatingly irrelevant thought of her sprang into his mind, and when, as he often did, he failed to distract himself, he thought about her anyway. He tried analysing his feelings about her to the point of their elimination, but the analysis was protectively dishonest, and availed him nothing. He tried to exhaust his thoughts of her by deliberately and exclusively considering her for an hour at a time. In desperation, he selected an attractive antithesis to her, but he found, and not soon enough to avoid considerable embarrassment, that he did not in the least want her. After this last experiment, which was both expensive and humiliating, he gave up, and returned to London.

In the aeroplane, he bolstered his defeat by such thoughts as her extreme youth – she was only twenty – and youth was resilient; that she was unlike many young women, in that she had a career to think about (she was learning to paint), and therefore was unlikely to become obsessed by him; and that in any case all young women were flattered by and attracted to any personable man considerably older than themselves who took trouble over them. Her vanity was amused and soothed, and her heart untouched: that he had always been honest with her – by which he meant that he told her only such truths as he thought she could take – and that he had already taught her a great deal. Gone was her contentment with dirndl skirts and ill-fitting trousers; her predilection for sweet white wine and sandals and ridiculous scent smelling of nearly dead flowers; her tendency to lose or forget telephone numbers, cheque books, latch-keys, and lighted cigarettes; her dangerous habits of impartial truthfulness, consistent inaccuracy, and utter unconsciousness of her own beauty. But when this last word came to his mind, he was shamed from thinking about her with such devilish selection.

All those aspects of her, he knew, were both true and absurd, because they might easily apply to any young girl of twenty, but he also knew, with the integrity born of experience and interest, that she was by no means any young girl of twenty. Apart from her startling, dazzling appearance, she had the innate quality of something beautifully made. Hers was not merely the resilience of youth. She had selected him (he was her first lover), from a mass of opportunities – wealth, he reflected, was hardly in this context, the word, as an attractive woman will automatically collect a plethora of men whose perceptions are sharp enough to perceive only her most obvious attractions, and who have not, consequently, very much to offer in return. Probably she thought she was seriously in love with him, and of this she must be most gently disabused.

For the rest, he reflected, she had learned not always to say what she thought, and the larger business of teaching her to think what she said could belong to the next man to whom she belonged.

He filled his ears with cotton wool as the aeroplane began its descent, concluding in his mind that he was simply a pleasantly instructive incident in the beginning of Imogen's life – neither significant nor damaging – that the situation was therefore well under control . . .

∞ ∞ ∞

When he telephoned her, Imogen, wearing out a dirndl skirt and a blouse with a great deal of unfortunate embroidery upon it, was making an elaborate soup. She thought she was thinking what she was doing: Conrad had once said that he was exceedingly fond of good soup, and so every day since he had been away she had made soup – thick soup and thin soup, and soup with bits in it and sieved things in it, hot and cold, brown and white and pale green and pink – she had not known before that there were so many kinds. There had been a heat wave, and neither she nor the girl with whom she shared the studio liked soup; but she told herself that it was a useful accomplishment, and she thought about Conrad as much while she made it as she thought about him at any other time – at her art school – in her bath – while she was talking to other people – while she bought paper, or charcoal, or bones for more stock – when she saw somebody who was not like him in the street – and when the telephone rang and it could not possibly be he, because he was in France.

It was he, and he was not in France. He was at the

airport, what was she doing? Well, he would be with her in two hours.

Two hours. She wound up the clock and looked at the hands. They stood at twenty minutes past eleven, but they could not be altered because the screw was broken. She wrote '11.20' on her drawing block, and propped it up on the table. She had time to look carefully round the studio and decide that it was fairly tidy (Mrs Green had been that morning), before she had to dash into the bathroom to be sick.

When she emerged green and shivering, she found Iris back, lying on the sofa, smoking.

'I thought you were out. My dear!'

'I wasn't out, I was being sick – awful waste – I've only got two hours.'

'You look frightful. I'll get you some brandy.' She rose neatly from the sofa and went in search of a glass.

'Conrad's back! He's come back five days early. He's coming here.'

'I gathered that,' said Iris dryly. 'Here you are—'

'Is it all right to drink brandy just before a bath?'

'It's always all right to drink brandy. Sit down to drink it.'

Imogen regarded her anxiously over the rim of the glass. 'I've got to wash my hair.'

'You washed it two days ago.' Iris looked at her – still palely green, but even in those pretentiously awful clothes, still tremblingly, absurdly beautiful, and forbore to add: 'Don't be ridiculous.' Instead she said: 'Wash it if you want to, and I'll trim the back for you first if you like. Where did you put the good scissors?'

'They're either in my dressing-gown pocket, or else they're in the bread-bin. The bread-bin,' she corroborated after thinking about it. Since Conrad had explained how wasteful and tiresome it was to lose things, she had taken to putting everything into what she described as a safe place. When Iris pointed out that this often made it difficult for her, Imogen replied reassuringly that it was much better because now she could find things for them both, whereas before nobody could find anything.

'He likes it to be cut down to a sharp point,' she said minutes later. She sat on a kitchen chair with a bath towel tied round her neck, and her hair so faintly gold that it was almost silver falling straight down to her shoulders. She looked up at Iris to strengthen this statement. She never had any colour in her face, but she had ceased to look green.

'Keep still. Have a cigarette. Calm down.'

'Have to scrub my hands. Conrad says if I held them properly the nicotine wouldn't go all over my fingers. Thank you. Good thing I've saved my decent clothes.'

'You would have.'

'I mightn't.'

'Look at all that disgusting soup we've nearly drowned in.'

She looked up again. 'Don't tell him about the soup.'

'I won't tell him anything, but I'll tell you.'

'What?'

'Just that you mustn't be so single-minded about all this. You mustn't let your life revolve round him.'

'But why not?'

There was something about her eyes – a simplicity, a kind of stark innocence which Iris found unanswerable.

Perhaps it is better to look like me, she thought afterwards, you don't get hurt so ingeniously.

When she went into the bathroom, Imogen, looking

like a carved angel whose hair has been washed away, said:

'He must love me or he wouldn't have come back early.'

'He may have had to come back.'

'Why are you against him, Iris? Do you dislike him?'

'Would it make any difference to you if I did?'

'No – but I can see that it's a bore for you to have the flat upset because of someone you don't like.'

'That's all right: he's your man. Anyway it is you who upset the flat and I must be devoted to you even to consider sharing a house with you. Hurry up, or your hair won't be dry. And for goodness' sake open the window when you've finished or you'll have the paper off the walls.'

'I haven't had that sort of bath.'

While she quietly emptied pans of unfinished soup, cleared the kitchen, and changed her clothes, Iris, witnessing the extravagant attention, the infinite care about detail, the mounting delight in her achievement that Imogen employed, said nothing. The discrepancy between the preparations, which were unexpectedly, even shatteringly, sophisticated, and the pure unadulterated passion of joy with which they were carried out, disturbed and paralysed her judgment. Only when, at the end of the two hours she went into the studio, and found Imogen standing by the window that looked on to the street, and Imogen turned to her and really wanting to know, asked: 'Please: do I look all right?' she answered inadequately: 'You look all right,' and then, quickly: 'Enjoy yourself. Make the most of it.'

'I do. I shall. He – Conrad – says that before he never knew the meaning of the word. Iris – You *don't* dislike him, do you?'

'No, no, of course I don't dislike him. Stopped feeling sick?'

'Completely. I feel ready for – oh – anything!'

∞   ∞   ∞

He had brought her a dress from Paris of a grey which, he said, would help him during the next week to determine about her eyes. Was there, then, a *week*? Well, five days. But her eyes were so dark with delight that he found only their shape – the clear downward curves at the ends of the heavy eyelids were memorable, and they would always be so, giving her face a quality almost pagan, older than any angel; no kind of morality, he thought, could attach to eyes set as hers.

During the spending of those five days, while he watched her making the universal, privately miraculous discoveries about love, he, walking and talking and watching and loving and sleeping, discovered that he loved her. Since, of all primary emotions, love is perhaps the least blind, he made a myriad quantity of discoveries about her, charming, alarming, breath taking, admirable, and fearful. He found her intense immediate capacity for enjoyment both entrancing and infectious. He forced her to show him her drawing and painting and discovered that it was simply a temporary translation of her creative impulse with people. She had a good, though undeveloped, sense of colour, and she could not draw at all. She had simply needed to make something of things, because she had not, until now, known how to make anything with people. But her beauty, now that all the lovely aspects of her interlocked with her happiness, glowed and glittered and shone – overrunning all the bounds of his imagination: it was there in a room after she had left it; she lent it to anything that she wore or touched; it lighted the faces of people who looked at her; it so charged anything they heard of, saw, or experienced together, that, to him, at least, she seemed its essence; there seemed no beauty in anything that did not originate from her. He observed how, in five days (they had not, until now, spent more than a few hours together) her feminine mind, the small darting intuitions that before had occasionally startled his admiration, became steadier and more confident; how with her concern for his pleasure and peace, she collected and guessed and protected and felt her way with him: how quickly she learned to embroider his wit, to rest on his silence, to entertain his interests, and respect his reservations.

Her only reservation with him had been her attempt to conceal any of her work from him. At first he had thought that this was because she thought that she was good, and that he would not recognize her ability: after he had seen it, he knew that it was because she knew she wasn't, and was afraid that he would confirm her knowledge. He tried to be encouraging about the drawings, but it was she who pronounced their death sentence.

'Anyway,' she said, 'I don't care about them any more.'

He looked down at her sharply: she was sitting on the floor, her head bent over the folder. One of the black tapes had knotted, and after trying for a minute to unpick it, she broke it off and shoved the folder out of sight under the sofa. When she looked up, she caught the end of his expression, and said:

'Were they very awful?'

'I've told you about them.'

'Unlike Ophelia, I was not deceived.'

178

'What *do* you care about?'

Her long delicate mouth slowly smiled.

'Oh you, my darling love – you.' She moved towards his chair, and put her hands on his. 'I love you as though you were God and had created me, and then as though you said, "Look, there is light, there are trees and stars, and days and nights, and this is life and this is rest, and I am always with you." Only,' she finished, 'sometimes, of course, I can't see you.'

In the short silence that followed, and long before the implications of her confession had begun to dam up his mind, his love and his fear were conceived.

SIX

On the sixth day, in the evening of which he expected his wife's return from France, he went back to work. He found himself as unable to tell Imogen that he loved her, as he found himself incapable of trying to diminish her love for him. While he was with her, these impulses, equally strong, effectively cancelled one another out, and as he could see no alternative while he remained with her but their strengthening with relentless impartiality, he escaped to the professional problems, which would, he knew, have accumulated during three weeks away from his work. He sent Imogen back to her art school, and Iris a tremendous bunch of the flowers of her name, with a note thanking her for her tactful accommodation. That day, with the desperate strength of a man who has at last uncovered his own weakness, he took decision after decision with the brilliant ease and force of indifference; straightened out what promised to be a major feud between two of his partners; prevented a maniacal architect from making the offices uninhabitable; interviewed five potential receptionists, turned them down, and procured a suitable sixth; wrote twenty-three letters and signed forty cheques; lunched with a kleptomaniac millionaire who divested him of all three of his fountain pens, but was otherwise amenable; and obtained counsel's opinion on a right of way recently discovered in Kent to run with admirable precision down the centre of his tennis court. On his way home, he collected three dozen oysters from Bentley's, and his luggage from his club.

They were back: she was back. As he let himself in, he heard sounds of the children bathing at the top of the house, of activity in the basement below. He faintly smelled her scent – saw that her pile of letters on the hall table had been examined – that she had put flowers in the dining-room – and knew that she would be upstairs unpacking and changing her clothes. He stood there for a moment, trying to meet her in his mind's eye, distilling her personality – trying to make her more like a well-remembered character in a book – collecting and reminding himself of her idiom, of how, chapters away, they had behaved on meeting after a separation: but there had not before been a separation like this, where skins of another life must be cast and cast until there seemed to be no skin left . . . Absurd: she would be glad to see him, and he had brought home oysters. He shrugged his shoulders at the image he had made of her, and took the oysters down to the kitchen.

She was lying on the Regency day-bed in their bedroom. He had bought it years ago, because, he had said, it was a piece of furniture perfectly designed for her, but although she had seemed delighted at the time, he had never before seen her lie on it. Strewn over her and the bed were samples of wallpaper; she dropped a piece as he entered the room: but she turned her head to greet him, ignoring the paper. He was unprepared at a distance of ten days and an immense quantity of feeling, for her burnished elegance. He picked up one of her hands to kiss it, but she withdrew it, saying:

'I don't think my nails are dry.' They were lacquered

white. She met his eye almost timidly: he thought she wanted approval for her hands and said:

'They are fascinating, but if you do that to them, you will have to keep them perfectly.'

'I know they are rather borderline,' she answered.

'How was the trip back?'

'Oh – hot, and considering the children, and Leila as she is at present, uneventful. Very smooth, really.'

'They are a couple with whom familiarity is breeding something pretty contemptible.' Then, he added: 'I'm sorry I find them so dull.'

It was most unlike him to say that. There was a silence while both of them wondered why he had said it.

'I find him dull,' she said at last. She was collecting together the pieces of wallpaper.

He said: 'You have got down to work very quickly,' and she answered with the quickness of faint irritation:

'It isn't work. It's only choosing.'

'It is choice that distinguishes the *artiste* from the common woman—' he began, but she interrupted:

'But I am not an artist either!'

'Oh darling! Are you obsessed with a need to be something?'

She looked up: 'Am I? I mean, is it an obsession?'

Of course, she's tired, he thought. Aloud he said: 'My dear, if I had been the kind of little boy who kept beetles in a match box, stamps in an album, or bricks in the brick sack, I might have grown up into the kind of man who wanted to keep a woman in a house. But I was always racing my beetles till they escaped, swopping and losing stamps, and building something with the bricks. The beetles weren't fast enough, the stamps were too often fakes, and there were never, by any chance, enough bricks. So you see, you may do what you like.'

'As long as I no more than like it.'

He was combing his hair with her comb.

After a silence during which she could hear the comb in his hair, she asked: 'Have you seen the children?'

'I laid oysters at Dorothy's feet, and came straight to you.'

She rose from the day-bed.

'I'll say good night to them, and join you downstairs.'

He stood still when she had gone, and then went to wash. The thought of the children suddenly crowded his whole day upon him: he realized that he was very tired, and wished that he had organized people for dinner as well as food. Early bed, he thought, turning off the taps, and remembered her behaviour in St Tropez. 'Early bed,' he repeated almost viciously to himself, surmounting a wave of angry guilt, and went down to the drawing-room.

∞ ∞ ∞

He asked her that first evening when she was going to Kent, and she replied that she was sending the children, but that she was not going down immediately. There were a number of things she wanted to do, she added quickly: she seemed to expect his resistance to this plan. He answered urbanely that she should, of course, do exactly as she pleased. He thought she intended watching him, and was secretly angry and alarmed at the prospect. She knew he was angry, and at the thought of his guessing the reason for her wanting to stay in London, a spasm of terror fled over her face, which she afterwards feared he had seen. But she caught no breath of his alarm, and he had not seen her face. They both found it difficult, if not impossible, to look at one another. They finished the evening with mutual exclamations of exhaustion; with that faint overemphasis of commiseration, the one for the other, which is designed more to underline than to comfort fatigue. She fell asleep at once, as all day she had determined to do; but he, overtired, and baffled by her behaviour, which had given him no chance to unwind – lay for hours with circular aching thoughts. He resolved not to see Imogen the following evening (in the small hours even this temporary negation of his desire seemed heroic), and finally having decided at once to transfuse some people into the flagging bloodstream of his private life, he slept.

That evening was representative of many days and evenings after it. They were like two people standing on distantly removed rocks in the sea, each of them holding the end of a heavy cable which was their only means of contact. If the cable was slack, it was heavy in their hands, and communication was impossible; if either of them tried to haul in their end, the weight became untenable and they trembled from the trembling tension. In the days that followed, the cable either dragged, while they stood hopelessly isolated – or shortened and shivered, burning their separate hands – precipitating the moment when one of them must cross the perilously taut line to the other.

When he returned one evening to dress for a theatre party, he found her asleep and unchanged, in the drawing-room. In the moments before she woke, to present him with her face but not her eyes, he made the terrible discovery inevitably experienced sooner or later by men who marry beautiful women: that her beauty, set in its immobile continuity of sleep, brought him to a sudden emotional standstill – he saw, perhaps more clearly than he had ever seen, that she was admirably beautiful, but he saw it with an utterly disinterested appreciation – he had no desire to identify himself with it. Afterwards he was always to have this curiously complete picture of her, annihilating desire, undoing love, jamming any movement of feeling, because in his mind she was always lying there, as complete, as still, and beautiful as death.

The notion that perhaps she was dead occurred to him in a sudden violently unreal crossing of his mind: dead, and finished for herself as well as for him. The perfect ending . . . To know all may be to forgive as much, he thought, but to see everything is to care nothing.

The telephone rang. Before he had moved, she was alive again and had reached it. He watched her, surprised at her urgent immediate interest in an instrument she so much disliked. It was clearly a call of no consequence. When she put back the receiver, she said with the faintly timid smile that prefaced much she now said to him:

'Wilfrid – Papa – is very ill. I thought it might be about him.'

'It wasn't.'

'No – it wasn't anything.' She turned from the telephone with the weariness of an impatience that has persisted too long. 'Shall we have a drink here before we change?'

'If you like.' Fatigue, he thought objectively, becomes her. She is reduced by it to an absolute of distinction. 'Sherry?'

'Brandy.' She perched unrestfully on the arm of a chair, and pulled out her watch. 'How long have we got?'

'Long enough to drink in. What is the matter with Wilfrid?'

'Something inside. They aren't sure, but his heart is bad and it's complicating their investigations. He looks dreadful.'

'You've seen him?'

'I was there this afternoon. He's in St Mary's, you know.' She spoke defensively – as though she thought he didn't believe her. She took the glass from him. 'Of course he's been feeling ill for months without seeing anybody. He didn't want to go to hospital. He hates it. I think he thinks he's going to die.' She drank some brandy, and her voice rose a little. 'He'd much rather die in his own house.'

He was silent; he knew how she suffered from the illness of other people. Even if she knew them very little, her imagination made no allowances for her ignorance; she did everything possible to alleviate their miseries, but under the agonizing pressure of her distress for them, she never believed that she did anything; her pity never retreated before the advance of any achievement, until the illness was resolved one way or another. She would have made a wonderful nurse, people said, watching her in one of those situations, and perhaps only he knew that she would never have survived six months of such a career.

He picked up a box of cigarettes and offered them to her.

Her fingers felt in the box while she looked at him.

'That is a Turkish cigarette which you detest. Have this one.'

She looked down. 'It's a French cigarette!'

'You used to like them.' He picked up a match. How odd that fear should always make women look ten years younger. But he was prevented from considering what it did to men by her saying:

'I'd rather have Turkish.'

He lit it for her, and did not move away in case she wanted to touch him for knowing that she wanted to smoke. Women's affections operate like insects – with tiny significant gestures: then he remembered Imogen putting her hands on his and dropping her heart at his feet – the gesture to end all others, he thought – and wished desperately that it did.

She had finished her brandy and was off the chair, stubbing out her cigarette.

'They are not habit-forming, at least,' she said.

'Do you very much not want to go to this theatre?' he asked her upstairs, and she answered with unconvincing vigour:

'Of course I want to, of course.'

'You are a very bad liar.'

'No.'

'Well, you have never managed to deceive me for a moment.'

'And you? Are you such a good one?' she said, after a fractional hesitation.

'My dear, I have passionately wanted to go to this play since five o'clock this afternoon. Can you imagine my feelings now?'

'Absolute indifference. Let's go then.'

SEVEN

He had not seen Imogen for several days, and when he arrived, she did not expect him. She had been bathing, and wore a robe of rough blue towelling.

'I was drying slowly inside it, but I haven't got very far.' Her confusion at seeing him always made her talk as though he had been away only five minutes. She threw open the studio door for him, and waited, poised to disappear.

'Come and talk to me while you dry.' He did not want to be in her surroundings without her animation. 'Where is Iris?'

'She's away for a week. She's inspecting things in the Midlands.'

'So you've been alone?'

'I've been thinking,' she answered gravely.

'Let us find something to drink, and tell me your conclusions.'

'Touch me first.' She smiled, to lighten the request, and held out her hand. He shook it carefully.

'I am delighted to see you,' she began carefully, but it did not stop tears from slipping down her face. 'Oh – really: they don't matter.'

'Imogen, I believe you capable of fainting for joy. Have you ever done that?'

'No: I simply get sick.' The tears made no difference

to her eyes. 'We could drink Dubonnet. I'll get it. You sit down somewhere. Are you very tired?' she called from the kitchen.

'You should never ask men whether they are tired. You should simply treat them as though they were, and then evince ravished astonishment later on when either you find that they are, or that they aren't.'

'Impartially?'

'Oh yes. Their vanity is easily whipped.'

'I don't need to know about men.'

'That is both arrogant and short-sighted of you.'

'I'm not arrogant,' she said anxiously – showing that she was used to the accusation.

'Aren't you? Well, you should be.' She was standing still in the kitchen door, with a lemon in one hand, and a knife in the other. He looked at her without seeing her, and then again observantly – but it was all right – he could make no picture of her: he found that he was relating to her lack of colour, the differently entrancing textures of her skin: there was no photograph, he discovered, when all the senses were employed.

When she saw him watching her so intently, she looked quickly down at herself as though she felt there must be something wrong. She has no vanity, he thought – I really must teach her a little conceit.

'At least nobody can say that last week they saw some-body rather like you in the street.'

'If they did, it would have been me they'd seen,' she said simply, and went to get glasses.

The flowers he had sent to Iris were nearly over. Bad shop, he thought, they ought to last a week, and then counted up the days that they had lasted. Until now, he had always liked to live in as many different environments

189

as he could either afford or contrive, but now, it was beginning to be disquieting. When he was at Campden Hill Square, he found himself wondering how life was being spent in this studio – whether there were wild student parties with night-lights in saucers and Spanish music on the portable gramophone, and Imogen dancing by herself – parties with black coffee and wine and very little to eat – or whether Imogen sat on the large yellow cushion which she dragged about the floor and on which she always sat, eating Bath Oliver biscuits and reading plays aloud to herself. He always thought of her by herself – even in a party.

And then, when he was here with her, he discovered that the moment she was out of the room, he was thinking about his wife and their house – enduring now the thought of her father's illness – enduring thoughts about him of which he was dreadfully ignorant: sitting alone with a tray of food in the drawing-room (she had sent the children to Kent in order that she might devote more time to her father). She would go to the hospital and read to him until his drug worked and he slept for a few hours, poor devil. Then she would go home and try to read herself to sleep, but she did not use drugs, and he knew that she was sleeping very badly.

He was about to switch his mind on to his work as a relief, when he realized that Imogen had returned with the Dubonnet and glasses, and was sitting quietly on the floor beside him.

'What an unobtrusive creature you can be!'

'I thought you were either thinking, or asleep.'

'I might have been both. Intellectual people are so used to thinking that, naturally, they do it in their sleep as well.'

She looked up, smiling. She was beginning to feel happy about his being there. 'Pour it out.'

'I'm not an intellectual, anyway,' she added, taking her glass.

'No? Nor am I then.'

'What *is* an intellectual?' She had a charming habit of tilting her head at the end of a question, really wanting the answer.

'Intellectuals are the intelligent theorists who are sneered at by the clever administrators. It is because of them that the world goes round the wrong way far too slowly.'

'Because of the intellectuals?'

'Yes – the administrators reverse their theories, you see.'

'Which *are* you?' she persisted.

'I'm a diabolically clever administrator. I make pounds out of the intellectuals, but I'm much kinder to them than most of my contemporaries.'

'But then, you are exceedingly kind,' she said.

He denied it – he resolved to be kinder – he wondered whether he had ever been kind before. Aloud, he said: 'Here I am kindly talking nonsense when you have conclusions to divulge. What are they? No, wait a minute. I will administrate the evening, or three hours hence, we shall still be sitting here and you will be quite dry but very, very hungry. Put some clothes on, and we'll have dinner while you tell me.'

'All right.' She stood up.

'Take that off first, would you?'

She made a small, self-conscious gesture with her hands, and the blue robe slipped to her feet. He tried to look at her carefully, but in the entirety of nakedness she was dazzling – it was not possible to look at her for long. I need her, he thought savagely – and if she loves me – why not?

'Go and get dressed.'

She picked up the robe, frowning a little.

'Conrad.' He saw that she was trembling. 'I don't understand you.'

'What don't you understand?'

'I was going to ask you whether you loved me.'

'You've picked a very bad moment.' He got up from his chair, and walked to the window. 'Go and get dressed.'

He heard the murmuring rub of her robe trailing from her hand on to the floor, and the door shut with a dejected quiet.

In the taxi, when his desire had subsided, he said:

'Of course I love you.'

Upstairs in their restaurant they were alone, and he chose their dinner and gave her a glass of vodka.

'I've never had it.' She drank, and said: 'You have to drink it in the present.'

'Now then.' He was beginning to feel curious to the point of apprehension.

'It was about my future.'

'Yes?'

'Well, you've made me see one thing very clearly.'

He was silent.

'You've made me realize,' she repeated steadily, 'that there is no point in my trying to paint.' She was staring at her empty glass – twisting it round and round in her fingers.

'Are you sure of that?'

'I am sure. I mind rather, at the moment.' Her voice

had become less steady – she shook it together with a little laugh. 'I expect I'll get over it quite soon.'

'You may not be a painter, but there are innumerable decorative possibilities.'

She relinquished her glass. 'I don't think of it like that. Either painting, or myself.'

'Designing, advertising, and so forth,' he persisted.

'Oh – clothes, and material and wallpaper. I shouldn't care twopence about any of that. So there would be no point in my trying to do it.'

'What are you going to do instead?'

She turned to him: she had an unusually intricate pattern of lines on her forehead. 'That is what I don't know. What could I do?'

There was a short silence while they both thought; then she continued: 'I never thought of not being able to paint. For years I was told that when I had finished my education I could come to London and go to an art school, and, of course, I always wanted to. It always seemed so far away, that I never thought beyond it. Stupid of me. None of it has turned out at all how I imagined.'

'Why don't you try to do it for a little longer?'

'I can't let my family go on paying for a training which I know is no use. You know what Tonks said to the student about knitting. Well, it seems to me that I'd better learn to type or something.' She gave him a bewildered meaningless smile, and began to eat her smoked trout.

'Good: well, now I know, I'll think about it.'

She turned to him. His face was closed and utterly unresponsive. She had thought that he would immediately produce a host of possibilities, and recoiled against what she felt was his reduction of the problem.

'You need more horseradish sauce,' he said.

After all, it is my whole future, she thought, watching his expert dissection of his fish. She remained wrapped in this thought for the rest of dinner, and asked him small dangerous questions such as why did they not go to the opera any more, and why had he not told her that he would be free that evening.

Afterwards, they walked slowly, until they were nearer one another. The hot dusty streets were smelling of horse-meat and garlic and cheap cooking oil; spattered with a few limp scurrying leaves; lined with the motor cars belonging to the theatre crowds; and cornered with women wearing thin black silk stockings and high-heeled dirty white sandals – with hair imitating Ginger Rogers and tied back with pieces of limp white chiffon. The sky above them reflected the neon lighting as the colour of a black grape skin against light. A noble-looking tramp was settling on a bench at St Giles-in-the-Fields for the night. His hair and beard hung nearly to his waist in luxurious ringlets and curls the faintly greenish black of a bad black dye. He wore a bowler hat and two overcoats, with a paper carnation pinned to the outer lapel. He had taken off his boots, and his toe nails – immensely long – gleamed like the black talons of some bird. He was eating soft bread which seemed ferociously white against his beard. When he observed them, he gave them a courtly, sardonic smile, and with a neat animal movement of his shoulders, turned his back on them.

'Did he mind our looking at him?'

'Shouldn't think so. I was wondering what the statistics were for men as opposed to women living that life.'

'I should hate it,' she began, and he interrupted with a stab of irritation:

'Oh – you would. The life is far too self-contained for most women.'

'*You* wouldn't like it either.'

He hailed a taxi without answering her, and thought: How continuously personal women are. They apply everything to themselves, or someone near them: they are incapable of general application. The effect of what she had said in the restaurant about painting and her future was beginning to knock about in his mind, hitting blindly at any blind or tender spot, piling up his resentment against her, and making him very angry that at his age he should have propelled himself into such a mess. She sat, miserably attendant upon his mood, her hands in her lap, her head a little bent, waiting for him to speak, even to be angry aloud (for his anger filled the cab and was stifling).

When they arrived at her flat, she slid from her seat and out of the door like a child imitating a lizard. He remained.

'Tell him to go to Campden Hill Square.'

'Will you please go to Campden Hill Square?'

She did not look at him, and she had moved to the door of her house before the cab moved.

He tried to settle down with his anger: he had meant to hurt her, and he had succeeded: by how much, he wondered; was she crying – had she flung herself upstairs into some dark corner to cry? Or was she angry – was she standing in a blaze of light, blazing and trembling with rage? Or perhaps neither; perhaps she had wanted him to go on, and had been simply tired and bored. Damn all emotions; they preclude any sort of planned existence; they are worth next to nothing afterwards, and provoke childish excesses of anticipation. In a minute he knew he would stop the cab, but in an ecstasy of self-destruction he allowed it to continue while he derided himself for what he knew he was going to do. Well, there was to be no sentimental reconciliation like anybody in a film. She had wanted to talk about her future: right: they would talk about it, and she should be made to see exactly how responsible she was for herself – the weapons of tears or sex should only be allowed a single, physical, edge, and if it became clear that she needed a few corners rubbed off her heart in order that she might in future live down to the accepted standards of being in love, tonight was the night for rubbing. This cauterizing philosophy of being kinder to her in the long run had the advantage of complying with his immediate need to cry down and depreciate. He stopped the cab. One could spend one's life, he thought, fumbling for silver which he had not got, being kinder to a number of different people in the long run. It was the neatest preclusion of kindness imaginable.

There was light in her windows. He rang the bell, and waited for what seemed to him an unnecessarily long time before she answered it. Her hair was untidy, but she had not undressed, and she looked at him with a curious blankness.

'May I come and talk to you?'

She moved aside for him, shut the door, and followed him up the unkempt stairs that belonged to no one living anywhere in the house.

The studio stove was lit, and the deathly smell of burning paper filled the air.

'What are you burning?'

'Paper,' she answered, and her voice was as blank as her face. He saw an empty drawing folder lying open on the floor by the stove.

'My dear, you aren't burning up all your drawings at this hour of the night?'

She moved to the stove and shut it. 'I don't suppose I shall manage all of them tonight – it takes much longer than I thought.'

He sat down: 'Well, I must say, it's intensely dramatic of you.'

She did not reply. He watched her moving about the room for a minute, and then said: 'I suppose it is all my fault that you are burning them?'

She was kneeling by the stove again unpicking the tapes on another folder. She flushed a little: 'It isn't your fault that I am unable to draw.' The drawings had to be torn before they would go into the stove.

'You know perfectly well what I mean. You could hardly have contrived anything more aggressively destructive.'

'I had no idea that you were coming back.' She did not look at the drawings before she tore them. There was something hard and elusive about her which he had not encountered before. She is older than I have ever seen her, he thought, although her head is still the head of an ancient young angel.

'But you would have taken care that you told me all about it afterwards.'

She turned her head, and answered honestly: 'Perhaps. I don't know. What was it that you wanted to talk about?'

'I can't talk with all this destruction going on. Come over here, and have a cigarette.'

'You want to be the centre of destruction.' It was the kind of remark that he had taught her to make, and he found himself bitterly surprised that she had learned so fast.

She took a cigarette, but remained standing in front of him, and looking up at her, he suddenly realized that she was intolerably unhappy: that she was so consumed by the overwhelming ache and burn of this discovery which she was attempting to conceal, that it was frightening her – she moved and spoke alternately with the quickness or deliberation of panic.

'Imogen,' he said her name almost as though he was afraid of waking her; 'if you don't tell me, I shan't know.'

She did not move. 'All one's life,' she said painfully; 'there is this little path, and that little path – hedges, I suppose, on either side – one can't see very much, just a narrow alternative from time to time, until quite suddenly – at least, I didn't expect it – one comes to the end of the path, one can see everything – an endless desert of possibilities. I suppose – everyone feels that?'

He said, as though it was a reassurance: 'I don't know. Some time in their lives, perhaps.'

'It is most solitary and blinding.' He could hardly hear her.

'It is a predicament of the courageous imagination,' he added.

'Is it?' He felt her seize upon this.

'I think so. Either people don't look, or they won't admit to what they see.'

'That isn't anything to do with imagination.'

'It is all part of the mind. Do you think that the imagination is always employed with the fantastic, the falsehood, the distortion, the wishful improbability? It is the single most powerful weapon for discovering a truth. A lot of nonsense is talked about the imagination, because, like most powerful implements, it is dangerous.'

She was regaining her balance. To give her more time he continued: 'When imagination is successful, it is called vision, and when it is abused or a failure, it is called morbid or worse. God has a hand in it when it is good, and the psychiatrists when it isn't. Don't,' he added, 'believe exactly what I say. I am approximating, or marking time, or something like that.' He smiled at her, and she began to smile back; stopped anxiously, and said:

'What was it you came back to talk about?'

'Oh, you, of course. The most fascinating subject in the world, excepting me. But I was forestalled by this – conflagration.'

She glanced at the stove.

'Sit down. It is much harder to be anything sitting down.'

'All right. I didn't do that on purpose to annoy you.'

'I see that now. But I am naturally so bloody-minded that I always expect other people to be the same. Why did you do it?'

'I wrote to my family about it last night. When I told you this evening, I thought – I thought that—'

'You thought that I would help, and I didn't.'

'A bit. I thought you would know exactly what it felt like. I see that that is silly, because nobody can know exactly what someone else feels like about anything.' There was a pause while she digested this discovery: then she said: 'And I suppose I thought that you would think of something else.'

'Yes?'

'Well then, as you didn't, I felt when I was alone here that I had better really burn my boats while I had enough courage to do it. I was afraid of waking up in the morning all soothing and dishonest with myself about it. If I burned everything, I thought I wouldn't, at least, be able to pick over my work and find excuses for it.' She looked at him, and her face was not blank any more, she was talking again as though she could see him. 'The trouble is that I don't see what to do at all.' She added violently: 'I don't want to exist and drift and make nothing. I would rather not be alive than do that.'

'You've had the idea of painting for a long time. You cannot expect immediately to be presented with an equally significant alternative. It takes time, but you will find one.'

'But *what* might I *find*?' she persisted like a child.

'I don't know yet. It will be your discovery, if you look.'

She looked so disappointed that he added unwisely: 'Anyway, you will marry and have children.'

'You? Could I possibly marry you, do you think?' Her face was lit with intention: so ingenuously without design, so passionately certain of her love, that his heart moved. He said:

'I didn't mean that. I am married, already.'

He saw her immediate acceptance: that he did not want her, or want her enough – the sudden death of that brilliant hope sinking to the bottom of her heart. She tried to smile and answered: 'I didn't really think I could, of course,' and folded her hands, one upon the other in her lap.

He wanted then desperately to protect her pride which was not vanity – to comfort and reassure her, but he could find nothing entirely safe to say or do.

She unclasped her hands, stared at the palms, and put them flat on the floor.

'It's probably very late,' she said at last. 'You'd better go.'

'I don't want to go.'

'Then, don't go. Stay – if you like.'

Shutting away the memory of that inflexion, he knelt beside her.

EIGHT

He went home early in the morning before anyone was up. On the hall table was one of Dorothy's notes: 'Madam Mr Tomson rang will ring again.' It was not until he was half way upstairs that the name clicked, and he remembered Marseille. Why on earth should – but there was only one reason why Thompson rang up any woman. She, and Thompson! No, but really, she would be little Thompson's Waterloo – must already have been, as Thompson was not the man to waste time . . . then why was he telephoning now? He shrugged and gave it up.

The bedroom was empty; she had not spent the night in it. He pulled off his clothes and fell asleep trying to imagine his wife calling Thompson by his perfectly ghastly Christian name; but he couldn't even remember the name, only howling with laughter when he had heard it first, and advising Thompson never to use it. 'It was my mother,' Thompson had said. 'She was very interested in the East at the time.'

He was half way through breakfast when his wife came into the room, wearing a coat and carrying her morning letters. She sank wearily into her chair without a word. He rose to get her coffee. 'Black, please, Conrad.' After he had put the cup before her and she had sat in silence warming her hands round it – the situation seeming

202

impersonally tense – the product of their separate fatigues
– she said:

'I suppose I ought to have told you. They rang up and
said that they were operating suddenly, so I went to the
hospital to be there afterwards when he came round in
case he wanted anyone, and by the time I realized I'd be
there all night, it seemed too late to ring you up.'

'Is he all right?'

'I don't think he knows much about it.' She drank some
coffee, and repeated: 'I don't think he knows much.'

Her face was absolutely worn by fatigue – expressionless, familiar, enclosed – he remembered that she had
looked like that after her first child, and how difficult he
had found it then to make contact with her. Now he said:

'But do they regard the operation as successful?'

She was stirring more sugar into her coffee. 'How can
one tell? He is not dead, and they say he is doing as well
as can be expected. They haven't dared say that he is
perfectly comfortable, because it is obvious to the meanest
intelligence that he is not.'

'You saw him?'

'Yes.' There was a pause, and then she said: 'Isn't it
extraordinary how everything shrinks about people in
pain except their eyes. But perhaps it isn't just pain.'

'Well,' he said sharply, 'what is it?'

She stared at her cup. 'Oh – agony of mind as well.
That is what one cannot bear to—'

'You torture yourself,' he interrupted. 'You were not
so devoted to your father. Be simpler – more subjective.
Bear those ills you know.'

She said nothing, and he fell back to the position of
practical concern. 'Are you going to sleep today? Dorothy

can answer the telephone. She'll give you any important messages.'

The faint animation of some new anxiety crossed her face. She looked up. 'I can put the telephone by my bed.' She gathered up her letters. 'I might want to talk to them myself.'

When he left to go to the office, he glanced at the ebony table. The message written by Dorothy was not there.

∞   ∞   ∞

The atmosphere of impending crisis enveloped him until he was not rid of it even in his office, nor walking about the streets, nor in his club. Certainly it was at its worst in Campden Hill Square. There, he felt the drag of a death struggle which his father-in-law illustrated, and which, he felt, was repeated in his association with his wife. He was unable to approach her: he had not with her been used to that effort; for many years she had come to him and been delighted to find him at the end of her journey; but now she was distant, and he knew only that she was distraught: her heart and mind were set entirely apart from him, her consideration the mechanical forethoughts of routine. Sometimes, he thought, she seemed almost glad to have him out of the house . . .

With Imogen, the situation was more transparently uncertain. She had stopped going to her art school, and although she did not discuss any alternative, he felt that she was obscurely, and perhaps unconsciously, dependent upon him. Since the evening when she had so simply asked whether she might marry him, he had laboured to devolve his emotional responsibility for her on to the practical. He tried to be commanding and kind, and watched her accept what he was determined to give, refusing in his turn to take anything from her until he had established it either as commonplace, or as an indulgence of her generosity. She was unhappy; he perceived this, and straightway canalized her unhappiness; imposed upon her the conflict of alternative careers – discussed her future with exhaustive enthusiasm, enclosed her heart and hedged his own with an ugly evergreen caution which preserved the immobility of balance between them; so that she wept alone, and he thought alone, and their love lay untouched, extant, but deeply frozen.

Alone, he probed and analysed, threw away excuse after excuse, and then anything which resembled an excuse, made up the separate parts of his mind, discovered that they did not fit, and tore them to pieces again. He tried seeing his wife as sentimentally bound up in dependants, her children, her father, as tediously, omnipotently maternal – as dependent upon him only for an environment where she might employ these instincts. He tried seeing Imogen as an infatuated adolescent, as a tentative young whore, as an imperfect schemer after destruction. He had only to be with either of them for these simplifying phantasies to resolve into a vortex of anxiety and ignorance – and worse, for the two women to dissolve into one another, until they were baffling and inseparable – a composite picture in his mind.

He worked feverishly these days. Long afterwards, he was to remember strafing a young office clerk for muddled thinking. 'I was in two minds about it at the time, sir.' (There were nearly tears in his eyes, he was so desperate to hold down his job.) 'It won't never happen again, sir.' Poor devil, thought Conrad, so uncharacteristically, that he was provoked into saying:

'Two minds are all very well, Blackburn. But never let your right mind know what your left mind is doing.'

'No, sir.'

'All right, Blackburn.' And the boy went, his escape as much a mystery to him as his muddle had been.

That evening, he went on an impulse of admiration for his wife to St Mary's Hospital, intending to collect her and at least see that she had a reasonable meal. She was not there, they said, she had left the hospital at five thirty – they did not know when she would return. Mr Vaughan was quite comfortable. He left the entrance to the private wing which was impregnated with the odours of ether and floor polish and carnations, which echoed with the starched shuffle of the night nurses going down to their first meal; stood outside in the weary little road which led nowhere but to the hospital, and then went home. But she was not there, either. She had gone out, reiterated Dorothy unnecessarily. He went to his club and dined alone, drank a glass of port with one of his oldest enemies, and went home to prowl aimlessly about his house.

She came in at eleven o'clock, into the bedroom as though she had not expected to find him there, for she halted at the door a moment before walking across the room to her dressing-table.

'I am not staying. I have to go back.'

'Back?' He watched her mercilessly until she was forced by the pressure of his eyes to look at him. He propped himself up in bed. 'You look as though you have a fever,' he observed. He had not forgiven her for the scene about Imogen before they went to France.

She flushed, and dropped her eyes, made the little nervous gesture with her hand across her hair, and said: 'Do I? I am just tired.'

'I should think you are utterly exhausted.' At that moment he was hating her; for deceiving him, for deceiving him so badly – she had positively forced his commiseration for her father – for sheltering beneath such an unassailable alibi. She had her back to him, she was searching for something in a drawer, and as he acknowledged his actually murderous instincts, he realized how deep, and he had thought impregnable, his regard for her had been. He had never, until now, questioned his admiration of her character; that she was neither dishonest, nor stupid, nor indifferent; that she had possessed the courage of her emotions, which, in his opinion, was the most to be expected of any woman. Now the whole structure slid like so much shale down a mountain, changing the face of his concept with a frightful, sudden, indifference. There was the frightful complete silence which follows such avalanches; then he asked:

'Are you going to be out all night?'

'I don't know. Perhaps only an hour.'

'Would it not be simpler to ring up the hospital first, and find out how he is?'

'I know how he is, far better than they will tell me.'

'Nonsense. There is no point in dashing about like this if it is to no purpose. He was quite comfortable when I left.'

'*You* left? When were you there?'

She had been tucking a scarf into the neck of her shirt, but now she turned her head, so that with the looking-glass he could see her three times.

'Earlier,' he replied after a pause: he was almost enjoying the simplicity of his hatred.

'I must have been dining,' she murmured; she seemed confused – aware that something was wrong, and afraid of knowing more. She pulled out the scarf impatiently, and started to tie it in a bow. 'Was he really all right when you were there? Did you see him?'

'I took their word for it. You must have had a remarkable dinner, if you have only just finished.'

He was still watching her: he saw her eyes cloud suddenly with something like fear, or pain. Then she said distantly: 'I dined – oh – ages ago. I have been walking. I have walked about for hours.'

He put down his book, and got up.

'I am not playing this game any more. Do you understand? I am out of it from this moment. You may do as you like, and I shall not care whether I like what you do. Your only ingenuity has been in landing me with a great deal of unnecessary guilt . . .' God knows what else he might have said, but the telephone rang, and she flew out of her frozen silence to answer it. The conversation was brief: there was not time for the haze of anger to clear – he had not known what he was going to say – and he found he was unable even to see her until she said: 'I have to go immediately. Conrad. Do you hear me? I *must* go.' She stared at him with a kind of urgent misery, and then ran out of the room, the rush of air from her departure stirring the pages of his open book.

Watching the pages hesitate and settle, he felt nothing but a sick astonishment.

NINE

'What is the matter? Please tell me.'

'Nothing to do with you.'

Imogen laughed, and he said: 'Why?'

'I never thought that one could say "Nothing to do with you" like that. I thought it was always cross.'

'Have you *always* thought the same things about the same things?' he enquired irritably, and she answered humbly:

'I suppose I have.' Then she added: 'But would it help to tell me what is the matter?'

'My father-in-law was very ill. I began last night to say unforgivable things to my wife, in the middle of which the telephone rang and she rushed to his side arriving just in time to see him die.'

'Yes?'

'That's all.'

'Oh. Of course, I don't know what it was like before.'

'No, of course you don't. The trouble is that I don't either.'

'You must know whether you love her.'

'I am not a woman, so I don't know anything of the kind. Responsibility succeeds desire – some men enjoy one, and some the other – that's all.'

'Don't you see it in *any* other terms?'

'There have been seconds when I have seen it in other, indefinable, terms.'

'Which do you enjoy – the desire, or the responsibility?'

'Both; provided I may engineer their proportions.'

'But you *are* attached to her,' she persisted.

'Clearly. She is my wife.'

'Is *she* unhappy?'

'You don't imagine that being married to me is fun, do you?'

She turned her head away.

'I don't imagine anything at all.'

∞ ∞ ∞

At home he discovered his wife stamping letters, while her young cousin (in London on his way up to Cambridge) discoursed to her upon his future.

'. . . what one really *craves* is some quite useless work for which one is grossly overpaid, and where one has all the time in the world for one's *interests* – mocking up a really brilliant biography of one of these dictators or someone – proving they're madly aristocratic, or it's all adrenalin for instance – only one knows people who are doing that – or one could simply found a bureau for giving people bad advice; make them pay like anything and then they'd do the opposite and it would all end happily ever after . . .' He had to breathe occasionally, and in the pause, when Mrs Fleming was about to say, 'Nonsense, Roland,' encouragingly, she saw her husband, checked herself, and gave him a little formal smile.

'Oh, good evening,' said Roland; 'I was worrying about the future.'

'Generally or specifically?'

'Oh, generally, with specific relation to me.'

Mrs Fleming threw away an empty stamp book and said: '*Is* there any other way of worrying about it?'

There was a pause, and then she said mildly: 'I had no idea that I should stop everyone talking. I shall post these while you decide what film you want to see.'

'She says she has to be taken to a film,' said Roland.

Fleming suddenly suggested: 'Why don't you post her letters for her?'

Roland looked faintly surprised, and began uncoiling the weedy waste of his legs, but she interrupted: 'No – I should like the air': and then as though she was afraid of what she had said, she held out the letters to her husband and added: 'Unless *you* want to post them?' In spite of the faint emphasis, she did not meet his eye. He shook his head, and, when she had gone, tried desperately to remember exactly what he had said last night.

∞   ∞   ∞

They travelled across the desert evening – eating, talking, watching the Marx Brothers – after which Roland thanked them politely, said that he thought he would have a Turkish bath, and lounged off into the night, 'As casually,' she remarked, 'as he arrived.'

Alone together, she was so self-possessed, that he began to feel frightened for her. He asked her about her father, and without any emotion she told him the arrangements she had made. She did not take long to tell them, and at the end they both wished that there was more to say: but there seemed nothing for it but to drive silently home. They got out of the car and she said: 'Oh – I could put it away tonight.'

'Don't bother.'

The monotony of agitation, he thought, trudging upstairs. Dorothy had left sandwiches in the drawing-room.

'Do you want any?'

'Why not?' She started to eat one as though it was filled with sand.

'Are you going to join the children?' he asked.

'I expect so: should I?'

'Wouldn't it be a good thing?'

She put the sandwich on a plate. 'If you want me to go.'

'I don't mind whether you go—' he began, and stopped, as she interrupted: 'I know.'

There was a silence. Then she said: 'Their terms start in about a week anyway.'

We had better talk, he thought wearily – talk it all out somehow – women usually respond to such a method, even if it results in pushing the balance further in either direction than they anticipate. Perhaps we ought to have Imogen here as well, and do the thing thoroughly – but Imogen wouldn't understand her: she would not see anything in our relationship. Perhaps that is because it seems entirely composed of a kind of middle distance memory – one cannot pretend that one doesn't remember, and one cannot pretend that one remembers clearly.

'Do you think that we had better try and talk to one another?'

She had been lying back in an armchair with her eyes shut; now, without any other movement, she opened her eyes and said: 'I don't think so, Conrad. At the moment I should be no good at talking. I don't care enough about anything at all.'

When the distant memory had faintly died, he said: 'Do you know that that was the first thing you ever said to me?'

'I don't remember. How odd that you should.' But she did not ask the circumstances of her not caring.

'Possibly indifference is useful for this sort of talk.'

'For men. Not for women. Women are quite useless for anything when they are indifferent.'

He looked at her thrown back in her chair; her feet and her hands lying elegantly useless, her attitude the epitome of indifference, as though she had finished everything in her life, and could not imagine why she was not dead. I used to be fascinated by her indifference, he thought, but then it had not the same quality about it – she was only lying in wait for something which it enchanted me to discover for her. Now, she seems disenchanted; I should have to think very hard before I loved her, and neither of us seems to care enough for the subtle sensitive effort which we should both have to make. But we cannot go on like this . . .

She sat up in her chair.

'I shall probably go to Kent, before the weekend. Make your plans as though I was going, anyway. That was what you wanted to know, wasn't it? But I am not going to bed yet. I still have a great many letters.'

He finished his drink. 'Don't stay up all night.' He got up, feeling strangely awkward.

'I won't. I shall feel much better when the letters are off my mind.' She felt his awkwardness, but she was unable even to make that the last straw. She gave him a social unconvincing smile on which she intended him to leave the room.

'Don't imagine anything at all if you can help it at the moment,' he said, and she answered with lightning clarity:

'I sometimes think that the only imagination we have is in thinking that we have it.'

She is not dead, he thought to himself; just badly shocked; she'll recover somehow and recognize herself again, but what the *hell* do I *do*?

He threw off his clothes, to indulge in the immediate escape of sleep, but he dreamed and dreamed, and woke sweating from elusive fears to sleep and dream again of the same unidentifiable anxiety and grief. When, eventually, he looked at his watch, it was after four, and she had not come upstairs. He was strung up to the point when her not being there disturbed him. All the evening he had dreaded the end of their day together, but now, at this hour, the suspense had degenerated to an almost physical alarm, when he knew that he must find out where she was.

She lay huddled at one end of the sofa. There was a lamp lit by her desk which made very little light in the room. She wore her coat, and there was a handkerchief clenched in her hand. Her face, touched by shadows and marked with the tears which had died on it, was the colour only of shadow and light, and absolutely still: her head propped in the extreme corner of the sofa seemed unnaturally disposed for such stillness. He stood, remembering the last time that he had found her asleep there, and how remotely, perfectly beautiful she had seemed – the picture presented itself and then faded before the reality of her now. Now she was not beautiful, she had no appearance for him; he felt only a confusion of gentle recollections – of when she had been vulnerable: afraid, or ill, or tired, or sad – of times when, afterwards, he had wondered what she would have done without him – to ease her safety, to free her from fears, and enclose her with affections. The price of sustaining their marriage at so high a tension of reality and love had been those casual infidelities which, from time to time, he had needed for the satisfaction of that aspect of him which dictated no fair bargain, but a simple gain – the something-for-virtually-nothing, assurance-of-vanity requirement: an instinct common to all men, and too often disastrously fulfilled in their wives or sublimated in their work. 'What you do every day must be better done,' his father had once said to him, advising him against what he precociously outlined to his father as a five-year plan; 'therefore, be cautious of routine: employ it only so much as you can live up to it. Let your second-rate behaviour be as random as your mistakes are various. Do not join that insufferable body who remain constant to their disabilities.' His father had been the only man with whom he had felt any affinity. He remembered how, when his father had died, old, impoverished, and sanguine, 'I have drawn the distinction between life and death: I have been a noble grasshopper!' he had actually wept, and turned blindly to his wife. Now her father had died, and she had not been able to turn to him because Imogen had not been, was not, a casual infidelity. With the heart you have no choice about chastity, he thought; it is not a question of morality: it just won't split. I love her, he thought, thinking of Imogen, and walked slowly towards his wife.

She stirred as he leaned over her; her hands shot upwards with a convulsive gesture as though to protect herself; a frown fled across her forehead with the curious lilting speed of a sharp breeze across water – her eyelids trembled – she woke with a hard desolate little cry, and shrank away from him as though he was some blinding light. Staring at him, she began weeping: even before she was awake her tears streamed uncontrollably – she put her fingers under her eyes to break the rush of tears, and as he knelt by her he thought she made some faint incoherent negation of something that was not to be said or done. He heard himself asking the gentle foolish questions that are asked of children or animals – meaningless words that discover nothing; a helpless attempt at comfort since there is never any reply – but she seemed beyond comfort. He saw her cast wildly round the room for escape, and then back to him immediately before her.

He stood up, and told her carefully what he was going to do; but when he bent over her she resisted him with a kind of weak frenzy, until she was in his arms, sobbing bitterly now as he carried her upstairs.

He laid her on the bed, and, shutting the door, watched her a moment before getting sodium amythal from their bathroom; but when he returned with the capsules and a glass of water, she lay as he had left her, her hands clenched by her sides, weeping, but more quietly. He offered her the capsules and she frowned twice and shook her head; he propped her up and told her to take them – she gave a deep sigh and did as she was told.

Swallowing the water helped her to some control of herself, and she asked for a handkerchief. When he came towards her with it, she said: 'Please don't ask me: please don't speak to me.' He shook his head, gave her the handkerchief, and began to take off her clothes. When he had found her nightgown and pulled it over her head, he collected the pins out of her hair until it was also undressed. He pushed her hair back from her face – she seemed much calmer – and thinking that she had reached that need, he kissed her forehead – but she twisted away from him with a small heartbroken sound. Better trust the drug and let her finish, he thought; it isn't a bitter sound any more; but what have I, or anyone else, done to her? I've never seen her break like this – she is far beyond anything I've ever known about her. Hysteria . . . but then if one thoroughly understood the reasons for anybody's hysteria, one would be hysterical oneself. He had continued rhythmically to stroke her head. He felt that she was very near sleep; her eyes were closed and she was quiet. He was just moving to switch out one of the lamps, when she whispered: 'Conrad. I haven't got my watch.'

'Do you want it?'

She nodded.

'Downstairs?'

There was a pause, and then she said slowly: 'I put it in the fireplace. I so much hated the time.'

He found the watch lying in a corner of the hearth where she must have thrown it, as the glass was shattered, and the lovely enamel back badly cracked. He pulled out the remaining splinters of glass and took it up to her.

'Is it broken?'

'It doesn't go, but you'd better wear it.' He fastened it round her neck, and as she looked at him with infinitely grateful calm before her eyelids closed again like heavy books, he said: 'I don't suppose it is irreparable. At any rate, I will try and get it mended.'

'*You* will,' she murmured, with content.

'Yes,' he answered. '*I* will.'

TEN

'What is the matter?'

'Nothing.' She went on studiously arranging the flowers he had brought her with unnatural finnicking concentration.

'That, my very dear Imogen, is just a time-wasting reply.'

She looked at him over the roses with defensive hostility. 'It is what you often say to me.'

'And then you ask me again because you really want to know.'

She took a rose out of the bowl, and broke the stalk. 'You ought to know without being told.'

'Is it because I cannot stay to dinner?' He knew that it was, but he felt too weary for an argument.

'Because you won't stay. Oh – not really even that. Because you don't want to stay. You say your wife will be alone if you do, and I shall be alone if you don't.'

'You must accept that. I told you on the telephone this morning.'

'I know. I do accept it – I try,' she corrected herself, 'but I can't help minding.'

'It is only one evening, and anyway, here I am now.'

'You mean I see so little of you, I should make the most of it?'

What an interminable brink, he thought; each thing

we say, or rather I say to either of them; lines of it, days, weeks . . . to either of them . . .

She swept the broken stalks off the table into a waste paper basket. 'Down on my knees, and thank God gorging for a bad man's love?' She was trying to play his game, and smiled unhappily.

'Where did you get that from?'

'Out of *The Taming of the Shrew* and out of my head.'

'Well! Does that mean that you are a shrew and I am a bad man?'

'Poor Conrad. You do look dreadfully tired.' She ran to get glasses. How few women run prettily indoors, he thought. With any luck we shall be all right in a minute.

When she had given him a drink, she dragged her yellow cushion up to him and they sat in an abstracted but amiable silence, until she said: 'I think really I meant that you are trying not to be a bad man, and I am trying not to be a shrew.' Then she looked up at him solicitously, and added: 'I'm sorry if I am one.'

He laughed, disarmed, and kissed her: and throwing her arms round his neck she clung to him, without speaking, or kissing him.

'I shall have to get rid of my glass if that's how you feel.'

But she slid away from him on to the floor again, and said hurriedly: 'Will it be like this for long?'

'Our being in love?'

'No – your worrying about her. Is she very unhappy about her father?'

'She is very unhappy, anyway, not entirely about her father.'

'Will it be like this for long?' she repeated.

'I don't know, darling. I'd tell you if I knew anything.'

She sat silent for a moment, picking the fringe of her cushion, and he felt her struggling to control herself, and knew that she could not, long before she cried out: 'I'm jealous of her! I've tried and tried not to be – it is the worst feeling I've ever had, and I don't understand it at all. I am so miserably awfully jealous I feel sick with it, and the rest of the time I am so ashamed. I thought if one was so dreadfully ashamed of a feeling one could get rid of it. It isn't hating *her*, really, I don't even know her – it is your house, and your furniture, and what the rooms look like that I've never seen which all belong with her; and your friends, and all the years and hours you've spent like that; making plans at breakfast, and then if you've planned that I should see you, you can't, because your life with her streams steadily on, and with me there are just isolated flashes.' She looked at him with miserable honesty. 'I don't expect you to understand about being jealous. *You* don't feel it, but with me it goes on and on however hard I try, until I can only try not to think about you at all, or I spoil you in my thoughts. I don't expect you to say anything, but I am so dreadfully ashamed, I thought you ought to know.'

'Why do you think that?'

'It wouldn't be fair,' she answered simply: 'you might be imagining me better than I am.'

There was a pause, and then she said carefully: 'Please could I have a cigarette?'

When he had lit one for each of them, he said: 'Have you thought at all why people fall in love or love one another?'

'I have thought, but I don't know.' She spread her fingers with a little movement of denial. 'I don't think I know anything.'

'It seems to me quite simple. It is always based upon some mutual requirement, or complementary need. The point is to concentrate on what you have got with anyone, and not on what you haven't.'

'Well?'

'Well? You work that out.'

'I know you want me,' she said, after thinking a moment, 'you find me attractive, and you need someone for that.'

'There have been moments when I thought that feeling was reciprocal.'

'Yes, but—' She frowned with the desire to make herself understood. 'I can't concentrate all my – my feeling into simply going to bed with somebody. It isn't all I want.'

'Then don't. Don't try to concentrate it. Split it up among more people.'

'That's what I can't do!'

'You want to spend all your time with one person, being everything to them.'

'No.' She was nearly angry. 'You are sophisticating the argument. Of course I don't want that. I just can't divide my heart, that's all. Perhaps you can, I can't. Perhaps men always can, or perhaps their hearts don't run over into all their life. I told you, I don't understand anything, I'm trying to find out because of what I told you just now.'

'You thought if you knew more, you would not feel jealous?'

'I thought it might help me not to,' she answered.

'There isn't time to talk now, but you are wrong about my being simply attracted to you. You really know that, but perhaps it needs saying.' He got up and smiled at her. 'I need you in more ways than one. We are not really so dangerously different. I am simply older, and consequently more dishonest. Don't be infected by me. I must go.'

She walked downstairs with him to the door. At the door, she touched his arm timidly: 'Conrad. Does *she* need – does she love you – do you think?'

'She – no – I don't think she really loves me.'

How curious, he thought, walking away from her, how curious that it should be so much easier to betray someone if you kiss them.

∞ ∞ ∞

He walked, past the taxi rank, half way up the wide dreary road to the park, and then stopped; neither wanting to go back to the rank, nor to finish the dreary road. There was nowhere to sit – he was forced, in this case, to employ an alternative. Then he saw a telephone box, and felt hopefully in his pockets for pennies, but there were none. I will put twopence into each suit, he thought, and was flattered by even so small a resolution.

He pressed button B in the box and twopence jostled forth. He began dialling Imogen's exchange – Really, the whole business is becoming positively Freudian, he thought, as he started again. He wanted to evade dinner at home with his wife, and he succeeded with unexpected ease. She answered; his brother Joseph had turned up, and invited himself to dinner. He asked whether he might return in time to drink brandy with them, and added on an impulse of candour: 'I have something to think out, and want to dine alone.' Afterwards, he wondered whether he had been foolish to say that: perhaps she would not believe him. He did not usually give such weak reasons for his absences. But the truth *is* weak, and very, very, flexible, he thought in his taxi, extraordinarily hard to break, however improbable.

All the time in the taxi, the crisis gained momentum, although he refused to acknowledge it until he was actually dining.

He chose his food and wine with great care, almost with the deliberation of a man for whom it was to be the last meal. He had not, he supposed, the Embankment mentality; in trouble, he was more of an Algernon.

He looked round the small restaurant: it was half full, and he had easily secured a corner. He was the only man dining alone; although often before he had observed somebody doing exactly what he was doing, and had wondered idly why they did it. Boredom and greed he had usually concluded. Perhaps he had been wrong. Perhaps they, too, had been unable to nerve themselves on to the merry-go-round without the support of good food and wine. He took a last look at the couples round him, decided that the best things in life were very, very expensive, and plunged into his private vortex.

He began with the premise that his behaviour was inexcusable: there could be no excuse for making two people who loved him continually uncertain of his affection or interest, and therefore extremely unhappy; but if the situation continued, this was inevitable.

If, as Imogen had confirmed, the heart could not be divided, why did they require the heart? Why could not his wife be content with his children, their houses, the certainty that he would not socially compromise her, and the knowledge that if she kept her head they would be old together? And Imogen . . . why could not she settle for his desire, the more exotic amusements, and spasmodic, but fairly regular attention? They might, of course, either or both of them, be induced to accept their portions, but, he realized, only at the expense of those virtues which made them in any way desirable. They were not naturally promiscuous, and therefore any attempt at imposing promiscuity upon them was bound to lead to disaster. On the other hand, he could hardly expect his wife indefinitely to lead a celibate life (he remembered Marseille, and her misery the previous night, and began to understand that situation) . . . nor could he expect a young and beautiful creature, designed for love, to live undamaged by his partial return. She would grow older – she would rationalize her real needs by something less attractive. She would, she must, to some degree become capricious and demanding, dishonest and resentful, as his wife must become dulled by their mutual deceit, and both discover that there is no humiliation so entire as not being quite good enough. If their lives continued like this, there was a far greater chance of Imogen being unfaithful to him. He realized with some shock that even the thought was intolerable. 'I don't expect *you* to understand about being jealous,' she had said: and then remembered what he had felt about his wife the night her father had died. He had then, he supposed, felt jealousy, of a sort, although it seemed odd, and really rather unpleasant to be jealous about somebody whom one did not want. Did he then, perhaps, want and need both of them, and was it simply their whole-hearted temperaments which made the business so exhausting? It was not until then that he understood their likeness to one another: Imogen was potentially his wife; his wife had been an Imogen. His reason snapped under the weight of this discovery, the clarity of his mind gave way to a mist of memories . . . of his wife when he had first seen her – so lovely, so young, so despairing of life . . .

Before he had spoken to her, before he had even known her name, he had wanted to be responsible for her peace and pleasure; he had known that her despair was deeply attractive to him (it had none of the second-hand chronic quality he usually associated with the word) and he had been certain of success for the simple (and, now, he thought, astonishing) reason that he had never wanted anyone so much. He had pursued her through her indifference, her almost savage shyness, her countless unpredictable fears, her secret prejudiced intelligence – she had succeeded, he found, in concealing from her family both her heart and her mind, they having vitiated her beauty for her by so constantly denying it, that when he had first told her she was beautiful she had lunged out at him wildly and cried that she knew what she looked like – he need not look at her. When, as a result both of his perseverance and his extravagant imagination, she had finally consented to marry him, he instantly removed her from her family – he remembered stopping the car, rushing into a chemist, and flinging a toothbrush into her lap 'for your new life'. That had been the beginning. That was years ago, and he did not want now to recall the landmarks which pointed their descent.

Imogen, however, had not been complicated by a singularly destructive family and that other misfortune (he did not choose to think of that now); she surely was not therefore so vulnerable? But he knew that she was as likely to be hurt by him as his wife had been hurt by anyone else: as he might now hurt his wife. I've simply picked the wrong characters for this situation, he thought, or at least, one wrong character, but when I picked the other kinds there wasn't a situation, because I didn't care in the least. But to manage *this* efficiently, I've got to care so much that I shall be good for nothing else, and I'd give a good deal to be clean out of it. He began to imagine himself clean out of it – away from both of them, irresponsible, and alone: he did not get very far because he now knew perfectly well that alone he would search for another responsibility – another Imogen – another wife. If one thoroughly knew oneself, he thought, one would be incapable of moving at all: the whole thing would be like a chess championship without any opponents. Of course it isn't ever like that; it is much more like seeing all the pieces of a jigsaw puzzle, and only being able to fit them together after the event, when it doesn't matter.

Whatever I do, they must leave me alone afterwards, he thought: for a while – if they will – if they can. But, of course, there will only be one of them left to do that, and I have already bruised their sensibility and undermined their confidence for too long to expect much intuition from either. They will know what it is like and talk about it, or they will be silent because they don't know – no, they won't be silent, and I'm not at all sure that I can stand anything that either of them will say. I have decided nothing! he thought, struggling with his disgust, nothing, except that it is intolerable to decide nothing. That is what I am here for, to make decisions and then go on living them until the very end of my life.

He did not want to eat any more. He asked for his bill and a shilling. When the waiter put the coin on the table, he said:

'No, toss it for me.'

The Cypriot smiled with pleasure, tossed the shilling, and covered it with his hand flat on the table, with a gesture both lightning and pedantic, like a man silencing a drum.

'What is it?'

'It is the head, sir.'

He had wanted it desperately to be the head; but now, it being the head felt entirely wrong. 'Toss again. Best of three.'

'Again the head.'

He felt a surge of terror opening across his brain like a fan, and asked sharply: 'You rigging it?'

'No, sir! I spin with gravity.'

'Spin again.'

'It is the third head.'

'Thank you.' He signed his bill, and got up. His legs were trembling.

The Cypriot hovered, anxious to finish the game – wanting to keep the coin. 'No doubts – same every time, sir – no doubts. You keep the shilling, perhaps, for luck?'

Fleming said heavily: 'Good night. No, you keep it. It is no earthly use to me.'

ELEVEN

'What is the matter?'

(She doesn't know, or she wouldn't dare ask.)

'Conrad!'

She doesn't know. He nerved himself – and failed. 'I am very tired. Let us both have a drink.'

'I thought you'd already been drinking.'

'My dear, you sound like the little woman in a Victorian *Punch*. Anyway, how do you know?'

'I smelled whisky when you kissed me.'

'*Did* I kiss you?' He looked so startled, that she laughed, and said: 'You've done it before, you know.' She gave him his glass. 'Iris is going to have a drink with us before she goes out to dinner.'

'Shall we take her out to dinner?' But at the same time she said: 'I've cooked ours; sorry – no, she's going out with some people she works with. She's always going out.'

'Why don't you go with her?'

'I used to – sometimes—' she hesitated: 'I'm perfectly happy as I am. I don't need new people.' She turned to him defensively: 'You don't mean go out with her tonight, do you? You aren't ditching me tonight?'

'You talk as though my ditching you was an everyday practice. Most unfair of you.'

'Darling – I'm sorry! I really am. I think I've been a

bore – wanting things I can't have, and letting you know it. I know you are having a bad time. I'll try not to make it worse.'

'Do you mean that it is all right your wanting things, provided you don't let me know you want them?'

'Yes – if they are things I can't have. I'm learning.'

He looked carefully at her face, which had now the variations for him of a piece of familiar beautiful country: this evening he found the discrepancy between her determination to learn these painful grown-up tricks and the candour with which she explained her learning heart-rending . . . his anxiety for her increased.

'It isn't all right, you know,' he said gently; he wanted to touch her like that: 'it is entirely wrong. It shows what a magnificent image you have made of me, and how little I am worth the gilding.'

Before she could answer, Iris, dressed as someone for whom the pleasure of going out to dinner was a duty, came into the studio.

The conversation was desultory: he was watching Iris – wondering how much she could or would help Imogen. Then he discovered Iris covertly watching him, and the atmosphere heightened. Imogen, intent upon these two people she liked and loved approving of one another, seemed oblivious of the cautious worldly appraisal which was exchanging.

'I think I have found a job for you,' Iris announced to her when Imogen returned from one of her many anxious missions to the kitchen.

'Oh! What? Iris feels I lead a very useless life nowadays. She is quite right, of course. Is it' – she made a wide gesture – 'is it going to increase my experience of life?'

'I thought it might increase life's experience of you,

229

which might be a good thing.' She looked at Fleming, to see whether he would identify himself with this challenge, but he simply asked:

'What is the job?'

'It is in my office, needless to say.' Iris got up and walked to the stove. 'It's – well to begin with, it's simply stooging for someone who does all the interviewing. Not simply interviewing people for work, but about their personal worries, and whether they ought to have grants, or leave, or a change of job. If you are any good, I thought you might do that in the end.'

'Iris, how could I? I don't know anything about money or people.'

'I think you might learn. *If* you took the trouble to learn, I think you might be good at it. They want someone, and I have suggested you. They would like to see you, anyway.'

'Thank you. Thank you very much. Yes, I will go and see them.'

Fleming said: 'What is the matter? Don't you like the idea?'

'Oh, I do. But it sounds so fearfully – responsible. I can't imagine my doing it.'

Iris said: 'You seem to take those responsibilities which have come your way quite seriously.' She did not add, 'too seriously', but Fleming knew that she meant it – as a second challenge.

'I think it sounds an excellent idea. Don't refuse it, and don't give up for at least six months,' he said, and felt Iris's attention.

'When do I go and see them?'

'I'll fix it tomorrow. I wanted to talk to you first.'

'Thank you *very* much, Iris. I'll try and be a credit to

you.' She was in the kitchen again, and they heard her thumping something. 'Oh, damn, we've completely run out of salt: I did know we had really, it's my fault, I forgot. There isn't a grain.' She returned shaking the tin.

'Get some off the caretaker, or buy a packet of crisps at the pub,' said Iris.

'You do have such *immediately* good ideas. I do see why you're so important in your work.' Iris made an affectionately ironical face. 'I'll take an egg-cup down to Mrs Green.'

When Imogen had gone, Fleming, for no reason that he could afterwards understand, said: 'You dislike me. Why?'

Unperturbed, she answered: 'I don't know you. I dislike what you are doing to Imogen.'

'Why?'

She regarded him silently for a moment, and then said: 'If you don't know why, you are also a fool.'

There are very few women, he thought, who can be as quietly completely rude as that, and get away with it. His respect for her increased.

'It isn't as simple as you think—' he began, but she interrupted:

'Oh yes, indeed it is. It is perfectly simple. You have no right to take a highly strung and totally inexperienced girl, inspire her with a whole range of emotions which you haven't the faintest intention of reciprocating, and expect her to drop the lot and get over it the moment you are bored. There is a word men use about women who do that to them in a rather different context, and the only distinction I can see is that what you are doing does more lasting damage.'

'You've left out one important factor.'

'You aren't going to tell me that you love her!' She gave a short incredulous laugh, and threw away her cigarette.

'Does that sound so impossible to you?' It had not occurred to him that she could disbelieve his loving Imogen: he had thought that he was the last person to make that discovery.

'Really, I think it does.' She lit another cigarette. 'I know that I am being rude.' She waved away his box of matches with her silver lighter. 'Oh, I'm not being coy and calling myself outspoken. I'm simply being rude. But I cannot understand why, if you care about her at all, you should pick Imogen for this role in your life. There are dozens of women to whom it would, no doubt, be the most frightful fun – why not one of them?'

'Why do you think Imogen needs so much more protection than anyone else? Why should *she* be so vulnerable?'

Iris was silent for a moment, staring past him out of the big window. 'I think, because, apart from her astonishing appearance, she has a heart,' she said at last: 'for other people – not simply the common set of egocentric reactions like most of us.'

He leaned forward – urgently – but before he could tell her, they both heard Imogen's step – and he leaned back.

Coming into the room, she caught the end of his movement; sensed the air of tension which had preceded it, and said: 'You look so – so *momentous* – like a still in a breathtaking film. What *are* you talking about?'

'Minorities,' said Iris. She smiled briefly, and got up, shaking specks of ash from her navy blue taffeta skirt.

'That explains it. Poor them – or do you think they like it? At the art school it was vulgar not to be in a minority; everyone was.' Nobody said anything, so she continued:

'Mrs Green grinds her salt! It's extraordinary how the proper things for cooking are always so much more trouble, isn't it?'

'The proper things for everything are always more trouble, I'm afraid. I must go, or I'll be late.'

Fleming said: 'Shall I get you a taxi?'

'Thank you, but the rank is only a few yards. I'll walk to it.'

Imogen was in the kitchen. Iris walked to the door.

'Goodbye,' said Fleming suddenly, and as she turned to face him Imogen called:

'Shall you be late; have you got your key?'

'Of course I've got my key. No, I shall be back early tonight.' She was still looking at Fleming. 'Goodbye,' she added quietly, and went.

All the while that he watched her laying the table with the care and concentration which he now recognized she peculiarly associated with him, he tried desperately to think how to hurt her less: what omissions, what emphases he should make; whether a line of near truths should be left her as props, or whether she would find it easier to be told the whole truth.

At dinner he made her talk, while bright mad visions rocketed up in his mind, to explode at the second before they became brilliant . . . of his taking her away with him – somewhere – anywhere – that night; casting the dried painful skin of his other life – of beginning with her, of starting again – of never again creaking up that steep hill in a taxi to his house, hesitating in the lock with a key that did not always open the door at the first turning, looking automatically to the left at the ebony table for letters that he never wanted to read; of the stairs – the sharp corner, and the drawing-room patterned with the furniture always in the same position – and she always there – lying, sitting; always in one of the familiar attitudes . . . there need be no preamble, no words; simply never, never, returning there – losing at once all memory of how he had done those things . . .

He had asked Imogen to tell him everything she knew about Iris: he did not think she had noticed that he was not really listening. Watching her, he imagined how she would be if he said: 'We are going away together.' 'Now?' 'Now. As soon as we have finished dinner, of course.' She would not hesitate: she would be radiantly simply confident that they could go away and start a new life. He had done that before: she had never done it, and so she would be certain.

'. . . when we've finished dinner.'

'What?'

'Oh, darling, you don't listen to a word I say. Such a waste of all my small talk.'

'I do listen with the greatest pleasure.'

'What did I say about Iris then? You see!'

'That she was in love with somebody once,' he began uncertainly, then remembering Iris, he improvised: 'but that he went away with someone younger and more attractive.'

'*Not* younger. Exactly the same age – the same everything; except that she was more attractive. Am I very boring? You did ask me, or I wouldn't have told you.'

'I did ask you. No. What was it you said about after dinner?'

'I thought I might play the gramophone – properly – I play it very well, and then we need neither of us talk.'

'After dinner,' he said painfully, 'I shall probably want to talk.'

'It's really after dinner now,' she said.

'Is it?' He looked at his plate.

'You don't want to eat,' she said gently, taking away his food. 'Please, Conrad, you are not simply tired. What *is* the matter?'

They moved, with one accord, to the upright uncomfortable sofa, and sat, one in each corner, so that they were nearly facing one another. As he began to speak, she raised her hand – as though, he thought afterwards, she already knew, and wanted to preserve the last minute of them – but she dropped it again, and he did not stop for the momentary instinctive gesture.

He told her quite simply in the end. That he could not sustain the present situation, either for himself, or for her, or his wife: that he had therefore to leave one of them: that his wife needed him, and must be his first consideration, and that for these reasons he must leave her – Imogen – altogether: 'Not see you any more.'

However slowly or gently one used those words, the speed, the impact, was like a bullet, he thought, as in so short a time he saw her face wither, and then begin to freeze into a kind of courage.

'I don't expect you to believe me, but I do know that it will be better in the end for you if I go. In the end it will be better,' he repeated, trying to reach her, but she had retreated already some separate agonizing distance.

'You are much younger than she – you see – it makes a very great difference. You have time to get over it: it is why it hurts so much now.' She nodded dumbly; he was not even sure that she had heard what he had said.

'You are young, and beautiful – and now she is not so much those things – she would not know – I do not think she would know how to do without me – either if I stayed, or if I left her altogether.' He remembered what his wife had said about people in pain: how everything seemed to contract, except their eyes.

'You are too young for me to be a tragedy. I don't suppose you can believe it, but you will forget about me entirely in the end, and that is a good thing for you to do. She wouldn't, you see. She couldn't. There are the children—'

'The children,' she repeated after him. He waited, and then she said: 'Is that why?'

'No. I am being entirely honest. They are not the reason. It wouldn't matter in the least to *them*, except through her. No – I have been thinking of her.'

'You told me she didn't really love you.'

'I lied to you,' he answered heavily. 'I lied. She does love me.'

'And really, you love her.'

He checked his instinctive denial: he could not now expose her to his miserable conflict and uncertainty, which must from this moment be his private affair.

'Yes. Yes, I love her also.'

He saw her face touched with a tremor of anguish, and then close again. She said nothing.

'I could have told you that I was leaving you because of the children, but it wouldn't be true. I have never cared about them, and consequently they do not care about me. They would not have been enough cause. There could be only one reason which would make me do this.'

'I know.'

He had been staring at her hands, clenched upon one another – locked together until the bones of her fingers seemed to show white through the skin – now he looked with sudden hope at her face, where the bones seemed white also.

'You *do* know. You do understand.'

She bent her head. 'Awfully difficult for you to say.'

There was a brief silence. She was still dazed, still collecting her courage; then she said: 'I didn't realize at all about her.'

'What didn't you realize?'

'About your loving her.' Then she added almost to herself, 'About your not loving me. You – don't – love – me.' She said the last slowly, as though she was learning something new – incomprehensibly difficult.

'You are wrong!' he cried: 'You don't understand – that isn't the reason – you must know that I love you.'

'You've just told me about loving her. You've only just told me that. You cannot love two people.' Then, very sadly, she said: 'I expect you thought you did.' She cleared her throat. 'Isn't it odd? Tonight, when you began telling me, I had no idea – I thought that you were going to tell me that we couldn't have so much time together: that I was becoming possessive – that I must be content with much less of you – and I wanted to stop you before you began – to tell you that I loved you so much that I *would* be content with very little – to see you once a week – once a month even, if that made it easier for you . . .' She stopped, as though she had suddenly realized the futility of saying any of that now.

'That wouldn't have been any good you know: for either of us. That just doesn't work, I know it doesn't. It only works if the people aren't in love. You see, I *do* love you.'

But she cried with suddenly passionate bitterness: 'You *can't*!' and he watched her leave the sofa and walk to the window, knowing now that she would never believe it – like Iris, but for different reasons, she found it impossible to believe. I can't even try any more to make her understand, he thought, any more than I can go to the window to comfort her: it would only last longer for her if she knew now that I loved her.

She had been standing very still with her back to him. Now she said: 'Why did you do this? You must have known how it would be. Why did you do it? Now that *I* know, I would never . . .' Her voice, which seemed to come from a long distance, tailed away, until she turned to face him, and asked, as though struck by a new and frightful thought: 'Has she – I suppose she has felt like this – all this time?'

He got up. 'I don't know how she has felt.'

'Of course, people aren't the same.' She met his eye, and smiled politely; she seemed to be waiting for the end; but he stood, not able to move, seeing her as though he had never seen her; loving her then almost as though he did not exist; aching to reach her, and knowing that he could not. Out of touch with her now, he thought, and that is the last thing I shall be to her now, until I become an uneasy aching memory, and oh God let that be soon.

'I didn't *know* you, you see. I didn't recognize you in time. That was our disaster.'

She shivered, and moved further from him.

'I think I had better go now.'

She was staring at the ground between them.

'I hope it is all right for you: with *her*, I mean.' She tried to look at him, and failed. 'Yes; I think perhaps you had better go. Now,' she added faintly, and he knew that she had come to the end of her strength about him. He walked quickly across the room without a word, and shut the door without looking back. As it shut, the first wave of despair for her flared up with such violence that seconds later he was still leaning against the door, moving his hand across his eyes again and again in an effort to see the stairs.

As soon as he could see where they began, but before he could distinguish them clearly, he went.

The easy hard way out, he thought, as the taxi strained up the steep narrow road to his house. 'It's heaven to be home,' people often said. He had once known some people with a coloured butler called Peter.

He walked up the path past hollyhocks grown to nightmare size, and fitted the key into the keyhole, noticing how the paint on the door had discoloured round the brass. Cleaning up one thing dirtied another. A few platitudes on compensation gibbered in his mind while he opened the door – succeeding at the third attempt. He picked up a catalogue from Sotheby's, a letter from one of his banks, and a couple of bills; looked at them, and put them back on to the table. Catalogues are really rather soothing, he thought, they divert the mind to a kind of freakish acquisitiveness, they take one's mind off anything else: but then it isn't on anything else – I think it has been painfully removed, and I am doing quite well without it. He hit his elbow on the banister and recoiled out of habit rather than hurt. I am absolutely heartless, as people would say. He opened the drawing-room door.

The furniture, which seemed to have been rotating, or perhaps swimming round the room, since in moving it made no sound, settled itself as he came in, to the pattern he expected of it – the dented cushions in the corners of the sofa made it look like a fat person winking at him in sudden knowing intimacy – and everything seemed to have its back to the wall, but to be concealing nothing. For she was not there. He remembered Coward's line in a play about a husband or wife – 'Oh no, she's not dead: she's upstairs.' That didn't, of course, mean that if she wasn't upstairs, she must be dead. The sofa leering at him – its expression was too prolonged to come under the heading of a wink, did not now contain her. She had slept on it, wept on it, read and talked and lain upon it, but now he was alone. The variations of which women were capable in disposing furniture about their drawing-rooms were uninspired, he thought, showing only the lowest and most conventional view of social intercourse. There were endless possibilities, by which he thought he meant that nothing need ever remain exactly as it was. Things could always suffer one change – the alternative, with dreary rigid singularity, always lay in wait to halve pleasure, to halve all experience, he felt, but pain. You cannot be in two places at once, and he dragged the sofa to its other possible position in the room. The operation made him strangely breathless. He took off his coat. The last time he had kissed her he had not known either that he had kissed her, or that it was the last time . . .

She arrived some time after he had finished (he did not know how long). He heard the car, and although he did not consciously associate its sound with her, a sense of apprehension collected the wandering insensibility into which he had sunk. He finished his drink, picked up a book, and resisted a mad impulse to look in a mirror to make sure that he was alive and recognizable. He heard the front door, and remembered that her feet would make no sound on the stairs. She might come into the room, see him . . . 'Conrad! What is the matter?' She, too, might say that.

'Conrad! You've changed it all round!' But she did not look at it. 'Oh I am so glad you are here.'

'Do you like it?'

'I don't know.' She gave it an agitated glance. 'Why did you do it?'

'I thought it was time for a change.'

She repeated nervously: 'Change? Oh, the poor Sickert! Nobody will see it now unless you change the lighting as well.'

'I could do that tomorrow.' He had been wondering what to do tomorrow.

'What are you drinking?'

He looked at his glass. 'I can't remember. Do you want some of whatever it was?'

'Yes, please. Are you going out?'

'No. Why?'

'You look fearfully poised for something.' She held out her hand for the glass, and, unwillingly, he saw that she was exceptionally nervous: her fingers, out of touch with one another, were trembling: had she been at ease she would have examined the room; if she had been happy she would have come nearer to him; but she had not been happy for some time now, and she had barely glanced at the room. He smiled (it felt most extraordinary, but he thought it was a smile), and said:

'What have you been doing?'

'I've been to Sevenoaks.'

'Oh.' An interest in the other person's activities is essential. 'Was that nice?'

'I didn't *go* to Sevenoaks. Sevenoaks was as far as I got. I was going to Tenterden.'

'To be with the children?'

'To get away from you.'

Something in his mind screamed loudly, once, and was immediately, deadly, quiet. The sudden close-up sound was such a shock, that he was unable to speak. He looked sharply at her, as though he thought that she must have heard it too; she was leaning a little forward in her chair, but her face had exactly the same expression of strained last-minute courage upon it as before the scream. 'How blue your eyes are, Ernest! They are quite, quite, blue.'

'What did you say?'

'Nothing.' He shifted his position. 'Shall we both have cigarettes?'

'I thought we didn't smoke.'

'We didn't. That's why we ought to have one now.'

'All right.'

When he had discovered, and lit them, she said:

'I was going to the country to get away – hoping that if I didn't see you for a bit things would get better – you know what I mean – that we should be more – habitable for one another. Then, after I had started (I only decided to go after dinner), I began to realize that my going wouldn't make the slightest difference. You see, I should only have to come back to the same situation.' She waited a moment, but he said nothing. 'There seemed to be no plans for the future at all. I thought perhaps that if we talked, we should know if there were any – or not.'

'Suppose our talking discovered that there weren't any?'

'There couldn't be none,' she answered steadily: 'either you want me to go away, or you don't.'

'And you? What about your requirements?'

'It is no good my wanting against your grain,' she said, 'I have only just discovered that, but it has always been true.'

'None the less, you must want something.'

'Yes. Oh, yes.' She frowned tentatively at the ground, stopping as she looked at him. 'But I think women nearly always have several sets of requirements.'

'Which cannot all be satisfied. I don't think you need confine those states of mind to women. We all want something which we cannot have.'

'Yes. That is tolerable. It's the having something which we cannot want.'

'Well?' She was looking directly at him now: he noticed the blood perceptibly travelling faint colour over her face up to the smooth peaked line of her hair. The room seemed suddenly airless, or perhaps packed with cold dead air – involuntarily, he shivered, and saw her slight movement of sympathy.

'Well?' He said it again, to bridge the silence for her.

'I am afraid of having become that to you. Something that you have, and cannot want. You know what I mean by that.' Immediately, he was not sure. 'If – if you do feel that, I would rather know now, and then I would go away. But I need to know *now*. I cannot bear any longer not to be sure.'

'Why should you go?'

'Because my staying would become unutterably painful to you – until perhaps it became something worse. I know that much of you, you see.'

'Do you, then, care about me, even *love* me?' he asked, before he could stop himself: it seemed incredible to him now that she or anyone else could love him; and she answered stiffly:

'I told you, I know something about you, and you are not easy to know. I was not talking about love.'

With a sudden, almost violent movement, he got up from his chair and knelt by her.

'I think you were.' He picked up her hand (it was very cold) and held it in his. He wanted then passionately to denigrate himself to her, to cry himself down, to insist upon her understanding the worst of him, to finish this siege of her confidence in his merit, but he continued to hold her hand and said nothing.

'Well?' She was trying to look at him dispassionately – trying to withdraw her hand. Then she added with a kind of jerky arrogance: 'I can easily do it if you tell me now.'

He shook his head; he had become too much afraid of words, but she continued to stare at him with such urgent questioning, that he had to say: 'No. I *am* telling you now. Don't go away – don't think of it. Antonia!'

Her eyes filled with tears. She drew a long breath, and he put his hand on to her eyes.

'Don't cry now.'

'My name. It is so very long since you used it. No, I won't.'

'My dear Antonia. Most people hate their names.'

He took his hands away from her eyes and touched her head gently. 'Is that settled? Is that all right?' He was so exhausted by the situation that he wanted to confirm the ending of it. But she seized his hand, leant towards him and began rapidly:

'No – no, it isn't. There are things I have to tell you first – to try to explain to you – they might make you feel quite differently.'

'Are you so sure that you have to tell me?'

'I must tell you. I could never forgive myself if I didn't.'

He translated this last into the feminine, and waited.

So she told him about Marseille after he had left, and in her attempt to be brief and calm it became an attenuated unreal little accident – only credible because he recognized that for her it was a difficult confession; only significant because she found it necessary to tell him anything about it. How odd, he thought, listening to her, a poet can see someone in the street, and thereafter intoxicate others with what he saw, but she or I can thoroughly love, or think we love, and immediately after it seems incommunicable, or dies from our poor expression.

He felt no jealousy now – for a moment he wondered whether *she* was at this moment destroying her love by telling Iris – extinguishing it with her tears and protestations of its immortality – then pain engulfed him: he stopped thinking of anything, and hung drowning on to his wife's words. Poor Antonia: what a little, continuous, business is pity.

'. . . in London,' she was saying: 'back in London it all seemed like a dream – not good or bad – simply a dream which had stopped too soon – like most dreams, before the proper end of it, I mean. Then Wilfrid – Papa, was so ill. That was separate: it was easy to be single-minded about him. You were working, and – busy, and Papa needed all the time I had. The whole thing seemed merely an incredible interlude – except that I thought he was coming back to London and might write or telephone, but I didn't think about that much: I see now that I was afraid of thinking about it. I must really have known . . .' She did not finish the sentence. She was trying so hard to be painlessly honest – telling him so many things that he did not want to know – trying carefully to hurt herself rather than him.

'Then Wilfrid got worse, and I realized that he was

actually going to die, and that he knew it and minded. And then *he* rang up. Then I really did know. Even Wilfrid so ill, and arranging about the children, and worrying about you, didn't stop it at all.'

'Didn't stop what?'

She dropped her hands like small deadweights on to the arms of her chair.

'This consuming, uncontrollable desire to be with him. I can't describe how it horrified me.' Her fingers curled over the ends of the chair arms. 'I couldn't stop it, or understand it.'

'So you saw him?' He felt now as though he was finding footholds for her, or one more rung in the ladder of this perilous descent.

'Yes – no. I rang him up and told him that Wilfrid was ill, and that it would be difficult for me to get away. I said I'd get in touch with him when I saw a chance of being free. He said – 'she frowned – 'he said, "Well, make it soon." I didn't tell him anything – but after we had stopped talking it was worse than before. I couldn't go to the country because of Wilfrid, and all the time I had only to make one telephone call to arrange a meeting. It went on being so easy to do that for so many hours of so many days – telephones are devilish – I had never realized what a torment they could be – Conrad, I haven't realized anything – or certainly I *hadn't*. If one only just manages to resist something, one is too frightened even to feel good about it: at any rate I went on feeling ashamed, I suppose because I knew that I wanted him to telephone me again, although I'd told him not to . . .' She was suddenly silent, and pressed her hands on to her forehead.

'My dear, do you really need to do this? It doesn't matter now – to me, at least. You need not tell me—'

But she interrupted: 'Yes, yes, I must – because of how it ended. *Doesn't* it matter?' The last with such an arrogant pang of curiosity, that he replied:

'I meant only that it need not matter too much to you.' But he saw that she did not understand him. I can't manage this without more alcohol, he thought, and got up to replenish their glasses. As he leaned over the table beside her to pour brandy into her glass, she covered it with her hand – too late – and the brandy slopped over her fingers.

'Darling, you *always* do that – you never look.' She said it with an uncertainty, as though it was an experiment with security, which moved him. The trouble with human relations, he thought, is that the damned ball is *always* rolling, or in the air, never peacefully in the charge of one person. He said:

'You used to lick it off each finger in the most endearingly greedy manner.'

'I'm not endearing any more.'

'That isn't a statement people are allowed to make about themselves. You have to pay through the nose nowadays for the privilege of saying that sort of thing.'

She was silent, and he saw that she was still strung up with nervous resolution. He sat down again.

'Finish it.'

'It was only—' Her voice, usually so steady, sounded uneven. She began again. 'The point about the end that you have to know, is that after days of miserable indecision, I arranged to see him – to tell him that it must be all finished. I had to see him for that. I couldn't think how to write it, and I couldn't bear the idea of the telephone – you see, I didn't realize about *him* then – I thought, and really I don't know why, that he would find it just as frightful. I arranged to have a drink with him at some horrible hotel in Earl's Court where he was staying. I couldn't imagine him in it – but there he was, exactly the same, and at the same time at home. He met me as though I'd only been away half an hour. We took our drinks into a dismal little room that smelt of soup and was crammed with gold-painted basket chairs, and he said: "How much time have you got?" I said not very long, because I didn't think I could manage very long with him and stick to my decision – even *then*, I *still* felt that – "Well, don't let's waste it," he said with that smile which never seemed to change. I told him then. But, Conrad' – she was blushing with extreme humiliation – 'this is what I have to tell you. He didn't mind at *all*! I mean, it was clearly a bore, and not really what he'd expected – but otherwise . . . I'm afraid he noticed in the end that – that we didn't feel remotely the same about it, because then he said things that made it much worse, and I felt more of a fool – more ridiculous – you see, I'd bolstered myself up by thinking that I was doing the right difficult thing – in the end, of course – about nothing at all. I'd thought that it was impossible for me to feel so strongly like that by myself – that it was the only time when one is not alone . . . It was a frightful shock – pride, I suppose – I walked about for hours after I left him, trying to balance the thing up – to manage feeling a fool, but justifiably – but I couldn't. I went on feeling bitterly ashamed – as though I'd behaved like some idiotic young girl – it wasn't *his* fault, you see, of course I realized that – he was perfectly honest – I'd simply behaved like an hysterical fool.'

She had stopped, at last. At last, she had finished.

He cleared his throat. 'And then you came back here, and the telephone rang, and it was Wilfrid dying?'

'Yes.'

'You don't connect these events with one another, do you?'

She got up from her chair, and went to the window. 'Why do you ask that?'

Clearly, she did. People were so painstakingly irrational, he thought, it was a wonder they survived at all. Perhaps superstitions, innumerable though they seemed to be, provided a kind of bedrock below which a few misfortunes were eliminated; some griefs were unconnected with some other fears, some failures unrelated to any subsequent tragedy: a magpie is not, after all, invariably under a ladder on the thirteenth of the month. He tried this last observation aloud on her, and after a moment, she smiled, but remained at her distance from him, and he knew that she was awaiting some pronouncement. It was extraordinary, he thought, how people childishly expected the right change from any gesture they made to one another. Although it had been a part of his decision never to tell her that he had had to make one, he realized now that he had nevertheless assumed the immediate reward of her tacit knowledge – an understanding of him which would have precluded the indulgence of her confession. But the fact that she clearly knew nothing of his gesture shifted her behaviour from the level of indulgence to a significant point of courage, where she, in her turn, was waiting – to be seriously condemned – to be thoroughly absolved (she needed both; since in diminishing the virtue of fidelity for her, he would merely diminish her to herself). After these reflections like a scurry of dead leaves, he was brought back to her waiting face and the knowledge that his structure with her was

249

now so fragile that the handing out of any more stones might be positively dangerous. He said aloud:

'If I were Shelley, there might *be* a piece of bread in my pocket,' and she answered immediately:

'Or a *raison d'être* for me.'

'Oh, I have that,' he replied gravely, but he was secretly delighted with her, for breaking the ribbon at the end of this marathon – although neither of them dared to laugh.

She said: 'You know, I don't really understand you at all. Why Shelley?'

'Never you mind.' (Now is the moment to move – to go out of this room with her.)

But on the stairs she said: 'Conrad – you haven't told me – I should perfectly understand if you were – if you were—'

His heart sank. 'If I were what?'

She was standing two stairs below him – he could scarcely hear her. 'If I had – revolted you – too much.'

He put his hands on her shoulders, and as he touched her, he realized with a distant shock that he was feeling very sick. All the ugly splitting terrors that he had buried in his youth returned in the lightning sequence of nightmare: the hideous fear of being entirely inadequate – or of his mind watching his body race out of control over a precipice, with the sudden cheap explosion of desire – so quick and so violent that afterwards it seemed to have dislocated memory . . . the empty, nauseating relief, and the urgent need to escape into complete darkness – to be touched by nothing but by air or water . . .

This was Antonia – his hands were still on her shoulders, heavily, to prevent their trembling – a little more weight, and she would stumble on the stairs below him, she would be hurt, and then he would carry her up, weak and grateful for his gentleness . . . but he had not the courage to do it . . . The impotence of knowing oneself, he thought again, as his mind began to grind a way out of the situation, and he could again take refuge in ingenuity.

'You cannot expect me to be quite indifferent.'

She shook her head, and looked down at the stair between them, but he knew that that was what she wanted to hear.

'I am not revolted,' he continued more honestly: 'I just don't want to talk about it any more. I want to sleep. Come along.'

He held out his hand to her – he was so tired, that unless he helped her, he felt he would never reach the top of the stairs. In their room she suddenly kissed his hand, and before he knew it, he turned on her, crying: '*Don't!*' and saw her face change, even before she dropped his hand.

In the bathroom he discovered that it was only four hours since he had left her. For a moment he thought his watch must have stopped – his hurting her already seemed so far away. She would be asleep by now, he thought – at her age one sleeps in the end from exhaustion – for a few hours, at least, he would not be hurting her. This afforded him the small agonizing comfort of freezing bones before a fire – one could not bear to be comforted for very long. He must stop being by himself; go back into the bedroom: the whole point of the operation was Antonia's happiness, and he didn't seem to be making a very good job of that. If it is impossible to be in two places at once, it ought to be impossible to make two people unhappy at the same time . . .

She was sitting on a window seat, shrouded in one of

the green velvet curtains which she had pulled back in order that she might stare into the dark, and she did not immediately hear him. Possibly she had been crying; from her position of strained immobility and her silence he guessed that she had. As he approached her, she drew the edge of the curtain across her face before letting it drop, and turned her head to see him. Her face seemed not white, but the faint composition of water that has no colour to reflect, and he knew that she was a little afraid, because her eyes were dark, but no colour at all.

He said gently: 'We are going away together.'

Her hands separated nervously. 'Now?'

'As soon as you have had a good night's rest.' The echo, burning, writhed, twisted, and shot up the chimney of his mind: he shook himself, and said more resolutely: 'Tomorrow.'

She said nothing, but looked at him with a confidence which he found astonishing and dear.

'To Tenterden?'

'No, by ourselves. Unless you want the children as well. Do you?'

It was the first time that he had ever offered her the children – without cynicism, or anger, or the difficult jealousy against which she had only succeeded in protecting them – never herself: for the first time since these conflicts had begun, they were not being presented her as an alternative, and she discovered that she was content to leave them, and go where he chose.

She said simply: 'No, I don't want them.'

She got up, and he saw a single tear, like an odd leaf from a tree, fall on to the ground. She was taller than Imogen.

He put her to bed as he had always used to do, and

she turned obediently on to her side without looking at him. He put his hand on her head. 'Bless you,' he said, and seeing that her eyes were no longer dark, he bent down to kiss her. The delicate warm smell of her skin, so elusive that away from her he could never remember it, so distinctive that blindfolded he would have recognized it as essentially hers, gently surrounded his senses, and he kissed her twice, on her forehead, and on her neck. 'There.'

When he was in bed, and had turned out the light, she said:

'Conrad.'

'You want a handkerchief.'

He felt her shake her head.

'A drink of water.' He prepared to move, but she stopped him.

'No – Conrad, it was the beginning of it all – that girl. I think it was my fault. I won't be foolish any more. You have her, if you want. I do really know you don't love her.'

It was her utmost generosity, and she was rewarded by immediate dreamless sleep.

PART FOUR
1927

ONE

The situation between them must, she supposed, have been changing, steadily, but imperceptibly, since the moment that they had married. Certainly when they had married, she had been subdued, out of love, and more than a little frightened: she had resigned herself to him at least, she felt, with honesty and a determination to do her share of the giving: she had told him truthfully that she no longer felt unhappy – or, indeed, anything at all.

She remembered her voice repeating 'anything', because she found it so difficult to go on. 'If, in spite of that, you are absolutely sure that you want . . . but I don't see how you can be!' she had finished suddenly. There had been a short silence. 'I do – I do *like* you,' she had then said, and felt herself colouring at the inadequacy of such a statement.

'Good,' he had said: he had been observing her intently: 'Good.' There had been another short silence during which she struggled with what she felt was her intolerable lack of feeling.

'I *am* sorry that it is such a crumb.'

He had smiled then. 'A most trusting crumb.'

That had been when she had first expected him to kiss her – but he had not. When she had said that she dreaded telling her parents, he had not turned left into the lane by the oast houses that led up to her family's house, but had gone straight on to London.

'What are you doing?'

'Abducting you, with honourable intentions. Most people conduct their lives the other way round. You need not go back to them any more. From now on, you are my concern.'

They had married, very quietly, by special licence. 'We shall spend nothing on our wedding, and everything on our honeymoon.'

'But I shall need my clothes!'

'You will not need clothes. We are going to Paris.'

They had been in Paris for a week, and the situation *had* changed. Now, after seven days of a life so different that every conceivable aspect of it was new, she did not, surprisingly, feel tired, and she was so much less afraid, that she was both grateful to him and elated with herself.

He had rented a furnished flat with its owner's staff, a couple who appeared each day to cook, clean, and drive the motor car (he detested driving, she discovered, and had privately resolved to learn herself). He had not told her about the flat until they were arrived in Paris, and without knowing why, she had been alarmed at the prospect. 'I think you will like it,' he had said: 'People should never begin their marriages in hotels if they can avoid it. It forces them to tiresome extremes of privacy and crowds. But we need not stay there, if you dislike it.' Then he had added: 'I see you disposing yourself towards liking it.' Too nervous to reply, she had stared out of the windows of their taxi cab at the foreign beautiful streets of a city where she had never been until now. Shutters and chestnut trees, and a kind of wide straightness, she had observed. It was spring, and it was raining a little, sharpening the greens of the trees, and dissolving the watery greys and stones of the houses and pavements until they became simply streets – foreign street colour, she thought. The sky was patched up with whites and blues, and, far away, a delicate, stormy, early-evening yellow. Beds of tulips glistened stiffly from the shower; awnings and umbrellas were double striped with their colours, and the greasy dark streaks of rain. They crossed the river by a bridge that seemed to her decorated with immense pieces broken off from a gigantic chandelier. 'The Left Bank,' he had said. When they reached the flat, the rain had stopped; evening sunlight crept and trembled about the street, and when she got out of the cab there was a smell of hot fresh bread.

The flat had immediately delighted her. It had an air of retired distinction; the furnishings (excepting a lovely Modigliani head of a girl) were faded, and very simple. There was an open fire burning with exactly the right degree of discreet energy, and there was a bowl which seemed to her to contain a thousand tulips. 'I *do* like it!' she had exclaimed: she still felt then as though she were a guest at a long festive party he was giving, and she was anxious that he should immediately know her gratitude. She walked a little hesitantly about the room to express her liking, and then, when she saw him watching her, stopped, and ran her hand through her hair. Immediately, he said:

'I was thinking that you ought to grow your hair.'

She waited: she had already learned that none of his remarks about her appearance were unconsidered.

'Yes,' he continued: 'it will be more trouble to keep, but you will look so wonderful, that you will not mind that.'

'I will start growing it at once.'

'Good. You have plenty of time. Now. Would you like a bath while I look for something to drink? Would you like to go out to dinner, or to dine in?'

'Which would you like?'

'My darling Antonia – I have what I want. It is your turn to discover your preference and enjoy it. I brought you here for that purpose.'

'But you see, I don't *know*! I really don't know.'

'I shall go on sowing little seeds of certainty in your mind until you find out. You would prefer to dine in tonight, and out tomorrow.'

'Well, then, I should also like a bath.'

But when he had left her in the bedroom, she had sat on the edge of the bed and looked at her hand which seemed entirely covered by her wedding ring, and wondered what on earth she had done. There seemed to be no reason why, after those few terrifyingly well-chosen words said early that morning in such incongruous surroundings, she should find herself in Paris, in a flat, with someone she felt she hardly knew. While she was with him, she was able to crush these feelings of guilt at her inadequate return for his tremendous certainty; but alone, she felt wickedly afraid. Supposing, for instance, he had married her simply because he had not believed her capable of accepting him without returning his love? If he was so secretly incredulous, the whole thing was merely a matter of time – for what would become of them when eventually he discovered beyond any shadow of doubt that she had not, did not, love him? But I *did* tell him – again and again, she thought – he can be under no illusion: after that, I suppose I succumbed to his overwhelming determination. At least I will try to do my share of it all – I will try to *do* what he wants, even if I am unable to be as he would like me. These conclusions, by now, were familiar: she always ended with resolutions about him which were as frantic as they were ignorant.

She had not heard him come into the room, and she was unused to this particular violation of her privacy. He felt that, almost as quickly as she smiled at him.

'I'm sorry, I haven't begun my bath.'

'Why should you?' He came over to her, and sat beside her on the bed. 'I think I know what you are thinking.'

'I've stopped thinking it,' she answered defensively. He touched her hand.

'I am so delighted that you have actually married me. After that confidence, I do not expect anything else of you.'

'But it is you who are trusting me; it is you who have married me blind.'

He smiled. 'Not quite blind. Not absolutely.'

'I meant – I have not told you anything – about – any of it.'

'Ah,' he interrupted quickly; 'we know nothing about one another's lives.'

'I will tell you, if you want to know. And if you think I should.'

He thought for a moment, and then said: 'I'll tell *you* something about duty: there is no such thing as duty until one is presented with a positive alternative.'

'Am I not?'

He saw that she did not really understand him. 'Not yet. At any rate, I do not want you to weigh yourself down with good intentions: they are a terrible deterrent to pleasure. After dinner we will consider how our lives are to be spent here.' He got up. 'When you have had your bath you will find a box on your bed containing what is vulgarly and quite inaccurately called a tea-gown. I thought you might drink champagne in it.'

As she went to the door which she imagined led to the bathroom, he called to her:

'Antonia!'

She turned round: he was leaning against the other door, and his eyes were as intent as they were pale. 'Darling Antonia – there is one more thing. I have absolutely no intention of making love to you at present. So do not have anxieties or intentions about *that*, either.'

And before she had had time to realize that she could think of nothing to reply, he had gone, and the door was shut.

At dinner, he had presented her with a programme which was perhaps so fascinating because it was so varied, and invited her to choose what she would do first. When she had several times proclaimed her ignorance either of a particular artist, or even one particular art, or couturier, or place, or food, he had laughed, and simply said: 'I am not trying to inform your mind. I want merely to employ your senses – as many of them as possible. You need only tell me that you dislike listening, or, alternatively, that you have never listened.'

'Would you then despair of me?'

'Good heavens, no!'

'You do not want a well-informed wife?'

'I am not an information addict. No. I want you to be informed about your pleasures. I do not like the people who read fifteen books by a man who has written three worth reading.'

'But if one enjoys reading, one must be resigned to many disappointments.'

'Disappointments – certainly. But if you read a book and are disappointed, it is because you intended to be pleased. I only want your intentions of pleasure to be as widely diffused as possible. I do not want you to embark upon any venture with me privately convinced that you are going to dislike whatever it is. When you feel that, tell me, and we won't do it.'

She said: 'This applies to a holiday, I suppose.' She had been brought up very differently.

'No, no, to our lives. Holidays only mean a change of enjoyment.'

'Were you brought up to think pleasure of such significance?'

'No,' he said: 'so far as pleasure is concerned, I am an entirely self-made man. And money,' he added suddenly. 'My father was a tremendous investor in roundabouts.'

'And you?'

'Oh – swings,' he said. 'But not any more. When we go back I shall get something to do. By then, I hope I shall have stopped speculating.'

He spoke of himself with a kind of detachment which made her relation to him seem incredible. He saw her look up suddenly from her soufflé, and said: 'Don't be anxious. You have not married a man determined to gamble his last penny. I spend: I don't gamble. I've bought you a house, you know.'

'Have you? I wasn't worrying. Why should I? Where is it?'

'Ah. I am not going to tell you tonight. If you don't like it, we will get another. But I haven't furnished it at all.'

'Then we shall not go straight back there?'

'Oh, no. The first step is to put you in it, and then choose things that will go with you.'

'Are they not to go with you also?'

'I am chameleon,' he said, with a gentle, sardonic gleam. 'Shall we drink our coffee in front of the fire?'

Much later, after hours of easy animated conversation, he got up from his stool and said: 'Now, you are tired. We will talk more tomorrow.'

She had been so absorbed that she felt childishly cheated.

'How do you *know* I am tired?'

He stood looking down at her with his particular kind of tender detachment. 'Because pale blue veins appear on your eyelids, and because you have a little muscle here' – he put his fingers on her face – 'that ticks. See? The most exciting aspect of your beauty – Oh yes,' he stopped her defensive interruption – 'You have beauty now, but the most exciting thing to me is that you are clearly going to become steadily more and more beautiful – for years and years, and I am going to see you do it.'

She felt herself blushing as she stared at him.

'Yes?' he said, a moment later, as she had continued to stare.

'I – I was looking at you, too.'

He raised his eyebrows (a movement which she was afterwards to discover meant anxiety, or embarrassment), and then said indifferently: 'What do I look like?'

She looked at him with careful, enquiring gravity. 'You look,' she said slowly: she was still very unsure of herself: 'as though you ought to look as though you might be any age.'

∞   ∞   ∞

She had woken in the night, trying to remember the face of the man sleeping beside her in the dark, and found that she could not assemble his features . . . Perhaps she could remember his eyes – grey-blue, nearly round, sometimes instantly reflecting his mind; sometimes covered with glass curtains – revealing nothing: or the broadly thumbed planes of his forehead, inclining back to where his hair grew thickly in wide undulating curves like low tide in a bay. Fine, bright brown hair – a little like the song – but with him, a curious dense effect – like one-ply jungle. Or his mouth: there was something complicated and inconsistent about his mouth, but she was not sure what. She could remember these separate aspects of his face, but she could not co-ordinate them into any one expression – any sum total, she found, was related to his voice; a phrase he had used illustrated him, but only for the moment that it took her to remember the phrase. She lay awake a long while trying to 'collect' him, and she lay carefully still, because she did not know how easily another person in a bed woke up . . .

TWO

They had been in Paris for a week. Each day, each evening, appeared not to have been planned, but she felt now that the pattern they made together had too much design about it for pure chance and the choice of the moment. He always presented her with a choice, and she had learned that he liked her to choose – but he selected the possibilities – *he* chose first, and she imagined that he chose from things that he wanted to do.

It was late afternoon, and she was alone in the grey and white room where they breakfasted and occasionally dined. He usually brought her back to the flat at about half-past three, and went out again himself for at least two hours. 'We must never spend every hour of the twenty-four together,' he had said the first day, and she discovered that she enjoyed these short solitudes. Dominique left the flat at midday, and did not return until early evening: she was entirely alone. She could read (she was secretly improving her schoolgirl French); she could look out of the tall windows; one opening on to the paved and cobbled courtyard with the concierge's cane chair, and the other on to the tops of trees and tall narrow houses, with pigeons and the sky – a conventional top-floor view – but one which afterwards was essentially Paris to her. She spent most of these times, however, idly unpicking layers of new experience, comparing, considering, reflecting, anticipating . . . Conrad raking a picture gallery for its most hidden and exciting pictures; Conrad defeating the ingenious determination of a *vendeuse* at Worth to dress her in beige; Conrad exposing to her the brilliant vulgarity of French pianists; Conrad's intricate, intimate knowledge of the inside of the Louvre; Conrad's passionate unmasculine attention to every kind of detail – the perfect balance of a meal – the exact shape and colour of her shoes, her handbags, her gloves (tomorrow they were going to buy gloves); his magnificent generosity in bookshops (her favourite shops): there seemed to be so much to think about, so many things to consider . . .

Sometimes she slept, curled up on the sofa: her mind was now so constantly stimulated, that alone, it healthily drowsed. She was no longer actively tormented with those agonies of the heart which she had once thought (so short a time ago) would never leave her. She did not care to think about them, but she no longer found that she could think of nothing else. She had not once communicated with her parents since that day in the car with Conrad. *He* had seen her father in the country, and her mother in London, and he had returned from both those interviews enigmatic, and very gentle to her. They did not object to his marrying her, was all he would say, to which she had retorted that she was nearly twenty-one. Invalid objections could be far more tiresome than those which were legitimate, he had replied.

Well, they had not objected; she did not want to think about them, and now she had a great deal else to think about. After a week, she had still the feeling that she was a uniquely favoured guest at a long party: their lives were so plainly spent for her pleasure, that she could not see how to relate this week to the rest of their marriage.

For surely it could not continue like this – in London, for instance? He had said that he was going to work; that he had bought them a house – she thought carefully for any other indication of what seemed to her the realities of their life together, but could find nothing. Presumably, it would be her business to manage the house. In London, then, she would have a share: she would not simply be a delighted pawn in this complicated, amusing, decorative pattern he was designing for her. She wondered what kind of work he was going to do in London, and realized then that he had said nothing which gave her any idea of his profession. It was extraordinary, surely, to have married somebody and not even to know that? It was more than extraordinary, it was downright absurd; that he should not have told her, and she should not have discovered so elementary a fact. 'Dear Toni,' her mother had so often said: 'always *so* impractical! Such a juggins!' How she hated to be called Toni – to be called impractical – to be called dear or a juggins by her mother! She began, with almost tremulous defiance, to count up what she knew about her husband. He had a father living. His mother had died several years ago. He had a brother who had been a baleful witness at the Registry Office. He was remarkably well informed about the arts – about women's clothes, about wine, about scent, about food. He spoke French with (to her) unintelligible fluency. He was therefore an enchanting, a perfect companion for the life they were now leading. She had vaguely supposed him rich – they were certainly spending what seemed to her to be a fantastic amount of money; but she remembered his saying 'I spend money', a simple, forcible statement, which did not necessarily mean that he had an unlimited amount to spend; indeed, would be more likely with him to mean that he spent everything he had, and started again. But *how* did he start again? What did he do to earn money? Suddenly, she remembered her passport, with 'Married Woman' written opposite 'Occupation.'

His passport lay, as she expected, on his dressing-table. She picked it up, and hesitated: frivolous or sinister possibilities packed her mind – 'Agent', 'Dilettante', 'Burglar', 'Artist' – what did he look like? But he looked like nobody she had ever seen; in all probability he did something she had never heard of. She opened the book. His passport photograph, bland and furtive, stared at her. 'Lawyer', she read, and read again, 'Lawyer'. She shut the book, and walked slowly back to the sofa. Lawyer! And why should that seem so improbable? He wasn't her idea of a lawyer, but had she ever known any lawyers? Only an uncle, and she was still too young for a relative to contrive looking anything beside a relative. Uncle Simon looked the spit image of an uncle, and incidentally, was a lawyer. I know very little about Life, she thought sadly. Filled with this deeply private confession (it was not one which in any company at all she would have made), she lay down again with her feet higher than her head, which Conrad said was good for her admirable ankles, and tried to imagine life as a lawyer's wife. The trouble was that they were not now leading a married life. She was not certain what she meant by this, but essentially she felt that Conrad was not treating her as an equally responsible person. From that point, her mind raced. He was kind, he was charming, but she felt like a child, or like that song that her mother's friends had hummed and whistled while they marked the tennis court, or prepared the bridge tables: a great big beautiful doll. He was deliberately preventing her from taking on those responsibilities which she felt should be hers – or even from discovering what those responsibilities were . . .

Alone, without the looking-glass of another person's presence, the mirrors of the imagination sometimes effect cunning distortions. By the time Conrad returned, she was firmly grasping the wrong end of an elaborate stick, with which, given any chance at all, she was fully prepared to beat herself.

He returned a few minutes after six – a few minutes later than usual – to find her nervously reading a French newspaper.

He seemed in high spirits. 'I have secured our seats.'

'For what?'

'*Manon*. Is that a good thing?'

'Yes.'

He looked sharply at her: she was still looking at her newspaper, frowning with an appearance of concentration which was not for one moment deceptive.

'Antonia!'

'Yes?'

'What is the matter, Antonia? Has something happened while I was out?'

'Nothing at all.'

'You have not had a letter, or anything of the kind?'

She put down her paper, whose pages were beginning to tremble. 'No. But supposing that I had: I can manage my own letters, surely?'

He sat down. 'Of course you can. Why not?'

There was a silence between them. Then, because he showed no sign of giving her an opening, she cried: 'You don't take me seriously.'

She said it too sharply, and brought tears to her eyes. When she had shaken her head, she saw that he was actually laughing. Laughing! She was filled with such anger that she could hardly speak. 'You see? You think it amusing! I assure that – I assure you that . . .'

'What do you assure me?' He was smiling now – leaning towards her and smiling: she had an instant of hatred, violent, and, she felt recoiling from it, unaccountable. She wanted to strike him (how terrible: that he should be so near, and that she should want to do that!) then she saw him clearly again; noticed with resentment that his eyes were kind.

'I think you should tell me things. You shouldn't treat me as though I were a child.'

'I will tell you anything that you want to know.'

There was another silence. She did not know where to begin.

'Well – for instance—' She was striving for the dignity of unconcern. 'You haven't told me what you are going to do when we go back to London – *or* where we shall live – or anything which I might reasonably expect to be told.' She was feeling more unreasonably unreasonable with every word.

'No, I haven't. I didn't know that such facts were of immediate importance to you.'

'But of course they are! Imagine somebody asking me what – what my – *husband* did, and my not even knowing! Imagine how foolish I should feel!'

'Whereas if you could say that he was an industrial consultant, or a top linkman, you would—'

'But you are a lawyer!' she interrupted.

'Ah. How do you know that?'

She was sitting up on her heels on the sofa.

'I read your passport,' she said. She looked very much ashamed. 'I'm sorry about that. Rather base behaviour.'

'And you wanted to know about me in order to tell other people?'

'No – not really. *I* wanted to know, myself. Curiosity!' She was beginning to look frightened.

'I admire curiosity,' he said; 'and you have a perfect right to read your husband's passport.'

'I always meant *not* to exercise perfect rights,' she said quickly; '*you* don't.'

He raised his eyebrows. 'Do you want me to?' He saw her cast round the room as he had begun to learn she always did when she wanted to escape. 'If you rush away now, I shan't be able to tell you anything. You will continue childishly uninformed. Think of what you won't be able to say to people!' But she was not fit to be laughed at, so he continued: 'Now – this house. It is on the top of Campden Hill. It is far too big for us, which means that we shall be comfortable. Do you like furnishing houses?'

'Yes. Of course, I've never furnished any.'

'Of course not. Well, apart from one or two things that my mother left me made in equal proportions of French polished mahogany and horsehair, we shall be starting from scratch.'

'Can we afford that?'

'My mother also, surprisingly, left me a certain amount of money: so we can. We share money, you know,' he added. 'When we get back, I'll make a proper arrangement for you. *Your* mother is going to give you some also.' He felt her instant withdrawal when he spoke of her mother.

She said stiffly: 'Do I need to take money from her?'

'Not if you very much dislike the idea. She wanted you to have some, you know. She believes that women should have some independence.'

'I'm sure she believes that!' This was said with so much bitterness, that he could see she had alarmed herself. Suddenly, she leaned towards him, and put her hand uncertainly on his arm.

'I – do not want to be that kind of wife.' She was blushing painfully. 'Perhaps I have been very stupid. But it was not what you intended with me, was it?'

'It was not what I intended.' He got up, hearing her little sigh of relief and acceptance; still feeling her hand on his arm. He did not then know what she meant.

THREE

When she was dressed for dinner, he told her in meticulous, measured terms what she looked like, and she acknowledged them formally, but because he was entirely strung up and obsessed he observed in her the very faint displeasure of uncertainty. She had, that evening, the extraordinary quality of beauty which has not arrived, and he thought that when he told her how she looked to him she was aware of this.

They dined, and he took her to *Manon*. She had read the book, and she had expressed a desire for the opera. It was not remarkably given, but she seemed enthralled. When he asked her why, she said that the character of Manon filled her with astonishment and terror. (He noticed, with amusement, that she unconsciously employed adjectives the period and emotional calibre of the work required.)

He had proposed that they dance afterwards, but as soon as they were seated in a hot dark corner with champagne, whose temperature did not, as he remarked, conceal its inferiority, she began to talk. She said that the most interesting aspect of Manon was the ease with which she attracted those people most likely to precipitate her doom. Des Grieux might, as she met him, have been any man; but he was not; he was des Grieux. Did Conrad think everybody was like that? Did they unconsciously collect people who brought out their strongest weakness and fears? It was a frightening thought, but if it was so, it explained a great deal to her. Then she added casually: 'I was thinking of my father.'

This thoroughly startled him for the simple reason that he had been thinking of his father. How absurd, he thought, how that man Freud would laugh. How simply complicated we all are (he thought he meant complicated in the same way) but her next remark disillusioned him.

'I think you admire and like your father. You see, I cannot admire mine. In the circumstances, it should be easy, but I cannot.'

'How on earth do you know that?'

She turned to him with a little smile, gentle and triumphant. 'You never talk about him. You protect him with silence.' Then, because she was very young, she spoiled the effect by saying: 'I *am* right, aren't I? You do like him, very much?'

'We are not here to discuss our fathers.' He knew it was a reply stiff with weakness. She said quietly:

'I thought they were a little alike.'

'Our mothers were not alike.' The touch of malice did not escape her. She coloured faintly.

'I expect not.'

'Would you like to dance?'

She shook her head, and then looked to see whether he wanted to. There was something unbearably touching about her secret, sensitive desire to please.

'I have a box for you,' he said, suddenly. All the time now, he found himself taking refuge in generosity. He took it out of his pocket, and put it on to the table. 'No, I want to pour them into your hands.'

'Peridots,' he said, as she stared at the necklace of green

stones flung on to her fingers. 'The Edwardians liked them: they are not fashionable at the moment, but they are your colour.'

'Like moss – or stained glass.'

He looked anxiously at her: her expression was incalculable – desirable, so that he could hardly bear it.

'Do you like them?'

'Yes: oh yes. Thank you. But you give me far too much.'

He said nothing.

'They are lovely: a lovely colour,' she repeated, and poured them slowly back into the box.

'Home?'

She looked at him again – not a breath of her stirring on her face. 'If you like.'

'It is what *you* like that matters,' he said in the taxi.

'Why? Why not you also? I am not an invalid, or a spoiled child.'

'Of course you are not.'

She said in a low voice: 'At least I know what I am *not*.' She was sitting in the extreme corner of the taxi, away from him in every possible respect.

'When can I learn to drive a car?' she asked, much later, and he wondered how far and how fast her mind had worked to reach this apparent irrelevance.

'Why do you want to learn?'

'You said you disliked driving, and I thought it might be useful. Then I could drive you everywhere.'

'That would be perfect. Of course I should have to buy you a chauffeuse's uniform.' Immediately, although he could not see her face, he felt her anger. 'Antonia!' He put out his hand to touch her.

'You seem absolutely determined that I shall be useless!'

He waited, not daring to risk a return shot in this dark.

'It is the least that you might allow me to do!'

He said, after thinking about it: 'You will have to explain that.'

'You make it impossible for me to explain! I don't understand how you can simply want to dress and decorate me and show me all the things we have seen and heard this week – if you do not find it worth taking me seriously in any other respect. You make my marrying you such an unequal business! I thought we had talked enough about it for an arrangement to be clear – but obviously we haven't – nothing like enough: even now you make me feel ungracious, ungrateful, as I said – like a spoiled child. I don't want everything for nothing – surely nobody wants that!'

'What would you consider something?'

'It is not what *I* consider, it is what *you* consider—' she began, and then stopped, as she realized that they had arrived. He noticed her concealed impatience while he paid the taxi, and also with the public distance between the cab and their flat. Once there, however, where anything could have been said, she was at a loss for anything to say. She walked about the room, refusing to allow him to take off her cloak, and finally perched or poised herself on the end of the sofa, ruffled, and nervously angry. 'Well?'

He was standing by the fire, with one arm on the mantelpiece, very nearly sure of himself, but determined to wait.

'Why did you marry me?'

'I wanted to marry you.'

'But *why*? *Why* did you want to?'

He said nothing.

'You don't even know! Or perhaps you thought you did – and have found that you were wrong.'

Still he did not answer her.

'You see, I am *not* a child. I am not just someone to be dressed up and amused and fed.'

'What *are* you, Antonia?' Everything he said – every gentle enquiring word, contrived to accent her anger – to provoke her unconscious determination for a scene.

'You see, you *don't* know. You don't know anything about me. You cannot answer a single question!'

'I can answer every question. I can tell you exactly why I married you, and exactly what you are – going to be. I will in a minute. Take off your cloak – you have caught the end of one of your earrings in it – and sit down calmly.'

Of course, he knew that he was making calmness impossible – that he was inciting her to reckless behaviour. 'I don't want to take off my cloak, and I can hear perfectly well from here.' She tried unsuccessfully to free her earring from the gauze ruffle.

'I think I had better do that for you.' But before he could reach her, she had gone to the mirror to do it herself. He took a deep breath.

'I married you,' he said slowly and clearly, 'because you are going to be extremely beautiful, which means for me that you will be a pleasure to see, a delight to be with, and because, possessing you, I shall be envied by others. Knowing this, I wanted you. I married you because you are not a fool, because you have innate good taste, because you have a vast capacity for enjoyment, and because, if I was to marry at all, I wanted at least the possibility of perfection. You will not be perfect: but the amount that you will fall short will be my fault – not yours – and that responsibility is more desirable to me than anything else.

Being what you are, you had also the potentiality of utter failure: of being tragically destructive. You require a certain amount of protection not to become that. You are fortunate to have found somebody to take you so seriously as I have been doing, and as I will do. *I* am very fortunate to have discovered somebody whose natural talents make the whole enterprise so fascinating; to have found even the *possibility* of perfection. You see why I cannot help laughing when you say that I don't take you seriously.'

She had been standing with her back to him, and he knew by her stillness that she had most carefully listened. Now, without moving, she said: 'But what do you want me to do? What – part am I expected to play in all this?'

'I was waiting to see whether you were prepared to play any at all.'

She turned to him eagerly, and the cloak slipped from her shoulders and collapsed at her feet without a sound. 'Oh, I am! If only you would tell me what you want me to do, I would do it!'

He was staring at her so intently, that she found it difficult to go on looking at him. There was a long silence, and then, with a great effort, he said:

'Perhaps – perhaps you would.' He seemed paralysed.

'That is why I thought if I learned to drive the car . . .' she faltered, and stopped; dimly aware of the absurdity of cross purposes. He said suddenly:

'You were a little drunk – and now it is wearing off. We will both drink some more. And damn the car,' he added, as he went to collect champagne.

'When you are a little drunk, you become very fierce and careless.' He handed her a glass.

'What do you do when *you* are drunk?'

'I do nothing at all. I watch the sum of all my sorrows floating about on my own surface. Nothing.'

'Nothing,' she repeated, and drank.

'Why don't we understand one another?' she asked a moment later.

'I am understanding you,' he replied.

'Oh, *stop* that! How on earth do you know? Men always think that they understand women. Women, at least, don't pretend to understand men.'

'An inversion of the popular theory. Quite untrue, of course. Nobody understands anybody.'

'Nobody understands everybody,' she corrected, and then looked faintly surprised.

'Were you being shocked by your perspicacity?'

'No – by my capacity for the platitude.'

'You see, you *have* some sort of mind!' he cried.

It was a remark which she recognized was, for him, so naïve, that she burst out laughing – 'My mind!' and champagne slopped out of her glass.

He said stiffly:

'If one is entirely obsessed by someone's body, it is difficult even to consider their mind.'

She stopped laughing: for a second, she was incredulously still. We should hear her cloak drop now, he thought. He could barely hear more than her astonishment when she said: 'Are you? Are *you*?'

When he touched her, he thought she shivered. He kissed her sensitively, and she had not dissolved before him. He had suddenly a feeling of power and joy, and kissed her again to communicate it. Touching her, he seemed now to be creating and possessing her mouth, her shoulders, her hands trembling at the back of his neck, her violently beating heart . . .

He thought of moving her, but before he could collect the cloak from her feet, she said:

'Conrad. Most extraordinary – but I don't believe I can walk.'

He picked her up. 'At last – at last – I have succeeded in sweeping you off your feet.'

FOUR

In the night, she lay tired, and stiff, and still, and awake
– there seeming no beginning or end to her mind or her
body: or the whole world was a vast, painful, practical
joke: everybody, excepting herself, was endowed with
some extra sense, or perception of this mysterious, ubiquitous secret – 'It's a secret! Don't let's tell Antonia: she
wouldn't understand!' Now, she couldn't understand: but,
until now, she had thought that her feverish, almost
unbearable needs of the past year – that being stretched
upon the constant extremities of ecstasy and despair
because of the presence or absence of someone else had
amounted to the secret centre of love. Then, she had
thought that she had uncovered the meaning of the quantity of lovers whom she had encountered in literature:
she had understood that they were people; just as she
had understood that of the people surrounding her many
were doubtless lovers – loving and beloved. She had
thought then that she had been able to shake this great
kaleidoscope of emotions and people and make a comprehensible pattern, whose theme, or motif, or impetus, she
had understood. Now, suddenly, she understood nothing.
Either there was nothing to understand, or her ignorance
was unique; an aching lassitude, or the sharp pain of
isolation. 'Don't let's tell Antonia: she *won't* understand!'

She longed, with the wrong degree of exhaustion, for

oblivion; but as she stirred with cautious discomfort, on to her side, he drew her into his arms. The shock of his being awake, when she had been sure that he slept, broke her last reserve before him, and as his hands met round her body, tears poured out of her eyes, falling suddenly on her breasts and on to his hands, vanishing silently between them into the dark.

He said nothing – he thought he was remaining comfortingly anonymous, until she said:

'Could there be light?'

'It's on your side. I'll do it.' He leaned carefully over her and pressed the switch. Immediately, she looked up at him.

'I am so sorry for crying.' She looked anxiously about the dimly lit room and back to him.

He gave her a handkerchief. 'People often do that. Would you like a drink?'

'Water, please.'

The Evian was in the bathroom. He poured some into a glass: his hands were shaking so much that he spilled water from the bottle. He wiped the glass on a bath towel, and tested it with his right hand to see that it was dry.

She was sitting up in bed blowing her nose with a serious care that made her seem, if possible, even younger. He gave her the water, and stood beside her while she drank.

'I don't want all of it. Thank you.'

'Lie down now?'

She nodded, and then, without looking at him, she said with a little laugh which was meant to sound desperately casual:

'I hurt, rather.'

He touched her head, and then stroked it. 'People do – quite often, at the beginning.'

Then she did look at him, and, for a moment, he saw her new terrifying prospect. '*Other* people?'

He sat on the bed beside her. 'Many people. It is not at all unusual. Only at the beginning, you know – the whole thing becomes entirely different.'

'Oh.' He watched her trying to accept this, and then trying to believe the best of it. He said:

'You know I am getting very cold. May I get back into bed with you?'

'Of course.' She was still sitting up, and he pulled her gently against him.

'My poor Antonia. Did you know absolutely nothing about it?'

She shook her head. 'Not very much.' He felt that she was going to say that she was sorry, that it was her fault, and put his hand over her mouth. 'My poor Antonia. My fault—'

Before he could tell her that he loved her, he felt her fingers pulling his hand from her mouth. 'Oh no! Because I know now, that I could not have – that it would have been impossible with anyone else!'

Afterwards, while she slept, peacefully, trustfully, in his arms, he lay awake, calming the small drifts, those little flurries of desire, which recurred, and then subsided – imperceptibly – like single feathers from the soft pillow which he shared with her. She lay in his arms . . . desire, he reflected, was not enough.

∞ ∞ ∞

In the morning he woke late to find her still in a deep dreamless sleep – she seemed not to have moved all the night. He ordered their coffee, and shaved, and she was still asleep. He began to be afraid of waking her; but the coffee was ready, and drinking hot coffee was an excuse for starting her day. He stood for a moment looking down at her. She looked remote – profoundly engaged with her sleep. He touched her: her eyes opened immediately and shut again.

'Antonia.'

She opened her eyes.

'Coffee, Antonia.'

She stretched slowly, and then lay perfectly still, looking at him. She seemed then to him incredibly, frighteningly beautiful.

'Is it very late?'

'Fairly late. Time for coffee.'

'I thought it was late,' she murmured, and sat up.

She was warm and naked: he saw her breasts start a little with the cold air as he gave her her dressing-gown. He was pouring her coffee when she said:

'Conrad!'

The dressing-gown lay loosely round her shoulders: she took a quick little breath, and turned her face up to him.

When he had kissed her, she said:

'Lighting me for the day – as though I was a fire,' and then looked at him with a kind of nervous affection.

'Put your arms in – you are still half asleep.'

But she answered: 'Oh no – I am perfectly awake now.'

It was her first experiment in loving him.

∞   ∞   ∞

The tempo of their life changed – became less designed, less charted with organized amusement. They spent hours walking slowly about the streets; hours sitting outside cafés with what Antonia described as 'practice drinks' (she was working her way through the vast repertoire of everything that could be drunk in a café or bistro) – days of idle discovery – outwardly exploring Paris, but, as he once remarked when they were hesitating over which street to take: 'Our destination is really one another' and when she asked:

'Haven't we arrived?' he said at once:

'Oh – we shall travel all of our lives: there is no arrival.'

They talked – and they were silent. There was privacy for intimate detail – there was leisure in which to mark time. Once – very late in the evening they were sitting inside a café; she was drinking her first Pernod – and he was watching her, concealing the amusement which her dogged and impartial experiments aroused in him. She put down her glass with a startled sigh, and said: 'I had imagined it clear – and bright green.'

'Are you disappointed?'

'Oh no. But now I have two ideas about Pernod.' She thought for a moment, and then added: 'Like Paris.'

'Have you two visions of Paris? You'd better drink some more of that or you'll never get used to it.'

She nodded and then said: 'I nearly always do – about everything. It's odd: but the actual experience of something never seems to interfere with the imagination of it beforehand. It just means that one has two of everything. Do you think when I'm ninety, I shan't remember which is which?'

'We shall have to wait and see.'

'How did you imagine Paris?' he asked a few minutes later.

She thought for a moment. 'All the trees pale green,

or with flowers on them. The buildings like slices of one enormous castle. Women wearing high heels and pink hats – very tidy animals with ribbon round their necks. The men with beards, and rather dark and boneless, and the children with long hair and white dresses and black stockings playing on neat bright green grass. Round tables out of doors with wine on all of them, and baskets made of plaited sugar with sweets made to look like something else. Fountains about everywhere, and sunlight with dust in it. At night, hundreds of lights in the streets – no curtains and the windows glowing: and steamers on the river with music coming from them. People going to the opera with monocles or black velvet round their necks. Large black pots with just water and carrots and things in them, but steaming deliciously – and butter made into swans and roses. Scent, of course, wrapped in beautiful little boxes, and people spending the whole day choosing a really pretty paper-weight . . .' She stopped for a moment, and then said: 'Of course, I'd never been here.'

He looked at her with such grave affection that she took the plunge.

'What I can't imagine properly,' she said at last, 'is our life in London – I mean about your work and everything.'

'Let's dispose of that quickly. What do you want to know?'

'Well – what kind of lawyer are you?'

'Company law – very lucrative and interesting. I've got another man to work with. You won't have to be nice to him – he is without exception the dullest man I've ever met in my life, but he's exceedingly good at his job. You needn't work up a wifely enthusiasm for my career: I am by no means dedicated to it and don't want it overlapping with our life.'

'I thought that all good lawyers took it very seriously!'

'I'm probably a very bad one. A real menace to society. If I turn out like that I shall have to think of something else to do, shan't I?'

She stared at him, perplexed by these uneasy proportions of mockery and truth.

He took her hand. 'Your first concern, my darling, is our house.'

FIVE

Back in London, he showed her their house. The first time she saw it, it was empty and very dirty, and during their visit there was a thunderstorm. When they arrived, the house seemed filled with dusty sunlight, which rose politely from wherever it had been resting on floors and window-sills, and then hung motionless and golden in the air until they moved to another room. But before she had seen the whole house, the sky had begun to darken, to behave like all the romantic pictures of storms: the flowering trees in the square were swaying – their leaves suddenly distorted by gusts of panic – a crescendo of movement before the first explosion of the clouds. The explosion – the violent implacable rain. As she turned to him he put his hand on hers.

'Does it frighten you?'

She nodded. She wanted, as suddenly as the storm had started, to be lying in his arms – to be entirely surrounded by him. This desire occurred with such furious single-mindedness that she clung blindly to him – until his arms went round her.

'Not fright,' he said, and there was just time before she kissed him to hear his amusement.

A minute later he said:

'What a mistake it is to take a *totally* unfurnished house.'

289

She did not reply. She was exhausted.

'Shall we go?'

She looked at the streaming beaten windows.

'Well, we shall just have to get wet. Do you mind very much?'

She shook her head, and they started down the steep dark stairs.

He said: 'You mustn't tell me you are frightened when you aren't – or I may not believe you when you are.'

When she remained silent, he put a hand on her shoulder.

'Antonia!' He felt her shiver. She looked up at him quickly, and away again.

'I won't then.'

'Shall we come back tomorrow?'

'Yes.'

As they slammed the front door, there was a clap of thunder immediately over their heads. She looked so white that he began again to think that it had frightened her, or, at least, that she very much disliked it.

'Take my hand and we'll run to the bottom of the hill.'

She took his hand, looked at him again with a kind of astonishment, and said faintly: 'I love you.' She felt so shaken by the violence of her discovery that it seemed hopeless to say any more. She dropped his hand, and they ran steadily separate down the hill to Holland Park.

They were staying in a small hotel in Kensington. It was what most of its inhabitants called quiet, which meant that it combined an air of restrained discomfort with bad food, and the apparently everlasting boredom of both the staff and the guests. It smelled faintly of Madeira cake. 'Contrast, my darling. It enables us to concentrate on one another and our house. And of course we provide a delightful contrast for them,' he had added. That had been yesterday, and today she considered the prospect of their rooms, decorated in shades of saxe blue and mud, with a contentment that flowered now in the taxi almost to ecstasy.

'You must have a hot bath,' he said, and she noticed they were both soaked.

'Both of us.'

'All right. Then an extra-large Ark Tea.'

They had discovered that tea in the hotel was graded in three stages of daintiness, but whatever its size, there was always a pair of everything they ordered.

By the time they had arrived, and paid off the taxi, she was beginning to feel cold: but her hair lying dankly on her head, the little icy shocks that seemed to originate from her throat or her wrists or her ankles, were all overlaid by a kind of joyful certainty – of ease and of excitement.

They walked out of the rain and into the warm brown afternoon paralysis of the Tea Lounge, and while he collected their key, and ordered tea to be sent to their room, she collected the battery of dull cardiganed curiosity which concentrated upon them. On the stairs she laughed and said: 'They always feed the animals half an hour earlier than one thinks. There were two llamas in the lounge.'

'Llamas will eat anything. Tea-cake, loose covers, paper napkins.'

'Serviettes! They've got bluebells round the edge.'

Their sitting-room seemed dark and cold.

'Now. We'll draw all the curtains, and light all the lights and the fires. I will. You get out of that ridiculous coat.'

But when, a few minutes later, he joined her in the bedroom, she was still standing just as he had left her, and with a little sigh – half sensual, half despairing – she threw herself into his arms . . .

After that, he was easily able to dissuade her from wearing innocent, sensible night-gowns. 'You really cannot wear wool next to my skin.'

∞   ∞   ∞

In the weeks that followed, before they moved into Campden Hill, he concentrated upon the house, and she upon him. She spent most of the days with him, and for those hours when she was alone (and without him, she seemed to herself to be alone) she thought, with a curious limited intensity, about Conrad, about her love for him, and about love. In love, she fell, as though in a dream, an incalculable distance – from a height where she had scarcely breathed, to the brilliant warm air of affection, down to an earth which was only inhabited by Conrad. Looking into water or a glass, her image seemed to be Conrad's, and she fell further, drowning in the composite reflection. She discovered that this delight of loving did not dissolve her perceptions into some shadowy amalgam of his own; nor did it dull the activities of her private mind (which before loving him had been her only resort to pleasure); but found herself living at a sharpened pitch, where her intellect was more alert, her judgment more apt, and her ability to express what she thought, and felt, and saw, and heard, was enhanced by this new passionate devotion. Her senses seemed now to be suspended at a level which, in fact, he had determined, just as her choice of colours or furniture for their house was set in his key; but from that level and in that key she became original.

The days were spent in choosing and buying: in taking things to be altered, or cleaned, or painted, or recovered, or sprung, or mended, or made into something else: in harrying the chimney-sweep, the plumbers, the builders, the house-painters and the various domestic agencies. In the evenings they would bath and change and escape from their hotel to the theatre or cinema or a restaurant. He did not suggest other people to her, and it did not then even occur to her that except for a nod, or his particular way of raising his hand across a room or a foyer, they never met any. She was utterly absorbed in him and in their house. At the end of each day she was physically tired, but she was so happy, that even her fatigue was a new kind of delicious contentment.

They had decided to furnish only their drawing-room, dining-room and bedroom, leaving the top floor of the house untouched. Their dining-room became green, their drawing-room white and yellow, and their bedroom (she wanted a wallpaper, but was imperceptibly over-ruled) a Venetian red with white furniture. Three times she endured the fearful ritual of interviewing a servant, unsuccessfully, and on the brink of a fourth attempt she lost her voice. 'I didn't know you disliked it as much as that,' he said; 'I'll do it.' She gazed at him gratefully un-comprehending.

'Got her,' he announced on his return. 'Not the one they sent. *She* was just another anaemic harlot with a squint.'

'Who *did* you get?'

'A nice young round one. She says she can cook, and she looks capable and greedy.'

'Where did you find her?'

'Coming out of the Agency, on her way to interview someone else. Her name is Dorothy,' he added.

'Dorothy what?'

'I haven't the slightest idea. We shall have to wait until somebody writes her a letter.'

SIX

He took her, without warning, one day to see his father, who lived in a little villa in Maida Vale, near the canal.

'Does he know we are coming to see him?'

'No, he dislikes plans.'

'How do you know he will be there?'

'He always reads in the afternoons.'

She noticed that he was almost snapping with irritation. He pulled the bell, and pieces of plaster fell off from round the knob. It was the first time that she had observed his nervousness. Before the watery jangle had died away, they heard a heavy uneven tread, and saw, through the blurred glass panes of the door, the dark stooping figure of a man. She touched his arm. 'Your father?'

'No, no. George. Good afternoon, George. Is my father at home?'

'Oh yes, Mr Conrad, 'e's *in*.'

'This is my wife.'

George finished shutting the door, and turned deliberately to face her. She held out her hand. 'How do you do?'

He looked doubtfully at her hand, and then shook it. 'How do *you* do?' He managed to make it sound like a shaky retort. She noticed Conrad prowling restlessly away from her, and followed him.

Conrad's father lay in a huge basket garden chair on

a wrought iron veranda so small that his chair occupied all of it. He was almost entirely covered by a paisley blanket, and was reading a small but she thought unusually heavy book; his hands shook so much with the effort of holding it that she wondered how he managed to read.

He put down his book and looked up at them as they stood in the tall narrow frames of the French windows: he looked quickly at his son, with a curious, almost photographic glance, embracing him in that short exposure of time – and then slowly at her – his eyes, she now saw, were as clear, as simply inquisitive, as the eyes of a child.

'Madam, you have bereft me of all words. Unfortunately, I am, for extraneous reasons, transfixed.'

She said nothing: she felt unaccountably shy – afraid of moving or speaking (moving forward was, in any case, virtually impossible).

'A triptych, Conrad, I have no doubt, but move me in, and get that lazy old devil to give us some tea.'

George immediately appeared out of the dusky room, and she retired into it while the two men carried the basket chair back into the house.

'Well – and how do you like Conrad?' he asked – but he asked with a kind of innocent malice, which was more endearing than offensive.

'Very much.' She looked up, and caught the crescendo of a gleam, before he turned to Conrad and said:

'I think that shows good taste – a trifle esoteric, perhaps. It is an extraordinary pity, considering the selection one is supposed to employ over all sorts of trivia, that one should be so powerless in respect of ready-made sons. I have no daughters, as you know, and I do not imagine that you expect me to make some queasy sub-sentimental remark about having gained one now. But I am delighted to see you, as indeed, anyone would be. I am ravished by this lovely appearance you have made.'

His voice was very like Conrad's, she observed – gentle, a little pedantic in pronunciation; but he spoke with an effortless flow, unusual, she felt, in someone of his age (his appearance was formidably ancient).

'I did not attend your wedding because I no longer go out – the conduct of my mobility is now so elaborate – such a precarious business, that I have ceased to feel it worthwhile. The hills remain green for too long nowadays to sustain my interest in their metamorphosis. And George,' he raised his voice as George trembled into the room with a gigantic tea tray, 'George has always been a man of inaction – a creature whose mind vacillates and whose body is unaccountably frail.'

'I'm not tied to me chair 'aving to read books all day.'

'He is deaf also,' said Mr Fleming sadly.

'We're none of us what we were.' She watched George rearrange the paisley blanket with shaky care. 'And you'll strain yourself insulting me one fine day. Water off a duck's back – shall I pour out?'

'Madam will pour out,' said Mr Fleming instantly.

'Arf a cup for 'im, or it'll be slop slop all over the blanket.' George grinned with sudden malice, revealing a set of startling aluminium teeth, and then, content with his last word, shambled out of the room.

She looked at the two men – at Conrad sprawling in his chair, uncharacteristically silent – at his father smiling faintly down on to his uncontrollably shaking hands.

'Antonia,' Conrad indicated the tray.

She asked hesitantly: 'Do you really want half a cup?'

'Oh yes. He's perfectly right: since my last stroke I produce a storm at once in a full tea-cup. Why were you called Antonia? I imagine your parents were expecting a boy.'

'Yes.' She began handing him his tea, but Conrad intercepted it. Mr Fleming continued gently: 'You must have been a most marvellous shock to them.'

She noticed Conrad arranging a bed table which he seemed to have procured from nowhere; as he put down the cup, the old man looked at him with a sudden, agonizing gratitude. She felt Conrad as suddenly withdraw; with a denial in him so violent that she thought he must have moved or spoken, but she could see that he had done neither. She remained frozen with concern upon the crest of a situation which she did not understand, until she felt her hand burning against the tea-pot and heard Mr Fleming's unexpectedly tranquil voice: '. . . and bramble jelly. I shall only want one, so I should like it exquisitely spread.'

The business of eating and drinking was painfully precarious for him, but he carried the situation with a courteous serenity – talking all the while – saying, not the first thing which came into his head – his mind seemed so freakishly packed that she could not imagine there being room for any casual thought – but freeing from his imagination a cloud of ideas which circled about the dingy over-furnished room like exotic birds. He did not ask them any questions, but she found herself telling him about Paris; discovering, as she told him, that she was also telling Conrad: and that the implications of her memory and her delight gave him pleasure. Fleming was attentive; Conrad seemed more at ease, and she was filled with grateful relief at finding herself so charmed and apparently so charming. Eventually, when she had reached the point of their new house, she stopped suddenly feeling that she had talked too long, and asked Mr Fleming whether he would come and see them there.

'Ah: that I might do.' Then, turning to his son, he said: 'Those houses are surely rather large. Are you going to keep great state, or are you merely providing for a host of healthy intelligent little sensualists?'

Conrad shrugged his shoulders, but she saw his face close up to a lack of expression so complete that for a moment she was afraid, but Mr Fleming, who could not have observed this, continued: 'Conrad, unfortunately, does not like children. I fear that this is the natural result of years spent with Joseph – and really he can hardly be blamed. Nor can I. Joseph would undoubtedly have been a suitable son for someone – even, indeed, an admirable brother – but from the earliest moment it was clear to me that that inability to select one's children would in the case of Joseph prove disastrous. You know how all babies have an ineluctable dignity which enables them to survive any quantity of humiliating circumstances? Joseph was the only baby I have ever seen without it. Now, of course, he has contrived a good deal of pomp with no circumstance whatever. But perhaps, on the whole, I have still been more fortunate than most parents.'

At the end of this speech, he turned affectionately to his son: she watched his expression – his older-relation-of-Conrad's face – close, like Conrad's, to a deadness which made them, for a moment, identical.

The crack of silence, like all terrible silences, came to an end – in reality, perhaps, almost at once, but in her frightened feverish ignorance its end seemed later than she could bear. During it, Conrad had got up and walked to the fire-place, his father had struggled with the last of his tea, and she had sat with her mind racing from one blank wall to the other. (Children? But why should he feel so passionately about them?)

'I want to give Antonia a present. Conrad: the object which is, I think, on the extreme right of the looking-glass.'

That was the breaking of the silence. Conrad picked it up and presented it to her. 'A present from my father.'

It was a snowstorm. She suddenly remembered having one as a child, and wondered where it had gone, even when it had vanished. Hers had been a small thatched cottage with two pine trees; this was a lighthouse on a rocky point surrounded by raging sea.

'You must shake it,' said Mr Fleming, and she felt him watching her intently while she shook it, and the little globe gently seethed with snow. She held it so that he could see. He watched it to the very end, and then murmured: 'The best illustration of casting bread upon the waters. Do you want it?'

'Yes, please. I used to have one, but I lost it,' she said to strengthen her desire for his present in his mind.

'Well, don't lose that one. I often fear that they will cease making them.'

'I won't lose it. Thank you very much.'

'I haven't much nowadays, to give,' he said: he looked suddenly very tired. Then he raised himself in his chair: 'He often comes to see me – you don't mind that, do you?' He shot this out with a kind of querulous anxiety – damn her if she stopped it, but he did hope that she wouldn't.

She said: 'Of course not. I should hate you to be wasted,' and wondered whether that meant anything to him. But he collapsed again in his chair and muttered: 'Every other day, you know. I read, and digest the matter, and then I am able to tell him a number of things which he probably does not want to know.' He looked up. 'At least he allows me to fulfil the function I have invented for myself. Divide your life so that you take longer over living than you take over dying: that's the ticket.'

Conrad nodded at her, and she rose to her feet.

'May I also come and see you again?'

'My dear, I should be desolate if you didn't.' He held out a shaking hand: she thought that she was meant to take it, and then realized that he was trying to point at something.

'That picture. I want to load you with presents. Go and detach it.'

It was a small upright panel; like no picture that she had ever seen. It presented a vast, pale coil of smoke rising upwards, into which were woven four figures. At the top and the bottom appeared a spirit, each holding by the hand a small child: but the children were being separated – their arms were stretched out to one another – their faces touched by an anguish of parting, as the spirits, the one with an inexorable serenity, the other with an inexorable evil, seemed, with soft silent motion, to be dragging one child up and the other down. All colour was subdued to the fantastic design, and the implacable contrasts of the four faces. Her attention at this moment was distracted by Mr Fleming's voice:

'It is a panel eighteen inches by ten, painted in tempera by William Blake. I want you to have it.'

'The man who wrote the poetry?'

'The man who wrote the poetry.'

She looked quickly from Conrad to his father.

'Oh! Thank you for it! It is the first picture that I have ever been given.'

'It is the last picture that I shall give.'

'For both of us?' She felt in some way that Conrad had detached himself from the present.

'No, no. I never give a present to more than one person. Diffuse giving in that manner and it becomes a public-spirited affair – generally vulgar and heartless.'

'I see.' She was thinking about it; delighted, and also a little anxious – that she should be given such a picture – that Conrad, obscurely, did not want her to have it.

'Like people, it is capable of many interpretations.'

Before she had thought, she answered aloud: 'And one at a time will never be enough.'

He raised his eyebrows. 'One person?'

'I meant one interpretation.' Again she looked at Conrad, and got nothing back.

'Now you must go.'

She put the picture on her chair, and moved nearer him, with some idea of taking his hand. 'Goodbye. I do thank you for both my presents.'

But it was he who took her hand in both of his, so that she felt their trembling on the palm and on the back.

'It is curious that once I thought I had married you. It took me so much time to discover that I hadn't.' There was a short silence while he gazed at her in a manner both penetrating and gentle; then he added: 'You see, I have *always known* what I have been missing.' He gave her hand a little shake. 'That is why I have given you my picture. Away you go.'

They left the house, and she had not forgotten the snowstorm.

SEVEN

She broke their silence in the taxi by saying:

'I *do* like your father,' and he answered politely:

'He, as you saw, liked you.'

In the minutes which followed this exchange, she discovered that words break only the crust of a silence, and that uneasy silence is fraught with unspoken words. She wondered why on earth she had not discovered these sad familiarities before.

'I don't know anything,' she said aloud.

'What is it that you want to know?'

She turned to him. 'I don't think you can tell me.' For a moment she saw him respond with a flicker of amusement at her surprise, then, as she added: 'I shall have to find out for myself,' his face clouded again to this new passivity which she did not understand.

After a long pause, he asked: 'Is it your intention to have a large number of children?'

This question, both bleak and blank, warned her that she was very near an edge, but she did not know how near, or how dangerous: in an attempt to shift her ground, she said: 'Do you dislike the picture? Why are you angry?'

Without looking at it, he replied: 'It is a good picture. I detest it. I detest it,' he repeated, as though that ended the matter.

'But, Conrad, *why*?'

303

He was silent.

'You haven't answered my question.'

He looked at her, she felt now, with deliberate hostility. '*You* have not answered mine.'

She realized suddenly that the taxi was grinding up the steep hill to their house. At the same moment, he said: 'We move in tonight. A surprise for you,' and she felt her heart drop down out of her throat.

When they stopped, she leaned towards the picture that had been propped on the floor of the cab.

'Give me your snowstorm,' he said, and took it, and shook it gently. 'Now that I *do* like. That is a present which I thoroughly approve your having.'

The way in which he said this angered her, and she retorted: 'Yes: because it is suitable for a child! I have been moved in here like a child. I do not want this kind of childish surprise.'

Instantly she felt his fingers murderously separate on her wrist – she thought that he was going to say something violent – that some fury of abuse must break from him, but he remained silent, and after he had dropped her wrist she became suddenly afraid of what he had not said.

They entered their house without a word, and he led the way upstairs to the drawing-room. Everything was completely arranged – there was even a bowl of wall-flowers burnishing the air with their brown velvet scent. She stood uncertainly in the middle of the room.

'Our unpacking has not been done,' he said; 'I thought we might do that now before dinner.'

She turned obediently towards the door. The room did not feel like her room. The contrast between his fingers on her wrist and his voice now frightened her again, and, for the first time with him, she felt alone and without him.

'I am going down in search of drink.'

She nodded: she could think of nothing to say.

Their luggage lay neatly stacked in the middle of the bedroom, which, orderly and exquisite, seemed, with a kind of superior detachment, to be waiting any attempts she might make to untidy it. In spite of her having chosen with Conrad how it should look, its finished appearance now defeated her: the white carpet and the red walls – even the simple white painted furniture seemed to her intolerably sophisticated: the white muslin curtains blowing gently from the open sash-windows seemed to arch their backs with a delicate indifference: the smooth coverlet on the bed made it look like a stage bed. The fire basket was carefully laid with clean paper, the twigs and small pieces of coal – to light it, she felt, would be a violation of its elegance. She remembered moving to the house in Sussex when she was a child – the disorder, the first picnic meal eaten in the kitchen with packing-cases and tools strewn all over the floor: the smoking oil-lamp, and the candles stuck on to saucers which everybody had had to carry about the half-furnished rooms – the sense of adventure which had pervaded her first night there – she had slept on a sofa wrapped in her father's old army sleeping-bag. In the morning they had boiled fresh eggs in the tea-kettle because the saucepans were not unpacked, and all the water had had to be pumped by hand from the well by the kitchen door. She had enjoyed those first days more than any other time there.

Now – this was her house – her home. I may live here for ever, she thought, and was suddenly, irrationally home-sick for the mud-coloured room in the Kensington hotel.

I *have* to live here now: I am married. I have to live in this house with him; even now, when I do not understand him and there is nobody I can ask. 'What is the longest river in the world, Miss Dawson?' 'The Amazon, my dear.' But she was no longer a child. She had graduated from these matters of fact to questions like the moral worth of such people as Napoleon and Henry VIII – problems whose solution she had early recognized were dependent upon the ethical views of first Miss Dawson, and later herself. These earliest discoveries of different points of view had been alarming, but they had also enchanted her. People did not resemble one another, and their differences were deeply and delightfully engrained beyond their physical appearance. Now, however, one could not run away and play with Napoleon's possible states of mind. She was no longer playing, and she certainly could not run away. She must unpack all those clothes which he had given her, but she stood looking at the trunks without touching them. They contained nothing, she then realized, that had belonged to her before she had married. She felt suddenly and utterly without refuge – like a child who has been sent to stay with people, and has not even its own railway ticket as means to escape. He was angry with her, and she did not know why – she did not even know why his anger frightened her so much – but she could neither avoid nor ignore it. 'If you are unsure of anything, dear, ask me.' Dear Miss Dawson; she had never thought uncertainty necessary. Perhaps it wasn't. Perhaps she had only to ask Conrad why even the thought of children drove him to such a distance of hostility . . . Did that mean that they would never *have* children? She most passionately did not want to consider this – she knew that that was why she had not answered his question in the taxi. Surely it was a situation which must simply arrive – by which she recognized that possibly she meant him to design it – but not, but *not*, a clash now about what were, after all, only potential requirements? He had precipitated the conflict; she did not know why, and not knowing that, she felt she knew nothing.

She heard him coming upstairs, and looked again at all their luggage marked with Paris labels. This seemed to collect all her experience of him: she added it rather defiantly to her courage, and turned to face him.

He came into the room carrying a tray of bottles – smiling – not to her, but rather as a part of his general appearance. For the first time since they had been married, she badly wanted a cigarette.

'You don't seem to have got very far.' He put the tray on her empty dressing-table.

She shrugged her shoulders. 'I wanted a drink first. It *is* rather formidable, isn't it?'

She felt him turn sharply to look at her: at least, she thought with a surge of arrogance, none of her behaviour was lost on him.

'Some of them are simply books, you know. They can be left.' He sounded matter of fact, almost soothing, but there was still something wrong about the way he said it.

She walked to a window, and looked out on to the square. There would not be a single cigarette in the house, and absurd though it seemed, she could not go out and buy any.

'What are you thinking about?'

She answered stiffly: 'I'm waiting for my drink.' He should not, she felt wildly, pursue and trap her thoughts – but as he handed her a glass, she heard herself asking: 'I suppose there isn't a cigarette anywhere about?'

Instantly he drew from his coat pocket her small silver case and handed it to her.

'I didn't know that you had that!'

'All the time. You have been admirably good about it.'

She answered honestly: 'It has not been difficult. I haven't wanted to smoke.'

'Until now.'

He did not produce a match for her, and she looked about the room.

'Over there,' he said: he did not move.

She walked with her drink to the fire-place, and picked up the box of matches. The obscure sensation of being 'handled' again struck and humiliated her: again she felt cornered by him; now with this petty habit of smoking which he had decreed bad for her palate and unsuited to her personality. In so short a time he had so much altered her that she felt lost, panic-stricken, almost unrecognizable to herself. Her fingers, shaking, broke the first match in striking it, and she felt suddenly, intolerably, self-conscious as the creature he had made of her – someone who was frightened and ashamed of lighting a cigarette.

'I left my picture downstairs. I want to hang it.'

He walked to the stool in front of her dressing-table and sat down. He said nothing.

'I want to hang it in here. There are no pictures in this room. It is unbearably bare.' Her ill-chosen words to describe the room made her angrier: she repeated: 'I left the picture downstairs.'

'If you want a picture in here, I will give you a picture.'

'I've already been given one. I don't want you to give me a picture – I want the Blake.'

He swung round on the stool to face her. Then he said deliberately: 'I have put that picture away. I do not want it hung in my house. I have told you, I detest it.'

'I thought this was also my house!'

'Don't you think that on so important a point as a picture we should agree?'

'Agree with *you* – I can see that you mean that. I see now that this is to be your house in which I am to live, and that I—'

He interrupted smoothly: 'This is my house, and you are my wife.' But behind his apparent urbanity, she felt that he was angry and involved.

'So that I am your property, and anything belonging to me is really yours!'

'The legal aspects of that situation are no longer what they were. I am not prepared to discuss this any more. I am sorry that I dislike your picture, but my feeling against it cannot be changed, and I will not have it hung in this house.'

There was a short silence. Then she said:

'We had better return it to your father, then, and you can explain why.' But he answered immediately:

'We must not do that! It would hurt him – it would hurt his feelings – and I won't have that.'

She turned on him to cry '*His* feelings!' but his face, lit by a look of profound humility and determination, stopped her: she said nothing, and in the silence that followed her anger drained heavily, reluctantly away.

When she tried to open her trunk, she found it locked, and from where he was sitting, he threw her the ring of keys. She had thought that the scene, or quarrel, or whatever it was drearily called, had finished; but with this gesture she knew at once that it had not. When she had opened her trunk, he began: 'I asked you a question in the taxi: you didn't answer it.'

'Conrad, wouldn't it be better to unpack now, and talk about that later?'

'Why?'

'All right: now, then.' She sat back on her heels – her heart had started again to thump. She added faintly: 'I can't really remember what it was you asked me,' and knew that he didn't believe her.

'I asked you whether it was your intention to have a large number of children?'

'Surely that isn't an intention which there would be any point in my having by myself?'

'You are again evading the question. Why can't you be honest about it?'

'Honestly, I haven't thought seriously about it at all. Yes, I suppose so. Not a large number – but I think I always imagined that I should have some children.'

'And it had not entered your head to say one word about it until now?'

'I tell you, I haven't been thinking about it. It was you who started it. It seems to be you who feel strongly about children. Why haven't *you* talked about it?'

She had left the matches by the fire-place, and got, with some difficulty, to her feet. As she struck her match, he asked: 'Do you feel, then, that without children, you will not be "fulfilling yourself" – whatever that may mean?'

She threw the match away into the beautiful fire-place. 'Oh do stop asking these – venomous questions! I tell you, I don't *know*! Why does it suddenly matter so much? Either we shall have children, or we shan't. I mean—' she felt colour flooding her face: 'I mean – if we decide to have them, of course.'

'Exactly. If we decide.'

She walked shakily back to her place on the floor. 'Well – couldn't we decide that later?'

'You thoroughly misunderstand me. I am talking about the principle – not some idiotic feminine timetable.'

'*Talk* about it, then! Stop *asking me*, and talk about it!'

This retort, reasonable and collected, actually broke from her because, while it no longer seemed to matter what she said, she could think of nothing else to say. But it *was* reasonable, she thought, forcing herself to continue looking at him (if his eyes were really made of glass, he wouldn't be able to see me). She felt with a kind of terror his anger distilling to hatred, and looked down away from him at the little white hairs from the new carpet which had come off on her skirt. ('Is there *no end* to what people can feel for one another?')

'Please – do – talk about it.'

At the very end of her asking him, the intricate balance of power and pain seemed suddenly to equate, to assume those half-hidden but familiar proportions which enabled them to communicate with one another.

'Yes. I will talk about it.' He got up and moved intently, silently, about the room, stopping when he began to speak.

'People generally get married for extraordinarily few reasons. Legalized sex; economic security; somebody to die with. Children seem to me simply an ingenious re-inforcement of these arguments. But supposing that one married for none of these reasons. Supposing that you take one desirable woman as you find her – and loving what you have found, you marry her. From the moment of your finding her she is not the same – nor is she ever

311

from that time on in any sense *fait accompli*, unless you choose, because it is easier, to recede to elementary behaviour with someone else – or, unless you so charge your life with activity extraneous to her that she is forced into isolation – or, unless you jam her intentions towards you with a whole lot of new intentions towards other people. Marriage could be the fascinating, difficult experience of living in two bodies instead of one – it matters far less than people think which alternative body they select – it matters far more than they imagine how they inhabit it thereafter.' He stopped abruptly as though he was considering what he had said. 'There, under the cover of these vast generalizations, you know what I believe about marriage.' He waited a moment, but she said nothing. 'The particular and the general provide endless refuge for one another. I was not beginning to talk about women. Only men – only myself.' He stared at her as though he was expecting her to question him, but she did not. 'And you? Women? They are a different mechanism. I don't think that anything of the kind – living in two bodies and so forth – applies to them. The most mysterious, intricate point about women is that they require someone else to teach them to live in their own body. Without that, they are lost, because they are never discovered.'

'And when they have learned?'

He seemed astonished. 'They have never learned, because they are always changing – always requiring something different. There is no end to the business – no end at all.'

'Don't men change also?'

He answered with the careless immediacy of irritation: 'But, of course, everybody changes all the time. The point with two people is that they should change at approximately the same speed in approximately the same direction.'

'I meant, don't the women teach the men *anything*? Is the whole thing really so unbalanced? Are women so passive – lying in wait for something they don't understand . . . how do the men know, anyway?' – interrupting herself – 'who teaches *them*?'

'My dear, I was not generalizing. Most people, men or women, know nothing, and, as they say, care less. I was talking about us. You ought to understand that: you are a woman.'

'But I *don't* understand! If you are going to have this – vast continuous effect on me, what am I going to do?'

He sat on the end of the bed, facing her.

'Be my wife.'

'That is another thing'; she was now too alarmed and distracted to be careful. 'If you think that children are such a frightful mistake, why did you marry me? Why marry, at all?'

He leaned suddenly towards her: she heard him draw breath with a little scorching hiss, and there was just time for the shock of knowing that now they were over the edge before he began:

'So you *did* determine on children when you married – if not before – you see? It was always your real intention behind this profound dishonesty – that *I* should be merely a means to an end – that you should order, and dominate and control . . .' He was pouring out words with a deadly facility again – as though he had trapped her, she felt frantically – only I can't be trapped; I haven't been dishonest – I wasn't lying – it is he making me feel like that. This is simply ridiculous – she thought uncertainly – but it wasn't – all these weeks we've been living on this edge, and I never knew. She realized with a shock that she had actually not heard the words which were streaming from him – felt only the waves of anger surging towards her, breaking over her with such painful violence that the whole room seemed to be rocking as they broke.

'. . . your attention distracted – your mind retarded by their ceaseless infantile demands – and for *what*? They will grow up *as I did*, to see us destroying one another in the illusion that we are preserving them.'

He stopped suddenly; and as suddenly she could not see him for the curious black mist that seemed to emanate from his silence. She put out her hands to tear the mist apart, but it was too far away from her hands – she could not touch it. After some immeasurable time, she heard her voice, distinct and calm: 'Let us – not – have – children.' She saw him through the mist for a moment as she said it – sitting on the bed, a long way away – a mere speck in the distance of conclusion. Words, love, reason, we don't need them any more: there has been an accident between us. It would be better to keep quite, quite still, or I shall discover how much I have been hurt. It is over now – the damage has been done – there can be no – more – damage. What relief – that it was over, and one didn't know beforehand what it would really be like: living in the future in such a protective dreamlike affair . . . I love my house. Soon, we shall actually move in, and be living there. I can still, *still* remember exactly how I imagined it would be . . .

She put her hands up to her eyes to press out this liquid memory of her imagination; but it still swam with a magnified distortion behind her fingers. She heard his voice again – saying something now about unpacking – about drink – and took away her hands to see whether he had resumed his ordinary proportions: but her hands were wringing wet, and she could not see him. She wrung her hands (that is why people say in books 'she wrung her hands'), smiled feverishly in his direction (princesses in fairy-stories 'weeping bitterly and wringing their hands') and suddenly he was beside her, his eyes enormous – too near – enormously concerned . . . He was touching her – repeating her name again and again – looming over her until she lay shrinking in his arms – protected, trapped by his comfort (*you* cannot comfort *me*: you are the last person to do it!). She tried to say that, turning her head away from him, but there was such bitter weeping that she did not think he could possibly hear. *He* would surely have comforted her – who was he – Geoffrey? – no, she had discovered him: after discovery, people were neither kind nor comforting – never confess your love; never, never come near anyone – the further you venture with them, the longer the way back by yourself . . . don't think of it – don't remember it – don't weep for it . . . 'I can do without you!' and flung herself hard into Conrad's arms.

As she said this, the weeping halted, and as her tears began, she understood that all the weeping had been hers.

He held her patiently – until she fell into the rhythm of his comforting – until he had entirely ceased to be her fear, her enemy, and become her refuge – from what? She lifted her head to ask, but she was stupefied by her returning ease: there seemed no need to ask, and no need to know. She pulled his handkerchief out of his pocket, and they wiped her eyes.

'There,' he said: 'Shall we unpack your clothes now, or would you like another drink, or shall we go down to dinner?'

She shook her head: she could not bear to think what to do.

'You choose,' he said. 'This is our first night here.'

'Don't let us stay here tonight!' She barely saw his look of astonished concern before her eyes clouded again with new scalding tears. 'I don't want to! I want to go back – to go back to where we were before – not like this—'

'To go back where? How far back do you want to go?'

She shook her head speechlessly: the places flicked backwards in her mind like the pages of a book – rootless, restless, incomprehensible – not a time nor a place occurred now as desirable, because her experience of them now was tainted with her knowledge of their future. This had always been waiting to confound and confine her: there were to be no children. Pictures of children – dazzling, unrecognizable illustrations – flickered instantly in this lightning sheaf; back, and back, and further back to the beginning of the book until she was a child herself. Bewildered and diminished far beyond choice, she said:

'I don't want to choose.'

'I have done too much to you! You need not choose.' He lifted her up and laid her on the bed. 'You don't weigh enough.'

'I hate milk.'

'Then you shan't have milk. But it can be made to taste quite unmilky, you know.'

'But all the time there is the *feeling* that it is milk.'

'Well, then, not milk. Other things. Now I'm going to run you a hot bath. You shall christen the bathroom.'

'Where are we going to have dinner?'

'Up here. You're going to have it in bed. I'm going to light the fire.'

'Oh no!'

'Darling, why not? It is getting cold.'

'It's too beautiful to light.'

'It can be made beautiful again tomorrow. Just the same.' He picked the box of matches off the floor by her trunk.

She put her arms behind her head and watched him touch the clean paper in three places with a match.

'Conrad!'

'Antonia?'

'I don't want you to make love to me.'

He put the matches on the mantelpiece and returned to her. 'I know that. I am not simply the person who does that to you, you know.'

'*I* know that.'

He pushed her hair back from her forehead, pressing it gently with his fingers. 'Now: your bath.'

While he was in the bathroom, she said: 'Really, you are the person who does everything to me.'

'I'm sorry: I didn't hear that.' He stood in the doorway, anxious, attentive. 'Is there anything you want?'

'Nothing. Only to go back *to* you. I want to go back *with* you – not by myself.'

'You will not be by yourself. I shall see to it that you are never alone. I love you, you see.'

'I see.' She knew now that now he was again protecting her, she was safe from him.

PART FIVE
1926

ONE

Their situation was beautiful. The house, lying half way up the incline of a small valley – like something poised on the shallow palm of an elegant hand – was fringed at the back with the fingers of pine and larch trees: before it was lawn and rough grass descending to the wrist of the valley where a concord of little dark streams met, and separated, and vanished into a cuff of willow and alder. Up the other side were fields casually picked out with single perfect oaks, beeches and Spanish chestnuts – and just below the skyline the branch railway track was laid – straight, like a ruler – with a small black train puffing across the backcloth twice a day; from right to left, and, in the evening, from left to right.

The house, secure and content in its position, presented a simple, good-tempered face – brick of an amiable complexion – widely spaced features of white windows and a comfortable door, the folly of its porch overwhelmed with clematis, honey-suckle and wisteria. Behind its façade, however, it rambled, changing its mind and its nature; no architect's dream – having slipped a hundred years before out of its corseted design into a comfortable spread of wasted space – of rooms which were not personally related to one another, and which seemed not to have been built for any particular purpose. At the back was a quantity of outbuildings: stables, sheds, greenhouses, and a garage, and, behind them, a tall tightly packed wood.

The place was really too large for them, Antonia's parents had said over and over again: but they had bought it, because it was cheap, because they had been unable to agree upon an alternative, because his health required him to leave London, and because, faced with the country, she was determined upon Sussex. The space had its advantages; she wanted a house large enough for weekend parties, and he wanted the room to escape her friends. For Antonia, the change had been miraculous. Her childhood had been spent almost entirely in London with occasional visits to the sea, until her mother had rented a cottage for weekends (a form of restlessness in which she excelled). Then Antonia had experienced the violent delight of pining not for 'the country', but for one particular bit of it – her distant London imagination made intimate as, season by season, she slowly learned their immediate landscape.

The final move from London had coincided with the end of her education, and the joy of her undivided country life outweighed even the exquisite shock of arriving as they had used to do at the cottage on a Friday evening in summer, and finding the orchard, which the last time had been frozen turf, so thickly grassed, so richly flowered, that there seemed not an empty pore in the earth. Even this kind of minutely finished splendour was not, she discovered, more marvellous than its barely perceptible appearance.

The earliest recollection Antonia had of her parents was people saying that her father had a very good brain, and that her mother was fearfully, divinely, attractive. As she grew up, she might have observed the subtle change in these generally idle opinions: her father became someone who knew a very great deal about something – an authority – and her mother someone possessing a tremendous zest, a gusto, a *joie de vivre*: but at seventeen, or even eighteen and nineteen, Antonia had not encountered the experience to conclude anything from the gradual devastation of her father's mind and her mother's appearance. A day school sandwiched between years of governesses had produced no lasting friends of her own age, and she accepted the friends of her parents without any great curiosity or interest. Her father had one or two people with whom he exchanged abstruse technical pieces of information; her mother had a floating crowd with whom she played games in and out of doors, went to parties, and used the telephone. As a family, they had no mutual interests, and virtually no conversation. The house embraced them all, and Antonia, at least, had been unconscious of their extremely separate lives in it. For nearly three years she had gardened, walked, and ridden, and (after emerging from the stupefied indigestion of her parents' library) read with increasing discrimination. She also made constant attempts to write down what she saw and heard and smelled – efforts which were remarkably free from self-consciousness, since she was simply interested in the subject of her writing, and not in its effect upon herself. She tried to draw; she tried to make her clothes; she tried to teach herself Russian; she collected books, and postcard reproductions of pictures; she made a garden entirely of wild flowers and herbs; she tried to cook from various ancient and exotic recipes – all these pursuits she followed entirely along with an enquiring content. She associated more nearly with the people out of her favourite books than with her parents or their friends. With the last she was neither communicative nor shy: she cleaned tennis balls, arranged flowers in their bedrooms, fetched the trays of lemonade and gin, made up a fourth at bridge, tidied the Mah Jong, and wound up the gramophone: went because she was asked and not particularly wanted, because she was asked and did not care whether she went, on the excursions to other people's houses, where different sets of people played the same games and drank the same drinks – all with a docility which was both indifferent and self-contained. When her mother unfavourably compared with other girls Antonia's ability to 'join in the fun' she was embarrassed: when (more and more frequently) her mother attempted with public ridicule and private interference to invade the rest of her daughter's life she was unhappy. Dimly she felt that from her mother's point of view she was not a success. Then she would make further, conscientious efforts at weekends, but this only seemed to shift the ground of her mother's criticism. She was, her mother said, too tall and far too thin; her hair, although positively dark, was too fine to be manageable and she had almost no colour. Her eyes were her only good feature, said her mother, and proceeded to dress her in every shade of inferior blue which detracted from them. Her mother, to whom colours were merely light or dark, put down the unsatisfactory results to Antonia's innate obstinacy and indifference, and Antonia, when her attention was thus drawn to it, was unhappily overwhelmed at being unable, as her mother said, 'even to look nice'.

Her mother also frequently told her that her father had wanted a son, and Antonia, who naturally saw intellectual achievement in her father's terms – the masculine scholar and recluse – accepted his disappointment, and even occasionally, on his behalf, wished that she had been a man. She supposed, quite simply, that had she been one she would have provided her father with the mind and company suited to him. She had tried to read his works – his books, his published lectures and articles – but although she generally managed to get to the end of them, and even at the time to understand what they meant, a week later the information she had absorbed dropped out of her mind like so much dead wood.

She grew up, therefore, feeling, not precisely a failure so much as an unnecessary appendage. Any brief, hesitant trials she had made with people had not in fact either rewarded or touched her. She had remained isolated; unaware that any ecstasy, despair, or pleasure could be a mutual business. Antonia – until she was nineteen . . .

Then, into this piece of elaborate, sensitive still life, dropped Geoffrey Curran. His entrance was inevitably simple. He was just one more friend of her mother's friends. He arrived, as they usually did, on a Friday evening; at the end of a day that for Antonia was so fraught with the restless anticipatory ritual to which her mother subjected the whole household on Fridays, that afterwards it was difficult to remember exactly how she first met him. It was he who told her about it, and then, of course, she could remember it perfectly. 'It was just before dinner, and you were the last to come into the drawing-room. You wore a blue silk dress and a wide silver bracelet on your delicate arm. Your mother introduced you, and you nodded your head carefully to each person's name. Then we all sat down again, and you sat with a quick little movement, holding the sides of the seat of your chair with your hands. The bracelet slipped down to your fingers, and you had to shake it back.' Then she could remember. She had been afraid of being late. She had been fetching drinking water from the spring down the road, and she had stayed too long turning her pony out afterwards. Then she had changed hurriedly, knowing by the silence upstairs that everyone else had gone down. It was an early summer evening – the sun had just set, and the air was fraught with the gently evening grumble of birds. Bats leered about with amazing silence; and when she opened her window, she let in an indiscriminate flitter of moths. Daisies lay faintly on the lawn, still staring upwards to the end of the light – floating on the dark turf – extinguished, drowned, out, one by one, as the mushroom shadows grew mounting out of the ground. It was the last time alone in her life.

Downstairs, she hesitated a moment by the drawing-room door, examining the clasp of her bracelet, trying to remember how many of this weekend's guests she had met before and should identify. They were so very much alike, she thought, and it was bad manners not to know who was who.

Her mother was wearing cream-coloured lace and had a long ivory cigarette holder. Four men got to their feet as she entered the room: her father was patiently mixing drinks.

'This is my huge daughter Toni. Enid and Bobby you know, Margot Trefusis, Geoffrey Curran, Alistair you met at the Framptons, and George Warrender. There! Now we can all sit down. Want a drink, darling?'

And she remembered, in that confusion of eyes, the second of blinding illumination when she looked at Geoffrey Curran (he looks as though he can *see*!) before she subsided, abruptly forgetting that she had thought anything so odd.

During dinner she discovered that he was Irish, that he took horses, and poetry, and people whom he did not know, easily in his stride: that he talked with abandon, and listened with care. They did not talk to one another – only, every now and then, if he was telling a story, he would collect her into his audience with a separate, charming, attention – his eyes inquiring, admiring, amused, holding hers until her interest was secure . . .

Back in her room, instead of immediately resuming her private life she found herself considering the evening and the guests; all of them – those she had met before, and those who were new to her. That her mind came to rest for the night upon Geoffrey Curran did not prevent her sleeping; she was subject to no disturbing thoughts – no intolerable curiosity: the aching uncertainty of loving secretly and in ignorance had not yet begun, and she knew nothing of it. She thought him interesting; his conversation had not been confined to gossip, or to games as he played them: she particularly enjoyed his voice and his range of description, which compared with the few imperative, overworked adjectives employed by the others, enriched his quietest, most commonplace remark. He was old, of course, he must be well over thirty, and perhaps his talking as he did was a result of his having led a long interesting life. Or perhaps because he is Irish, she thought. She fell deeply into sleep on the edge of the conclusion that she had never known anyone whom she had known was Irish, and perhaps that accounted for him.

TWO

Saturday was a very fine day. At breakfast, eaten in the small sunny morning-room, everybody remarked on it; the first really beautiful day of the summer. The tennis in the afternoon was safe – and the Framptons' cocktail party afterwards would take place out of doors. Antonia's mother was dynamic with last-minute plans for the success of these arrangements. There was to be one expedition to Battle for fish and various other provisions, and another to Hastings to collect two racquets that had been restrung, some drink, and a new housemaid who was arriving from London that morning. Somebody must roll and mark the court.

'Ooh! Let me be the marker!' cried Enid. Her voice was so high-pitched that it had become husky with the strain. 'Bobby can roll: good for his figure. I've always *longed* to mark a court all by my small self. Absolute heaven: Minty, darling, I'll be dreadfully careful.'

'Do you mind rolling, Bobby, dee-ar?' Antonia's mother switched her personality like an arc lamp on to Enid's husband.

Bobby made a good-tempered but hideous face. 'I can see I'll be doing it all right. I *always* do it – it's my broad shoulders or something. The moment people see me they think – there's someone to roll the lawn.'

'It's your *shape*, darling. Like horsy people ending up by looking like them.'

Curran turned to Antonia. 'Do we look like horses, would you say?'

She regarded him gravely. '*You* don't.'

'And what about yourself?' he teased. 'You keep a horse, don't you?'

'A pony. A large pony – I suppose she's nearly a horse. She's just over fifteen hands.'

'Oh goodness! No horsy talk *now*, Toni, dee-ar! We must get started. George! You are my chauffeur for the morning. You're coming to Hastings to collect the new maid. Just your line, darling. You can sit holding hands with her all the way home.'

'Tricky – if I'm driving.' (George Warrender was a huge square man who laughed indiscriminately to be on the safe side.)

'It's your marvellous, marvellous company I want, not your marvellous driving. Alistair, will you terribly *sweetly* take Margot and Geoffrey into Battle and be an angel about the fish and things? Wonderful. Then Wilfrid can have a heavenly peaceful morning.' She got up from the table, and ruffled what remained of her husband's hair. 'Just what you'd like, Wilfrid, dear. You don't want a hot journey in a car, do you?'

And he replied obediently: 'I do not.'

'There! Everybody happy? Now I must go and do a teeny bit of housekeeping, and then we can all start. Twenty minutes, George?'

'Whatever you say.'

Araminta swept out, and Wilfrid smoothed his hair.

Margot said: 'Isn't Minty *marvellous!* The *amount* she manages to get through!' (Margot was one of those young women whose social reputation rested upon her public approval of everyone surrounding her.)

Curran said to Antonia: 'And what will you be doing with yourself this lovely morning?' She looked startled, he observed, as though she was unused to any enquiry or interest about her movements.

'Oh – things in the house. We're a bit short-handed until the new maid arrives. And I shall probably put up the hammocks. And pick the asparagus for dinner. Things like that.'

Her father said: 'Antonia, will you ask Araminta to come and see me before she goes to Hastings? I should very much like some books I have ordered collected from the library. If she has time.' He retired with the *Morning Post* under his arm, and his going made no difference to the room.

The morning, which earlier had been tentatively decorated by sun, became slowly charged with a dazzling, beating heat. As the haze was stripped and scorched away, the garden colours feverishly heightened; the pulsing dynamo of insects quickened; the hot air was loaded with lavender and sweet briar.

Antonia, her housework over, went slowly out to pick the asparagus. Enid and Bobby were quarrelling on the tennis-court. She slipped by without them seeing her, wondering whether they ever noticed the kind of day it was. She passed her father's study, and saw him chewing his pipe over a book. *He* didn't notice either. She went to the greenhouse to collect her trug, and urged a frantic, boiling bird to freedom. Thomas the gardener was fiddling with his precious sweet peas. She waved to him (he was stone deaf and it was too hot to shout) and followed the narrow cinder path past the buddleia which was already a riot of butterflies to the kitchen garden. Here was the smell of warm twine from the fruit nets mixed with the faint purposeful aroma of slowly ripening fruit. There were patches of marigolds and pinks and sweet williams, and the expanse of strawberries lying on their fresh golden bed. The marrows were flowering like pale paper hats out of crackers. One or two of the smallest tomatoes were ripe – little hot red and yellow buttons – she ate some: the skins were tough, but they were incredibly sweet. The rows of asparagus fern looked effeminate and cool, like people at the beginning of a garden party. She picked a cabbage leaf so vast that it covered the bottom of her trug, and carefully cut her asparagus. Thomas, after three years, trusted her, but she knew that he watched all her picking with a sternly critical eye, and once or twice he had spoken to her – gently, repetitively – more resigned than angry at her folly, but at the end of those half-hours she had felt like an indiscriminate thief. Thomas was a very beautiful man, she thought; it was curious how gardeners nearly always looked very bad-tempered or beautiful. Thomas had an expression of gentle nobility which lightened only when he smiled, when complimented or congratulated upon some prize he had won. Then he contrived to look angelically malicious; translating what was an innocent triumph of skill into terms of immense secret cunning. He approves of me, thought Antonia, he simply tolerates my mother and Wilfrid because they live in the house belonging to his garden, but I think he even likes me sometimes, because I like the garden so much. Curious: she had never bothered before whether Thomas liked or disapproved of her . . .

By the time she had taken the asparagus to the kitchen, she was too hot to want anything but to lie in the garden with the end of *Northanger Abbey*. There were the hammocks, however, which had not been up this year. She sighed:

something always went wrong the first time one tried to hang them; however carefully one rolled them up, they rotted malevolently in the garden room all the winter. 'At *least* you might put up the hammocks,' her mother had said. Anyway, she would not have to play tennis in the afternoon. There were already too many people; and she, an unenthusiastic and poor player, need not be called upon to make up a single set.

Everybody was exhausted by luncheon time. The court was rolled and marked, but Enid and Bobby were not on speaking terms. Only Araminta and George seemed gay. They were late for luncheon; they had stopped at a pub for a tiny drink: the maid had felt sick in the car, and they had had to stop anyway. Margot said that she had a headache, and Alistair said that Battle was far too crowded on a Saturday. Wilfrid hardly ever contributed to general conversation: he discovered that Araminta had forgotten his book, and settled into resigned silence. Curran was the one who tried to talk to him, Antonia observed during the meal; she watched her father gradually drawn into explaining the purpose of his present book, and then watched Curran listening with every appearance of intelligent interest. She began by thinking that Curran was simply employing his manners, but by the end of luncheon she was half-convinced that he really cared about sixteenth-century social customs. She wanted suddenly to ask him, but did not dare.

At three o'clock they began playing tennis – all the party assembled to watch, excepting Margot, who had retired to her room. The court was laid at the bottom of a steep bank of rough grass, on which lay those of the audience who could bear the sun. The sun blazed. Antonia began by pretending to watch, and reading her book, and ended by pretending to read, and sleeping.

She was woken by her mother's voice, and someone tickling her arm with a dandelion.

'. . . on to the court with you,' Curran was saying. He was smiling down at her, and it was he who held the dandelion. 'Your mother wants you to make up a four.'

She sat up, dazzled with waking.

'Margot's with us again. We want a women's doubles. Bobby and George are exhausted.'

'All the men will watch from the bank.'

'I'm umpire,' said George Warrender. Everybody seemed to be talking to her. An infinity of time seemed to have passed while she had slept.

'Hurry *up*, Toni. That child's capacity for *sleep*!' her mother again.

She looked round helplessly. 'Must I? You know I'm no good. Won't somebody else . . . ?' But her father and Alistair had disappeared, and the women were standing about the court in various attitudes of impatience. As she got to her feet, she became aware of her throbbing head. Curran smiled encouragingly and said: 'Go on. I'll watch your every stroke, and, when you win, I'll strike the skin off me hands with delight.'

Suddenly, she wanted more than anything in the world not to have to play bad tennis in front of Geoffrey Curran. Discovering that she was to partner her mother seemed only the last part of some plot to expose her incompetence. Her head ached: the sun seemed to explode in her eyes, and press itself together again at the back of her head. After the tossing for sides, she walked to her place facing the sun feeling sharply, freshly, self-conscious; with that terrible sensation of having lent her own critical eyes to someone else for the single purpose of watching the worst of her.

The set opened with her mother's service, which went smoothly enough. Her mother was the best player, and with George and Curran applauding her, she won the game easily, without Antonia being required for a single stroke; but while she collected balls, and kept out of the way, her nervousness unbearably increased. After this game, I shall *have* to play – eventually, I shall have to serve, and I *can't*: they all go into the net or miles outside the lines. And it was all worse than she had imagined. To begin with George said: 'Bad *luck*!' every time she lost them a point, and with a dry mouth she apologized to her mother, but in the end he stopped saying anything, and she did not dare to apologize. She lost count of the points or even the games. After she had completely failed to serve a single ball in, her mother suggested she serve underarm for the rest of the afternoon: the suggestion, made overtly in tones of good-tempered resignation, masked, she knew, such anger and dislike, that her eyes burned with unshed tears, and she could not see any of the white lines. She no longer looked at her mother, and never in the direction of Curran. She knew that the game could not go on for ever, but her anguish of humiliation seemed unending – the escape that would have to be made – the lawn that must be crossed, towards Curran, there being no other reasonable exit – the eyes – the talk – the hearty commiseration concealing the profound contempt . . . 'I have a headache – I am so sorry to have let you all down – to have let myself down . . . I have only just discovered that I cannot bear being watched doing anything so badly . . .'

It was over: nearly a love set. She walked slowly

towards the grass bank, her legs shaking: she apologized, and felt their eyes turned upon her – 'It didn't matter a *bit*: it was only a game . . .' With trembling shreds of dignity she did not offer them her headache. Half way up the steps she turned as her mother called to her, and saw the corners of her book warping in the sun where it lay beside Curran.

'Toni! Your petticoat is nearly an inch down below your skirt – *do* try and hoist it up somehow, it looks definitely odd like that.'

She left her poor book to its fate: left them all having looked at her petticoat, and then immediately, at anything else.

In her room, she bathed her face, and then went to the bathroom for drinking water. The bathroom looked out on to the little back lawn where tea was laid, and the window was open.

'. . . I don't know,' her mother was saying. 'Of course, I should understand if she was simply bad at games – if she had any other interests! Wilfrid says she doesn't really know a thing in spite of years of governesses, and she hasn't the sort of brain to do much good at a university – although heaven knows a blue-stocking daughter would be a ghastly enough prospect – even *that* would be better than this total lack of interest in anything. Nobody has ever *noticed* her, if you know what I mean – and personally, I don't blame them. Her appearance – you'd think the average girl would mind frightfully about that, but *she* doesn't. When I think of myself at that age! The fun I used to have! It's shattering! Of course I was a perfectly ordinary young girl . . .'

Through the clamour of interruption – of gallant denials, she heard Curran's voice – startling; incisive; calm:

'She has the most remarkable eyes I've ever seen in my life.'

She heard no more. Looking suddenly up to her reflection, she saw her own eyes, hurt, astonished, before the tears ran out of them, and she fled to her room.

It was like being born a second time: this violent picture – this seeing of her own appearance through other people's eyes. Unable to think, she wept, huddled in the hideous leather armchair in which she had spent so many hours reading about imaginary people, until the instinctive reasons for crying incoherently occurred . . . She *was* bad at games – but she was not interested in games – it was not that she didn't care about anything: she simply cared about different things, and that hadn't seemed to matter until her mother had drawn everybody's attention to her – to her dullness, lack of interests, and generally un-attractive appearance. She hadn't *wanted* to be noticed at all, and to be unfavourably noticed in this way made the prospect of seeing any more of the house party intoler-able.

Curran's remark about her eyes only filled her with the terror of unbalance – seemed only an unwelcome con-fusion, interrupting the accepted view of her otherwise complete insignificance. She felt then that it would be somehow easier to be considered entirely unremarkable – that a single grace would neither save nor console her; and the thought of a single person defending her, simply prevented her from sinking into the camouflage of her background. Her eyes would give her away. He was prob-ably being polite, she thought, and then, because he had not known that she would hear him, she wanted to look for herself. But her eyes looked now merely blurred and dark; staring back at her with solemn, searching anxiety, and just as she turned away from the glass with a wavering disapproval: 'My mother is perfectly right.'

When, an hour later, her mother came to chivvy her to the Framptons, she found Antonia curled up in the leather armchair as easily and deeply asleep, in spite of her tortuous position, as a young animal. She had not changed, her mother told the others, and if they waited for her, they would be late. So of course they did not wait.

She woke to the empty pleasure of the house – the sunlit evening after a hot day. While she had slept, the roses in the bowl beside her had yawned so widely that they had shed their outside petals in an ecstasy of exhaustion: the room was cooler, and outside there was a soothingly distant cuckoo – saying it again and again, and then a pause – assuming for her the responsibility of sound and silence.

She woke refreshed, and with a violent curiosity; as though, asleep, she had been presented with some tremendously exciting discovery, which awake, she was to discover and pursue. She stretched herself out of her chair, and looked at her watch, but watches galloped on her wrist with such extraordinary disregard for their function that she had no idea of the time. She was reflecting contentedly that they must all have gone to the party – that she had, at least, escaped them for a bit – when there was a knock on her door. It was the new maid, who had been sent to tell her that her mother and everyone was staying on at their party, and would not be back for dinner. Her father wished dinner half an hour earlier than had been arranged, and did this suit Miss Antonia? While she delivered this message, her eyes roved round the room, nervously, with a kind of inexpert collection of the scene. Her eyes were red, Antonia noticed, her face was puffed and a dull pink – her apron looked paper stiff and new, and the absurd frill round her damp straw-coloured hair seemed pathetically incongruous. As she observed this, and discovered that it was about seven – but the maid would go and make sure if Miss Antonia wished – she realized that she knew nothing at all about the new maid excepting what she had just noticed.

'I don't know your name, I'm afraid.'

'Dorcas, miss.' She stared at the floor.

Antonia asked awkwardly: 'Are you all right? Have you got what you need?'

'It's a bit strange at first. I've to find my way about. I've not been away in service before. Ever.' This confidence seemed nearly too much for her; she glanced hurriedly at Antonia with the shadowy attempt at a smile, and began screwing the corner of her apron with soft pink fingers.

'Are you homesick?'

But Dorcas stared at her with a kind of dogged incomprehension, and answered: 'It's strange, at first, but I'll manage, miss,' and Antonia was left feeling clumsily curious, which was not at all what she had felt when she had asked the question.

'I'm sure you will.' She smiled, but the little maid was staring at the floor again, and she did not dare ask her any more. 'Dinner at half-past seven, then?'

'Yes, miss.'

'Thank you, Dorcas.'

'Thank you, miss.' And she went, shutting the door with such nervous caution that it sprang open. They both arrived face to face to shut it. 'I'm sorry, miss.' Antonia saw a large pear-shaped tear rolling across her face, but this time they managed to smile at one another – a tentative acknowledgement of the door . . .

As she dressed for dinner she began to imagine the evening: sitting opposite her father with the green glass bowl filled with polyanthus between them – their appearance for one another across the table – the possibility that alone together they might embark upon the great unknown areas of communication that she felt now must exist between sixteenth-century social customs and what her mother and George Warrender had done that morning in Hastings – that he might christen her curiosity with his personal experience: as she knew nothing about him, so she felt that there must be everything to know . . . Her father – Papa – his name was Wilfrid . . .

He put down his book with an obvious reluctance when she came into the room, and as she walked over to him, feeling almost as though she was meeting him for the first time, she saw his eyes flicker a second from her and back to the book with a glancing regret which she now realized was so habitual that he had ceased to conceal it.

He said: 'Shall I get you a glass of sherry?' His manner with anyone but another enthusiast upon his subject was uniform: she might have been someone he was meeting for the first time.

'I'll get it.' When she had poured it out, she perched on the arm of the sofa, and said: 'Supposing that we had never met?'

She saw him screw up his eyes – adjusting himself to this complicated, unimportant idea: then he said: 'I think I should still have offered you a glass of sherry wine.'

'That's what I thought.' She looked at him expectantly, but he did not turn this particular pebble, so she continued:

'And then what would you do? What would you talk about with me at dinner?'

He looked at her with wary resignation. 'There would probably be other people there. I don't expect that I should talk to you much.' He made his little dry unnecessary cough. 'My small talk is rather limited you know.'

'But would it have to be small? I mean if there weren't other people there, of course. Wouldn't you want –' she hesitated, trying to discover exactly what she meant – 'Wouldn't you want us to find out what we were like?'

'Really, my dear Antonia, I don't know.' She felt the sliding edge of alarm in his voice. 'In any case, this is an absurd hypothesis. We have known one another for years.'

'I don't think I know anything about you.'

He coughed again. 'There is remarkably little to know.' He finished his sherry with a conclusive gesture. 'In any case, families don't pioneer with one another much, you know. They seek fresh fields to conquer. One can only occupy oneself with research upon one's family, and I don't think yours is a mind which could easily apply itself to research. Shall we go into dinner? It was waiting for us before you came down.'

'I am so sorry!' She looked despairingly at her watch. 'I set it a little while ago. It doesn't stop – it simply doesn't go at the right speed. You should have told me.'

He picked up their glasses and put them carefully on the tray of drinks, saying: 'It doesn't matter. The meal is cold.'

His voice, she thought, was exactly like the meal.

They ate their cold tongue by the light of six candles – she had remembered that there would be polyanthus, but not their deep-set appearance by candlelight – this piece of slipshod imagination lying diagonally across her mind in the way of her perfect attention to the present – while he filled her few startling gaps of clarity, the moments when she could have recorded, or observed, or anticipated, with the landscape clutter of words; mechanically, carelessly spoken – laid like the familiar objects strewn in familiar disorder upon a dressing-table. So, they ate their tongue: but during the silence while their plates were being changed, she looked carefully at him – he had the appearance of an indifferent portrait, consistent and incomprehensible – and resolved to try again to break through this palisade of filial platitudes . . .

'What do you think I ought to do?'

Distrusting action of any kind, he simply said: 'I don't understand you.'

'Well, then, what do you think I am like? How do I seem to you?'

'You must remember that I am not acquainted with many, indeed any young women of your age. I have therefore no standard of comparison.'

'Do you need one? Can't you just consider me – and – tell me? I do want to know,' she added.

He looked at her steadily for a moment. He was perfectly still, and there was something about his rigid, humourless expression which she found both pathetic, and a little frightening.

'Women are invariably concerned with the appearance of things. Generally, I think, with the effect of their own appearance upon other people. I expect you want me to tell you that you are pretty – although I should have thought that there were enough young men incessantly in and out of this house to inform your conceit without my doing it – but yes, you seem to me suitably equipped to make a number of men unhappy, if that is an object.

You will doubtless marry one of them one day, and as you have not shown any particular interest or ability in any other direction, I assume that, in common with most young women with an attractive appearance and a commonplace mind, marriage, and all that goes with it, is to be your metier.'

There was a dead silence. Then he said: 'Wasn't that what you wanted to know?' The edge had gone from his voice, but she was too much distressed to notice.

'I am not an authority upon appearances. I may be wrong. But you have every opportunity to find out.'

She could not reply. His indictment of her mind (*he*, of all people, must be an authority upon the *mind*!) struck her with the dreadful accuracy of a truth: no shallow injustice, no glancing indifference, but straight and deeply to the heart. She said nothing. He finished his asparagus, and thought deeply about something else.

Outside the dining-room, he suddenly remembered her again, and said: 'Come to my study. I have something for you.'

Her warped copy of *Northanger Abbey* lay upon the foolscap on his desk. He picked it up and gave it to her.

'Your book. Geoffrey Curran brought it into the house. He said that you had left it in the sun on the tennis court this afternoon. Nobody, I think, who really cared for books could treat even a novel in this fashion. Now I shall work. Good night, my dear.'

THREE

The next morning there was no sun, but a grey, heavy, almost tangible, heat. Everybody agreed that there was to be a thunderstorm, and spent the morning in listless disagreement about everything else. Antonia breakfasted early to avoid the others, and then went out to garden. 'I'll weed for at least two hours, and then I'll read a book, not a novel, but something really serious.' Thus did she plan the aimless isolation which she had suddenly discovered to be surrounding her; but alone in her garden, she thought all the time about it, and afterwards, alone with her book (she did not choose one which presented her with any company) she began to find the precision of the little sledge-hammer question 'But what shall I *do* about it all?' both painful and frightening. By the end of the morning she was almost grateful for the ordeal of luncheon.

At luncheon, even before she had had the time to live through her first self-conscious moments with the house party, the storm began. Then, as the first crash of thunder echoed heavily away, Curran leant across the table to her and said: 'When this is all over, and the country is fresh and sweet, would you consider taking me with you for a ride?'

She sat facing the window, and he saw the lightning reflected in her eyes as she looked suddenly to him to say: 'Yes!'

Later on during the meal he noticed that without lightning, her eyes had still the appearance of astonishment and joy.

It was about five in the evening when they set out – he on the stout grey which her father occasionally rode, she on her neat, pretty, little liver-chestnut. She had asked him whether he wanted to go anywhere in particular, and he had said that he knew nowhere, and left it entirely to her. They had time, picking their way down the steep hill to the spring, to notice and approve one another. He sat as though he had grown up on a horse, and she, he thought, with a kind of graceful tension which physically became her. They rode in silence, past the spring where the full chuckling gutters emptied into the stream, past a hop field, rampant and dripping, to the corner where there was a disused mill. Its pond had silted into a swamp – there was the custard smell of marshmallow, and she saw one or two delirious dragonflies. As they turned off the road down a bridle path, the little church clock struck five in its usual, childishly abrupt manner. The evening sun was out, lighting the dandelions in the damp misty grass, giving to the tall hedges on either side of them a fresh glinting golden haze: cobwebs clinging to their wild rose and blackberry were so encrusted with seed pearl drops that they hung in broken glittering swags – the delicate mist on the fields beyond lay softly, like shallow smoke – and the sky, washed clean and calm of its cloud, mounted this quantity of brilliant detail with a vast, blank serenity. She looked down from looking up at the sky, and felt him, watching her.

'There's a good gallop later on,' she said; 'I was just looking at things while we walked.'

'So was I. I was discovering the meaning of seeing through someone else's eyes.'

'Were you?' she said awkwardly: she did not like his saying that. Immediately, he withdrew from this stock personal position. She doesn't like it! he thought – She's different; very young – and shy, I do believe. Aloud, he said: 'Even more than anything to be seen, I adore the multicoloured smell – so violently fresh. Do you notice that, also?'

'Fresh and sweet, you said before.'

'Did I? And when did I say that?'

'At luncheon,' she replied diffidently.

'Isn't your memory the tall book!'

But she gave him a solemn glance, and said: 'My father says that my memory is practically non-existent.'

They were approaching a wood: their path was edged now with young bracken, the fronds were tightly curled, as though snarling from the damp. She started a gentle jog-trot, and he followed. Her mare began to get competitive, edging ahead, laying and pricking her ears, tossing her head so that the rings of her running martingale creaked against the leather, and her neck started to darken with sweat. Curran dropped back to watch Antonia. In spite of her tension, her hands were quiet, good hands, he thought, with professional approval.

They were in the wood now; and the trees met over their heads, making an exotic light of lush gloom and slippery sun. She was bareheaded, and the noisy drops from the trees made darker streaks on her dark hair, and soaking circles on her thin white shirt. The rich brown mud splashed up their horses' legs, and Antonia said: 'I'm afraid I'm splashing you. We shall be out of the wood soon, and she knows she can gallop. She always starts this sort of thing exactly here.'

'You don't really need that martingale, do you?'

'It's supposed to help a bit. It's when she's jumping. She gets so excited – up goes her head, and I can't collect her.'

'Then you need a proper one. Those contraptions just give an animal an idea of its own importance.'

She liked the way he said 'contraption', and looked back at him, laughing. 'Is it because you are Irish that you know about horses?'

'It could only be that, now, couldn't it? I was born with a silver bit between my teeth.'

'You wouldn't have been *born* with teeth, you know.'

'Oh, but I was. I was the little ready-made article. My mother had scarcely thrown away her orange blossom before I made my appearance – complete with hair, and nails, and one or two teeth.'

'By the skin of your teeth,' she said, and blushed.

He smiled, delighted with her. 'That's right. You see, our priest was a very powerful man. My father stood six feet in his stockings, but Father O'Rorke had the breadth on him. "You should marry Patsy Gallagher now, considering the way you've persuaded her." "I will not!" said my father. "Consider the shocking shame you'll be bringing on her and your own damnation into the bargain," said Father O'Rorke, gripping me father's jacket with a hand like a spade. It was no good. My father stuck to it that he had no mind for the business. "Then God is witness of my awful unwillingness, but I'm compelled to lay me hands on you. Unhitch your jacket, my son – you'll be imploring me to marry you in it." Well, he pounded me poor father to a pulp, extracted the promise from him, blessed him as he lay in the mud, and was on his way. He married them three weeks later.'

When he told the story, his brogue became rich and pronounced – the rest of the time his voice had only the faintest suggestion of accent and inflexion. He had told it with such a lively unselfconscious pleasure that, fascinated, she had forgotten that the story was about his parents. Now she remembered, and asked:

'And were they happy?'

The question did not seem to be one that he had considered, and he thought a moment before replying: 'Where they were matched they were happy. My father had a terrible temper on him, but my mother was a creature of such elegant pride that she was entirely fearless. It was she read up such quantities of poetry, and French books in the language – she could gallop through those faster than my father could read a horse's pedigree. But she was always expecting something wonderful to happen to her – up to the very day that she died, she believed that. She married beneath her, you see,' he concluded, as though he had explained everything.

'Oh.' It was all beyond her horizon, and there was nothing she dared to say.

'And now, tell me about yourself.' They had unconsciously slowed to a walk while he had been talking, but now they were coming to the gate at the end of the wood.

'This is where we can gallop,' she said, and trotted ahead to open the gate.

'After our gallop, then. You lead, to keep your little mare happy.'

Their ride was round two sides of a large corn field, over a small stile, past a field of clover – it would be flowering now, she thought, and then they were off, and she thought of nothing – feeling only the air on her skin, and the hard quickening rhythm of the mare's shoulders beneath her. Curran kept up with her until they came to the stile, when he checked, to let her over first. Her mare jumped it big and carelessly, fumbling a little the other side. He's right about getting a standing martingale, she thought. The scent of the clover mingling with the delicious heat of her animal – her short hair blowing across her eyes – it was getting too long – and then out of them again – the air – the everlasting joy of it – and then they were slowing for the sloping track down to the lane. She turned to him, flushed with excitement.

'I must have done that dozens of times, but it is always wonderful.'

'Yes?' For a moment their eyes met, and the moment was so violently charged that anything he might have said would have diminished it. But he had an instinct for timing a silence, and exactly at the height of her confusion, he said: 'Now, you were going to tell me about yourself. Come now – use up this dreary lane so determined to make us pay for our gallop. Embroider it with the story of your life. All I know about you is your ravishing face – your pretty voice – and that you ride far and away better than you play tennis.'

She said stiffly: 'My mother feels that my appearance leaves a great deal to be desired.'

He whistled, and then looked carefully at her. 'Does she now?' he said slowly. 'And would you be regarding *her* as the last word on the subject?'

'There – there haven't been any other words.'

'The first word, then. That's a different matter – entirely. I wouldn't go placing your whole heart on her judgment. She's a very attractive woman herself – one might say.'

'I know,' she answered quickly, 'of course I don't.'

'Women are sharp at discovering each other's little faults. It's the men who can tell you what you look like. You'll find that's the way of it.'

She considered this inversion of her experience for a moment, and then said, hesitantly: 'Don't – doesn't anybody ever do both? I mean, notice one's appearance *and* one's character?'

'Now you're going too fast. That is the fairy story. The princess who was as good as she was beautiful.'

'Of course. I suppose that people are *never* as good as they are beautiful: usually the more they are one – the less they are the other.'

'I wouldn't be too sure of that. It is all, as the damned scientists would say, a question of degree, and the story-tellers like extremes. The ugly wicked witch, and the good beautiful princess. People are more beautiful if they are admired, more lovable if they are loved.'

'Oh yes!' She suddenly discovered this.

'Look at yourself. Getting more heartbreakingly attract-ive throughout this ride, all because I've been admiring you from the second we started.' He said this with such wicked determination to confuse her again, that she deter-mined to outface him.

'And *then* what happens?'

But he was not in the least outfaced. 'Oh – after a while of it, you would begin to see how perceptive I was – how clever to see you in such a beautiful light.'

'And then?'

'Then, because you observed it in me, I should become fifty times more perceptive – I should see you through a rose-coloured veil, but it would not in the least obscure you – it would suit you more than anything you could contrive for yourself, I should be a better man in your eyes, and therefore a better man in my own. So would your beauty and my character develop in these magnificent strides of our imagination.'

'Then?'

'Then we should fall madly in love, and live happily ever after,' he finished gaily.

They were almost home. They rode up the drive in a silence swollen with secret, dissimilar delights.

∞ ∞ ∞

After dinner, somebody asked whether he had enjoyed his ride, and Curran said: 'A dream of a ride. When I do eventually start my riding school, I shall ask Toni to be my riding mistress.

'Indeed, yes – it's all planned,' he added, as he saw her look of astonished pride.

The dream had begun.

After dinner, they all danced to the gramophone, and, of course, he danced with her. He had the kind of face which went with dark colouring; incisive, sensual, animate – but he was fair. He danced with enjoyment of the music, and attention to the other couples – sometimes he spoke to them, and they nearly always laughed. Whenever he looked down at her and saw her change from rapt content-ment to the little serious smile she offered him when she felt his eyes on her face, his heart turned over with a remembered, tilting excitement. Once, her mother brushed past them, saw Antonia, and cried: 'Wake *up*, Toni! The child looks as though she's sleepwalking – in a trance!' Then he saw her, utterly unprepared, painfully wake from her enchantment, and assume an expression of careful neutrality – an attempt to feel nothing at all – which made him more sharply aware of the contrast – which uncomfortably touched him.

He danced with everyone else, and twice with his hostess. He wanted to be asked again, and he had a general, instinctive desire to please. The second time that he danced with Araminta, she said:

'You have been an angel, bringing my Toni out of her shell. She is just terribly young for her age – of course, she *is* terribly young, I suppose.'

The answer to that was easy. 'And *you* are terribly young to have even a young grown-up daughter.'

She settled into the crook of his arm (she was half a head shorter than Antonia), and murmured: '*You* are an absolutely *divine* dancer. You must come and stay with us again.'

'I'd love that.' He smiled down into her prettily shaped eyes, and noticed how when they did not appear shrewd, they were vacant.

When, a little later, he looked round for Antonia, she had disappeared.

'Toni's gone to bed,' said Enid, 'aren't you *heartbroken*?'

He had known Enid for years, so he simply seized her round the waist, saying: 'It was *you* I was looking for, my darling.'

She gave her husky incredulous laugh. 'There's nothing like a good roll over the haystack to find the needle, as hardly anybody I know knows better than you.'

'Talking of needles, what about that gramophone?'

They went to its rescue.

Antonia had not gone to sleep. For a while she had watched him dancing with the others – they all, she felt, danced better than she – and she did not anyway want to dance with anyone else, so she said good night to the nearest couple, and slipped away.

In her room she undressed as quickly as possible, put out her lamp, and drew back the curtains. The moonlight crept coldly over the room with a soft secret silence. Images, steeped in this silver light, shifted about in her mind – idle, disordered, repetitive: her face burned with a fever of recollections, and she lay perfectly still. She suffered no anxiety then about the future. She did not need or imagine any return – and, she thought, simply, that he need not know.

FOUR

He went away the next morning when the house party broke up, and she felt calm, and curiously relieved that he had gone. She had only a continuous, almost insupportable need to be alone; but on Mondays the clearing up after weekends made privacy impossible: her mother skimmed the house of flowers, gramophone records, bedside books and biscuit tins, cigarette boxes and house linen, and distributed a fresh supply. It was on Mondays that her mother suddenly decided to rearrange a room, or to move a piece of furniture from one end of the house to the other. These activities were usually accompanied by a post-mortem upon Antonia's weekend behaviour which always made her more or less unhappy, but on this Monday she was struck with a sudden indifference to everything her mother said, and instead of miserable silence while she searched for an apology or an excuse, she found herself replying with an immediate, agreeable equanimity. Yes, her clothes *were* awful – she was going to do something about them. It was no good expecting her to play tennis well, she didn't enjoy it and had decided to give it up. She hadn't particularly wanted to go to the Framptons, and it seemed to her almost rude to one's hosts to go unwillingly to their parties. When, somewhat baffled, her mother set about Antonia's inability to make small-talk, Antonia retorted: 'Nor can my father make small-talk. Unfortunately, unlike him, I also have, he says, a commonplace mind. You had much better stop worrying about me. I am perfectly happy.'

During the hot empty summer week, however, her happiness became less perfect – became tinged and tainted with the fear that perhaps she might never see him again – not once more in her whole life.

Araminta often went to London for Wednesday or Thursday night, and this week, Antonia suddenly asked whether she might go with her. This did not suit Araminta. Why did she want to go? To buy two lengths of linen for summer dresses. 'Oh, I'll get *them* for you. You want blue, I suppose.' 'No. I'll mix the colours on to a piece of paper, and I shall want them exactly like that.'

She mixed for a whole afternoon, and produced a deep sage green, and a daffodil yellow.

'They'll be too dreadfully difficult. Greens are always tricky, and yellow is practically impossible. I shouldn't have thought either of them were *you* – but I'll do my best.' And Antonia knew that she would, because in small matters her mother was extremely conscientious.

Her mother (and George Warrender) returned on Friday morning, with a perfect green, a paler version of the right yellow, and a deep terracotta dress, also linen, with a plain top, and a pleated skirt. 'You can't possibly manage with two. I don't suppose for a moment it will fit, but Miss Hilder can come up and alter it.' But it did fit, perfectly.

'Oh, thank you! It does fit – it's perfect, and I'd forgotten this colour.'

'That's marvellous, darling. It looks marvellous on you. Doesn't it look marvellous on her, George?'

'Marvellous,' said George, and laughed admiringly.

Antonia felt suddenly that her mother was very much kinder than she had realized, and kissed her. Araminta looked pleased, and, to hide her confusion and surprise, lifted her arm which was weighed down by a bracelet strident with lucky charms, and said: 'And look what that *angel* George gave me. This sweet little platinum fiddle. Isn't it a dream?'

And Antonia, while she dutifully admired the platinum fiddle, thought how much prettier her mother looked when she was being kind.

The weekend guests arrived – and apart from George Warrender they were all different from the weekend before: another man sat opposite her in the dining-room. She watched (as she must have watched so many times, only before she seemed not to have noticed it) various guests making dabs and stabs at conversation with her father, and remembered exactly a week ago (no, it had been Saturday luncheon) that Curran had engaged him in easy, animated discourse. She sat longing for the evening to be over, so that she might escape to the understandable loneliness of being by herself . . .

But alone, her happiness, the extraordinary peace of mind which had been hers when he had gone, seemed now to have dwindled to a little painful pin point of anxiety to which, however restless her mind, she seemed fastened. No thought matched with any other: she felt bereft, and she did not know why; she felt sadly isolated from everybody else in the house, and yet she did not want to be with any of them; she wanted this long, empty day to be finished, but had no desire for the next one; she could no longer bear to remember minutely the evening ride after the storm, and yet she was terrified of forgetting any moment of it. She felt exhausted – wasted, and sleep seemed not only more exhaustion, further waste, but impossible. Burning, shivering, from these irreconcilable longings and rejections of longings she lay, until, just before her thoughts ran down to sleep, she wondered how all the countless people who must have felt as she was now feeling had managed to bear it.

On Saturday, she decided that she must accept the likelihood of never seeing him again, and on the strength of this strength, the day spent itself for her in a consciously usual manner.

On Sunday afternoon, without any kind of warning, he arrived. The house party were playing tennis, and Antonia was preparing strawberries for the cook to make jam. She had collected the trug, a vast pan, and a basin for the stalks, and settled herself on the front lawn. The strawberries, beautifully piled, completely filling the trug, smelled warm and delicious: the distant sounds of tennis were soothing, even enjoyable, she decided, and began to feel familiar solitary happiness flowing steadily back into her – the pleasures of the sun hot on her hair, of twisting each stalk and its white conical root out of each strawberry, of her fingers becoming transparent pink, and tasting sweet, but more sophisticated than sugar. She could almost, she thought, experiment with those mysterious, curiously unsatisfying sensations which had so much possessed her – that tide was now so far out that she could hardly imagine when it had been in, concealing the pleasant, empty wastes which before had always contented her. 'You want to be the only pebble on the beach,' a governess had often said. This did not seem to her now to be a question of desire or choice, but simply of acceptance.

Then she heard a car in the drive, and the tide gave a

little lurch towards her, so that she could see it quite clearly. More people to play tennis, of course.

She heard the gate open and shut, and saw him. Her heart gave one violent leap, and then settled into an entirely different position. He had seen her, and came quickly across the lawn – without speaking, but smiling with a kind of conspiratorial friendliness.

'I've just sneaked over. I've no invitation to come. Do you think that will cause a rumpus?' He was exactly as though he had not been away at all.

'No – no, I'm sure it won't.' She felt as though he had been away for a year.

'I like you with all the strawberries round you. I can't tell you how delighted I am to set eyes on you. May I eat one?'

'Of course.'

'Choose it for me. Won't you?' he added, as he saw her fingers hesitate over the pile.

'I was choosing a good one. They are only jam strawberries, you know. Some of them are rather squashed.' She held one out, and had, for the first time, to look at him.

'Perfect,' he said, and ate it watching her.

'You look hot, and a little sad,' he observed, his eyes still on her.

She began twisting stalks out of strawberries again. It was surely not charming to look hot, and sadness was out of the question. But he persisted.

'Have you had secret troubles, then, my poor Toni?'

'If I had, they would, as you say, be secret.'

'Ah, but one has to tell secrets to *someone*. That is what friends are for.'

'They are the people to whom one betrays secrets?'

'To whom one betrays oneself. "I love you: I wish I saw more of you" people say: they don't necessarily mean more *time*, you know – they nearly always mean more of *you*.'

'So time doesn't count very much? I mean – how long one has known somebody – or how much time one has spent knowing them?'

He smiled gently at her. 'With you and me it doesn't count at all.'

She felt the blood rushing over her face, and realized that that was why, a few minutes ago, he had said she looked hot. 'Anyway, I haven't any secret troubles.'

Then her mother appeared: saw them, and came straight over – calling – shouting, and then talking – swinging her racquet against her neat, childish knees.

'. . . how lovely to *see* you! Where *have* you sprung from? George will have a spare pair of flannels. Toni, you juggins, why didn't you come and *tell* me?'

She was up to them. Curran was on his feet – explaining that he was weekending with the Leggatts, and, discovering how near they were to one another, had got them to drop him here for the afternoon – he couldn't resist seeing them – he did hope that was all right?

'It's marvellous! Algie's turned his ankle, and we're desperate for a really reliable man. You must stay to dinner. George will drive you back. It's only Roberts-bridge, isn't it? It's the Edmund Leggatts, isn't it? I've met her at a party somewhere, but I can't remember a *thing* about her, except that she had a madly attractive husband who she was meanly incarcerating at home with malaria. *Is* he madly attractive? But of course you wouldn't know – men are absolutely hopeless about that sort of thing. Come into the house and find clothes for tennis. You don't want to play, Toni, do you? She's given it up – isn't it *middle-aged* of her!'

He was swept into the house, and she was left, alone with her strawberries, and the tide – a spring tide – approaching, galloping in – overwhelming her peace.

∞ ∞ ∞

He stayed to dinner, and talked charmingly to her father. After dinner, Araminta was insistent that everybody dance, so of course they danced, and he danced with Araminta. (George Warrender said that actually he preferred to work the gramophone.)

When, much later in the evening, he came up to her and collected her for a record which they had danced before, she felt a wild release of happiness: although, not alone with him, hardly speaking to him, she had felt happy all the evening.

After a minute, he said: 'Tell you something.'

She looked up.

'You don't look sad any more.'

And she answered joyfully: 'I'm not sad, at all.'

But after that record, Araminta said that George must drive him home.

'I'll come with you, George, darling – to cheer your lonely return.'

George, as usual, laughed, but he looked much more cheerful than when he had been changing the records.

When Curran said goodbye to her, he touched her hand, and said: 'It was you I came to see. You have eyes like stars in the sky at night. It was you I came to see.' Then they were both overwhelmed by the communal leave-taking, and breaking up of the evening.

So – the point of no return: the last moment before a distant approaching figure is recognizable and can be identified – has seen and been seen; before there is no turning back, and they must be met, suffered, or enjoyed, or a mutual indifference underlined. He had come to see *her*, and at the instant of their parting in the crowded room, they met.

In the night she woke, and all the time of her life seemed concentrated on the moment of waking, and all the meaning of her existence on her being deeply, irrevocably, in love.

FIVE

A fortnight later, he was invited to stay with them for ten days. He arrived with everyone else on a Friday; she heard them arrive, and for nearly an hour afterwards, she could not bring herself to go down: the joy of knowing that he was in the house was so great, that she was afraid that she could not meet him calmly. Her fear that anyone – particularly her mother – should guess or know anything at all about it filled her with sickening terror, and she wondered whether he would understand her need for absolute secrecy. She did not know.

His manner, when she walked into the drawing-room, was impeccably casual; indeed at first he seemed really not to notice her, and her pendulum of anxiety swung to the end of his indifference, but later, as she drank sherry and listened to an argument about whether hard or grass courts were the most fun, he was suddenly at her side, muttering:

'I have a curious feeling that *I* shall turn me ankle tomorrow, so that I shan't be able to *move* except on a horse.'

Which was how they came to have their second ride.

They went out for the day, talking sandwiches with them. Araminta, initially exasperated by Curran's unfortunate accident with his ankle, seemed uninterested in any other plan for him, and when Antonia suggested taking him to see the famous Battle Great Wood, her mother immediately agreed in the way that she always did when she wasn't even listening.

As soon as they were a few hundred yards up the lane, Curran leapt off his horse, and undid the long crêpe bandage which he had wound round his ankle.

'Remind me to put it back,' he said, and stuffed it into the pocket of his old riding jacket.

'There really is nothing wrong with you?'

Even now, she hardly believed him, he had been so convincing earlier in the morning: so courageous, and distressed, and apparently so crippled. But he laughed his curious glancing laugh that without him she could not precisely remember, and said: 'Play acting – the whole affair. Did I take *you* in as well? I must have surpassed myself.'

'I think I am easily deceived. At least I was sorry for you.'

'Bless your gentle heart. Now – tell me about this wood of yours.'

'It is called Battle Great Wood. It isn't as great as it used to be – although people can still get lost in it.'

'Have *you* ever got lost in it?'

'Oh no! I think one would have to be on foot and very stupid. I just ride there sometimes.'

'Would this be good country to start a riding school, do you think?'

Without answering, she asked eagerly: 'Are you really going to start one?'

'Would you really help me if I did?'

'Oh, I should *love* it! But I thought you were going to have the school in London.'

'It's the obvious place. There's a little more money in it there, I'm afraid.'

'I don't like London,' she said, suddenly remembering her dislike of it.

'Then it can't be in London. What country shall it be – you choose.'

'I like woods—' she began, and then said: 'Do you mean what *kind* of country, or simply *which* country?'

'I meant which kind,' he replied, watching her. 'How old are you, Toni? Seventeen?'

'Nineteen,' she said, shocked at the amount he was wrong. She waited a moment, and then, elaborately casual, asked: 'Do I seem to you to be only seventeen?'

'Well, yes, I think you did. Does that offend your dignity?'

'Of course not.' She sounded so deeply offended that he laughed outright.

'Oh dear! Toni, *don't* be cross with me. Many women, you know, like to be thought younger than they are.'

'I know that, of course.' She had begun to trot ahead of him on the verge at the side of the road. 'Anyway, you can't just tell people what you think they would like to hear.'

'But if you like people you want them to like what you tell them.'

'Flattery,' she said, without looking back. The simplicity of her contempt both annoyed and fascinated him, and he rode level with her, but, to his consternation, her eyes were filled with tears.

'Toni?' When she did not reply, he asked gently: 'What have I done to you?'

There was a short silence, and then she said:

'You are not to say things to me which you do not mean. I won't have it,' she added stiffly.

'But I've never done anything of the kind!' he cried, wondering what on earth he had said to her.

363

'Do you *promise* you haven't?'

(Heavens, she was young!) 'Toni, why should I flatter you? I've meant every single word I've ever said to you. Will you do me the honour of believing that?'

'Of course; if you ask me to.' Then she smiled at him, her immediate acceptance startling him as much as had the appearance of her tears. (Heavens, he thought again, she is *young*!)

'We go to the right in a minute, and then we are nearly there.'

'We have good weather for our expeditions,' he said, following suit.

She looked about her. 'Yes, but it isn't drawing *attention* to itself, like it was the other evening after the storm.'

They turned to the right of the road, into a narrow sunken lane, its high banks covered with wild strawberries and dog violets. On their right, the wood had now mysteriously begun.

'The thing about the wood,' she said, 'is that when you are well into it, there doesn't seem to be any weather, or time.' She looked to see if he had understood her, but he was attentively at a loss, so she went on: 'I mean, whatever the weather, or whenever one is there, it seems as though it is always like that. No evening, or night, or rain, or darkness – it seems complete, and separate, and permanently the same.' She stopped, and then added thoughtfully: 'Of course, it is different every time one goes there.'

'Is that how you think to yourself?'

'Only sometimes: only about some things. It's odd: it seems perfectly clear when I'm thinking it, and absolutely stupid when I try to talk.'

'Always?' he asked, and she answered at once as he expected.

'I've never tried before.'

(The sky above the heavy tapestry of the wood was a piercingly tender blue.)

'I *like* flattery,' he said unexpectedly.

She turned to him.

'You see, I'm flattered that you haven't tried to talk to anyone else.'

'But that is true!'

'Yes, but you might not have bothered to tell me.'

'You asked me, so of course I did.'

He groaned aloud. 'Toni, you frighten me! Do you not allow yourself any comforting deceptions with people or yourself?'

She considered, and he noticed that she was faintly blushing.

'I don't know. I don't think I know exactly what you mean. I think I am absolutely ignorant. Have you noticed how, if they *are* that, people nearly always sound priggish? I didn't mean to be.'

He thought – There is a difference between ignorance and innocence. Aloud he said: 'I know you aren't a prig. Well, if I promise never to flatter you, and you promise constantly to flatter me, we shall be happy for ever.'

She turned to him, laughing – but her eyes were really like stars – he thought – she'll break my heart with eyes like that.

She said: 'Here we are. Here we go into the wood.'

The entrance to the wood seemed casual enough, but in a few minutes they might have been in the middle. It was laced by endless paths and tracks, flecked with glades where timber had died or been cut for fencing – presenting enormous proportions of contrast: of heat from the strips of sky above the sun – baked tracks; of cold from its infinite shades and greens: of immense silence and the miniature orchestration of insects – of no colour – the trunks of the big oak and Spanish chestnut trees were simply lighter or darker, like shadows – the ground a rich texture of dust – the old, odd, dead leaves the mere bones of their bronze – the snapped-off twigs like silver ghosts, as though they had once been drowned in moonlight; and then the pink-purples of loosestrife and foxgloves, the warm yellow of toadflax, the cold yellow of celandine, and the greens of moss, of lords and ladies, of wood anemone, of bracken, and of oak leaf – rich, glossy, delicate, luxuriant and simple.

'Where are we going to eat our lunch?'

'Why? Are you hungry? Do you want to stop now?'

'No – I was just wondering whether you knew your way, or had some mysterious plan.'

'I was going to take you to the only stream that I've found. It isn't very far, and then the horses can have a drink. Are you afraid of being lost?'

'I am sure that *you* won't get lost. I am only afraid of losing *you*.'

'I won't let you get lost,' she replied.

However, after another half an hour's riding he decided that, without her, he would undoubtedly have been lost. They had changed their track so many times, that with the sun at its midday height above them, he had no longer any sense of direction.

'Nearly there. In the spring you hear the stream before you see it. But now it is far too languid to make a sound.'

They came out into a clearing in one corner of which was a vast oak, and on the far side of it a bank down to the stream. She jumped off her horse and looked round with a proprietary triumph which he found endearing.

'Don't you think it is a good place for a picnic?'

'Perfect,' he agreed. Watching her, he had forgotten to dismount.

'That is what you said about the strawberry.'

Perhaps she is not so unselfconscious after all, he thought, as he led his animal to the stake where she was tying hers. She has an infallible instinct for timing these memories of hers. Women nearly always know what is in the wind, after all . . .

She was scrambling over the bank to the stream.

'There is a deepish place where I thought we'd put the cider. At least it might cool the bottle a bit.'

He followed her. She had jumped down from the bank on to a small triangular island, so small that there was scarcely room for her and the hopeful little oak tree which grew at one end of it. On one side was a broad gravel bed over which the water lay as shallow as a biscuit, on the other a narrow swooping channel, dark green with the weed washed like long hair by the rush of water.

'I deepened it a bit, once,' she said, and wedged the bottle under a root.

'Do you want a hand up?' he asked, but she pushed her hair back from her face with wet fingers, and said carelessly:

'Oh no – I can easily manage.'

They tried watering the horses, who sniffed the stream slowly, with a delicate, contemptuous indifference.

'Proverbial horses,' she said, and they tied them up again.

They settled under the oak tree for their lunch. She unpacked the canvas bag, while he fetched the cider.

'Don't spoil my oak tree,' she called.

'Why? Did you plant it?'

'Oh no. It did it, itself. But I like it there.'

As soon as they were still, with their food unpacked, the insects seemed to gather in ceremonious clouds.

'It might help if we smoked.'

'You smoke. I don't. At least, I never have.'

'Have one now? They're gaspers, I warn you.'

She looked doubtfully at the packet.

'Gaspers? Are they nice? Honestly, I really haven't ever smoked.'

'People always smoke their first cigarette in a wood. It's traditional.' She took one, and he lit it for her. 'You draw on it and puff.'

She answered stiffly: 'I know how people do it, of course.'

He watched her, puffing jerkily with a carefully composed expression.

'All right?'

She nodded, and some smoke got into her eyes.

He poured out the cider and said:

'Nobody ever smokes *all* of their first cigarette, you know.'

'Don't they?'

'No. That's traditional, too.'

'I did like it,' she said, and stubbed it out very carefully.

They ate their lunch – talking very little – contented by the heat and the leisure of being alone with no possibility of interruption. For her this meant simply the perfect delight of a lazy summer day spent privately with him: for him the delicious mounting certainty that with all this time he would (in some sort) be able to make love to her. He was discovering the difference between her unselfconsciousness – the confiding ease which she displayed towards him, and her sudden, abrupt withdrawals into a confusion, an extreme shyness, and this was to him as fascinating as it was unaccountable.

They had drunk all the cider, which, she said, made her almost want to sleep, and now she lay on her back against the gently sloping bank, with her hands clasped behind her head, and her eyes shut. She had refused a second cigarette, but when she heard the match strike for his, her eyes opened for an instant, and she smiled: 'Wake me up, if I *do* go to sleep.'

He nodded, and settled himself against the oak tree with the appearance of drowsing over his cigarette, in case she should feel that he wanted to look at her.

The heat, and the silence which was disturbed only by the sensual conglomeration of insects, sharpened his senses to the point when he wanted nothing but to watch her, until simply watching her should become unbearable. Her position, her stillness, was in itself attractive – lying still, he thought, she was attractive almost to the height of beauty – and there was at last time now for him to enjoy all the details of her attraction. Her head, turned a little to one side, showed the long line of her neck, from the purely white skin down to the small hollow of her throat faintly powdered with gold from the sun. Her shoulders under the white shirt seemed almost childishly boned – no smooth, secretive flesh rounding their shape – giving to her arms the appearance of being not straight – not curved – but of some third elusive linear distinction. He imagined her breasts – small and white, they would grow with a different whiteness, enhanced by their delicate decoration. After them, the long hesitant lines resolved, slipped away to her waist into which the shirt was neatly tucked. She seemed to be all length and qualities of whiteness: no colour but her hair and her startling eyes – Irish

369

colouring – but she had told him that she was a part Welsh, and not Irish at all. He remembered her pretty hands, which were now hidden by her head: a short strand of hair lay with a sharper dark across her forehead, and he imagined her wet fingers, or the sweat of a hot day. She slept now, he was almost sure of it: that curious composition of a vulnerable repose was hers: the soft even breathing, and her eyelashes with the instant's poise of a butterfly . . . He remembered her asleep on the grass bank by the tennis court; how he had observed then how gracefully she slept, how he had been struck by the sudden, violent colour of her eyes when he had woken her . . .

'This is the second time of waking.'

She opened her eyes slowly: she had been fast asleep.

'No dandelion, this time.'

She stared at him – waking – beginning to smile: he saw the second's alarm in her eyes as he bent over her – then felt the smile dissolve under his mouth as he kissed her. Her hands, locked behind her head, were suddenly crushed by the weight; he stopped kissing her for a moment to free them, and she flung her arms round his neck. He held her head a little away from his to ask: 'Has anyone ever kissed you before?'

When she shook her head, a passionate tenderness overwhelmed his desire for her; he pushed the strand of hair back from her forehead with the absolute gentleness of possession. 'You'll never be able to say that again.'

They looked at one another in silence, she with astonishment, he with delight. Then he said: 'You are so *lovely*! I've never seen anyone *like* you! This is the beginning of your life, and it's I who have the fantastic luck to be there! Toni, Toni *darling*, sweet creature, say you love me a little!'

'Do you love me?'

'I'm mad about you! I adore you – I've never felt like this in my life before!'

He lifted her into his arms, and she, touching his face with her fingers, started to say: 'I *do* love you,' before he began kissing her again – touching, exciting, overwhelming her with their senses. Loving him, she startled him with her response, until he wanted her so urgently that he had forgotten that it was she he wanted. When the confusion of love and desire between them was at its height, he laid her breathless and trembling on the ground, and began wrenching undone the buttons of her shirt. Her hands flew up instinctively, and he said: 'Yes, you undo them: you'll be much quicker than I.'

She sat up.

'Don't stare at me – don't waste a second. Take off all your clothes.'

She was still dazed, but somewhere a distant pounding terror had begun.

'My clothes?'

'I want to make love to you – because I want you. Oh, Toni, don't pretend you don't know what I want *now* – after that.'

She looked wildly round at her sunlit wood: something had gone incomprehensibly, terribly wrong. 'I – I *can't*!' The pounding came from her heart. 'I – *can't*! I *can't*.'

His hands, which had been heavily on her shoulders, pushed her heavily away. 'Do you mean to say that you can behave like that, kiss me as you did just now, and then calmly stop when it suits you, like any little cold-blooded bitch? I'm not so likely now to believe the tale that you've never been kissed.' He was so furiously frustrated, that he hardly knew what he was saying. 'You make me mad with wanting you, and then, with your clothes half off

371

your body you say that you can't!' There was an angry silence, until the palpable injustice of this last remark pulled him up, and for the first time since he had laid her on the ground, he looked at her – pulling her shirt together, staring speechlessly at him – with an appearance so stricken, so utterly at a loss, that he was seized suddenly with an uneasy, exasperated remorse.

'It was my fault, really: I'm sorry. I was carried away.' It was intolerable, he felt bitterly – she said nothing; she looked so dead white; he wished she would *say* something. He tried to smile at her. 'It's all right – I know you didn't understand.' Then, in spite of himself, he added: 'I thought you loved me,' and felt the instant quickening of response, before, in a very low voice, she said:

'I *do* love you. I've never loved anyone else, and I love you with all my heart. I – I wouldn't have – kissed you, otherwise. I'm very sorry. I didn't know that it was a bad thing to do.'

'Poor little Toni – you don't have to say that, when I'm the one who has made such a mess for you: forgive me, darling, for upsetting you so badly – will you do that now?'

She nodded; but when he took her hand, she made a little, painfully resistant sound, and twisted away from him face downward on to the ground.

Now he did not hesitate: her saying that she loved him had restored all his confidence and kindness – he picked her up and held her in his arms, stroking her hair, and comforting her as though she was a child. She *isn't* much more than a child, after all, he thought; I've never made such a mess of anything in my life.

When she was nearly calmed, he felt in his pockets for a handkerchief, and out came the crêpe bandage.

'Will this do, do you think?'

She nodded, and the last tears spurted out of her eyes. He mopped her face carefully, and kissed it; and then, feeling her stiffen, he said: 'That's just kiss and be friends, like the children. You don't have to worry about it.'

She smiled, and it seemed then a minute adventure in her face. Nearly home now, he thought, if I'm careful. Aloud, he said: 'I think the time has come for me to indulge myself with a cigarette.'

She slipped instantly out of his arms.

'Would you like to try again?'

She turned to him, and for some reason – inexplicable to him – blushed scarlet pink.

'Oh no! Thank you.'

She began packing up the remains of their lunch with careful neatness.

'I wish we hadn't drunk all the cider—' he began, but she interrupted him:

'Geoffrey!'

'Toni!'

'There is one thing I have to ask you.' She was sitting back on her heels, not looking at him.

'Ask me anything you like.'

'No – but it isn't easy,' she cried, and then stopped completely.

Filled with an apprehensive curiosity, he urged her on, until, eventually, she said:

'It may sound absurd to you – but I would be terribly grateful if you wouldn't tell my mother anything about me. I simply couldn't *bear* her to know. I – *couldn't – bear* – it,' she repeated.

No request of hers could possibly have startled him

more. The idea that he would tell her mother, or, indeed, *any* mother, that he had attempted, and failed, to seduce her daughter, seemed to him so incredible that he looked searchingly at her, but her expression of nervous anxiety remained. At last, he said slowly:

'Of course, I wouldn't dream of telling your mother. It shall be just between our two selves. Yes?'

'Yes,' she said, with such deep gratitude, that he could no longer doubt her sincerity. There was a slight pause, and then she went on: 'She might suspect, you see – but if she asked me, I should *lie* to her!' She looked so passionately determined, that he found himself nodding gravely, as she finished half to herself: 'For the first time.'

'Well, but if I promise that, will you promise to come riding with me sometimes?'

She looked up, and he saw that her eyes were alive again.

'Do you *want* me to?'

'Of course I do! We'll make elaborate plans to fox your mother, hey?'

She smiled with a charming secret delight, and they went to untie their patient fly-ridden horses.

Perhaps everything will be all right, after all, he thought, in spite of getting away to such a bad start.

She rode, light-headed, with an exhaustion of which she was hardly aware. He knows that I love him, and he understands about not telling my mother, she thought again and again. He knows, and he entirely understands.

The journey out of the wood and home, therefore, was easy and peaceful.

∞ ∞ ∞

When they had returned, and joined the others, she was amazed at the ease with which she felt able to behave as though nothing had happened.

He, however, still feeling guilty, felt that her studied calm was extraordinarily unconvincing, and wondered whether, with her mother at any rate, she would get away with it. He devoted himself to Araminta for the rest of the day, observing George Warrender's helpless discomfiture with a streak of cynical malice.

Antonia thought that she had successfully avoided any conversation with her mother, but when she was undressing, Araminta tapped lightly on her door and opened it immediately before there was time for a reply. Antonia, who was brushing her hair, stopped with the brush defensively poised.

'Don't look so startled. It's only me, popping in to say good night.'

There was a slight pause, during which Antonia put down the brush, and Araminta skimmed restlessly round the room, eventually pouncing on the terracotta dress which Antonia had just taken off.

'Darling, you really *should* hang your things *up*! How can you *expect* anything to stay wearable if you don't?'

'I was going to hang it up. I've only just taken it off.'

Araminta's light, incredulous laugh sharpened her weariness to the pitch of nervous action. Her mother never came to say good night to her – she had obviously come for something. She swung round on her stool.

'What is it?'

Her mother was stooping to the glass on the dressing-table, patting her shingled waves into shape, and Antonia saw her second's anger at being attacked, before, with deliberate good temper, she said:

ELIZABETH JANE HOWARD

'Well, darling – far be it from me to criticize, but I think you were really a teeny bit rude to poor George this evening: he had nobody to talk to, and you simply read a book! Of course, nobody could be more delighted than I that you have at last found somebody you like – but you must try not to – well – *throw* yourself at somebody's head at everybody else's expense – if you see what I mean.'

There was a silence, during which Antonia thought of so many things to say that she could (fortunately) say none of them. Eventually, as she felt that this was simply provoking her mother's remorseless curiosity, she said flatly: 'I see – Was that all?'

Her mother had retreated to the door. 'That was all, darling. For goodness sake don't sulk about it, it was entirely well meant – for goodness sake don't take everything so *to heart*.'

She was gone, and at last, it was the very end of the day.

SIX

The rest of Curran's visit was conducted with perfect summer weather, and a faint but unmistakable tension, of which, in some degree, everybody was aware. Antonia, who was perhaps most aware of it, probably understood it least. She thought, simply, that every shade and degree of all her senses, which seemed to her exquisitely, unpeacefully heightened, were because she was in love: but she did not exist in a private world which contained only herself and Curran. Now, when she saw the little train from the morning-room window at breakfast, she felt that she could exactly smell its blue-puffed smoke: when her father arrived late for luncheon she felt that she could tell whether his morning's work had pleased him: she was sharply aware that George Warrender's behaviour was not, as her mother said, merely liver, but unhappiness of some kind; felt sorry for him – and tried, hesitantly, to take his mind off whatever it was. She knew that her mother was mysteriously, deeply angry with her, and tried, without any success, to annul the anger: but she was protected from understanding any of this by the screen, the filter, the instinctive relation that everything now had for her to Curran. So sudden had been this process of relating everything to her love, and then so continuous and complete, that almost immediately after acknowledging the change, she became unconscious of it. She was entirely possessed by her new and perfect pitch of happiness: entirely sensitive – entirely subjective – without even her earlier capacity to compare or analyse or understand the implications – like being suddenly able to read a set of foreign languages without translating a word of any of them.

The scene in the wood seemed miraculously not to have wrecked the situation; after a day or two not even to have altered it, and she was unquestioningly grateful to him for that. She was content to be very seldom alone with him, and his discovery that she neither sought nor avoided his company seemed to him as extraordinary as it was intriguing. If she loved him surely she would attempt some sort of private plan; if she did not, surely she would prevent any effort he made? But she seemed not calm, but passive about arrangements, although she responded eagerly to affectionate teasing, and easy, intimate, small-talk, whenever they were alone. For a few days he established this relationship with her, finding that her silence with the others was not so much colourless, as watchful and acutely observant – afterwards she would tell him what she had been thinking; they would continue the conversation from wherever it had been carelessly dropped – and he noticed with amusement her honest memory, her breathless care in reconstructing the scene. For the rest of his visit, he listened and argued and encouraged her to talk about herself – to tell him what she thought and felt – exploring the length and breadth of her inexperience, but finding, also, that there was nothing stale in her mind.

Once, when they were picking raspberries, she asked him about himself, and he laughed and turned easily aside from her question – a bird was caught in the nets, and they freed it together; she held the creature, breathing like a mill race, its beak wide with terror, while he carefully cut the twine from its little cold feet, until with a single, silently explosive jerk it was entirely gone – and she had forgotten the question.

The evening before he left he kissed her again. They were sitting on a stile at the end of the spinney behind the house. At their back the wood was unevenly dusk and dark – in front the end of the sunlight lay on the thick summer grass.

'It is rather like sitting in the front row of a theatre.'

'Have you been to many theatres?' he asked, watching her.

'Not very many. I've never sat in the front row.' She seemed to feel that this was an admission. 'But it is what I imagined the front row would feel like.'

'Will you come to a theatre with me? We'll sit bang in front if that would please you.'

'Would that be a good thing?' She did not really want to see him in London, but did not like to say so. There was a little silence, and then she asked: 'What about your riding school?'

'Oh, that will progress, I have no doubt, but I've yet to meet the man with more money than I to start it, and I have to go home first.'

'Home?' She stared at him – she hadn't thought of him having a home.

'To Ireland,' he said; 'that is my home, you know.'

'Oh, yes.'

'I shall be back, though. I shall come back to see you.'

'And to start your school,' she said, and he smiled, liking and knowing that she was not being prim, or coy, but simply, anxiously, accurate. He said: 'I shall miss you.'

She turned suddenly to him, and he felt that it had been both an inadequate and a stupid thing to say.

'Will you jump down, and let me kiss you?' She hesitated, and her colour slowly vanished.

'This is a different wood: it won't be at all the same.' He saw her fingers tighten on the top bar of the stile before she jumped.

This time, knowing now how to assail her confidence, he told her that he loved her.

∞   ∞   ∞

He went, and the sharp shock of his absence – even after she had imagined and dreaded it – astonished her.

A day or two after his departure, her mother had a letter from him at breakfast.

'Geoffrey's b. and b.,' she said, having flipped through it. Her husband looked up from his catalogue enquiringly.

'Geoffrey *Curran*,' she said impatiently. 'He seems to have enjoyed himself, and he sends his love. He's off to Ireland some time or other – awful writing – the kind one simply can't be bothered to read.' There was a pause, and then she continued: 'That wretch, Thomas, wants dozens of wilting little bundles of damp moss fetched from Battle station. Anybody want to go to Battle?'

Her husband shook his head: Antonia, trying not to stare at the letter, said nothing.

Araminta, who hated silence, said: 'You never want to go *anywhere*, Wilfrid,' as though Battle was a great opportunity lost. 'I suppose, as usual, it will be poor little me.'

'I'll go on the bus, if you like.'

'I do wish you'd learn to drive the car, Toni. No, I'll

do it. The Parkers are down, I'll drop in and see if they'd like a spot of bridge sometime.'

There was another silence: Araminta sighed restlessly, and flicked Curran's envelope across the table. Wilfrid made a note on his catalogue and asked: 'Are you going to London this week, Araminta?'

She shook her head. She seemed more than usually wrought up.

'There's no point in this heat. Nothing to do when I get there. Goodness! I wish we were all *abroad*, or something!'

'Well, my dear, *you* could go, and take Toni with you, if you like. I shall be perfectly all right by myself.'

Antonia got up from the table and went to the window.

'I often think you're *better* by yourself! What on earth do you think would be the fun for either of us trailing about the Riviera with Toni? I *do wish* that sometimes – *only sometimes* – you would occasionally do what somebody else wanted for a change. You think you make it perfectly all right by telling *me* to do whatever it is by myself – you think that lets you out of any effort – it doesn't occur to you that I don't *want* to do everything alone—'

He interrupted: 'I wouldn't have described you as a solitary creature. You have an enormous quantity of friends . . .'

But she retorted: 'What on earth should I do if I hadn't? We can't all spend our lives musing over books while everything else is being done for us, you know.'

'It is not a ubiquitous pursuit,' he agreed mildly.

She stared angrily at him.

'You are absolutely *extraordinary*! It doesn't matter what

anyone says – you don't seem in the least hurt – you don't even seem to care!'

Antonia turned round to them, wanting desperately to cry: 'You can't *do* this – *I'm* here. Stop it!' Pointless, illogical – far too late.

Her father was looking steadily across the table with no trace of expression.

'Do you *want* me to be hurt?'

Her mother stared defiantly back. 'Yes! I do! Yes!'

He got heavily to his feet, and went to the door.

'It would be too difficult for me to know where to begin.'

He was gone. Her mother gave a little sharp gasping cry, and burst into tears.

Panic – agony – somebody was awfully hurt – so awfully, that she could hardly bear to touch them. She went to her mother, and stood with her arm round the shaking shoulders. Her mother suddenly and wildly clung to her. 'I didn't mean it. Can't bear people who don't *feel* anything. That's why I say such awful things – it was only because of *books* he asked whether I was going to London – I can't bear being lonely—' Tears were pouring down her face: her long beautifully kept nails dug into Antonia's arm. 'I didn't mean to be a cad about France with you, darling – of *course* you shall go to France, to Paris, perhaps, by yourself for a bit – but two women careering about France – mother and daughter *en pension* –' she tried to laugh – 'It isn't as though I'd *choose* to live here – I'm sorry, darling – I've run clean out of sleeping pills – always makes me feel like hell – it's only if one felt he cared in the *least* – that's what makes me so bad-tempered . . . Have you got a hanky – can't seem to find one. Oh, darling! I've hurt your *arm*! How did I – the grip of emotion – I'm terribly sorry – darling, how dreadful it *looks*! I must look a sight too – I can feel my mascara running for dear life – it doesn't hurt too terribly, your arm, does it?'

'You do love him really, don't you?'

Her mother looked up – the crisp black of her eyelashes had dissolved to soft colourless fringes round her streaming eyes. 'My dear, you don't know the first *thing* about love! Poor little baby – those dreadful marks I've made, and you were being so sweet.' She blew her nose and picked up Curran's letter. 'I tell you what we'll do. We'll *both* go to Battle and fetch the plants, but we'll go to the Gateway first and gorge on coffee and cakes. Then the plants, and the Parkers on the way home. How's that?'

She had folded the letter so that Antonia could see the blue scrawl 'Geoffrey' upside down. Looking at her daughter's drawn face, she laughed, and patted her arm.

'Of course I love him. Why do you think I put up with living in this backwater? Ring for Dorcas to clear, darling. I'll be ready in a jiffy.'

She went, and Antonia was left standing by her empty chair. In a little while she would be going to Battle with her poor mother. She thought of the Gateway, with its warm smell of home-made cakes, and felt a little sick. She rang the bell for Dorcas, and then went back to the break-fast table, picked up Curran's envelope, and, ashamed of feeling so rich in comparison to either of her parents, went upstairs with it.

SEVEN

He did not write to her. July burned – the sun rose, glinted, yawned in the wide sky, and reluctantly, voluptuously, sank spreading colours of a dying violence each night. They sat on the front lawn after dinner and watched the sky carelessly, delicately, brushed of cloud. They did not talk very much: Antonia thought that one should be able to have wonderful conversations in the dusk – but nobody seemed to want them. She was discovering that it was better if her parents did not talk about anything in particular, and also that there was nothing which she could say collectively to her parents. So she sank into the mysterious frenzy of her private mind – half resting upon his return, half living with him as though he had never gone away. She had tried to imagine him in Ireland, 'the Emerald Isle', his 'home': it became a magically small island – very green, with wild horses and gentle rain – and no other people, except, she once supposed, their children; one house for them – no roads, and round them, lurching, lasting out for ever, the climate-coloured sea. He had said that he loved her – as the weeks went by she returned more and more easily to the exact intonation of his voice – to the moments before and after his saying it, until it was the single dazzling speck of memory set in the centre of her imagination.

She did not expect him to write to her.

July—August. The usual guests at weekends (excepting George Warrender who had gone abroad) – the same country summer life. Her father worked with his study window open; the smoke from his pipe exactly matched the lavender hedge beneath his window. Her mother changed her clothes to play games, and then changed her clothes because she had been playing them. Her arms became thickly powdered with freckles, her hair bleached by the sun: she was thinner, Antonia noticed – why, she is even thinner than I am! She seemed to play all these games more intensely – several times, Antonia observed, palpably minding if she lost. She had one habit of laughing so wildly at something anybody said at a party that everybody had to hear her repeat it: and another of asking Wilfrid in an intentionally childish voice whether she might do a number of foolish things which Antonia knew he could not possibly prevent, and about which in most cases he was too uninterested to have an opinion. 'Wilfrid, shall I grow my hair and wear it in two plaits like a little German girl?' 'I'd adore to see their faces if I rode through Battle on a bicycle in my bathing-dress. Wilfrid, *may* I?' 'I wonder whether rolling *stark* naked in the dew before breakfast *is* good for the skin? Wilfrid, would you mind too terribly if I tried – just once, Wilfrid?' – and so on. But perhaps, Antonia thought, she has always done that kind of thing and I simply haven't noticed it before. Underneath all her mother's behaviour she sensed the swift undercurrent of unhappiness which checked the shaming, flaming anger that she sometimes felt on her father's behalf, and left her questioning and afraid. Nobody, surely, would say those things if they were happy, and if people were unhappy, one was instinctively sorry for them. It seemed such bad luck – and so extraordinary.

It wasn't exactly her father's fault, although she didn't think that he tried: he seemed to continue his life – mildly, indifferently – very seldom stabbed by her mother into some sort of temporary bewildered resentment, which dissolved as soon as he could disassociate himself again, and which left no emotional residue for his wife at all. Either, Antonia thought, one had to be self-contained like her father, or contained in another person, like herself.

August – soon it would be September. A wonderful summer, people said; but the shock of his going had had time now to change. For a long while she had been not unhappily resigned; then, suddenly, and for no apparent reason, she began to regret his absence – no more, she thought, than that; but the regret grated and burned – spread over all the hours when she was alone, until it coloured and corrupted all the times when she was not. It was like homesickness, she thought, only not for one's home. If only he would write to her – a few lines, simply saying when he would be back – she would be able to bear it more easily; she would be able to sleep. For sleep, which had always been a simple, unconscious business, played with her now each night, like a cat with a mouse, pouncing upon her at the last point of her fatigue and resistance – knocking her out for the few remaining hours before it was breakfast. She woke slowly – the morning post urged her downstairs, and the small expected stab of disappointment of no letter from him, started day after day.

Eventually, even Araminta noticed that she was not looking well. They were having tea in the garden after a bathing party to Cooden Beach. Araminta looked up from the match that had lit her cigarette, and saw her daughter's strained and listless inattention – for a second Toni looked exactly like Wilfrid – which made Araminta say:

'Toni, darling – what on earth is the matter? You look absolutely *rotten*, darling; are you feeling ill?'

To her consternation, Antonia's eyes filled suddenly with tears – she sat rigid and still for a moment without speaking, and then, with a clumsy movement, got to her feet and ran into the house.

The guests drank some more tea, fingered their coloured necklaces or their old school ties, and cast desperately about for some means to escape the incident. Too much sun on the beach, someone said with a burst of social inspiration: but Araminta was concerned – she hadn't meant to upset poor little Toni like that. Perhaps she *was* ill. When, however, she followed Toni into the house, she could not find her anywhere.

Antonia had used the last vestiges of self-control to hide herself in an attic where the apples were stored. This was impossible; she must pull herself together – she *must*! Either she must endure the situation or she must find a way of ending it: she stopped crying, and thought carefully . . .

At dinner her mother explained that they were right about the sun, and that Toni had retired for the evening with a headache.

A few days later, when plans were being made for forthcoming weekends, Antonia said:

'What about asking that man, Geoffrey Curran, some time?'

Her mother stopped sorting bridge pencils. 'Isn't he in Ireland or Scotland, or somewhere? Sharpen the blue stripey one, darling, it looks all right, but the lead has broken inside.'

'Wouldn't Enid know whether he was back?'

'She might. I shall see her on Thursday. I'll ask. You

rather adored him, didn't you, darling? Thoroughly unsuitable, but, I must admit, fascinating. Why *do* people always pull the tassel off the *yellow* pencil – extraordinary – I must have mended it at least three times. You'd adore *anyone* who adored horses, you juggins – I suppose one day you'll grow out of it.'

She was silent – laughing secretly at the idea of such general adoration – and because she was suddenly sure now that he would return – even finding it pleasant to be so thoroughly misunderstood.

On Friday her mother announced that he *was* back, and was coming to stay the next weekend.

No sudden shock this time – but a whole week in which to collect her imagination and fear and delight. The time spent itself with unbearable slowness – reluctant to drip from one minute to the next – almost as though it was running out. In a sense, she thought, it was the end of time: these were the dregs of suspense – after Friday it would be new again – at a starting-point.

The days grew longer – seemed more and more drawn out with trivial incident: her mother loaded her with the minutiae of weekend preparations, and found her unusually acquiescent, but as she never bothered to account for her daughter's behaviour unless she was being a bore socially, Araminta observed nothing.

On Tuesday and Wednesday it rained: a series of heavy gusty showers. Unripe fruit was beaten off the trees, flowers were sodden of colour, high wet branches in the copse creaked hysterically. The tennis lawn grew green again – but Araminta bewailed the weather. The least it could do in the country was to keep fine. Antonia, who had decided to take Geoffrey to Bodiam, realized suddenly how much every private plan with him was dependent upon its being fine, and dutifully echoed her mother's complaints.

On Wednesday night the wind got up: on Thursday there was nearly half a gale blowing all day: a young cat belonging to the cook went mad chasing leaves and twigs and minute imaginary terrors, and the morning-room fire smoked everybody out of the room at breakfast.

Antonia spent the day cleaning tennis balls for her mother and taking the horses to Battle to be reshod. She had saved the shoeing until Thursday because she enjoyed it, and because it took up a whole afternoon. The blacksmith hardly ever spoke. He had a deceptively savage appearance, with a huge black beard, and his forearms heavily tattooed: he muttered and slapped his horses over – working with incredible speed. There was always a crowd of children who hopped in and out of his way, like sparrows, telling him all about their lives. Horses and children relied upon him, his appearance and taciturnity were just what they wanted – and even that day, Antonia found his skill and his few grunts soothing. At half-past three his sister brought him his blue enamel mug of tea – they lived together in a tiny white cottage at the back of the smithy, and she kept poultry. She was small and dark and wiry, and talked all the time; like the children, she told him everything that had happened to her since their dinner: he grunted without looking up, and went on paring the mare's hooves with gentle dexterity. The children fell silent while she was there – she asked one of them about its mammy, but it subsided into an agony of reserve, and so, with a remark to Antonia about the terrible wind, she went.

When the job was done, and Antonia had paid him – he

fetched the change out of an old tobacco tin – they led the horses outside, and Antonia mounted.

'Do you think it will rain again?'

He handed her the leading rein and looked at the sky. He had brown gentle eyes.

'Blow out, I reckon.' He ran his hand down the grey's neck and added warningly: 'Termorrer, though.'

The air was cold after the warmth and sizzling smell of the forge. There was a cart-horse waiting inside. She asked anxiously:

'You mean it'll rain tomorrow?'

'No – it'll blow out – twenty-four hours, I reckon – round about.' He wet a black splayed thumb. 'Don't fret,' he said, and wiped his thumb on his leather apron.

She thanked him, he touched his forehead, and turned back to the forge. As she adjusted her leathers, she heard one of the children: 'Teacher asked Ireen what she had in her mouth, but she swallowed it so then it was quite fair for her to say "Nothin", Mr Jarvis, wasn't it?'

It was the longest conversation she had ever had with him, Antonia reflected, as she jogged home. She stopped fretting about the weather.

Thursday evening – she would never have believed in the length and breadth of such an evening. They dined early – she and her father and mother. The meal seemed endless, but it was barely a quarter to nine when they had finished, and were back in the drawing-room with their coffee. A state of amiable indifference prevailed: her parents were not exasperating one another, and in her anxiety to conceal her private tension, Antonia was being exactly what they expected her to be. She even told them about the blacksmith, which ordinarily she would never have done – and her father listened politely. Her mother laughed and said: 'I bet he has a terrific past. Those strong silent men . . .'

Antonia looked up, and saw her mother's eyes seriously imagining this. Perhaps she *does* care about other people, she thought, and said quickly aloud: 'He doesn't seem at all unhappy, though.'

Her mother laughed again – shortly. 'Unhappy? I shouldn't think so. I must pop upstairs for a spot of telephoning. I want to remind Bobby about the peach bitters – he's got a head like a sieve, poor lamb.'

She was alone with her father, and it was far too early to go to bed. Unexpectedly, he saved her from this predicament, by asking her to play chess – a game which neither of them enjoyed, but which was recognized as something they did together.

When Araminta returned, she found them sitting on low chairs opposite one another, their heads bent over the pretty board. Wilfrid had his back to her, but Antonia looked up and smiled. She's really turning out quite attractive, thought her mother with a little two-way stab of triumph and envy: she would not have wanted a really *plain* child. Anyway she is dark, and I'm fair, so we couldn't be less alike. Of course, she is really like Wilfrid – She was far more like Wilfrid, but what with him added up to a general weakness of appearance was translated to a certain delicacy in his daughter.

Her father won the game. It was just after ten: Antonia said that she was tired, and escaped, but even that was not the end of the evening. Alone, her mind bounded with relief, that she need not any longer conceal her exquisite impatience, but there were, she discovered, many variations upon this theme. Apprehension: that something would prevent his coming; that he had not intended coming at all; that in all this time her appearance had mysteriously changed to disappoint him; she tried to determine whether this was so by looking carefully at herself, but it was very difficult because she did not really know how she had looked in the first place. He had not written to her; he had not even sent her a message in his letter to her mother. Perhaps, in spite of what he had said, he did not love her. She tried to remember his saying it, and immediately could not. She had flung herself on to her bed, but the angry uneven gale was tearing at her half-open window – and now she was cold and afraid. She pushed the window open before shutting it, and leaned out. Instantly, the wind seemed softer, wider – no less urgent – it was travelling too fast to smell of a summer night – but below its racking of the sleepless trees – beneath these irregular peaks of force – there was a steady barrier of such violent air that she could hardly collect breath from it. The trees tossed and creaked and shifted; branches strained, sprained, out of position – pitched against one another in agony – screeched, wrestled, and were shudderingly free until the next assault.

When, at last, she shut the window, and turned to the calm air of her room, her fears had blown out into the night, and she could remember perfectly what he had said.

On Friday, the wind still blew, suiting the tempo of the day, which, unlike the others before it, rushed to its conclusion. At six Araminta went to the station to meet Bobby's train. 'Bobby who?' her father had enquired.

'Bobby *Rawlings*, darling. The Brewers are bringing Geoffrey Curran down with them. It's only Bobby to be met. For goodness sake, don't go *off* somewhere, Toni;

show them their rooms and give them a drink if they arrive before I'm back.'

Her father went back to his study, remarking mildly that a great many people were called Bobby nowadays.

She dressed – in the terracotta linen – and prayed that the Brewers would arrive before her mother got back. She brushed her hair until tears came to her eyes – excitement – she was shivering with excitement, and the minutes running out. She had only one very unobtrusive lipstick, too pale to accentuate her dress, but she dared not go to her mother's room to steal another, in case she missed the car in the drive. If the first car was her mother, she would go and get it, she would not go down without it. If the first car was Geoffrey, she would go down wearing the pale lipstick. This foolish little bargain became terribly important as the minutes dropped one by one into the back of the week, and neither car arrived.

All her jewellery was oxidized silver and semi-precious stones. She had never thought about it much before, but now it seemed wrong – both clumsy, and muted. She put it on, and took it off again – tried to look at herself without it – but her mind's eye was too crowded, overwhelming, blotting out her finished appearance. Half-past six: there was a sulky, fitful sun, but the wind was dropping: the sky was streaked with furious blue. She opened her window, and heard a car turning into the drive. She stayed long enough to see, and there were the Brewers waving at her, and a third person in the back of the car. Shutting the window, she ran – her blush subsiding with her down the staircase.

Going to the car, greeting them, explaining about her mother, carrying Alison Brewer's hand luggage into the house, she was conscious of his eyes upon her, although she did not meet them. Would they like a drink immediately, or would they like to see their rooms first, and wash? Alison, immaculate and brittle as a biscuit, said she was simply filthy, and could they go up first?

So she led them upstairs, the Brewers down one passage to the Strawberry Room (he came, too, because the Brewers had so much luggage), and then back down the passage and round the corner to the small room in which he had slept the last time he had stayed. It faced south, and the transparent red curtains were drawn as Dorcas had once been told to do when it was hot. She crossed the room to draw them apart, and heard him put down his case. She pulled one curtain – in a minute she would have to turn round – he did not speak, and her heart was too high in her throat to say anything. The second curtain was sticky – she tugged it, and it flew suddenly right off the end of its rod. She turned to him then, to laugh, to apologize – but he was standing perfectly still, watching her – very near her – and she could do neither. He suddenly, simply, held out his arms – she took one hesitant step, and he was kissing her.

'May I put my hand on your heart and say you love me?'

He said it so softly, that for a second there was a confusion of hearts: he knew this, and said: 'You know me. I haven't changed: at all,' and saw her uncertainty resolve again to delight.

A car door slammed faintly, and she started from him. He nodded, the small conspiratorial smile which she remembered came and went on his face, and they moved together to the half-open door.

'You go down first. Just a minute.' He took her head in his hands, and kissed her quickly. 'Sweeting.'

The evening was very gay. They drank, and had dinner, and then they played vingt-et-un. At dinner he sat next to Araminta, who asked him in a perfunctory manner about Ireland. He had bought a couple of horses, he said, and, gradually collecting his audience – he gave such an account of his buying them, that everybody was listening and watching him, and Antonia was able to watch him as well – to relate her memory of him to his actual presence. He was thinner – no, browner, and that made him seem thinner, but otherwise exactly the same – not precisely the man she had imagined all these weeks, but the man who had stayed here all those weeks ago. The two pictures of him became one . . .

The story took up a whole course of dinner.

'Oh, I'd give *anything* to imitate people!' cried Araminta, dabbing below her eyes with her table napkin. 'But anything! Wouldn't you, Bobby – or *can* you, secretly?'

Bobby began to say that he couldn't begin—

'It doesn't matter, darling – one can't have everything . . .'

Curran leaned across the table to Antonia, and asked after her horses.

'She took them to be shod yesterday, especially for you, Geoffrey. She's dying to take you riding, aren't you, darling?'

Curran said quickly: 'I'm dying to be taken. Where shall we go?'

She saw his eyes, encouraging, protecting her – and filled with a new assurance, she began: 'I thought you might like to see Bodiam—' but her mother interrupted gaily:

'You know perfectly well that you don't care a hoot for Bodiam, Toni, my sweet. It's any excuse for a long ride. Anyway, not tomorrow. Tomorrow, we're going to have a positive tournament – Bobby and I were planning it in the car.'

'Bodiam Castle,' began her father mildly to Curran, 'is of considerable interest for more than one reason . . .'

(Safe. It isn't as difficult as I thought, but I can't do it for very long.) But the rest of the evening was much easier. Everybody was in a good humour – particularly Araminta, who felt that her house party was being a success. When Noel Brewer suggested vingt-et-un, 'He simply adores gambling – any form of it,' Alison assured everybody – everybody fell in with the suggestion. While the others collected drinks, Antonia and Curran counted chips together, and she had her first conversation that everybody else could hear, but which nobody else could understand. She was so lit with love – so much seething and glittering with it, that all her movements, her sorting and counting of the coloured chips, were neatly deliberate, and her voice carefully self-contained: only every now and then, when his fingers touched, brushed hers, or he made her look at him by a persistent question, the memory of him in the little room blazed up in her – his holding out his arms – his putting his hand on her violent heart – and she burned with joy.

Noel Brewer won steadily. Curran was the first to go bankrupt – although Wilfrid retired early from the game leaving him his pile – Curran went through it with a careless abandon. He was such a good loser that everyone wanted him to take longer over losing: his reckless misfortune quickly became a focal point of the game.

'Shall I lend you some?' She had not thought before she said this, and felt the blood running into her face.

'You'll have to give it to me – I've small chance of returning it – quicksilver is all it is for me tonight.'

Antonia began counting some of her chips, but her mother cried:

'Oh, *Toni*! You're so careful! What's a chip between friends?' and pushed half her pile over to Geoffrey.

Antonia looked mortified: 'I wanted to give him exactly half.'

'It doesn't matter, darling. My wretched husband'll win it all. It's devastating! He's like some awful professional!' A remark which, from the way in which he denied it, seemed to please Noel Brewer.

'Give me one for luck,' said Curran, and Antonia put a white chip into his hand.

But he lost, and retired with unruffled good temper. The game, somehow, had no impetus after that, and so, with much frenzied calculation, Noel was paid. Everybody talked about bed for five or ten minutes, and the evening was over.

It was a clear, calm night – the sky flooded with stars. She thought that she would never sleep, but she had scarcely time to think it before she slept.

∞　∞　∞

Saturday was fine. She spent the day in an ecstasy of frustration. The good weather meant tennis – nearly all day, and he played his fair share of the tournament. Antonia comforted herself with the possibility of their riding before dinner; but at luncheon, it became clear that Araminta had got him to ring up the Leggatts at Roberts-bridge (she had determined to meet the fascinating Edmund Leggatt) and they immediately issued a general invitation to the whole party to drinks either before or after dinner.

'Oh – after – please Geoffrey darling – who knows when we shall finish the tennis?' and Curran returned to the telephone.

'They want us to change, and dance,' he announced, when he came back. Araminta gave a little yelp of delight.

'Goody goody! *What* nice accommodating friends you have, Geoffrey!'

That means ironing my long frock, and I hate it, it's much too young for me, thought Antonia miserably. She had refused to play tennis, and was suffering a general reaction from the evening before.

At tea-time she took the horrible blue organdie dress to the pantry to iron it. A small barred window looked on to the drive. She noticed suddenly that it was darker, looked up, and there he was, holding the bars with his hands, and smiling at her.

'Is that your pretty dress for tonight?'

'It isn't pretty – I hate it, but I haven't got another one.' Her face had lighted up when she saw him, and then quickly clouded again.

'What is it, darling Toni? Drop your iron and come and tell me.'

She hesitated, looked at him; then put down her iron. He seized her hand through the bars.

'Secrecy looks like neglect – is that it?'

'It's just that – Oh you are much *better* at this than I am! Or perhaps you don't—'

'Oh, but I *do!* I do all the time. I couldn't sleep last night for thinking of you.'

'I went to sleep at once!' she said, just discovering this.

He dropped her hand. 'You see? I have just as much

reason as you to feel in the cold, but I won't. You have such a delectable candour – that's what it is. Give me your hand again: no, give me your little face – your eyes are too wide apart for the bars, but I can just manage to kiss you.'

The bars pressed, hard and cool, down the sides of her face. A bluebottle droned breathlessly about the room.

'It's hurting you, this prison,' he whispered, 'I'll have to get you out of it.'

She stroked his hair with her fingers.

'I'd like to take you away with me now. Carry you off! I will, too.' He gave a little triumphant laugh.

'Where?'

'To Bodiam Castle – tomorrow.' Then he saw her eyes, and said: 'Or further afield?'

'Anywhere,' she answered simply.

'Don't look at me like that when we dance tonight – I shan't be able to bear it,' he said, at last. 'Damn this contraption.' He shook the bars between them.

She laughed then with pleasure at the way he said that word. 'At other people? Am I to look like that to them?'

'You are *not!* You are entirely mine – you don't belong to *anybody* else. Is that crystal clear to you now?'

She shut her eyes for an instant, and repeated: 'I am entirely yours,' so low that he scarcely heard her. It seemed to her the most solemn moment of her life.

Then they called him, and he went. She heard him shouting cheerful, unimportant lies, and thought that she would never be able to match the courageous presence of his mind.

∞ ∞ ∞

The rest of the day, which ended with the evening at the Leggatts, swirled round her, slipped past her – like a long dream. Afterwards, her recollections of it were a confusion – a haze of time and people, without the sense of time or proportion. It might have been a minute, or a whole life – but it seemed neither her minute, nor her life; as though she was enchanted from it.

She remembered, at some point, coming slowly down a beautiful staircase – the steps were of stone, and so shallow that she seemed hardly to descend, to a crowd of people: not until she saw him standing by a window, aware that she had been seeking her love, although when she reached the window, he had gone . . .

She remembered a wide grass path set between borders of sweet-smelling herbs – the scent of verbena crushed in her fingers – and beyond, the luminous glow of pale roses. Someone was with her then, but it was nearly dark, and she was almost alone . . .

Somebody played the piano, and dancing with him she did not know whether they talked or looked at one another at all . . .

A piece of lemon drifting in her wine cup – the rind beaded with silver, the fruit magnified by the glass which he had given her . . .

The thought occurring that she was invisible, that she made no sound: that her senses were lost to him: she was some ghost, some rich shadow of what she had been: that only he could see or touch her – without him she did not exist.

A clock striking one – an isolated marking of the time. 'Late,' she heard them cry: and later: 'Here's Toni's wrap – Where is Toni?' He took the wrap and put it round her. Her mother's voice: 'You look tired, my pet.' They could see her now that she was wearing the wrap, and she was suddenly very tired. White mist on the lawn – a clamour of headlights. He put her into the back of a car, and got in beside her.

'Home,' they said. She put her face against him and slept, her fingers clutching his sleeve . . .

EIGHT

'I carried you out of the car and up to your bed. When I laid you down, you opened your eyes, sat up, and said: "Don't leave me: if you go, I shall vanish again." I promised I'd come back, and then your mother came in, and I went.'

'What did she think?'

'She just thought you'd drunk a little too much wine. *She* didn't mind.'

'I *hadn't*!'

'I know that, but it was wiser to agree with her, and – anyway – I wanted to see your room.'

'*Did* you come back?'

They were actually on their way to Bodiam: he rode for a moment without replying.

'I tried, once,' he said at last: 'but your mother was still flitting about the passages – so I had to retreat.'

'What on earth was she doing?'

He looked at her curiously, and then looked away. 'Seeing to you, I expect.'

She frowned. 'It sounds exactly as though I *was* drunk. Horrible! I *know* I wasn't.'

'You wouldn't look like you do this morning if you had been. How do you feel?'

She turned to him, checked herself, and said instead: 'Thank you for carrying me.'

'I adored carrying you. You must promise not to throw your weight about in any other direction.'

'I did promise that – yesterday.'

They were picking their way uphill – diagonally across a large field.

'Beware of rabbit holes,' she said. 'I came down badly once because of one. But it's better riding than the road.'

'Can we keep right off the road?'

'Not all the way. It depends on farmer to farmer. Most of them don't mind now – they know I shut gates and ride round things. What is the time?'

'Just after half-past eleven.'

'Is that all? Have we really got the whole day? Was it easy to arrange?' She had been late for breakfast, and, when she had come down, had found her anxious plan miraculously readymade.

'It wasn't difficult. Your father had fortunately interested me so much yesterday in the castle – that the whole thing went like clockwork. So here we are, for the whole day.'

'The whole *day*,' she repeated, and they smiled at one another.

It was fine, with the promise of heat, and they rode for some time without talking. At the top of the hill they could see more country – shimmering in the haze – like someone holding their breath, to keep absolutely still, she thought. They were skirting a small wood, and the flies came out of it in hordes. He warned her before slapping a horse-fly off her mare's quarters – but otherwise there began to be the faint tension of silence between them.

'A bit of road in a minute, I'm afraid,' she said, but he simply nodded – he did not answer.

When they were through the gate, and walking on the

broad grass verge by the road, she began asking him about his riding school. He had found some possible stables, he said, off Knightsbridge – they were cheap, but in a bad state of repair – it would take time to put them right.

'You have decided on London?'

He heard the faint disappointment in her voice, and said:

'I'd no real choice in the matter. Will you mind that very much? I can charge people more for the hour, and perhaps keep one or two private horses at livery. It's handy in several ways.'

She remembered saying 'Anywhere' to him, and thought, no – of course, she could not mind.

'After all,' he said, sensing her acceptance: 'if I come to Bodiam, you will have to come to London.'

'How much does it cost people to ride in London?'

'Five shillings an hour – sometimes seven and six. A special rate for *you*, of course.'

'For me?'

'Oh yes,' he said gravely. 'Everybody has to pay to ride in London, you know.'

'But I thought I was going to *help* with the school!'

'Darling! So grave and gullible – you'll never know how much I love to tease you! Of course you are. But I shall have to speak to your parents first, before they're likely to trust their only daughter to my wild life.'

'Will you *really*? Will you . . .' She was overwhelmed – unable to speak at the prospect so suddenly before her – her whole life coming out like the sun – dazzling, immediate – it was far too much to bear . . .

'Dear, *dear* little Toni: don't mind everything so much. It's *easy*, most things are no trouble at *all*, unless you make them troublesome.' He seized her reins and stopped their horses. 'Of *course* I'll talk to them. You've been too much alone in your life – you take it all too seriously, and it's all a wonderful business.' He smoothed her hair back from her eyes. 'It should be more wonderful for you than anyone I've ever met, if you don't shy at every new prospect. Look, when do we get off this devil of a road?'

She pointed ahead. 'Just beyond that white house. Why?'

'So that we can get off these damned animals, and I can give you a serious talking to about not taking everything so seriously. This is too narrow for the pair of us. You lead – and away with you!' He hit her mare with his hand; she snorted, and broke into a resentful hand-canter ahead of him.

'You can take two things seriously, if you've a mind to,' he called, a few minutes later.

She turned her head; she was laughing now.

'What?'

'Your own health – and money.'

But when they did get off the road, and had tied their horses to a bit of hedge, he did not talk seriously to her at all – the tension had exploded, and there seemed no need. They must move, if they were ever to get to Bodiam, she said for the third time, slipped from him and was on her mare before he could stop her.

The rest of the journey they spent partly on an amiable argument about why he thought that health and money were the only things to take seriously – she did not agree with him, but did not know why not – and partly on the pleasure of their ride. It grew hotter: white convolvulus wilted in the hedges – the road when they encountered it was like blue steel, and patched with mirages – the animal smell of cow parsley, and the caramel scent of drying hay filled the warm air. She noticed these things from private habit, thinking about him with a kind of private experiment – she was not used to this minute impassioned consideration, any more than she was used to her own feelings swinging so far from the end of anxiety to such a certainty of peace. The thought that he would have to go away tomorrow occurred, but did not interrupt her pleasure. She said something about it to him: he said that he could stay any time he liked with the Leggatts, and the answer seemed perfectly good to her. Buttercups glistened in the sun – the wild roses paled from the heat . . .

They were nearing Bodiam: the hop fields stretched across the valley before them, and he told her about the River Liffey, and how its water made the best stout in the world. Could they drink some, she asked. It was a very hot day for stout, he said. Oh, *please*, she wanted to – she didn't mind about the heat. She was like a child, he thought – she would eat ice cream before breakfast in a snowstorm if she wanted it. She was wearing a lemon-coloured shirt with her sleeves rolled up – Oh, all right, but not until they reached Bodiam. She wouldn't like the stout, he added: she said she *would*, and he saw her resolving to like it.

The hops, an aromatic sea, were on either side of them: showing alternately the dense green embroidered poles, and a bare narrow vista with geometric precision; but alternating with a slight jerk, like lantern slides, as they passed. Had he ever had a hop pillow, she asked. No – he slept too well – he had never needed one. Had she? No – she had smelled one – delicious – but she slept well too

– usually – and briefly she remembered, and he wondered, when she had not.

Then they were over the last rise, and the castle was before them: thrush coloured, and surrounded by very green turf. It was placed half way up the rise, commanding a view of the little river. It looked very simple, and apparently complete. Antonia stopped to look at it.

'At this distance people might be living there. It was the last fortified castle to be built in England.' Then she added: 'We can go up one of the towers.'

He stared painstakingly at it. He was not very interested in castles – but the mixture of love, information, and adventure with which she presented it to him, touched some secret spring – of compassion – tenderness – concern for her separate happiness, which he had never felt in his life before. The moment, with its responsibility and regret, passed – and he said:

'It doesn't look as though it was built there – but as though some giant set it down complete.'

'And then scooped his finger round it to make a moat. Yes! Are there castles like this in Ireland?'

'There are castles. I don't know. You see, I've never really looked at them.'

They started to pick their way down the hill.

'You don't tell me very much about Ireland,' she said.

'I'll tell you anything you want to know.'

'But I don't *know* what I want to know! I want to be told.'

'Do you want your glass of stout before we see the castle?'

'Yes please. We can eat our sandwiches inside. There is a grass courtyard. We'll have to tie the horses somewhere, though.'

She was easily deflected.

'How do we get across the moat? Or is it dry?'

'It's not *dry*!' she said, shocked. 'It has a lot of water, and water lilies. But they built a causeway on the north side – oh – years ago.'

At the pub he ordered her stout, and beer for himself. 'You *won't* like it, and then I shall have to drink it for you.'

'I shall! I know I shall!'

But she didn't, and in the end he poured it into a bed of phlox that grew by the door of the pub.

'I don't suppose they've ever drunk it before, either, but they'll love it,' he said. '*Now* what would you like, Miss Vaughan, crème-de-menthe?'

'Ginger beer,' she said meekly.

The village was very quiet. There had been one or two fishermen by the bridge, but no one came in or out of the gate which led to the castle.

'If we go soon, we shall have it to ourselves. A bus arrives some time in the early afternoon, and then there are always people. We can ride in the first gate, and leave the horses up by the man's little cottage.'

'What man?'

'The man who looks after the castle. He has a lot of rusty nails and things that they found in the moat. We have to pay him. Shall we go now?'

She wiped her mare's eyes clean with a wisp of grass, and it whinnied softly, thrusting its nose into her neck.

'We must find them some shade. There are a lot of oak trees round the castle.'

'They've got a pair of good tails. They'll help each other out.'

'I should think so! I wouldn't dream of having an animal docked!'

'Oh,' he said, half laughing. 'It's all very well to say that you yourself wouldn't dock an animal – but you can't deny your loving care to a poor beast just because somebody else has docked it – is that fair now?'

'I hadn't thought of that.'

'Domestic creatures never have any choice, you see – not like the wild ones.'

'You could divide people up like that, couldn't you? Wild, or domestic?'

'I don't know. I wasn't being serious. Could you?'

'But you *could*,' she persisted eagerly, and then stopped. 'I believe you are laughing at me.'

And he answered solemnly: 'I believe I am.'

They were waiting for some bicycles to pass before crossing the road.

'Health and money,' she muttered furiously, but she was not at all cross.

'*Your* health – *your* money. Don't make abstractions.'

'I'll *make* you care.' She was struggling to unlatch the gate that led into the castle grounds. 'I'll make you care about horses that aren't yours, and people, and—'

'I care about you – my darling love, and you aren't mine – entirely – yet.'

She said nothing, but he saw a faint tremor run down from the back of her head like wind on a field of grass. He shut the gate, and she gave him a quick nervous smile which melted to a look of such radiance that his heart turned over.

They rode, past the tiltyard and up the slope to the castle. As they drew nearer, it became a little more of a ruin. Tufts of grass and ragwort grew on the battlements, or simply out of cracks in the walls where the mortar had decayed: greasy black rooks flew heavily backwards and forwards from the tops of the towers to the tops of trees; their ceaseless cries sounding like the end of a fractious, inconclusive argument: but from the smooth round towers, the dark slit windows – no sign of life. The moat was still – like thick glass, perfectly reflecting the walls, except where there were great pads of water lilies in full flower. They rode slowly round to the north side where there was the cottage of the man who kept the rusty nails.

'There are yellow iris down by the river,' she said suddenly.

'How deep is the moat?' he asked, without thinking much – he was as absorbed in her, as she in her castle.

'Deeper than people, of course,' she said, after thinking about it. 'I don't know how deep. Are you hungry? Shall we go in and have lunch there?'

'Let's do that.'

They found a suitable place for the horses, bought their tickets, and walked across the causeway. When they reached the portcullis, she looked up at it to show him, and he put his hand on the back of her neck.

'When you shiver – you start there.'

'Geoffrey – I don't believe you are noticing the castle at *all*!'

'I am! I am!' he said – with no intention that she should believe him.

'It's my kind of building. I don't really like churches much.'

'Just castles. Or just this castle?'

'I haven't seen another castle as beautiful as this. I like houses too. I like places made for people to live in.'

Through the great gateway, there was a large courtyard,

covered with short green turf, and, round its edges, foun-
dations and bits of castle – the neat grass contriving to
make these pieces of ruin very suave in their appearance.

She said that she was too hot, and could they eat first,
and look properly at the castle afterwards? So they had
lunch on the site of the Lady's Bower – leaning comfortably against the smooth masonry, with small birds
hopping round them for crumbs. When they had eaten,
he offered her a cigarette, but she smiled and shook her
head. His pale blue smoke drifted, the hot moments spun
out on the golden air – even the rooks' argument seemed
desultory . . . She pressed the back of her head against
the stone, and felt its warmth penetrating her hair. Life
seemed endlessly beautiful – even the rooks, she thought,
were hardly bothering now to make the worst of it. She
looked up at the cream blue sky and opened her eyes to
the sun: an immediate burning flurry clutched at her nose,
and she sneezed. Emerging from the sneeze, she felt his
hands holding the top of her shoulders – his presence
blocking the sun and the sky: he kissed her – and at once
she was carried out of her depths.

'When I kiss you, you cling to me as though you were
drowning. Did you know that?'

She shook her head, and his face was in focus again.

He pulled her closer to him.

'Hay – clover hay – and new potatoes, and your hair
a little sweeter.'

'What?' She was whispering – so urgent seemed their
privacy.

'How you smell, my darling love. I adore it so. Promise
me something, darling – will you do that now? Wait one
moment before you do.'

But they were interrupted by a batch of sightseers, and

he exclaimed violently under his breath: 'Damn!' They broke apart and looked at one another, his eyes subsiding to a humorous despair – her alarm to confusion.

The sightseers trickled heavily through the gate – glanced casually at them, and then looked again; their general curiosity which they had expected to be leashed to the castle – enlivened, diverted by the spectacle of two lovers. Somebody said something – they looked again – somebody else laughed. Antonia, her face burning, started to pack lunch.

'Let's go,' he said; 'I don't want to see the castle with them.'

She nodded gratefully, and thought: How exactly we know one another's mind.

And so they rode away almost in silence; only when they reached the last point on the road from which the castle could be seen, she stopped, looked back and said:

'The people don't really matter at *all*. They don't make the slightest difference to it.' Then she thought for a moment: 'Of course, *we* don't, either: but you would have liked the castle without them,' and made a little gesture of dismissal with her hand.

'I'm very glad to have seen it.'

She looked at him sharply, not believing this, and he said: 'With you. It's you – not the castle – you know that,' and she was so sure that he loved her that she simply thought: Well, at least he's *honest* about the castle.

Much later, past the windmill at Staplecross, she broke the long silence by saying: 'There is a different way home,' and they turned to the right off the road on to a track. Here were a few straggling cottages in front of which were tiny gardens, crowded with honeysuckle, roses, beehives and hens, fuchsia and sweet briar hedges, and a smell of moss, and phlox and warm cabbage leaves and cinder paths. The track ended with a jerky gate: a small empty field and then woods stretched before them. She remembered the next bit of the ride for the rest of her life.

They rode slowly across the small field to the entrance of the woods – a bridle path roundly vaulted by trees. It was dark after the baking field with a chequered streaking light – the sensation of the hazy golden air had resolved to a frantic exchange of sun and shade. There was the slippery uncertain movement of the sun between the branches – slanting, shifting across her mare's neck on to the ground, against the larger rhythm of their progress: and her mind possessed by the starting darting uncertainties of loving him (what was she to promise?) against the vast certainty of love itself. For she felt now that each movement, each moment, was propelling them towards some mysterious ecstasy of accomplishment, and she was poised within herself for it; her senses confined to each step along their dark streaking path, and therefore sharply aware of each step. Sometimes the path lightened to a patch of clear yellow sunlight – then she looked up, and there was a patch of sky like a deep blue pool above them. Height, depths, distance – the yellow patch balanced the blue: she wondered whether love matched so easily, and it occurred to her with a discovering thrill made up of arrogance and humility, that if he loved her as she loved him, there could be no end to the beautiful distance of their lives. She turned to look at him, and at once his eyes met hers – urging her on without a word.

'There is a little meadow a bit further on.'

He put out his hand as though he was going to touch her, and changed his mind.

It was hardly a meadow, simply a narrow slip of open land, dotted with ancient molehills, and covered with very short fine turf. The sun lay over it like a fine golden film, and leaning against the edge of the wood were bramble bushes winking with black and red fruit.

'Beware of rabbit holes,' she said, and remembered the hours ago when she had last said that.

'This is the place,' he said.

'For me to make my promise?'

'Your promise?'

'You asked me to promise you something – just before the people came.'

They had stopped.

'Yes, yes, so I did.' He dismounted, and stood beside her. 'Jump now – with all your might. I want all your weight hurled down on to me.'

But she sprang lightly down into his arms, and laughed. 'I promised *that* this morning.'

'What?'

'You don't remember *anything*! Not to throw my weight about in any other direction.'

'You promised that yesterday.' And, reassured by his memory, she leaned forward to kiss him, but he said: 'Let's tie these animals out of the way first. Give me your beast.'

She sat quietly, hugging her knees, while he tied the horses to the edge of the wood behind her, thinking slowly: I am so happy. Whatever happens, I shall never, never be happier than now. But even such a thought seemed only to salt her content to an extremity of happiness, and she flung herself down, wanting suddenly to feel the turf like short green fur against her face – imagining the whole world – and touching this particular piece of earth's surface to exchange and share her life with it.

When he returned to her, and saw her face pressed against the ground, he thought that perhaps she was crying, and remembering that he had got very near her when she had last done that, he flung himself down beside her, prepared to be sensually comforting.

'What is it, darling love?'

And she answered solemnly: 'I am so beautifully happy.'

He took her into his arms, and then sighed, so that she, in her turn, asked: 'What is it?'

'I am so beautifully *un*happy. There's the difference.'

'Why, darling – *why* are you?'

He pulled her lemon shirt away from her neck to kiss it.

'I don't want to tell you now.' His hand slid round to the back of her neck. 'I *must* kiss you. You *must* kiss me. Now.'

His breath was like smoke on her face – his eyes near, nearer still – grey, with black pools – then all black . . . She kissed him passionately because he had said that he was unhappy; then because she loved him and he was kissing her, and then there ceased to be any reason. Her head lay hard against the palm of his hand; his other hand stroking her skin with quick, nervous, possessive movements, until it enclosed her breast – she gave a little fainting cry of astonished ecstasy as her heart leapt under his hand, and her mouth had suddenly a furious sweetness. At the height, on the brink of this torrent, he stopped, and said roughly:

'Now you see why I'm "beautifully" unhappy. I want you – I want you entirely – want, want, *want*! You're beginning to understand what that means, now, aren't you? Wait a few minutes more.'

There was no chance to reply; she heard her shirt tearing a little, but the sound seemed to come from a distance: it was as though they were galloping – their bodies racing one another; the only near things were his mouth and his requiring hands.

When, at last, he released her, she was aware of nothing but the loss of him – that the race was not over, but stopped, and a sense of intolerable anguish that was almost anger assailed her at his abandonment. Bruised and breathless, she saw him staring down at her – searchingly – and then with a little, hard, triumphant smile at what he saw: her eyes dark, and filled with tears of desire; her mouth printed the shape that he had left it. She felt his fingers tighten on her bare shoulder as he bent over her and whispered:

'You understand now, don't you? You want *me* now, don't you?'

And she repeated, 'I want you,' like the echo of his whisper.

His expression changed – and still whispering, she said:

'Will you speak to them tonight?'

'Who?'

'My parents.' Her eyes shone with a suppressed and delicious excitement. 'As soon as we get home?'

He frowned, in a genuine effort to understand what she meant, and seeing her face cloud, he felt suddenly tender towards her: 'Oh darling, don't start to be sad! The least little thing upsets you—' but she interrupted:

'I don't call our marriage "the least little thing"!'

'Our – *what*?'

'You said this morning that you would have to speak to my parents first.'

'Oh! Yes, so I did, but that was about the riding school. I didn't say anything about marriage!'

Some instinct made her prop herself up. 'But I thought you meant – don't you *want* us to be married?'

He turned sharply towards her, and then looked away.

'It wouldn't be any good if I did. I am married already.'

The silence was as though he had suddenly flung something down a deep well, and they were both intently waiting to hear it touch the bottom, as, after the time which was a little too long, they both stirred at exactly the same moment.

'You – are married – to someone else.'

She put her hand over her forehead, as though she was brushing something away.

'Yes.'

'In Ireland.' She thought of his saying he must go home, and the island that she had made.

'Yes,' he said again, and looked at her. She had gone very white, but she seemed perfectly calm. There was another silence while she stared at his hands, and watched him nervously picking the skin from the sides of his fingers.

'I don't love her, you see,' he said at last. 'We were married when I was too young to know my mind, but of course she's Catholic, and wouldn't hear of a divorce. I'm very unhappy with her.'

'But you go back to see her sometimes?'

'To see her – and the children.'

'Are there a lot of children?'

'Two – and the baby.'

'The baby,' she repeated, and then asked: 'What is *her* name?'

'Ellen. But, Toni, it's you that I love! You must believe that. You must know that I love you.'

She put her hand up to her forehead again, and then said almost confidingly: 'You must think I'm an awful fool, but I still don't understand why you didn't tell me this.'

He thought for a moment. 'I would have, of course, in the end. I didn't immediately, *because* I love you, can't you see that?'

She shook her head, and said simply: 'No.' She was still staring at his hands.

'I had no idea – I didn't know that there was such a – such a misunderstanding about everything.'

She tried to look at him then, but felt suddenly so sick that she did not dare move at all – even her head. She shut her eyes, dug her fingers into the ground, and the sickness lurched heavily away.

At the end of its going, she heard him say: 'I'm sorry if it was such a shock to you.'

Misunderstanding – shock – the words thudded distantly at the bottom of the well. She opened her eyes, and it was then that she discovered her shirt, hopelessly torn off one shoulder. She picked at the frayed cotton ends, to pull the pieces over her breast, and heard herself say: 'It must have been a very old one.' The pieces would not stay unless she held them there. 'How do I get home with a shirt torn like this?' She repeated the thought aloud, because it seemed so worrying.

'I may have a pin,' he said surprisingly. He had. 'It isn't a safety pin, so mind you don't get hurt.'

She took the pin clumsily, and stared at it.

'Better let me,' he said uncertainly.

She was so passive, so still, while he pinned the shirt that he thought that perhaps after all – all was not lost – although it seemed odd that she wasn't crying. He was just going to put his arm round her, when she said:

'Why – why don't you live with her? If you have all those children – and a baby?'

'She bores me. I'm bored to death there after a week.' There was a pause, and then he added desperately: 'And if it's the baby you're worrying about, I may as well tell you that she just likes having children. *She's* got the where-withal to look after them, and it keeps her quiet. She won't be coming to London, you know.'

'I wasn't worrying about the baby.' She said it politely, almost as though she was afraid of having embarrassed him. She looked down at her shirt – it covered her breast, but the top of her shoulder was still bare.

'I'm sorry, darling. I'm afraid I've done it all very badly.'

She shrugged her shoulders experimentally.

'It's all right. It will last until I get home, but—' He thought that she meant to misunderstand him, and was immediately angry.

'Am I to understand that you don't want me to speak to your parents about the riding school?'

He saw her face contract for a second, and she put her hand up to her forehead again, almost as though she thought he was going to hit her. Then she said:

'Please don't speak to them. I'm sorry I misunderstood you. I would like to go back now.'

'Sorry,' he muttered, as they went to their horses. He felt drearily ashamed. Obviously, he had hurt her – he'd made an awful mess of everything. He had no idea that she was so oversensitive. Her innocence! he thought with

419

a kind of horror – really one ought to be warned about people like that. No good thinking about it – he'd concentrate on trying to be nice to her. He went to help her on to her horse, but she had climbed up before he got there.

'Toni – I am sorry. That was a beastly thing to say. Will you forgive me now?'

But she answered in an unnaturally high clear voice: 'Oh no! It wasn't beastly at all! Come on.'

She rode ahead of him, and she rode hard. The horses were soon in a muck sweat, but still the way back seemed long. Whenever the tension of silence seemed to him to have become intolerable, she made some commonplace remark for which he was disproportionately grateful. For what seemed hours they rode through the rest of the woods, across a road, and then endless fields – she opened gates and waited for him to shut them. He said once that they would have to cool the horses off when they got back, and she said that she would do it; 'You can play tennis.'

They were trotting along a stretch of road, and he had ridden level with her: he looked at her as she said this, hoping to detect something in her face that he could understand – some trace of emotion – pique, anger, spite – he felt that almost anything would do, but nothing seemed to be there, and she added in the same closed voice: 'Not if you don't want to, of course.'

When, eventually, they reached the drive, she slowed down and said:

'I'll drop you at the garden gate, and take them round the back.'

'Toni, are you very angry with me?'

She shook her head, and rode a little faster.

'Well, let me come and cool off my animal with you.

Don't let's have an uncomfortable situation, darling – there wouldn't be any sense in that, would there?'

'Toni! I *am* sorry – cross my heart. I'd no idea—' He wanted to say that he'd no idea about her, but somehow he couldn't quite say that. She took the reins without a word – in spite of the heat she was still very pale. He watched her ride away very straight on her horse: he had no idea that the moment her back was turned, the tears streamed out of her eyes until she was entirely blinded.

Afterwards, she could never clearly remember the rest of the day. Walking the horses round and round the big meadow by the side of the copse until long after they were cooled – faint with pain – the same phrases recurring in her mind with the corners of the meadow – saying to him: 'I am entirely yours'; his saying, 'I must go home first'; and her imagination of the 'Emerald Isle': 'I must speak to your parents first before they trust you to my wild life'; 'Two – and the baby'; 'I want you'; 'Misunderstanding – shock –' when she had said that she was entirely his! He asked me to say that. Misunderstanding! The sickness lurched back at the word, so that she had to stop to endure it – clinging to the pommel of her saddle. The island was full of other children, and a baby that he had had with Ellen. She said that name aloud, and thought how familiar a sound it must always have been to him: and still her own island hovered resolutely before her – and her mother's streaming protective contempt when she had said: 'My dear, you don't know the first *thing* about love!' the morning that his letter had arrived. She didn't know anything, because he had not told her that he was married. He said he loved me. Had everyone else known? Enid? Her mother? Had the – misunderstanding – been entirely her own? Sickness again invaded the pain.

Her father's indictment of her mind made an ugly rush at her; only stupid people had misunderstandings (she was desperately trying to adapt herself to the squalor of that word, because it was the word that he had used). Then her mother fidgeting about her bedroom saying that one mustn't throw oneself at somebody's head at everybody else's expense. This now made agonizing shame, as she thought how desperately she had wanted him to think that she was pretty, to love her, to go out riding with her, to make plans to be alone with her, to write to her (which he had never done), to make plans for the future – she dropped her head into her hands – scalding, blistering shame – she did not know how to bear it.

The sunlight on the oak trees was very thin, very yellow, and the horses' sweat had dried, roughly matting their coats. Time to move – to do the next thing – but she did not know how to begin. The field had been a kind of suspension: the house would be full of people who had spent the day differently – and he would be there. Her tears occurred, dispersed, recurred, and she seemed to have no control over them – she was terrified by their treacherous command.

In her room, she unpinned the lemon shirt and took it off.

It took her a long time to dress; she kept crossing the room and forgetting what she was looking for; dropping things and looking at them for a long time before she picked them up. She wasn't aware of thinking about anything at all, until she saw a bumble bee trapped in the sashes of her window, and went instinctively to let it out. Here, again, she was clumsy – the bee escaped, but she pinched her finger; and then, with no very clear idea or reason, put the injured hand on the ledge of the sill and with her free hand dropped the sash on to it. That hurt very much, and it took her an agonizing second to lift the sash again. The skin was broken; she watched the separate dots of blood appear, until they got larger and ran into one another. Her hand throbbed with an irregular kick – she had bruised it badly – possibly cracked or broken a bone. She clutched her left wrist tightly with her right hand to stay the pain, and felt the tears pricking again in her eyes. But she was one up on her tears now. She had provided their reason – for the evening if necessary – and the moment that she thought this – they unreasonably stopped.

Going downstairs; entering the drawing-room – the sun blazing on her face as she opened the door so that at first she could see nobody; collecting a drink; her mother exclaiming about her hand which she had clumsily bandaged – and everybody looking at her hand: his eyes on her – looking up, meeting his faint conspiratorial smile (exactly as though nothing had changed!) and knowing suddenly that he didn't believe that she had hurt it, that it was another ruse like his sprained ankle: wanting him so desperately to believe her that she stared stiffly beyond his head, until she heard herself saying that she had only bruised it, and she didn't care any more.

At dinner – after the soup – picking up her fork her hand snarling, shooting with pain, so suddenly that she dropped the fork with a clatter on to the table and everybody looked up. Somebody boned her fish for her then, and her father was asking him about Bodiam. She heard him talking easily, volubly, but she didn't listen. Eating seemed difficult, and half way through she managed to think: It's fish. I don't really like fish, and stopped trying to eat it. She smiled a great deal; if anyone spoke to her, or when anyone said anything. Occasionally, he said something to her, and then she found that she couldn't smile; she felt that he was watching her, and she said something without really looking at him.

Dinner over: getting stiffly out of her chair, thinking then for the first time in her life: I am so tired: I'm very, very tired; and following the women into the drawing-room – the curtains were drawn now, and there was no sun. Holding her wrist again while they poured coffee – Alison Brewer saying: 'Have you put anything *on* that hand?' and her mother mentioning Friar's Balsam and Pomade Divine in the bathroom cupboard. She could escape on that. No, she hadn't really put anything on it, if nobody minded she would do so, and go to bed. Nobody minded the teeniest, weeniest bit.

In the bathroom cupboard she found some of her mother's sleeping pills. She took one out of the bottle, but somehow, when she got back to her room she couldn't find it. She put the lemon-coloured shirt into the waste paper basket. The sleeping pill didn't seem to matter – she ached just to be lying absolutely still in the dark: if she kept still enough she wouldn't disturb her mind . . .

In the same dark she woke violently: crying with terror at some unendurable anguish, some dreadful secret violence that had disappeared with her waking, had slipped below the surface of a dream – leaving only a panic of confusion and pain. As the pain in her hand touched her senses, she wept more quietly – more and more, and quietly, until, in a tremulous, irregular silence, she slept.

NINE

She had never been unhappy before, and there was
nobody to whom she could talk; and so, lacking the equipment of experience or sympathy, she travelled painfully
through the weeks, with the kind of stolid courage often
seen in unhappy children, and with a pride which was
her own. Her pride was like some kind of brace; it was
always uncomfortable, and sometimes agonizing, but it
held her upright: it staunched the curious internal drip
from her heart; it concealed her weakness, and supported
her against the sudden recurring shocks of misery that
slammed at her without warning round the corner of a
calm and dull day. Particularly it enabled her to conceal
everything from her mother.

'You never said goodbye to Geoffrey,' she had said the
next morning, and Antonia had immediately replied:

'Oh dear, how awful of me! Well, I don't expect he
minded too dreadfully. I think I'd better go and see Dr
Atkins about this hand – it's swollen up like anything.'

Interminable weeks later, her mother returned from
one of her London trips unusually good-tempered and
gay, and after dinner said:

'Oh! I met Geoffrey – *riding in Knightsbridge* – just as
I was coming out of the hairdresser's – too romantic!'

'Is he – have you asked him down?'

'I *did*, but he can't, poor lamb. He's up to his eyes in

his school. I'm lunching with him next week. He sent his love to you.'

It took her some time to throw his love (casual, meaningless, untrue – exactly, she thought, what Miss Austen meant about people sending their love) over her shoulder. 'Give my love to Toni,' he must have said, and she could imagine the expression on his face when he said it: or, perhaps – 'Give my love to everybody.' That would be better – but that involved her father and she realized with a pang of dismay that there was nobody who would ever send even casual love to her father.

Her mother seemed to go away more frequently, or for longer – either two separate nights a week, or two or three days on end, and Antonia spent most of those evenings alone with her father. They took to doing the daily crossword puzzle together: he was much better at them than she, but politely preserved the myth each time that she might possess the necessary knowledge or ingenuity to manage what he could not. She was grateful to him for this, and longed to please and dazzle him with achievement, but on the rare occasions when she got something right, he merely wrote in the word in his painstaking script and turned to the next clue – he did not seem particularly surprised or pleased.

Frost – mushrooms – the swallows gone – berries violently cheerful in the hedges – the trees stripping gracefully, the patient evergreens becoming smug – coming into their own like an Æsop's fable – outdated butterflies and roses frozen crisp – the smoke and romance of autumn turning into the brisk settlement of winter. The horses had to come in for the nights – she did not ride them.

One day her father asked her whether she was going to Hastings – which meant that he wished she would. He wanted some books, and she went on the afternoon bus, glad of an errand.

It was a raw slate-coloured day, and she walked straight on to the sea front. Hastings was empty. A few old gentlemen, immutably wrapped and muffled, were being pushed in Bath chairs by gaunt women wearing sensible shoes and ugly gloves; one or two ill-chosen persons were being forced to chase the magically absurd movement of their blown-off hats; the people who are always leaning over railings and staring at the sea were there; a child was being bludgeoned into bowling its hoop. But the whooping, yelping peach-coloured crowds were gone: the shingle over which they had sprawled for their tightly packed picnics – bald head and bathing cap almost touching sandalled, sandy feet – was dry and bright: even the orange peel, the chocolate papers, the paper bags, the newspapers, were gone; and overhead, aimless, ravenous gulls played with details of the wind.

She walked towards the cliffs and the fishermen's harbour; the damp salty air stiffened with tarred hemp and fish. The boats were in, lolling and beached; the cork brown nets hung from poles between the tall black pitched huts. The seagulls were more strident here. She stood to watch the sea, running grey and heavy – plunging dispassionately against the harbour wall, breaking from grey to a shower of white drops and oily bubbles – and swooning out again under the next sleek diagonal wall of water. Watching the sea, she could think about anything – it provided that mysterious repetition of movement which made rhythm. She seemed then to herself to have been walking for weeks down a long narrow passage, with all the doors on either side shut, and her thoughts were like the carpet: she trod on them, but their pattern repeated itself, so that again and again, like the waves of water breaking on the harbour wall, the same memory recurred to be shattered – to swoon away under her feet. The passage seemed endless, and in spite of her movement in it, she seemed imprisoned. It's just the passage of time, she thought sadly, and began a cautious wondering about the doors. People? Opportunities? People to whom she could not talk, things she did not want to do? Shut, or actually locked? I can't talk to my mother, and I can't bear to ride. What a shattering situation! she jeered, and watched the tight-lipped jeering horizon below the chalky sky. I ought, she thought solemnly, to think more about other people, and less about myself – and remembered writing this sentiment in her diary when she had been fourteen, and it had been very new. Then, the mere writing of things had disposed of them – a welter of priggish little dictates, written out and forgotten until now – rose in her mind, and settled uneasily again like hot ash: she had not known what she was writing about. People, then – but she was tired of the passage analogy – her father – the people who came for weekends – but her father was very much alone, and now she knew that the only time she had tried to talk to him had been when she had wanted him to talk about her. I must get his books, she thought, that's what he wants, and it's what I came for, after all.

Walking away from it, she wondered if that was why there were always people leaning on railings and watching the sea.

∞ ∞ ∞

That evening, she asked her father whether there was anything that she could do to help with his book. On the whole he thought not, he said, after thinking scrupulously of the whole. Was there not *anything*? Some donkey work that didn't involve intelligence but that had to be done?

She was sitting with her feet tucked up under her in the large chair in his study (they did not use the drawing-room when they were alone) and her face tilted towards him. Something of her eager humility reached him – he had the scholar's profound respect for humility – and he smiled suddenly at the pleasure of understanding it.

'There is, of course, the Index.'

She was attentively silent.

'A tedious business – it will contain many cross-references – and when it is done it would have to be carefully checked before the amended version is begun upon.'

She said: 'Yes,' and waited, until he added sternly:

'There must be nothing slipshod about the Index to this book, or what little use it might ever become would be dissipated.'

'Do you think you could teach me to do it?'

'There is nothing *difficult* about it. It is entirely a question of patience and concentration.' He looked doubtfully at her.

'I promise you that I will concentrate,' she said.

So he taught her, and for hours a day she laboured at a task which was by no means entirely dependent upon patience and concentration for its success. Her father, she discovered, had such an intimate, detailed grasp of his subject, that he assumed a knowledge of it in her which she was far from possessing. Her mother laughed at her – carelessly, and then with a hint of something nearer jealousy or alarm (surely Toni wasn't turning into a dreary *bookworm*?), but it did not interfere with *her* life, and Toni seemed now to fit in with people at weekends much more easily than before, so apart from inciting a little general mirth at dinner on Saturday nights about Toni's occupation, she left it at that.

Then, one day, she said:

'Really, I must do something about my figure this winter. The summer's all right, with all the tennis, but in winter one simply eats like a *hog* – I'm getting fatter every single minute, and it just won't do.'

Antonia looked at her. She had put on a little, a very little weight, but it suited her – she looked much better and more contented, Antonia thought. Aloud, she said:

'You were a little too thin before. Now, you're just right.'

Her mother laughed nervously.

'It's sweet of you, darling: I don't want actually to *lose* weight – only to stay exactly as I am. I thought I'd take up riding again.'

Antonia was really startled. 'I thought you *hated* it!'

'Not if I've somebody amusing to ride with.'

There was a pause, as awkward as it was brief, while they both wondered separately why on earth she had used the word 'amusing'; then her mother said:

'I thought we might ride in the afternoons. Then I can do my little domestic chores in the morning while you're being madly intellectual with Wilfrid. How's that?'

'I have to work in the afternoons as well, or I won't get it done in time.'

'But, darling, you must have *some* fresh air!'

'I do. I go for walks, apart from gardening.' She said this very sulkily, because she could see what was coming, and was frightened by it.

'But don't you *ride* any more? I thought your whole life revolved round horses!'

'Well, it doesn't. In fact I'm bored with riding. I shan't do it any more.'

'Really, Toni, your whole life seems to consist of giving things up! First tennis, and now riding!'

Antonia said nothing. Araminta lit a cigarette angrily, inhaled, and said: 'It isn't good for you, you know. At your age, you ought to be *adding* to your interests, not simply giving everything up all over the place. You've got frightfully washed-out looking again, all pale and bony, and honestly, darling, it doesn't suit you.'

But Antonia cried:

'If riding is going to make you thinner, I don't see how it can make me fatter, and anyway, I've told you, I don't want to!'

Araminta looked at her daughter. She was trembling – well, shaking, actually – and a little pulse was beating in her face (just like Wilfrid, on the few, now happily distant, occasions when he went round the bend about something), and all about *riding*! But something quite different started to run into this – a fleeting, uneasy, intuition . . . She put her hand uncomfortably on Antonia's arm.

'Darling – I'm sorry to have been a bore about it. You do *exactly* what you *like*. Just tell me some good rides, and I'll see whether I can take Wilfrid out. He never walks a step, and he certainly doesn't do a thing about the garden.' She smiled, to put paid to the whole tiresome business, and escaped. She did not at all want to pursue her intuition . . .

When she had gone, Antonia, still trembling, reached out for her mother's packet of cigarettes, lit one, and inhaled as she had seen her mother do. A comforting dizziness blacked out the trembling, and at the end of it she felt better – indeed, she felt nothing at all.

Winter was no longer a brisk business, of frost and clear crisp light; of sudden sounds and sharp branches. Now, sometimes, the days began with a cold milky quiet, and the sun, enormous and unwinking, hung in the sky like a tinned fruit, giving everything a dirty varnished appearance: the birds looked dusty – the sky was oil. Now, sometimes, the sea mists rolled in, white in the distances, but with you, their sensation changed to a raw freezing dampness, and distance was concealed: trees, bushes, hair, were encrusted with tiny iced beads – newspapers were limp and silent to read, and the roads were slippery. Then, sometimes, it rained all day – noisily, quietly, sadly, angrily – in chuckling life-size drops that slammed and bounced, or with a thin driving spite that dissolved into an icy slush – and the sky was tumbled and smothering – like old bedclothes.

Araminta said she *loathed* November, and went to London more than ever.

December: snow, and berries, and silence: the birds dark and lumpy with the cold; the sky loaded, stiff, weighty, with yet more snow, which slipping, drifting down, fell to cover each ledge and crack of the country, making neatness of disorder, and disorder of what had been neat. At night, it froze, and snowed again – the trees shook it like fruit from their overladen branches; all tracks, stolid and pattering, were smoothly covered, but the flower beds became untidy heaps of sugar, and the poor rabbits had no life at all. Icicles, and little streams of warm air breathed out; sharp violet shadows like the lids of dazzling eyes – water glazed, corseted, frowning with ice: sparks from logs on the fire, from brushed-out hair, and in the sky at night from the smallest whimpering stars. In the mornings, the sun staggered out, suffused and ineffective, like a drunk in *Punch*.

Then, one Friday afternoon, Antonia, going to Hastings, met Dorcas on the cook's bicycle in the drive. She was clearly unmoved by the weather, for she was wearing a shirt with rolled-up sleeves. It was only after their greeting – Dorcas seemed more than usually embarrassed, blushing and swerving on her bicycle before riding ahead – that Antonia recognized the lemon shirt she had thrown into the waste paper basket so many weeks ago. It had been carefully mended. I don't suppose she has many clothes, she thought. It cost her no more than a pang of recognition. I'm better, she thought; I hardly care at all, if I'm careful. But, somehow, she lingered at Hastings – she did not want to go home, so that when she did get back on a later bus, her mother's weekend party had already arrived. All she knew about the guests was that she did not know them: a couple, she believed, and an unknown young man. She was late changing because she had to wait for her bath, and, from the noise in the drawing-room, she guessed that she was the last down. She walked into the room, prepared to be apologetic, docile and helpful with the cocktails, prepared to be observant and more interested in other people than herself . . . utterly unprepared to meet Geoffrey Curran.

He had his back to her, but her mother had not.

'Here's my huge daughter, at *last*! Toni, this is Muriel and David Morrow – and – Bobby Dermot couldn't come – he's got a hideous cold, poor lamb – so I persuaded Geoffrey instead – whom you *do* know.'

It was just the shock, she told herself, drinking the sherry which he had handed her, just the having no warning – being ambushed when she least expected it. She had not dared to light a cigarette because of her hands, but now David Morrow offered her one, and she took it. It was over, she kept repeating – he had said something, and she had replied – but the ice round her heart was broken. He had seemed uneasy – for once uncertain of himself – he had not met her eye – and she had seemed – what? Collected? Calm? At the moment, the presence of her mind was more than she could bear.

At dinner, they talked about horses (excepting, of course, her father) and she said very little. The four of them, the Morrows, her mother, and he, seemed very used to one another's company: their efforts to include her father or her were perfunctory; explaining something at which they had all laughed so that it was not in the least funny or even comprehensible; referring to a host of unknown people and places: whoever was speaking said 'we'. He did not ignore her – but his manner, though apparently easy, was odd – both bluff and patronizing. He's treating me like a child! she realized. Not even like someone who he thought was seventeen, but really like a child! Perhaps, she thought, her mother had forced him to come down, and he was miserably embarrassed, and having thought this, it was easy to detect embarrassment in him.

Araminta was on the extreme edge of gaiety, her attention fully taken up with the two men. To Antonia, however, she was alternately maternal and conciliatory – 'the child smokes like a *chimney*, it isn't good for her'; and: 'Toni knows every inch of the riding country round here, don't you, darling?'

The thought that it was odd how well her mother seemed to know him, considering that she had said nothing since announcing their meeting at Knightsbridge, crossed the confusion of her mind, but she reflected that her mother hadn't mentioned the Morrows at *all*, and she seemed to know them equally well. Weekend people were always like that: but not knowing what it was that she was trying to reassure herself about, she did not feel reassured. She turned her attention rather desperately to Muriel Morrow who sat opposite her. Hair of an indeterminate red – an expanse of face too large for unhappily delicate features: minutely thin pale eyebrows, small blue eyes, a child's nose, and a tiny mouth; so that her expression was constantly like somebody trying to have a large party in a room with inadequate furniture – her gaiety uncomfortable, her enjoyment anxious – her refuge the constant assertion of what fun she was having. She had an attractive clear little voice, like a bell, and pretty, helpless hands. Antonia, having got so far, tried to consider Muriel in relation to the others, but her own feelings were so negatively jammed, that they did not seem to move in any direction at all.

After dinner, the women sat in the drawing-room, and conversation dropped like the wind. Araminta powdered her face for a long time with critical care, because she had nothing much to say to the other two. Muriel, who had dabbed furtively at her nose and made no impression on it, started all over again, coating her face with broad despairing sweeps. Antonia sat still, smoking. There was a long silence, except for the fire, and the ceaseless tinkle of Araminta's charm bracelet. Antonia thought: Soon they will come in, and I'm frightened; I don't know why, but I *am* frightened.

Eventually, Muriel put her powder away with a small sigh, leaned forward to Araminta and said:

'*Do* let me see it!'

'What?' Araminta shook her arm. 'Oh that. It *is* fun, isn't it?' She unclasped the bracelet, and threw it, so that it fell noisily into Muriel's lap.

Muriel, desperately anxious to please, said: 'It's absolutely *marvellous*! You've got so many things! Has it taken ages to collect them?' But Araminta merely said:

'I've been given nearly everything.'

But Muriel, clinging to the conversation, began dropping the bracelet from the palm of one hand to the other, saying: 'It's frightfully heavy: I shouldn't think you've room for any more things,' and like a child she began counting the charms aloud, and exclaiming over them. 'I *adore* the monkey with ruby eyes. That's sweet – *that's* rather sinister – oh dear, I wish I had one of those! Oh look at the little fiddle!' Then after more counting: 'Do you know, you've got *seventeen*? What's that, an old seal, or something?'

'Wilfrid gave me that years ago. Put another log on, Toni. It doesn't go with the others, but I can't hurt his feelings.'

And Muriel said admiringly: 'Of *course*, you can't. It's rather a funny colour, isn't it? Don't *you* think so, Toni?'

And Antonia, wrapped in her insensate fear, agreed without thinking that it was, and then loyalty to her father made her add: 'It's probably a pretty design. You could try it with sealing wax.'

One of the others said, yes, you could, without much interest, and then, as they heard sounds of the men joining them, and Antonia was steeling herself to being in the same room with him again – to his moving about the room – talking – talking sometimes to her, with everything dead and gone between them – Muriel suddenly cried:

'I *knew* there was something missing! Where's the little silver riding crop that Geoffrey gave you?'

They were opening the drawing-room door: Araminta simply said:

'I haven't put it on, yet,' but Antonia looked at her, and then could not look away – her senses suddenly sharpened to a pitch of feverish discovery – her mother was furiously angry! She almost snatched the bracelet from Muriel, who, her attention diverted by the men's return, had not noticed – had possibly not even heard Araminta's reply, for she babbled on:

'Oh, *Geoffrey*! Minty hasn't even bothered to put your dear little riding crop on to her bracelet! There's ingratitude for you!'

There was only a fractional pause, but tension infected the room. Then Curran said easily:

'Do you mean the one you asked me to buy for you? The little *silver* crop?' and Araminta replied:

'Yes. I'm not sure if I like it yet, but you must remind me to pay you back.'

They did not look at one another, and it was then, that, as certainly as she knew that they were lying – Antonia knew that he was in love with her mother.

Afterwards, it seemed as strange to her that she had not known this before, as it seemed strange that she should know at that moment. At the time, however, recoiling violently from this, terribly certain, intuition – she told herself that she had no proof of it – that she did not really know. But that was no good: all the evening she had been drifting with her fears – now, without warning, she was suddenly hit, cast, thrown up by a vast wave of emotion, on to some bleak shore of a reality – and for a while she lay where she had been thrown, winded, gasping for reason. No time for reason – the next wave assaulted her, she was dragged out by another murderous sea clutching the straw of his having loved her (but love, for him, meant only want – he must now want her mother) – and then she was beached again with the certainty that her mother was his mistress.

Her father had disappeared: they were going to play bridge, and she picked up the newspaper and pretended to do the crossword puzzle. She heard her voice telling her mother that she would be quite happy doing this. *Her* mother! *His* eyes, his hands, his voice saying: 'I want you entirely. Want, want, want! You're beginning to understand what that means now, aren't you? Wait a few minutes more!' She waited, enduring everything that she had most passionately tried to shut out of her memory; until there was nothing left that he had said or done to her, and she was forced on to the present; the reasons against his saying or doing those things to her mother coming and going – more straws that would not bear the weight of her panic. People who were married did not do this! But he was married, and he did. But not her *mother*! Surely, surely not her mother! Then her mother suddenly wanting to ride again, with somebody 'amusing' – the little silver riding crop for the bracelet – the sweet little platinum fiddle that George Warrender had given her . . . she was sucked out from her beach and drowning again – her mother had been given everything on the bracelet . . . she was thrown back this time high and dry of emotion – beyond the reach of another wave. Still, somehow, she could not leave the room: it did not occur to her that she was able to move, although her mind was working perfectly now, and with a kind of logical skill and speed which it had never done before – remembering, selecting, adding and subtracting – arriving always at the same answers.

At the end of some unknown time, the bridge party broke up, and she got stiffly to her feet with the others. At the head of the stairs everybody said good night, and Araminta warned them not to wake Wilfrid: 'He'll have gone to bed hours ago, and there's no light from his room, so he's asleep, poor old poppet.'

Antonia, sleepless, with no light from her room, lay rigid in the dark: the capacity to think had left her the moment that she was alone, and only the edge of a kind of animal instinct remained. At some point far on in the night, she thought she heard footsteps, and, at the moment when she was deciding that they were too quiet to be more than a shadow of her imagination, a door closed – too quietly – clicked back, and shut again less quietly. She turned then, on to her face, and wept with a most sudden bitterness, for her father.

TEN

The next morning, when she got down to breakfast, she found that her mother and Curran had already gone riding, leaving the Morrows and her father almost paralysed with uncongeniality, amid the wreckage of the breakfast table. The Morrows seized upon her eagerly – Araminta had said that Toni would take them somewhere – where should it be? Only for the morning – the others would be back for a late lunch, and there was some vague scheme for the afternoon, but David didn't know what it was. Come on – entertain us – they said. We aren't fussy about how it is done, but we must be entertained somehow. Her father slipped thankfully from the room with his newspaper. 'What about the Professor?' Muriel asked, almost before he had closed the door. 'Do we take him too?' He would be working, Antonia replied, and reflected wearily that this was her father's house, and that he, more than she, must object to his being treated in it as he was.

All through the morning, while she entertained the Morrows for her mother, she suffered from the incessant, frightful outrage which it seemed then to her they were all practising upon her father: for now, suddenly, everything that Araminta and her guests had ever said or not said, done, or omitted to do, took on a new, and horrible significance. Now their attitude to her father – which

before had seemed to be largely composed of embarrassment and indifference (Muriel's remark about the Professor
was typical) – meant very much more: the indifference
was insulting, the embarrassment guilty – calling him
'Professor' which he was not, but which they often did
– seemed to her insufferably patronizing. Bad manners,
and it taking all sorts to make a world no longer seemed
to apply and with a deadly facility were replaced by
squalid little phrases like: 'under his nose', or 'behind his
back': this last, because having stumbled upon something
which so much shocked and revolted her (and part of the
shock was the amount of time that she had not known
it), she felt that everybody else must always have known
– everyone, of course, excepting her father . . . *He* was so
calm, so quiet! He disassociated himself from them with
such an unassuming dignity; and his manner, untouched
by theirs to him, was invariably courteous and serene.
The Morrows, she decided, simply neither knew nor cared
what they were doing – but Curran! He could have picked
anyone else . . . and then, because all her sensibilities had
shifted from him and herself to her father, and she could
therefore observe Curran with an entirely new detachment, she realized that he *might* have picked anybody,
but that, in fact, her mother had picked *him*: and he had
simply responded. Her mother, then, on top of her careless indifference, her sledge-hammer preoccupation with
her own interests, was practising a deceit on her father,
a continuous accumulating treachery the discovery of
which, Antonia felt, might very well kill him. For he, of
all people, seemed to her not made for this: he knows
nothing about *people*, really, she thought; even I know more
than he does about them. His potential bewilderment,

shock and destruction haunted her, all the time that she was driving about the country with the Morrows. The thought that Araminta might really love Curran did once enter her mind, but the string of his predecessors dismissed it. Her mother's fitful interest in a particular game attached now to whatever man had been most frequently to stay at the time that she was playing it: her visits to London, her spells of hysterical restlessness and discontent with her surroundings – everything that had packed Antonia's mind while she had been ostensibly doing the crossword puzzle – returned now to confirm and enlarge her anxiety.

Now that *I* know, I suppose that I am deceiving him too, she thought. But I couldn't tell him – I couldn't bear to see his face – and I wouldn't dare even to try and comfort him – poor, poor papa. And I suppose when they are in London, they all laugh about it, and say what a bore he is, and how easy it is to deceive him. They don't realize how simple it is to tell lies to trusting people. And it was then that some dim but passionate idea of protecting him came into her mind.

When Curran and her mother returned, Araminta sped upstairs for a bath before lunch, which was already late, and the Morrows, placated with strong cocktails, asked him how he had enjoyed his ride.

'I adored every minute of it.' Then, defensively aware of Antonia, he added: 'But then, I always enjoy riding. I wish you'd been out with us.'

Araminta shrieked down the stairs for Muriel to be a *lamb* and bring her a drink in the bathroom. When she had gone, Curran offered Antonia a cigarette.

'No, thank you.'

He raised his eyebrows. 'Minty says you smoke all day and all night.'

'It's too near luncheon.'

'She says you've given up riding since the summer. She's worried about you, Toni.' He dropped his voice – glancing at David Morrow who was immersed in a newspaper. 'I'd hate to think that I was to blame in any way.'

She said nothing.

'Look, why don't we go for a short ride this afternoon? It's all right, your mother suggested it,' he added, seeing, and misinterpreting, the expression on her face.

She faced him coolly – her heart hammering with anger and contempt.

'I'm working this afternoon with my father, and anyway, I can't imagine anything that would bore me more.'

That touched him – she saw him flinch, and then the anger before he said: 'Still a child! Won't anything make you grow up?'

She answered steadily: 'Some things do.'

And after that, he left her alone.

All the afternoon she worked in her father's study with him. She had looked forward to being safe and alone with him, but she was exhausted from lack of sleep and the grinding confusion of her morning with the Morrows, and now she found that she could not concentrate on her work or her private anxiety. Again and again she found herself staring at her father staring out of his window, his face screwed to a tension of thought – at the same time withdrawn and exposed. It's a good thing he is concentrating on *sixteenth*-century social customs, she thought with bitter protectiveness: whatever he finds out about them can't destroy his life. For the first time she was looking at him with an outside eye: her anxiety for him and her fatigue equated their difference in age – seemed almost to invert their relationship: he looked spent, he did not look well, he added up to a general impression of weakness. He wasn't a very *strong* man, she began to think, and remembered quickly that he had been badly gassed in the war – he certainly did not look like somebody who could survive any more shocks. Then she realized that he was looking at *her* – noticing only that she wasn't concentrating upon her work, and she smiled at him with a deliberately guilty air – as though her attention had merely wandered to something frivolous. It occurred to her then that perhaps the only certain way of protecting him was to take him away from the house – leaving her mother with a clear field to do what she pleased in it; but she was at the stage of fatigue when although once she had had this idea, it persistently recurred, she could not think how to achieve it.

The day dragged through: ending with all the ritual – now ghastly – gaiety of a Saturday evening. Curran talked to her father at dinner, but now she hated him doing it, and interrupted him more than once with a savage assurance: whatever anybody did about her father seemed impossible to her now. If they spoke to him, she imagined their tongues in their cheeks; if they ignored him, their rudeness accumulated in her mind. She watched him with a jealous and despairing concern; observing for the first time a dozen details of his behaviour: the neat and orderly way in which he ate his food; how, with a minute adjustment of surprise, he always blinked and screwed up his face when he was spoken to; his deprecating little cough before he disagreed with anybody; his fingers stained with ink and nicotine; the sleeves of his coat shiny at wrist and elbow, and his sparse soft grey hair straggling hopelessly over his rather ragged collar. He had a dry toneless voice which tailed off into a barely audible quiet at the end of a sentence – as though he never expected anybody to wait for the end of what he had to say. All these things now seemed to her unbearably, dreadfully, pathetic, just as his painstaking quantity of knowledge inspired her utmost respect: and because she was so much on edge, she felt all the time that if for one terrible second, he applied the force of his mind to the situation round him, he would immediately understand it, and as suddenly, be destroyed. All the evening, until he retired to his study, she imagined that the others were propelling him inexorably towards this precipice of worldly knowledge, and that she stood by herself between him and them, pushing him back to safety. And that is only one evening, she thought, there is tomorrow, and all the other weekends of our lives; and, strained and drained by the last twenty-four hours as she was then, she could not bear to think of the prospect.

She lay awake for hours trying to think how she could get her father away; where they should go, and what reason she could give for their going – arriving at no solution: and woke from a sleep which was full of her mother – telling her mother frantically over and over again that she must *stop*, and her mother, who was dressed as a doll, opening her china eyes and saying: 'Stop what?' 'You know what I mean! You are a – a –' but then she couldn't find the word she meant, and her mother laughed, twitched her frilly skirts, and cried: 'You poor baby – you don't know the *first* thing about what you mean!' and she was crying with anger because she *knew* that she knew, only she could not bear to think of the word. 'Won't anything make you grow up?' he had said; and she thought that she had grown up so fast that she seemed to be looking from a great height at what she had been, and had so suddenly got so far away that she could see nothing at all. But I can't talk to *her*! she thought, as the dream surged back: I'm simply not brave enough: I don't know what to say, and wept then, at her own lack of courage: weakness of any kind was not going to protect her father.

∞   ∞   ∞

Sunday seemed indistinguishable from Saturday, except that more snow fell. She spent nearly all of it with her father, and in avoiding one second alone with Araminta. When they were all together, however, she continually found herself watching her mother – having thought that she could never again bear to look at her, she now had difficulty in looking at anyone else. Her language, her laughter, the way that she threw herself into a chair, the mock intensity of her undivided attention, the apparently careless but ruthlessly competent way in which she swept everybody up into any one of her immediate plans; her extraordinary energy about each separate part of the day, the particular covert impression of herself that she was making for Curran – all of this fascinated and repelled Antonia, almost to the point of hypnosis. Her own self-possession with the Morrows and Curran, however, astonished her – it seemed in those two days, to have become unpainful and complete. In the evening she even played card and paper games with them, as though she had always known all about them, or, alternatively, still knew nothing.

On Monday morning, the Morrows left before breakfast in their car, because David had to get to work. Araminta had said, that if he liked, she would take Curran to a train at a more civilized hour – for some reason she was determined upon this plan, and so, naturally, it became the plan.

Antonia overslept, and hurried anxiously down with the picture of a trio at breakfast accusingly in her mind, to find that her father had already eaten and disappeared into his study: Curran and Araminta were alone. Her self-possession shrivelled at the sight of them, their heads bent over a newspaper together: they were not reading it – she had the impression that they were arguing about plans – that they had expected, but did not want her. They both looked up, an expression of good-humoured blankness replacing their intimate discontent, and Araminta said:

'Well! I was beginning to wonder what on earth had happened to you! I suppose it would be tactless to ask you whether you've slept well?'

Antonia said: 'Terribly tactless,' and poured herself coffee.

Curran observed: 'When I was Toni's age, I could sleep the clock round,' which made Araminta say immediately:

'I *can* sleep for ages and *ages*, but it seems such a sickening waste of time. Anyway, you'll be nice and fresh for the party tonight, darling – I've been trying to persuade Geoffrey to stay down for it, but he's too sickening – he won't.'

'What party?'

'Oh, Toni! *Really!* The *Leggatts!*' *Don't* try to tell me that you've forgotten, or I shall scream.'

'I'm afraid I had.' She had, completely.

Araminta let out a neat little practised scream, like an engine, and turned laughing, to Geoffrey: 'You see what I mean? The child's hopeless! The next line will be: "I don't want to go, and anyway, I've got nothing to wear." The answer to that is that you said you'd go when they asked you, I've accepted for us, and you've got your white dress, which is perfectly ravishing if only you'll bother to put it on properly.'

Antonia, who was coldly angry, said: 'This picture of me as an absent-minded tomboy is so convincing that you must long for it to be true.'

Curran raised his eyebrows; Araminta, really startled, stared, laughed nervously, and said: 'You juggins! I was only teasing you. I'd forgotten you'd only just woken up. Geoffrey, *what* about changing your mind? Edmund will be delighted – he so adores you.'

'Edmund must languish. No, Minty, I must get back. I've had my holiday.'

'Well, when are you coming again?'

'As soon as you ask me.'

'Really – you are impossible! You know perfectly well that that's utterly untrue. Well – I shall hold you to one weekend in three, if that's all you allow yourself. Now we must *fly* for that train. Toni, do you know where Wilfrid has got to?'

'In his study, I expect.'

Araminta leapt to her feet. 'Come on, Geoffrey – you've just got time to say goodbye to him – after all, he *is* your host.' Geoffrey opened the door for her. 'You'd better say goodbye to Toni now, because we shall have to fly as it is.'

Antonia looked up from her paper.

'Goodbye.'

'Au revoir, Toni. I hope I shall be seeing you soon.'

She said nothing to that, and through the closed door she heard her mother's voice . . .

'Really, my family . . . I must apologize . . . their heads in the clouds or buried in books . . .'

Alone, Antonia drank some of her coffee, and lit a cigarette. One weekend in three! And he would come down to them because her mother wanted him to: she would only stop wanting him when she found somebody else who might be far more available – might, like George Warrender, or the young man called Bobby, come every weekend. This future was too much for her – there was nothing now that she could do about it – but, she suddenly realized that if she could prevent Curran coming down every third weekend, her mother would simply spend more of each week in London: it would serve the double purpose of protecting her father, and lessening the time she would have to spend alone with her mother. The remains of her anger at her mother's treatment of her during breakfast flared again – they had clearly discussed her, and she could easily imagine the dishonesty of the terms they had employed. She would prevent his coming – she was no child, but somebody as ingenious and determined as they. She lit another cigarette: she would go to her father. She knew that on occasions as rare as they were surprising, her father became absolutely, immovably obstinate, that having made up his mind about something, nothing or nobody could change it. She remembered her mother wanting to lay the tennis court outside his study window; wanting on another occasion to keep a Bedlington; wanting to give a fancy dress party in London years ago; wanting to send Antonia to school in Switzerland (she remembered the last with shuddering clarity because she had been so terrified by the prospect); she remembered the arguments, the scenes between them, and her mother sulking for days, but whenever he had opposed this minute proportion of her requirements, having to give way to him in the end. She must therefore get her father to be against having Curran to stay. Put as simply as that, the problem actually seemed simple: she did not doubt or question how to set about it – she was strung to a point where any action seemed easier than none. She had heard the others leave in the car, and knew that her father would be in his study finishing the newspaper before he started work . . .

Outside his door, she thought: I haven't thought properly what to say; and then thought that if she had given herself time to think her courage might have failed.

He was sitting exactly as she expected, with his feet on a small stool, smoking his pipe and reading the *Morning Post.* He looked up as she came in, and smiled absently at her.

'You're early, Antonia.'

She noticed with gratitude that he always used her proper name, and felt a rush of affection for him: he was returning to his paper, so she said quickly:

'I wanted to ask you something.'

'Yes, my dear?' He lowered the paper, but did not put it down.

She sat opposite him in silence – her heart was beginning to thump a little: it would be easy once she had started, but it was difficult to start.

450

'Papa – this may not seem serious to you – but it is serious to me.'

'Serious,' he repeated, and put down his paper. There was a second's silence, and then she said:

'Please don't have Geoffrey Curran to stay any more!'

He waited a moment, and then said: 'My dear, that's nothing to do with *me*. You must ask your mother.'

'No! I'm asking you, instead.'

He looked at her – he was beginning to screw up his face, and then without any real curiosity, asked: 'Why don't you want him to stay?'

'I don't like him.' She searched for a word that would impress him. 'I dislike him profoundly.'

He remained mildly uninterested. 'That does not seem to me adequate reason. He doesn't come here very often, does he? I don't seem to remember his being here for some time.'

'No – he hasn't. But he's been asked again, quite soon, and I know he'll come.'

'Well – when the occasion arises, can you not detach yourself and control this unfortunate opinion?'

'Papa – you don't *understand*! It's not just what I think about him, it's what he is – what he *does*,' she corrected herself.

His pipe had gone out: he lit it carefully before asking with resignation: 'What does he do?'

'He rides the horses into a muck sweat and doesn't cool them off properly'; she was getting desperate; 'and he drinks far too much, and won't play games except for money. He marks books by folding down the pages and shutting them,' she added – perhaps *that* would touch him – but then she could see that it hadn't.

'Well, my dear Antonia, the horses are, of course, your

province, and you must see to it that he does not endanger their health. I cannot recollect having seen him the worse for drink, and your mother enjoys a little mild gambling. What was your other objection?'

'The books,' she said hopelessly.

'Ah yes. I agree that that is a lamentable habit, but as all the books of any value or interest are in this room, I think I can protect them. You must exercise tolerance, my dear. It was not so very long ago that your own treatment of books was open to question. I cannot share your dislike of Mr Curran: he seems to me to have wider interests than many of our guests. Now. Let us stop worrying, and settle to a little work,' and he shifted his chair up to his large desk.

It was over, she thought, wildly, and she had got nowhere – had accomplished nothing. Her reasons had not been good enough – he simply thought that she was indulging in some feminine freak, or a childish whim. She looked at him bent over his papers, which he was methodically laying out all over his desk. He was probably quite happy, had already dismissed the subject from his mind; was safely concentrated upon – what was he immersed in? – midwifery; in a moment he would be unfavourably comparing Victorian methods with those of his beloved epoch, and she was the only person who knew and cared that he was *not* safe. She knew now why she had not dared to consider what she would say to him. The only convincing reason that she could give to prevent Curran coming, with its ingenious humiliating distortion, was one which filled her with nauseating fright.

She looked once more at her father. I do love him, she thought; one should be able to do anything for somebody one loves.

'I said that this might not seem serious to you, but that it is serious to me.'

'What, my dear?'

'About Geoffrey Curran.' She was patient now, with fear and courage. 'Papa – *please*! I didn't give you the real reason just now for not wanting him to stay.'

'I didn't think that you had.'

'Didn't you?' She clutched this straw of his perspicacity eagerly.

He smiled his humourless smile. 'Women are devious creatures. It would have surprised me if you had been direct.'

'I'm sorry.' She was blushing now – feeling that he could never know how much she deserved this stricture on her honesty.

'But if I am – if I do give you the real reason, I'm sure that you will understand.'

There was a silence, and then, staring on the ground, she said: 'He pursues me all the time. Of course, he *says* he's in love with me, but he isn't. He's tried to seduce me – he's married already – to somebody in Ireland – but that doesn't stop him in the least. He's always getting me alone somewhere, and trying to – trying—'

'To seduce you?'

She nodded. 'I hate him, but that doesn't seem to make the slightest difference. I hate him,' she repeated with relief at finding this to be true.

'Do you?'

Something about the way he asked – something cynical and controlled – made her retort: 'Of *course* I do! Don't you believe that?'

There was a dreadful little pause, which afterwards she was always to remember, before he said:

'I believe none of it.'

'Why – why do you think that I'm asking you to stop his coming here, then?'

'Oh – I believe that you don't want him here. But the reasons you give – particularly the last one – seem to me – shall we say, an ingenious distortion of the truth?'

She could say absolutely nothing.

He gave her a moment, and then continued relentlessly: 'You say, eventually, that you don't want this young man here because he pursues you, tries to seduce you, and is constantly getting you alone for this purpose. How does he manage to do that, unless you are, to say the least, acquiescent? This house is full of people, and on the occasions when he has been here, you are under no obligation to remain one minute alone with him. I suggest that you have done so, because your feelings about him are, to put it mildly, ambivalent.'

With difficulty, she said: 'If all that is true, why do I want him to stop coming here?'

'That, as I said, is a separate business. If it is true that he is married, you *might* want to escape from the possibility of conflict.' Again there was the cynical emphasis on the word 'might'.

She said slowly, dully: 'I don't know what you mean.' All she did understand was his unaccountable, startling hostility.

He made an impatient, waspish movement with his right hand, and leaned suddenly towards her over the desk.

'I am not *blind*. You have come to the wrong person with this story, which convinces me of nothing but how much a woman you are. All these excuses, rationalizations, distortions entirely feminine in their concept –

always blackguarding the wretched man – concealing any real motive you have, because you know very well how unattractive the motive is – does not all this excite *some* shame in you? Or are you so much a woman now that you do not understand the meaning of that word?'

'I can't tell you the real reason!' Tears were running down her face – he was attacking her, and she didn't understand a single word. 'I can't! You *must* believe me –' *she* had come to protect *him*: 'I can't tell you the real reason!'

He looked at her – his more savage anger draining away until, almost kindly, he said: 'If you had told me in the first place that you were simply, intolerably, jealous – I should have understood you.'

She stared at him – trying to see his face clearly.

'Jealous? Of whom?'

'Of your mother, of course.'

'My *mother*?'

He looked out of the window, and then at her: the cynical unpleasant control was back in his eyes and his voice. 'Who else?'

It was like being plunged into the dark, with some-where, anywhere, an open pit – a matter of seconds, but after one foot was in the pit, no time at all. She must have repeated: 'My *mother*?' because he cried:

'I am not deceived by this melodramatic reiteration! Not in the least! You are no Emilia – I know that you are not so innocent as you pretend, and as for me, I have known it, lived with it so long, that it has ceased to be a matter even of the smallest importance – only I am not prepared to be hoodwinked or pitied or drawn into any aspect of the squalid intrigues that seem to revolve round these situations! I have told you that Mr Curran seemed to me a little better than the usual run . . .'

She slipped violently into the pit – bottomless, nowhere for her feet, and blinded by its blackness – recovered to hear his voice rasping above her; '. . . at least I am not *blind*,' and realized that one foot was pressing hard upon the other, the pain mounting to an exquisite relief. His face was twitching on one side below his cheekbone; she put her hand up to her face, and then her head to adjust the extraordinary dead weight of her mind. The usual run . . .

He had always known; *he* was not blind – she thought he was angry at *her* blindness – she could not then begin to think that he had ever cared.

She nodded silently, almost solemnly, as though they had reached some momentous agreement, and left him.

∞ ∞ ∞

In the evening, as she was driving the two of them to the Leggatts'; Araminta said:

'Really, Toni, you must try not to be so devastatingly *rude* to me in front of other people. I mean, I'm sorry if I irritated you this morning, but you really must control yourself.' She laughed, and added: 'It's so *embarrassing!*'

Antonia said: 'I'm sorry.'

'Now you're sulking, darling, which is worse.'

'I don't think that I am.'

'Well, you might at least say you're sorry as though you cared!'

And Antonia replied: 'I don't care, in the least.'

It seemed suddenly to her the formula, the solution – one didn't care about anything. All day she had accepted, felt distantly that she had knowledge now of people and life – and kept the knowledge distant because it seemed to her not power, but the machinery of terror. Now, in the dark, feeling her mother's irritation, and finding herself unmoved by it, her indifference spread and stiffened, poured slowly over everything like lava down a mountain, obliterating all terror and concern and affection, until there was nothing left in sight. Emotionally, she thought, it must be rather like lying down in the snow to sleep – and didn't care about that, either.

The car was draughty, and it was very cold. Araminta, after a little gusty sigh of pure anger, had subsided – had dramatically resolved not to say another word all the way to Robertsbridge. So they drove through the frosty winter silence – Araminta sinking from anger at Toni into the hectic sentiment which invariably occupied her private mind – Antonia entrenching in her new overwhelming conviction.

They drove slowly round the large lawn in front of the Leggatts' house, looking for somewhere to park: and she remembered leaving the party there in the summer.

They walked in silence from the car. Inside the Victorian porch, with glass doors, the warm scented house was like the centre of some dazzling flower. Edmund Leggatt stood inside the second door, beside an enormous steaming punch bowl.

'Drink!' he shouted cheerfully, managing to make a personal greeting of the word: 'nobody is allowed one step further without they warm their vitals. Araminta, my dear, how mysterious you look – up to the ears in fur – cold, and mysterious, and very, very seductive.' He slopped some punch with a silver ladle into a small green glass and handed it to her. '*And* Toni. I can see how lovely you're going to look under that red shawl. Drink!'

'Edmund, darling, how delicious! Wilfrid's awfully sorry, but he couldn't get away.'

'Wilfrid?' For a moment, Edmund looked blank, but his face cleared. 'What a shame! Here are the frozen fragments of the fjords. Drink!' and he began again.

Antonia drank her punch quickly – her mother was already engaged upon the party – was not even going upstairs to take off her coat – a young man was removing it for her. The punch burned with delightful power, and she felt immediately and thoroughly warm. She seemed almost to float up the shallow stairs to the warm bedroom to take off her wraps. The room was dim – splashed with little dull pools of light, and their watery reflections in the many glasses hung about the walls. It smelled of freesias and face powders, and it was empty. Somebody had left three-quarters of their punch on the dressing-table; the delicate steam was misting the mirror. When she had taken off her coat and shawl, she sat down in front of the misted glass, drank the punch and looked at herself. Her appearance was blurred, and even when she wiped the mist away, it did not seem as clear-cut, as decisive as her mind: 'Women are chiefly concerned with the appearance of things', her father had said – but now, she was not concerned about anything at all. To see that the intricacies of her dress were properly fastened – to comb back her hair so that the line on her forehead was smooth – to note that the indeterminate shifting shadows on the bones of her face were not smudges, but only shadows – was, she supposed, no more now than habit, since she did all these things as a piece of unemotional ritual – the reasons for it lost and gone. Only, perhaps, her appearance was not quite right for the state of her mind; she did not look as old as she felt, and the second glass of punch seemed merely to continue her warmth without adding to it.

At the top of the staircase she paused to look down at the heads and hands and shoulders of the throng below her. Their voices, their laughter seemed to run up to the tremendously high encrusted ceiling, and stick there – an inversion of gravity, she thought – and started down the gentle stairs. At the turn of the staircase she could not, in the distance, see over all the heads – there were too many of them packed right up to the large window, where, in the summer, she had seen Curran standing. Now he was not there – was replaced by an anonymous crowd – and she was simply relieved that he was not there: perhaps not even relieved – merely indifferent, not caring about anything.

On the last step of the staircase, somebody took her hand.

'Were you looking for someone?'

She shook her head.

'You had an expression of searching.'

She looked at him.

'As though you were concerned about something.'

'I couldn't have. I don't care about anything at all.'

She looked at him calmly – wondering why she had actually said that, and they stood silent for a moment.

'Do you know anybody at this party?'

She withdrew her hand. 'My mother is here.'

'I don't suppose you know her very well.'

'Well enough to know that she will stay to the very end.'

'And you wish that it was the end now?'

She made a small, instinctively escaping movement of her head.

He said gently: 'This isn't the end: it may very well be the beginning': and picked up her hand again as though it was a piece of essential equipment without which neither of them could begin to move from the end of the staircase.

picador.com

blog
videos
interviews
extracts